A SAUCER
OF LONELINESS

Theodore Sturgeon with his children
Robin, Tandy, and Noël
on Grenada Island, West Indies
1958.

A SAUCER
OF LONELINESS

Volume VII:

The Complete Stories of

Theodore Sturgeon

Edited by
Paul Williams

Foreword by
Kurt Vonnegut, Jr.

North Atlantic Books
Berkeley, California

A Saucer of Loneliness

Published by
North Atlantic Books
P.O. Box 12327
Berkeley, California 94712

Cover art by Ed Emshwiller

Printed in the United States of America

A Saucer of Loneliness is sponsored by the Society for the Study of Native Arts and Sciences, a nonprofit educational corporation whose goals are to develop an educational and crosscultural perspective linking various scientific, social, and artistic fields; to nurture a holistic view of arts, sciences, humanities, and healing; and to publish and distribute literature on the relationship of mind, body, and nature.

Library of Congress Cataloging-in-Publication Data
Sturgeon, Theodore.
    A saucer of loneliness / Theodore Sturgeon: edited by Paul Williams
      p. cm. — (The complete stories of Theodore Sturgeon ; v. 7)
    Contents: A saucer of loneliness — The touch of your hand — The world well lost — And my fear is great — The wages of synergy — The dark room — Talent — A way of thinking — The silken swift — The clinic — Mr. Costello, hero — The education of Drusilla Strange.
      ISBN 1-55643-350-6 (alk. paper)
      1. Science fiction, American. I. Williams, Paul, 1948– II. Title. III. Series: Sturgeon, Theodore. Short stories: v. 7.
    GV1149.5.C6 C54 2000
    PS3569.T875 A6 2000
813'.54—dc21   00-042356

1 2 3 4 5 6 7 8 9 / 04 03 02 01 00

EDITOR'S NOTE

THEODORE HAMILTON STURGEON was born February 26, 1918, and died May 8, 1985. This is the seventh of a series of volumes that will collect all of his short fiction of all types and all lengths shorter than a novel. The volumes and the stories within the volumes are organized chronologically by order of composition (insofar as it can be determined). This seventh volume contains stories written between autumn 1952 and autumn 1953.

Preparation of each of these volumes would not be possible without the hard work and invaluable participation of Noël Sturgeon, Debbie Notkin, and our publishers, Lindy Hough and Richard Grossinger. I would also like to thank, for their significant assistance with this volume, Kurt Vonnegut, Jr., Carol Emshwiller, the Theodore Sturgeon Literary Trust, Marion Sturgeon, Jayne Williams, Ralph Vicinanza, Nicole George, Paula Morrison, Catherine Campaigne, Jennifer Privateer, Eric Weeks, Robin Sturgeon, Kim Charnovsky, T. V. Reed, and all of you who have expressed your interest and support.

BOOKS BY THEODORE STURGEON

Without Sorcery (1948)

The Dreaming Jewels [aka *The Synthetic Man*] (1950)

More than Human (1953)

E Pluribus Unicorn (1953)

Caviar (1955)

A Way Home (1955)

The King and Four Queens (1956)

I, Libertine (1956)

A Touch of Strange (1958)

The Cosmic Rape [aka *To Marry Medusa*] (1958)

Aliens 4 (1959)

Venus Plus X (1960)

Beyond (1960)

Some of Your Blood (1961)

Voyage to the Bottom of the Sea (1961)

The Player on the Other Side (1963)

Sturgeon in Orbit (1964)

Starshine (1966)

The Rare Breed (1966)

Sturgeon Is Alive and Well ... (1971)

The Worlds of Theodore Sturgeon (1972)

Sturgeon's West (with Don Ward) (1973)

Case and the Dreamer (1974)

Visions and Venturers (1978)

Maturity (1979)

The Stars Are the Styx (1979)

The Golden Helix (1979)

Alien Cargo (1984)

Godbody (1986)

A Touch of Sturgeon (1987)

The [Widget], the [Wadget], and Boff (1989)

Argyll (1993)

The Ultimate Egoist (1994)

Microcosmic God (1995)

Killdozer! (1996)

Star Trek, The Joy Machine (with James Gunn) (1996)

Thunder and Roses (1997)

The Perfect Host (1998)

Baby Is Three (1999)

A Saucer of Loneliness (2000)

CONTENTS

FOREWORD

I CREATED A CHARACTER, Kilgore Trout, an impoverished, uncelebrated science fiction writer, who made his debut in 1965 in my novel *God Bless You, Mr. Rosewater.* Trout would subsequently make cameo appearances in several more of my books, and in 1973 would star in *Breakfast of Champions.*

Persons alert for wordplay noticed that Trout and Theodore Sturgeon were both named for fish, and that their first names ended with "ore." They asked me if my friend Ted had been my model for Kilgore. Answer: Very briefly, and in a way. Kilgore, like Ted when we first met in 1958, was a victim of a hate crime then commonly practiced by the American literary establishment. It wasn't racism or sexism or ageism. It was "genreism." Definition: "The unexamined conviction that anyone who wrote science fiction wasn't really a writer, but rather a geek of some sort." A genuine geek, of course, is a carnival employee who is displayed in a filthy cage and billed as "The Wild Man from Borneo."

Genreism was still rampant in late autumn, 1958, when I was living in Barnstable, Mass., on Cape Cod, and Ted and his wife Marion had just rented a house near the water in Truro (also on the Cape), no place to be when winter came. We knew each other's work, but had never met. Bingo! There we were face-to-face at last, at suppertime in my living room.

Ted had been writing nonstop for days or maybe weeks. He was skinny and haggard, underpaid and unappreciated outside the ghetto science fiction was then. He announced that he was going to do a standing back flip, which he did. He landed on his knees with a crash which shook the whole house. When he got back on his feet, humiliated and laughing in agony, one of the best writers in America was indeed, but only for a moment, my model for Kilgore Trout.

Kurt Vonnegut, Jr.
New York, New York
November 1999

A Saucer of Loneliness

IF SHE'S DEAD, I THOUGHT, I'll never find her in this white flood of moonlight on the white sea, with the surf seething in and over the pale, pale sand like a great shampoo. Almost always, suicides who stab themselves or shoot themselves in the heart carefully bare their chests; the same strange impulse generally makes the sea-suicide go naked.

A little earlier, I thought, or later, and there would be shadows for the dunes and the breathing toss of the foam. Now the only real shadow was mine, a tiny thing just under me, but black enough to feed the blackness of the shadow of a blimp.

A little earlier, I thought, and I might have seen her plodding up the silver shore, seeking a place lonely enough to die in. A little later and my legs would rebel against this shuffling trot through sand, the maddening sand that could not hold and would not help a hurrying man.

My legs did give way then and I knelt suddenly, sobbing—not for her; not yet—just for air. There was such a rush about me: wind, and tangled spray, and colors upon colors and shades of colors that were not colors at all but shifts of white and silver. If light like that were sound, it would sound like the sea on sand, and if my ears were eyes, they would see such a light.

I crouched there, gasping in the swirl of it, and a flood struck me, shallow and swift, turning up and outward like flower petals where it touched my knees, then soaking me to the waist in its bubble and crash. I pressed my knuckles to my eyes so they would open again. The sea was on my lips with the taste of tears and the whole white night shouted and wept aloud.

And there she was.

Her white shoulders were a taller curve in the sloping foam. She must have sensed me—perhaps I yelled—for she turned and saw me kneeling there. She put her fists to her temples and her face twisted, and she uttered a piercing wail of despair and fury, and then plunged seaward and sank.

I kicked off my shoes and ran into the breakers, shouting, hunting, grasping at flashes of white that turned to sea-salt and coldness in my fingers. I plunged right past her, and her body struck my side as a wave whipped my face and tumbled both of us. I gasped in solid water, opened my eyes beneath the surface and saw a greenish-white distorted moon hurtle as I spun. Then there was sucking sand under my feet again and my left hand was tangled in her hair.

The receding wave towed her away and for a moment she streamed out from my hand like steam from a whistle. In that moment I was sure she was dead, but as she settled to the sand, she fought and scrambled to her feet.

She hit my ear, wet, hard, and a huge, pointed pain lanced into my head. She pulled, she lunged away from me, and all the while my hand was caught in her hair. I couldn't have freed her if I had wanted to. She spun to me with the next wave, battered and clawed at me, and we went into deeper water.

"Don't ... don't ... I can't swim!" I shouted, so she clawed me again.

"Leave me alone," she shrieked. "Oh, dear God, why can't you *leave*" (said her fingernails) "*me ...*" (said her fingernails) "*alone!*" (said her small hard fist).

So by her hair I pulled her head down tight to her white shoulder; and with the edge of my free hand I hit her neck twice. She floated again, and I brought her ashore.

I carried her to where a dune was between us and the sea's broad noisy tongue, and the wind was above us somewhere. But the light was as bright. I rubbed her wrists and stroked her face and said, "It's all right," and, "There!" and some names I used to have for a dream I had long, long before I ever heard of her.

She lay still on her back with the breath hissing between her teeth, with her lips in a smile which her twisted-tight, wrinkled-sealed eyes made not a smile but a torture. She was well and conscious for many moments and still her breath hissed and her closed eyes twisted. "Why couldn't you leave me alone?" she asked at last. She opened her eyes and looked at me. She had so much misery that there was no room for fear. She shut her eyes again and said, "You know who I am."

"I know," I said.

She began to cry.

I waited, and when she stopped crying, there were shadows among the dunes. A long time.

She said, "You don't know who I am. Nobody knows who I am."

I said, "It was in all the papers."

"That!" She opened her eyes slowly and her gaze traveled over my face, my shoulders, stopped at my mouth, touched my eyes for the briefest second. She curled her lips and turned away her head. "Nobody knows who I am."

I waited for her to move or speak, and finally I said, "Tell *me.*"

"Who are you?" she asked, with her head still turned away.

"Someone who ..."

"Well?"

"Not now," I said. "Later, maybe."

She sat up suddenly and tried to hide herself. "Where are my clothes?"

"I didn't see them."

"Oh," she said. "I remember. I put them down and kicked sand over them, just where a dune would come and smooth them over, hide them as if they never were ... I hate sand. I wanted to drown in the sand, but it wouldn't let me ... You mustn't look at me!" she shouted. "I hate to have you looking at me!" She threw her head from side to side, seeking. "I can't stay here like this! What can I do? Where can I go?"

"Here," I said.

She let me help her up and then snatched her hand away, half-

3

turned from me. "Don't touch me. Get away from me."

"Here," I said again, and walked down the dune where it curved in the moonlight, tipped back into the wind and down and became not dune but beach. "Here." I pointed behind the dune.

At last she followed me. She peered over the dune where it was chest-high, and again where it was knee-high. "Back there?"

I nodded.

"So dark . . ." She stepped over the low dune and into the aching black of those moon-shadows. She moved away cautiously, feeling tenderly with her feet, back to where the dune was higher. She sank down into the blackness and disappeared there. I sat on the sand in the light. "Stay away from me," she spat.

I rose and stepped back. Invisible in the shadows, she breathed, "Don't go away." I waited, then saw her hand press out of the clean-cut shadows. "There," she said, "over there. In the dark. Just be a . . . Stay away from me now . . . Be a—voice."

I did as she asked, and sat in the shadows perhaps six feet from her.

She told me about it. Not the way it was in the papers.

She was perhaps seventeen when it happened. She was in Central Park in New York. It was too warm for such an early spring day, and the hammered brown slopes had a dusting of green of precisely the consistency of that morning's hoarfrost on the rocks. But the frost was gone and the grass was brave and tempted some hundreds of pairs of feet from the asphalt and concrete to tread on it.

Hers were among them. The sprouting soil was a surprise to her feet, as the air was to her lungs. Her feet ceased to be shoes as she walked, her body was consciously more than clothes. It was the only kind of day which in itself can make a city-bred person raise his eyes. She did.

For a moment she felt separated from the life she lived, in which there was no fragrance, no silence, in which nothing ever quite fit nor was quite filled. In that moment the ordered disapproval of the buildings around the pallid park could not reach her; for two, three clean breaths it no longer mattered that the whole wide world really

belonged to images projected on a screen; to gently groomed god-
desses in these steel and glass towers; that it belonged, in short,
always, always to someone else.

So she raised her eyes, and there above her was the saucer.

It was beautiful. It was golden, with a dusty finish like that of an
unripe Concord grape. It made a faint sound, a chord composed of
two tones and a blunted hiss like the wind in tall wheat. It was dart-
ing about like a swallow, soaring and dropping. It circled and dropped
and hovered like a fish, shimmering. It was like all these living things,
but with that beauty it had all the loveliness of things turned and
burnished, measured, machined, and metrical.

At first she felt no astonishment, for this was so different from
anything she had ever seen before that it had to be a trick of the eye,
a false evaluation of size and speed and distance that in a moment
would resolve itself into a sun-flash on an airplane or the lingering
glare of a welding arc.

She looked away from it and abruptly realized that many other
people saw it—saw *something*—too. People all around her had
stopped moving and speaking and were craning upward. Around
her was a globe of silent astonishment, and outside it she was aware
of the life-noise of the city, the hard-breathing giant who never inhales.

She looked up again, and at last began to realize how large and
how far away the saucer was. No: rather, how small and how very
near it was. It was just the size of the largest circle she might make
with her two hands, and it floated not quite eighteen inches over her
head.

Fear came then. She drew back and raised a forearm, but the saucer
simply hung there. She bent far sideways, twisted away, leaped forward, looked back and upward to see if she had escaped it. At first
she couldn't see it; then as she looked up and up, there it was, close
and gleaming, quivering and crooning, right over her head.

She bit her tongue.

From the corner of her eye, she saw a man cross himself. *He did
that because he saw me standing here with a halo over my head,
she thought.* And that was the greatest single thing that had ever

5

happened to her. No one had ever looked at her and made a respectful gesture before, not once, not ever. Through terror, through panic and wonderment, the comfort of that thought nestled into her, to wait to be taken out and looked at again in lonely times.

The terror was uppermost now, however. She backed away, staring upward, stepping a ludicrous cakewalk. She should have collided with people. There were plenty of people there, gasping and craning, but she reached none. She spun around and discovered to her horror that she was the center of a pointing, pressing crowd. Its mosaic of eyes all bulged and its inner circle braced its many legs to press back and away from her.

The saucer's gentle note deepened. It tilted, dropped an inch or so. Someone screamed, and the crowd broke away from her in all directions, milled about, and settled again in a new dynamic balance, a much larger ring, as more and more people raced to thicken it against the efforts of the inner circle to escape.

The saucer hummed and tilted, tilted ...

She opened her mouth to scream, fell to her knees, and the saucer struck.

It dropped against her forehead and clung there. It seemed almost to lift her. She came erect on her knees, made one effort to raise her hands against it, and then her arms stiffened down and back, her hands not reaching the ground. For perhaps a second and a half the saucer held her rigid, and then it passed a single ecstatic quiver to her body and dropped it. She plumped to the ground, the backs of her thighs heavy and painful on her heels and ankles.

The saucer dropped beside her, rolled once in a small circle, once just around its edge, and lay still. It lay still and dull and metallic, different and dead.

Hazily, she lay and gazed at the gray-shrouded blue of the good spring sky, and hazily she heard whistles.

And some tardy screams.

And a great stupid voice bellowing "Give her air!" which made everyone press closer.

Then there wasn't so much sky because of the blueclad bulk with its metal buttons and its leatherette notebook. "Okay, okay, what's happened here stand back figods sake."

And the widening ripples of observation, interpretation and comment: "It knocked her down." "Some guy knocked her down." "He knocked her down." "Some guy knocked her down and—" "Right in broad daylight this guy ..." "The park's gettin' to be ..." onward and outward, the adulteration of fact until it was lost altogether because excitement is so much more important.

Somebody with a harder shoulder than the rest bulling close, a notebook here, too, a witnessing eye over it, ready to change "... a beautiful brunette ..." to "an attractive brunette" for the afternoon editions, because "attractive" is as dowdy as any woman is allowed to get if she is a victim in the news.

The glittering shield and the florid face bending close: "You hurt bad, sister?" And the echoes, back and back through the crowd, Hurt bad, hurt bad, badly injured, he beat the hell out of her, broad daylight ..."

And still another man, slim and purposeful, tan gabardine, cleft chin and beard-shadow: "Flyin' saucer, hm? Okay, Officer, I'll take over here."

"And who the hell might you be, takin' over?"

The flash of a brown leather wallet, a face so close behind that its chin was pressed into the gabardine shoulder. The face said, awed: "F.B.I." and that rippled outward, too. The policeman nodded—the entire policeman nodded in one single bobbing genuflection.

"Get some help and clear this area," said the gabardine.

"Yes, *sir!*" said the policeman.

"F.B.I., F.B.I.," the crowd murmured and there was more sky to look at above her.

She sat up and there was glory in her face. "The saucer talked to me," she sang.

"You shut up," said the gabardine. "You'll have lots of chance to talk later."

"Yeah, sister," said the policeman. "My God, this mob could be full of Communists."

"You shut up, too," said the gabardine.

7

Someone in the crowd told someone else a Communist beat up this girl, while someone else was saying she got beat up because she was a Communist.

She started to rise, but solicitous hands forced her down again. There were thirty police there by that time.

"I can walk," she said.

"Now you just take it easy," they told her.

They put a stretcher down beside her and lifted her onto it and covered her with a big blanket.

"I can walk," she said as they carried her through the crowd.

A woman went white and turned away moaning, "Oh, my God, how awful!"

A small man with round eyes stared and stared at her and licked and licked his lips.

The ambulance. They slid her in. The gabardine was already there.

A white-coated man with very clean hands: "How did it happen, miss?"

"No questions," said the gabardine. "Security."

The hospital.

She said, "I got to get back to work."

"Take your clothes off," they told her.

She had a bedroom to herself then for the first time in her life. Whenever the door opened, she could see a policeman outside. It opened very often to admit the kind of civilians who were very polite to military people, and the kind of military people who were even more polite to certain civilians. She did not know what they all did nor what they wanted. Every single day they asked her four million, five hundred thousand questions. Apparently they never talked to each other because each of them asked her the same questions over and over.

"What is your name?"

"How old are you?"

"What year were you born?"

Sometimes they would push her down strange paths with their questions.

"Now your uncle. Married a woman from Middle Europe, did

8

he? Where in Middle Europe?"

"What clubs or fraternal organizations did you belong to? Ah! Now about that Rinkeydinks gang on 63rd Street. Who was *really* behind it?"

But over and over again, "What did you mean when you said the saucer talked to you?"

And she would say, "It talked to me."

And they would say, "And it said—"

And she would shake her head.

There would be a lot of shouting ones, and then a lot of kind ones. No one had ever been so kind to her before, but she soon learned that no one was being kind to *her*. They were just getting her to relax, to think of other things, so they could suddenly shoot that question at her: "What do you mean it talked to you?"

Pretty soon it was just like Mom's or school or any place, and she used to sit with her mouth closed and let them yell. Once they sat her on a hard chair for hours and hours with a light in her eyes and let her get thirsty. Home, there was a transom over the bedroom door and Mom used to leave the kitchen light glaring through it all night, every night, so she wouldn't get the horrors. So the light didn't bother her at all.

They took her out of the hospital and put her in jail. Some ways it was good. The food. The bed was all right, too. Through the window she could see lots of women exercising in the yard. It was explained to her that they all had much harder beds.

"You are a very important young lady, you know."

That was nice at first, but as usual it turned out they didn't mean her at all. They kept working on her. Once they brought the saucer in to her. It was inside a big wooden crate with a padlock, and a steel box inside that with a Yale lock. It only weighed a couple of pounds, the saucer, but by the time they got it packed, it took two men to carry it and four men with guns to watch them.

They made her act out the whole thing just the way it happened with some soldiers holding the saucer over her head. It wasn't the same. They'd cut a lot of chips and pieces out of the saucer and, besides, it was that dead gray color. They asked her if she knew anything about that and for once she told them.

"It's empty now," she said.

The only one she would ever talk to was a little man with a fat belly who said to her the first time he was alone with her, "Listen, I think the way they've been treating you stinks. Now get this: I have a job to do. My job is to find out *why* you won't tell what the saucer said. I don't want to know what it said and I'll never ask you. I don't even want you to tell me. Let's just find out why you're keeping it a secret."

Finding out why turned out to be hours of just talking about having pneumonia and the flowerpot she made in second grade that Mom threw down the fire escape and getting left back in school and the dream about holding a wine glass in both hands and peeping over it at some man.

And one day she told him why she wouldn't say about the saucer, just the way it came to her: "Because it was talking to *me*, and it's just nobody else's business."

She even told him about the man crossing himself that day. It was the only other thing she had of her own.

He was nice. He was the one who warned her about the trial. "I have no business saying this, but they're going to give you the full dress treatment. Judge and jury and all. You just say what you want to say, no less and no more, hear? And don't let 'em get your goat. You have a right to own something."

He got up and swore and left.

First a man came and talked to her for a long time about how maybe this Earth would be attacked from outer space by beings much stronger and cleverer than we are, and maybe she had the key to a defense. So she owed it to the whole world. And then even if the Earth wasn't attacked, just think of what an advantage she might give this country over its enemies. Then he shook his finger in her face and said that what she was doing amounted to working *for* the enemies of her country. And he turned out to be the man that was defending her at the trial.

The jury found her guilty of contempt of court and the judge recited a long list of penalties he could give her. He gave her one of them and suspended it. They put her back in jail for a few more days, and one fine day they turned her loose.

That was wonderful at first. She got a job in a restaurant, and a furnished room. She had been in the papers so much that Mom didn't want her back home. Mom was drunk most of the time and sometimes used to tear up the whole neighborhood, but all the same she had very special ideas about being respectable, and being in the papers all the time for spying was not her idea of being decent. So she put her maiden name on the mailbox downstairs and told her daughter not to live there any more.

At the restaurant she met a man who asked her for a date. The first time. She spent every cent she had on a red handbag to go with her red shoes. They weren't the same shade, but anyway they were both red. They went to the movies and afterward he didn't try to kiss her or anything, he just tried to find out what the flying saucer told her. She didn't say anything. She went home and cried all night.

Then some men sat in a booth talking and they shut up and glared at her every time she came past. They spoke to the boss, and he came and told her that they were electronics engineers working for the government and they were afraid to talk shop while she was around— wasn't she some sort of spy or something? So she got fired.

Once she saw her name on a juke box. She put in a nickel and punched that number, and the record was all about "the flyin' saucer came down one day, and taught her a brand new way to play, and what it was I will not say, but she took me out of this world." And while she was listening to it, someone in the juke-joint recognized her and called her by name. Four of them followed her home and she had to block the door shut.

Sometimes she'd be all right for months on end, and then someone would ask for a date. Three times out of five, she and the date were followed. Once the man she was with arrested the man who was tailing them. Twice the man who was tailing them arrested the man she was with. Five times out of five, the date would try to find out about the saucer. Sometimes she would go out with someone and pretend that it was a real date, but she wasn't very good at it. So she moved to the shore and got a job cleaning at night in offices and stores. There weren't many to clean, but that just meant there weren't many people to remember her face from the papers. Like clockwork, every eighteen months, some feature writer would drag it all out again in a magazine or a Sunday supplement; and every time anyone saw a headlight on a mountain or a light on a weather balloon it had to be a flying saucer, and there had to be some tired quip about the saucer wanting to tell secrets. Then for two or three weeks she'd stay off the streets in the daytime.

Once she thought she had it whipped. People didn't want her, so she began reading. The novels were all right for a while until she found out that most of them were like the movies—all about the pretty ones who really own the world. So she learned things—animals, trees. A lousy little chipmunk caught in a wire fence bit her. The animals didn't want her. The trees didn't care.

Then she hit on the idea of the bottles. She got all the bottles she could and wrote on papers which she corked into the bottles. She'd tramp miles up and down the beaches and throw the bottles out as far as she could. She knew that if the right person found one, it would give that person the only thing in the world that would help. Those bottles kept her going for three solid years. Everyone's got to have a secret little something he does.

And at last the time came when it was no use any more. You can go on trying to help someone who *maybe* exists; but soon you can't pretend there is such a person any more. And that's it. The end.

"Are you cold?" I asked when she was through telling me. The surf was quieter and the shadows longer.

"No," she answered from the shadows. Suddenly she said, "Did you think I was mad at you because you saw me without my clothes?"

"Why shouldn't you be?"

"You know, I don't care? I wouldn't have wanted ... wanted you to see me even in a ball gown or overalls. You can't cover up my carcass. It shows; it's there whatever. I just didn't want you to *see* me. At all."

"Me, or anyone?"

She hesitated. "You."

I got up and stretched and walked a little, thinking. "Didn't the F.B.I. try to stop you throwing those bottles?"

"Oh, sure. They spent I don't know how much taxpayers' money gathering 'em up. They still make a spot check every once in a while. They're getting tired of it, though. All the writing in the bottles is the same." She laughed. I didn't know she could.

"What's funny?"

"All of 'em—judges, jailers, juke-boxes—people. Do you know it wouldn't have saved me a minute's trouble if I'd told 'em the whole thing at the very beginning?"

"No?"

"No. They wouldn't have believed me. What they wanted was a new weapon. Super-science from a super-race, to slap hell out of the super-race if they ever got a chance, or out of our own if they don't. All those brains," she breathed, with more wonder than scorn, "all that brass. They think 'super-race' and it comes out 'super-science.' Don't they ever imagine a super-race has super-feelings, too—super-laughter, maybe, or super-hunger?" She paused. "Isn't it time you asked me what the saucer said?"

"I'll tell you," I blurted.

> 'There is in certain living souls
> A quality of loneliness unspeakable,
> So great it must be shared
> As company is shared by lesser beings.
> Such a loneliness is mine; so know by this
> That in immensity
> There is one lonelier than you."

"Dear Jesus," she said devoutly, and began to weep. "And how is it addressed?"

"*To the loneliest one . . .*"

"How did you know?" she whispered.

"It's what you put in the bottles, isn't it?"

"Yes," she said. "Whenever it gets to be too much, that no one cares, that no one ever did ... you throw a bottle into the sea, and out goes a part of your own loneliness. You sit and think of someone somewhere finding it ... learning for the first time that the worst there is can be understood."

The moon was setting and the surf was hushed. We looked up and out to the stars. She said, "We don't know what loneliness is like. People thought the saucer was a saucer, but it wasn't. It was a bottle with a message inside. It had a bigger ocean to cross—all of space—and not much chance of finding anybody. Loneliness? We don't know loneliness."

When I could, I asked her why she had tried to kill herself.

"I've had it good," she said, "with what the saucer told me. I wanted to ... pay back. I was bad enough to be helped; I had to know I was good enough to help. No one wants me? Fine. But don't tell me no one, anywhere, wants my help. I can't stand that."

I took a deep breath. "I found one of your bottles two years ago. I've been looking for you ever since. Tide charts, current tables, maps and ... wandering. I heard some talk about you and the bottles hereabouts. Someone told me you'd quit doing it, you'd taken to wandering the dunes at night. I knew why. I ran all the way."

I needed another breath now. "I got a club foot. I think right, but the words don't come out of my mouth the way they're inside my head. I have this nose. I never had a woman. Nobody ever wanted to hire me to work where they'd have to look at me. You're beautiful," I said. "You're beautiful."

She said nothing, but it was as if a light came from her, more light and far less shadow than ever the practiced moon could cast. Among the many things it meant was that even to loneliness there is an end, for those who are lonely enough, long enough.

The Touch of Your Hand

"Dig there," said Osser, pointing.

The black-browed man pulled back. "Why?"

"We must dig deep to build high, and we are going to build high."

"Why?" the man asked again.

"To keep the enemy out."

"There are no enemies."

Osser laughed bitterly. "I'll have enemies."

"Why?"

Osser came to him. "Because I'm going to pick up this village and shake it until it wakes up. And if it won't wake up, I'll keep shaking until I break its back and it dies. Dig."

"I don't see why," said the man doggedly.

Osser looked at the golden backs of his hands, turned them over, watched them closing. He raised his eyes to the other.

"This is why," he said.

His right fist tore the man's cheek. His left turned the man's breath to a bullet which exploded as it left him. He huddled on the ground, unable to exhale, inhaling in small, heavy, tearing sobs. His eyes opened and he looked up at Osser. He could not speak, but his eyes did; and through shock and pain all they said was "Why?"

"You want reasons," Osser said, when he felt the man could hear him. "You want reasons—all of you. You see both sides of every question and you weigh and balance and cancel yourselves out. I want an end to reason. I want things done."

He bent to lift the bearded man to his feet. Osser stood half a head taller and his shoulders were as full and smooth as the bottoms of bowls. Golden hairs shifted and glinted on his forearms as he moved his fingers and the great cords tensed and valleyed. He lifted the man clear of the ground and set him easily on his feet and held him until he was sure of his balance.

"You don't understand me, do you?"

The man shook his head weakly.

"Don't try. You'll dig more if you don't try." He clapped the handle of the shovel into the man's hand and picked up a mattock. "Dig," he said, and the man began to dig.

Osser smiled when the man turned to work, arched his nostrils and drew the warm clean air into his lungs. He liked the sunlight now, the morning smell of the turned soil, the work he had to do and the idea itself of working.

Standing so, with his head raised, he saw a flash of bright yellow, the turn of a tanned face. Just a glimpse, and she was gone.

For a moment he tensed, frowning. If she had seen him he would be off to clatter the story of it to the whole village. Then he smiled. Let her. Let them all know. They must, sooner or later. Let them try to stop him.

He laughed, gripped his mattock, and the sod flew. So Jubilith saw fit to watch him, did she?

He laughed again. Work now, Juby later. In time he would have everything.

Everything.

The village street wound and wandered and from time to time divided and rejoined itself, for each house was built on a man's whim—near, far, high, small, separate, turned to or away. What did not harmonize contrasted well, and over all it was a pleasing place to walk.

Before a shop a wood-cobbler sat, gouging out sabots; and he was next door to the old leatherworker who cunningly wove immortal belts of-square-knotted rawhide. Then a house, and another, and a cabin; a space of green where children played; and the skeleton of a new building where a man, his apron pockets full of hardwood pegs, worked knowledgeably with a heavy mallet.

The cobbler, the leatherworker, the children and the builder all stopped to watch Jubilith because she was beautiful and because she ran. When she was by, they each saw the others watching, and each smiled and waved and laughed a little, though nothing was said.

A puppy lolloped along after her, three legs deft, the fourth in the way. Had it been frightened, it would not have run, and had Jubilith spoken to it, it would have followed wherever she went. But she ignored it, even when it barked its small soprano bark, so it curved away from her, pretending it had been going somewhere else anyway, and then it sat and puffed and looked after her sadly.

Past the smithy with its shadowed, glowing heart she ran; past the gristmill with its wonderful wheel, taking and yielding with its heavy cupped hands. A boy struck his hoop and it rolled across her path. Without breaking stride, she leaped high over it and ran on, and the glass-blower's lips burst away from his pipe, for a man can smile or blow glass, but not both at the same time.

When at last she reached Wrenn's house, she was breathing deeply, but with no difficulty, in the way possible only to those who run beautifully. She stopped by the open door and waited politely, not looking in until Oyva came out and touched her shoulder.

Jubilith faced her, keeping her eyes closed for a long moment, for Oyva was not only very old, she was Wrenn's wife.

"Is it Jubilith?" asked Oyva, smiling.

"It is," said the girl. She opened her eyes.

Oyva, seeing their taut corners, said shrewdly, "A troubled Jubilith as well. I'll not keep you. He's just inside."

Juby found a swift flash of smile to give her and went into the house, leaving the old woman to wonder where, where in her long life she had seen such a brief flash of such great loveliness. A firebird's wing? A green meteor? She put it away in her mind next to the memory of a burst of laughter—Wrenn's, just after he had kissed her first—and sat down on a three-legged stool by the side of the house.

A heavy fiber screen had been set up inside the doorway, to form a sort of meander, and at the third turn it was very dark. Juby paused to let the sunlight drain away from her vision. Somewhere in the dark before her there was music, the hay-clean smell of flower petals dried and freshly rubbed, and a voice humming. The voice and the music were open and free, but choked a listener's throat like the sudden appearance of a field of daffodils.

The voice and the music stopped short, and someone breathed quietly in the darkness.

"Is . . . is it Wrenn?" she faltered.

"It is," said the voice.

"Jubilith here."

"Move the screen," said the voice. "I'd like the light, talking to you, Jubilith."

She felt behind her, touched the screen. It had many hinges and swung easily away to the doorside. Wrenn sat cross-legged in the corner behind a frame which held a glittering complex of stones. He brushed petal-dust from his hands. "Sit there, child, and tell me what it is you do not understand."

She sat down before him and lowered her eyes, and his widened, as if someone had taken away a great light.

When she had nothing to say, he prompted her gently: "See if you can put it all into a single word, Jubilith."

She said immediately, "Osser."

"Ah," said Wrenn.

"I followed him this morning, out to the foothills beyond the Sky-tree Grove. He—"

Wrenn waited.

Jubilith put up her small hands, clenched, and talked in a rush. "Sussten, with the black brows, he was with Osser. They stopped and Osser shouted at him, and, when I came to where I could look down and see them, Osser took his fists and hammered Sussten, knocked him down. He laughed and picked him up. Sussten was sick; he was shaken and there was blood on his face. Osser told him to dig, and Sussten dug, Osser laughed again, he laughed . . . I think he saw me. I came here."

Slowly she put her fists down. Wrenn said nothing.

Jubilith said, in a voice like a puzzled sigh, "I understand this: When a man hammers something, iron or clay or wood, it is to change what he hammers from what it is to what he wishes it to be." She raised one hand, made a fist, and put it down again. She shook her head slightly and her heavy soft hair moved on her back. "To hammer a man is to change nothing. Sussten remains Sussten."

"It was good to tell me of this," said Wrenn when he was sure she had finished.

"Not good," Jubilith disclaimed. "I want to understand."

Wrenn shook his head. Juby cocked her head on one side like a wondering bright bird. When she realized that his gesture was a refusal, a small paired crease came and went between her brows.

"May I not understand this?"

"You *must* not understand it," Wrenn corrected. "Not yet, anyway. Perhaps after a time. Perhaps never."

"Ah," she said. "I—I didn't know."

"How could you know?" he asked kindly. "Don't follow Osser again, Jubilith."

She parted her lips, then again gave the small headshake. She rose and went out.

Oyva came to her. "Better now, Jubilith?"

Juby turned her head away; then, realizing that this was ill-mannered, met Oyva's gaze. The girl's eyes were full of tears. She closed them respectfully. Oyva touched her shoulder and let her go.

Watching the slim, bright figure trudge away, bowed with thought, drag-footed, unseeing, Oyva grunted and stumped into the house.

"Did she have to be hurt?" she demanded.

"She did," said Wrenn gently. "Osser," he added.

"Ah," she said, in just the tone he had used when Jubilith first mentioned the name. "What has he done now?"

Wrenn told her. Oyva sucked her lips in thoughtfully. "Why was the girl following him?"

"I didn't ask her. But don't you know?"

"I suppose I do," said Oyva, and sighed. "That mustn't happen, Wrenn."

"It won't. I told her not to follow him again."

She looked at him fondly. "I suppose even you can act like a fool once in a while."

He was startled. "Fool?"

"She loves him. You won't keep her from him by a word of advice."

"You judge her by yourself," he said, just as fondly. "She's only a child; in a day, a week, she'll wrap someone else up in her dreams.

"Suppose she doesn't?"

"Don't even think about it." A shudder touched his voice.

"I shall, though," said Oyva with determination. "And you'd do well to think about it, too." When his eyes grew troubled, she touched his cheek gently, "Now play some more for me."

He sat down before the instrument, his hands poised. Then into the tiny bins his fingers went, rubbing this dried-petal powder and that, and the stones glowed, changing the flower-scents into music and shifting colors.

He began to sing softly to the music.

They dug deep, day by day, and they built. Osser did the work of three men, and sometimes six or eight others worked with him, and sometimes one or two. Once he had twelve. But never did he work alone.

When the stone was three tiers above ground level, Osser climbed the nearest rise and stood looking down at it proudly, at the thickness and strength of the growing walls, at the toiling workers who lifted and strained to make them grow.

"Is it Osser?"

The voice was as faint and shy as a fern uncurling, as promising as spring itself.

He turned.

"Jubilith," she told him.

"What are you doing here?"

"I come here every day," she said. She indicated the copse which crowned the hill. "I hide here and watch you."

"What do you want?"

She laced her fingers. "I would like to dig there and lift stones."

"No," he said, and turned to study the work again.

"Why not?"

"Never ask me why. 'Because I say so'—that's all the answer you'll get from me—you or anyone."

She came to stand beside him. "You build fast."

He nodded. "Faster than any village house was ever built." He could sense the 'why' rising within her, and could feel it being checked.

"I want to build it, too," she pleaded.

"No," he said. His eyes widened as he watched the work. Suddenly he was gone, leaping down the slope in great springy strides. He turned the corner of the new wall and stood, saying nothing. The man who had been idling turned quickly and lifted a stone. Osser smiled a quick, taut smile and went to work beside him. Jubilith stood on the slope, watching, wondering.

She came almost every day as the tower grew. Osser never spoke to her. She watched the sunlight on him, the lithe strength, the rippling gold. He stood like a great tree, squatted like a rock, moved like a thundercloud. His voice was a whip, a bugle, the roar of a bull.

She saw him less and less in the village. Once it was a fearsome thing to see. Early in the morning he appeared suddenly, overtook a man, lifted him and threw him flat on the ground.

"I told you to be out there yesterday," he growled, and strode away.

Friends came and picked the man up, held him softly while he coughed, took him away to be healed.

No one went to Wrenn about it; the word had gone around that Osser and his affairs were not to be understood by anyone. Wrenn's function was to explain those few things which could not be understood. But certain of these few were not to be understood at all. So Osser was left alone to do as he wished—which was a liberty, after all, that was enjoyed by everyone else.

There came a twilight when Jubilith waited past her usual time. She waited until by ones and twos the workers left the tower, until Osser himself had climbed the hill, until he had paused to look back and be proud and think of tomorrow's work, until he, too, had turned his face to the town. Then she slipped down to the tower and around it, and carefully climbed the scaffolding on the far side. She looked about her.

The tower was now four stories high and seemed to be shaping toward a roof. Circular in cross-section, the tower had two rooms on each floor, an east-west wall between them on the ground floor, a north-south wall on the next, and so on up.

There was a central well into which was built a spiral staircase—a double spiral, as if one helix had been screwed into the other. This made possible two exits to stairs on each floor at the same level, though they were walled off one from the other. Each of the two rooms on every floor had one connecting doorway. Each room had three windows in it, wide on the inside, tapering through the thick stone wall to form the barest slit outside.

A portion of the castellated roof was already built. It overhung the entrance, and had slots in the overhang through which the whole entrance face of the tower could be covered by one man lying unseen on the roof, looking straight down.

Stones lay in a trough ready for placing, and there was some left-over mortar in the box. Jubilith picked up a trowel and worked it experimentally in the stuff, then lifted some out and tipped it down on the unfinished top of the wall, just as she had seen Osser do so many times. She put down the trowel and chose a stone. It was heavy—much heavier than she had expected—but she made it move, made it lift, made it seat itself to suit her on the fresh mortar. She ticked off the excess from the join and stepped back to admire it in the fading light.

Two great clamps, hard as teeth, strong as a hurricane, caught her right thigh and her left armpit. She was swung into the air and held helpless over the unfinished parapet.

She was utterly silent, shocked past the ability even to gasp.

"I told you you were not to work here," said Osser between his teeth. So tall he was, so long were his arms as he held her high over his head, that it seemed almost as far to the parapet as it was to the ground below.

He leaned close to the edge and shook her. "I'll throw you off. This tower is mine to build, you hear?"

If she had been able to breathe, she might have screamed or pleaded with him. If she had screamed or pleaded, he might have dropped her. But her silence apparently surprised him. He grunted and set her roughly on her feet. She caught at his shoulder to keep her balance, then quickly transferred her hold to the edge of the parapet. She dropped her head between her upper arms. Her long soft hair fell forward over her face, and she moaned.

"I told you," he said, really seeing her at last. His voice shook. He stepped toward her and put out his hand. She screamed. "Be *quiet!*" he roared. A moan shut off in mid-breath. "Ah, I told you, Juby. You shouldn't have tried to build here."

He ran his great hands over the edge of the stonework, found the one she had laid, the one that had cost her such effort to lift. With one hand, he plucked it up and threw it far out into the shadows below.

"I wanted to help you with it," she whispered.

"Don't you understand?" he cried. "No one builds here who *wants* to help!"

She simply shook her head.

She tried to breathe deeply and a long shudder possessed her.

When it passed, she turned weakly and stood, her back partly arched over the edge of the parapet, her hands behind her to cushion the stone. She shook the hair out of her face; it fell away on either side like a dawnlit bow-wave. She looked up at him with an expression of such piteous confusion that his dwindling rage vanished altogether.

He dropped his eyes and shuffled one foot like a guilty child. "Juby, leave me alone."

Something almost like a smile touched her lips. She brushed her bruised arm, then walked past him to the place where the scaffolding projected above the parapet.

"Not that way," he called. "Come here."

He took her hand and led her to the spiral staircase at the center of the tower. It was almost totally dark inside. It seemed like an age to her as they descended; she was alone in a black universe consisting of a rhythmic drop and turn, and a warm hard hand in hers, holding and leading her.

When they emerged, he stopped in the strange twilight, a darkness for all the world but a dazzle to them, so soaked with blackness were their eyes. She tugged gently, but he would not release her hand. She moved close to see his face. His eyes were wide and turned unseeing to the far slopes; he was frowning, yet his mouth was not fierce, but irresolute. Whatever his inward struggle was, it left his face gradually and transferred itself to his hand. Its pressure on hers became firm, hard, intense, painful.

"Osser!"

He dropped the hand and stepped back, shamed. "Juby, I will take you to . . . Juby, do you want to understand?" He waved at the tower.

She said, "Oh, yes!"

He looked at her closely, and the angry, troubled diffidence came and went. "Half a day there, half a day back again," he said.

She recognized that this was as near as this feral, unhappy man could come to asking a permission. "I'd like to understand," she said.

"If you don't, I'm going to kill you," he blurted. He turned to the west and strode off, not looking back.

Jubilith watched him go, and suddenly there was a sparkle in her wide eyes. She slipped out of her sandals, caught them up in her hand, and ran lightly and silently after him. He planted his feet strongly, like the sure, powerful teeth of the mill-wheel gears, and he would not look back. She sensed how immensely important it was to him not to look back. She knew that right-handed men look back over their left shoulders, so she drifted along close to him, a little behind him, a little to his right. How long, how long, until he looked to see if she was coming?

Up and up the slope, to its crest, over . . . down . . . ah! Just here, just at the last second where he could turn and look without stopping and still catch a glimpse of the tower's base, where they had stood. So he turned, and she passed around him like a windblown feather, unseen.

And he stopped, looking back, craning. His shoulders slumped, and slowly he turned to his path again—and there was Jubilith before him.

She laughed.

His jaw dropped, and then his lips came together in a thin, angry seal. For a moment he stared at her; and suddenly, quite against his will, there burst from him a single harsh bark of laughter. She put out her hand and he came to her, took it, and they went their way together.

They came to a village when it was very late and very dark, and Osser circled it. They came to another, and Jubilith thought he would do the same, for he turned south; but when they came abreast of it, he struck north again.

"We'll be seen," he explained gruffly, "but we'll be seen coming from the south and leaving northward."

She would not ask where he was taking her, or why he was making these elaborate arrangements, but already she had an idea. What lay to the west was—not forbidden, exactly, but, say discouraged. It was felt that there was nothing in that country that could be of value. Anyone traveling that way would surely be remembered.

So through the village they went, and they dined quickly at an inn, and went northward, and once in the darkness, veered west again. In a wood so dark that she had taken his hand again, he stopped and built a fire. He threw down springy boughs and a thick heap of ferns, and this was her bed. He slept sitting up, his back to a tree trunk, with Jubilith between him and the fire.

Jubilith awoke twice during the long night, once to see him with his eyes closed, but feeling that he was not asleep; and once to see him with his eyes open and the dying flames flickering in the pupils, and she thought then that he was asleep, or at least not with her, but lost in the pictures the flames painted.

In the morning they moved on, gathering berries for breakfast, washing in a humorous brook. And during this whole journey, nothing passed between them but the small necessary phrases: "You go first here." "Look out—it drops." "Tired yet?"

For there was that about Jubilith which made explanations unnecessary. Though she did not know where they were going, or why, she understood what must be done to get them there within the framework of his desire: to go immediately, as quickly as possible, undetected by anyone else.

She did only what she could to help and did not plague him with questions which would certainly be answered in good time. So: "Here are berries." "Look, a red bird!" "Can we get through there, or shall we go around?" And nothing more.

They did well, the weather was fine, and by mid-morning they had reached the tumbled country of the Crooked Hills. Jubilith had seen them from afar—great broken mounds and masses against the western sky—but no one ever went there, and she knew nothing about them. They were in open land now, and Jubilith regretted leaving the color and aliveness of the forest. The grasses here were strange, like yet unlike those near her village. They were taller, sickly, and some had odd ugly flowers. There were bald places, scored with ancient rain-gullies, as if some mighty hand had dashed acid against the soil. There were few insects and no animals that she could see, and no birds sang. It was a place of great sadness rather than terror; there was little to fear, but much to grieve for.

By noon, they faced a huge curved ridge, covered with broken stones. It looked as if the land itself had reared up and pressed back from a hidden something on the other side—something which it would not touch. Osser quickened their pace as they began to climb, although the going was hard. Jubilith realized that they were near the end of their journey, and uncomplainingly struggled along at the cruel pace he set.

At the top, they paused, giving their first attention to their wind, and gradually to the scene before them.

The ridge on which they stood was nearly circular, and perhaps a mile and a half in diameter. In its center was a small round lake with unnaturally bare shores. Mounds of rubble sloped down toward it on all sides, and farther back was broken stone.

But it was the next zone which caught and held the eye. The weed-grown wreckage there was beyond description. Great twisted webs and ribs of gleaming metal wove in and out of the slumped heaps of soil and masonry. Nearby, a half-acre of laminated stone stood on the edge like a dinner plate in a clay bank. What could have been a building taller than any Jubilith had ever heard about lay on its side, smashed and bulging.

Gradually she began to realize the peculiarity of this place—All the larger wreckage lay in lines directly to and from the lake in a monstrous radiation of ruin.

"What is this place?" she asked at last.

"Don't know," he grunted, and went over the edge to slip down the steep slope. When she caught up with him near the bottom, he said, "There's miles of this, west and north of here, much bigger. But this is the one we came to see. Come."

He looked to right and left as if to get his bearings, then plunged into the tough and scrubby underbrush that vainly tried to cover those tortured metal bones. She followed as closely as she could, beating at the branches which he carelessly let whip back.

Just in front of her, he turned the corner of a sharp block of stone, and when she turned it no more than a second later, he was gone.

She stopped, turned, turned again. Dust, weeds, lonely and sorrowful ruins. No Osser. She shrank back against the stone, her eyes wide.

The bushes nearby trembled, then lashed. Osser's head emerged. "What's the matter? Come on!" he said gruffly.

She checked an impulse to cry out and run to him, and came silently forward. Osser held the bushes briefly, and beside him she saw a black hole with broken steps leading downward.

She hesitated, but he moved his head impatiently, and she passed him and led the way downward. When he followed, his wide flat body blocked out the light. The darkness was so heavy, her eyes ached.

He prodded her in the small of the back. "Go on, go on!"

The foot of the steps came sooner than she expected and her knees buckled as she took the downward step that was not there. She tripped, almost fell, then somehow got to the side wall and braced herself there, trembling.

"Wait," he said, and the irrepressible smile quirked the corners of her mouth. As if she would go anywhere!

She heard him fumbling about somewhere, and then there was a sudden aching blaze of light that made her cry out and clap her hands over her face.

"Look," he said. "I want you to look at this. Hold it."

Into her hands he pressed a cylinder about half the length of her forearm. At one end was a lens from which the blue-white light was streaming.

"See this little thing here," he said, and touched a stud at the side of the cylinder. The light disappeared, came on again.

She laughed delightedly, took the cylinder and played its light around, switching it on and off. "It's wonderful!" she cried. "Oh, wonderful!"

"You take this one," he said, pleased. He handed her another torch and took the first from her. "It isn't as good, but it will help. I'll go first."

She took the second torch and tried it. It worked the same way, but the light was orange and feeble. Osser strode ahead down a slanting passageway. At first there was a great deal of rubble underfoot, but soon the way was clear as they went farther and deeper. Osser walked with confidence, and she knew he had been here before, probably many times.

"Here," he said, stopping to wait for her. His voice echoed strangely, vibrant with controlled excitement.

He turned his torch ahead, swept it back and forth.

They were at the entrance to a room. It was three times the height of a man, and as big as their village green. She stared around, awed.

"Come," Osser said again, and went to the far corner.

A massive, box-like object stood there. One panel, about eye-level, was of a milky smooth substance, the rest of black metal. Projecting from the floor in front of it was a lever. Osser grasped it confidently and pulled. It yielded sluggishly, and returned to its original position. Osser tugged again. There was a low growling sound from the box. Osser pulled, released, pulled, released, each time a little faster. The sound rose in pitch, higher and higher.

"Turn off your light," he said.

She did so and blackness snapped in around them. As the dazzle faded from her eyes, she detected a flicker of silver light before her, and realized that it came from the milky pane in the box. As Osser pulled at the lever and the whine rose and rose in pitch, the square

28

got bright enough for her to see her hands when she looked down at them.

And then—the pictures.

Jubilith had never seen pictures like these. They moved, for one thing; for another, they had no color. Everything in them was black and white and shades of gray. Yet everything they showed seemed very real.

Not at first, for there was flickering and stopped motion, and then slow motion as Osser's lever moved faster and faster. But at last the picture steadied, and Osser kept the lever going at the same speed, flicking it with apparent ease about twice a second, while the whine inside the box settled to a steady, soft moan.

The picture showed a ball spinning against a black, light-flecked curtain. It rushed close until it filled the screen, and still closer, and Jubilith suddenly had the feeling that she was falling at tremendous velocity from an unthinkable height. Down and down the scene went, until at last the surface began to take on the qualities of a bird's-eye view. She saw a river and lakes, and a great range of hills—

And, at last, the city.

It was a city beyond fantasy, greater and more elaborate than imagination could cope with. Its towers stretched skyward to pierce the clouds themselves—some actually did. It had wide ramps on which traffic crawled, great bridges across the river, parks over which the buildings hung like mighty cliffs. Closer still the silver eye came to the scene, and she realized that the traffic was not crawling, but moving faster than a bird, faster than the wind. The vehicles were low and sleek and efficient.

And on the walks were people, and the scene wheeled and slowed and showed them. They were elaborately clothed and well-fed; they were hurried and orderly at the same time. There was a square in which perhaps a thousand of them, all dressed alike, were drawn up in lines as straight as stretched string. Even as she watched, they all began to move together, a thousand left legs coming forward, a thousand right arms swinging back.

Higher, then, and more of the city—more and more of it, until the sense of wonder filled her lungs and she hardly breathed; and still more of it, miles of it. And at last a great open space with what looked like sections of road crossing on it—but such unthinkable roads! Each was as wide as her whole village and miles long. And on these roads, great birdlike machines tilted down and touched and rolled, and swung and ran and took the air, dozens of them every minute. The scene swept close again, and it was as if she were in such a machine herself; but it did not land. It raced past the huge busy crossroads and out to a coastline.

And there were ships, ships as long as the tallest buildings were high, and clusters, dozens, hundreds of other vessels working and smoking and milling about in the gray water. Huge machines crouched over ships and lifted out cargoes; small, agile machines scurried about the docks and warehouses.

Then at last the scene dwindled as the magic eye rose higher and higher, faster and faster. Details disappeared, and clouds raced past and downward, and at last the scene was a disc and then a ball floating in starlit space.

Osser let the lever go and it snapped back to its original position.

The moan descended quickly in pitch, and the motion on the screen slowed, flickered, faded and went out.

Jubilith let the darkness come. Her mind spun and shook with the impact of what she had seen. Slowly she recovered herself. She became conscious of Osser's hard breathing. She turned on her dim orange torch and looked at him. He was watching her.

"What was it?" she breathed.

"What I came to show you."

She thought hard. She thought about his tower, about his refusal to let her work on it, about his cruelty to those who had. She looked at him, at the blank screen. And this was to supply the reason.

She shook her head.

He lowered himself slowly and squatted like an animal, hunched up tight, his knees in his armpits. This lifted and crooked his heavy arms. He rested their knuckles on the floor. He glowered at her and said nothing. He was waiting.

On the way here, he had said, "I'll kill you if you don't understand." But he wouldn't really, would he? Would he?

If he had towered over her, ranted and shouted, she would not have been afraid. But squatting there, waiting, silent, with his great arms bowed out like that, he was like some patient, preying beast.

She turned off the light to blot out the sight of him, and immediately became speechless with terror at the idea of his sitting there in the dark so close, waiting. She might run; she was so swift . . . but no; crouched like that, he could spring and catch her before she could tense a muscle.

Again she looked at the dead screen. "Will you . . . tell me something?" she quavered.

"I might."

"Tell me, then: When you first saw that picture, did you understand? The very first time?"

His expression did not change. But slowly he relaxed. He rocked sidewise, sat down, extended his legs. He was man again, not monster. She shuddered, then controlled it.

He said, "It took me a long time and many visits. I should not have asked you to understand at once."

She again accepted the timid half-step toward an apology, and was grateful.

He said, "Those were men and women just like us. Did you see that? Just like us."

"Their clothes—"

"Just like us," he insisted. "Of course they dressed differently, lived differently! In a world like that, why not? Ah, how they built, how they built!"

"Yes," she whispered. Those towers, the shining, swift vehicles, the thousand who moved like one . . . "Who were they?" she asked him.

"Don't you know? Think—think!"

"Osser, I want to understand. I truly want to!"

She hunted frantically for the right thing to say, the right way to catch at this elusive thing which was so frighteningly important to him. All her life she had had the answers to the questions she wanted to understand. All she had ever had to do was to close her eyes and think of the problem, and the answers soon came.

But not this problem.

"Osser," she pleaded, "where is it, the city, the great complicated city?"

"Say, 'Where was it?'" he growled.

She caught his thought and gasped. "This? These ruins, Osser?"

"Ah," he said approvingly. "It comes slowly, doesn't it? No, Juby. Not here. What was here was an outpost, a village, compared with the big city. North and west, I told you, didn't I? Miles of it. So big that ... so big—" He extended his arms, dropped them helplessly. Suddenly he leaned close to her, began to talk fast, feverishly. "Juby, that city—that world—was built by *people*. Why did they build and why do we not? What is the difference between those people and ours?"

"They must have had ..."

"They had nothing we don't have. They're the same kind of people; they *used* something we haven't been using. Juby, I've got that something. I can build. I can make others build."

A mental picture of the tower glimmered before her. "You built it with hate," she said wonderingly. "Is that what they had—cruelty, brutality, hatred?"

"Yes!"

"I don't believe it! I don't believe anyone could live with that much hate!"

"Perhaps not. Perhaps they didn't. But they *built* with it. They built because some men could flog others into building for them, building higher and faster than all the good neighbors would ever do helping one another."

"They'd hate the man who made them build like that."

Osser's hands crackled as he pressed them together. He laughed, and the echoes took everything that was unpleasant about that laughter and filled the far reaches of the dark room with it.

"They'd hate him," he agreed. "But he's strong, you see. He was strong in the first place, to make them build, and he's stronger afterward with what they built for him. Do you know the only way they can express their hatred, once they find he's too strong for them?"

Jubilith shook her head.

"They'd build," he chuckled. "They'd build higher and faster than he did. They would find the strongest man among them and *ask* him to flog them into it. That's the way a great city goes up. A strong man builds, and strong men follow, and soon the man who's strongest of all makes all the other strong ones do his work. Do you see?"

"And the ... the others, the weak?"

"What of them?" he asked scornfully. "There are more of them than strong ones—so there are more hands to do the strong man's work. And why shouldn't they? Don't they get the city to live in when it's built? Don't they ride about in swift shining carriers and fly through the air in the bird machines?"

"Would they be—happy?" she asked.

He looked at her in genuine puzzlement. "Happy?" He smashed a heavy fist into his palm. "They'd have a *city*!" Again the words tumbled from him. "How do you live, you and the rest of the village? What do you do when you want a—well, a garden, food from the ground?"

"I dig up the soil," she said. "I plant and water and weed."

"Suppose you want a plow?"

"I make one. Or I do work for someone who has one."

"Uh," he grunted. "And there you are, hundreds of you in the village, each one planting a little, smithing a little, thatching and cutting and building a little. Everyone does everything except for how many—four, five?—the leatherworker, old Griak who makes wooden pegs for house beams, one or two others."

"They like to do just one work. But anyone can do any of the work. Those few, we take care of. Someone has to keep the skills alive."

He snorted. "Put a strong man in the village and give him strong men to do what he wants. Get ten villagers at once and make them all plant at once. You'll have food then for fifty, not ten!"

"But it would go to waste!"

"It would not, because it would all belong to the head man. He would give it away as he saw fit—a lot to those who obeyed him,

33

nothing to those who didn't. What was left over he could keep for himself, and barter it out to keep building. Soon he would have the biggest house and the best animals and the finest women, and the more he got, the stronger he would be. And a city would grow—*a city!* And the strong man would give everyone better things if they worked hard, and protect them."

"Protect them? Against what?"

"Against the other strong ones. There would be others."

"And you—"

"I shall be the strongest of all," he said proudly. He waved at the box. "We were a great people once. We're ants now—less than ants, for at least the ants work together for a common purpose. I'll make us great again." His head sank onto his hand and he looked somberly into the shadows. "Something happened to this world. Something smashed the cities and the people and drove them down to what they are today. Something was broken within them, and they no longer dared to be great. Well, they will be. I have the extra something that was smashed out of them."

"What smashed them, Osser?"

"Who can know? I don't. I don't care, either." He tapped her with a long forefinger to emphasize. "All I care about is this: They were smashed because they were not strong enough. I shall be so strong I can't be smashed."

She said, "A stomach can hold only so much. A man asleep takes just so much space. So much and no more clothing makes one comfortable. Why do you want more than these things, Osser?"

She knew he was annoyed, and knew, too, that he was considering the question as honestly as he could.

"It's because I . . . I want to be strong," he said in a strained voice.

"You *are* strong."

"Who knows that?" he raged, and the echoes giggled and whispered.

"I do. Wrenn. Sussten. The whole village."

"The whole world will know. They will all do things for me."

She thought, but everyone does everything for himself, all over the world. Except, she added, those who aren't able . . .

34

With that in mind, she looked at him, his oaken shoulders, his powerful, bitter mouth. She touched the bruises his hands had left and the beginnings of the understanding she had been groping for left her completely.

She said dully, "Your tower . . . you'd better get back there."

"Work goes on," he said, smiling tightly, "whether I'm there or not, as long as they don't know my plans. They are afraid. But— yes, we can go now."

Rising, he flicked the stud of his torch. It flared blue-white, faded to the weak orange of Jubilith's, then died.

"The light . . ."

"It's all right," said Jubilith. "I have mine."

"When they get like that, so dim, you can't tell when they'll go out. Come—hurry! This place is full of corridors; without light, we could be lost here for days."

She glanced around at the crowding shadows. "Make it work again," she suggested.

He looked at the dead torch in his hand. "You," he said flatly. He tossed it. She caught it in her free hand, put her torch on the floor, and held the broken one down so she could see it in the waning orange glow. She turned it over twice, her sensitive hands feeling with every part rather than with fingertips alone. She held it still and closed her eyes; and then it came to her, and she grasped one end with her right hand and the other with her left and twisted.

There was a faint click and the outer shell of the torch separated. She drew off the butt end of it; it was just a hollow shell. The entire mechanism was attached to the lens end and was now exposed.

She turned it over carefully, keeping her fingers away from the workings. Again she closed her eyes and thought, and at last she bent close and peered. She nodded, fumbled in her hair, and detached a copper clasp. She bent and broke off a narrow strip of it and inserted it carefully into the light mechanism. Very carefully, she pried apart two small strands of wire, dipped a little deeper, hooked onto a tiny white sphere, and drew it out.

"Poor thing," she murmured under her breath.

"Poor what?"

"Spider's egg," she said ruefully. "They fight so to save them; and this one will never hatch out now. It's been burned."

She picked up the butt-end housing, slipped the two parts together, and twisted them until they clicked. She handed the torch to Osser.

"You've wasted time," he complained, surly.

"No, I haven't," she said. "We'll have light now."

He touched the stud on the torch. The brilliant, comforting white light poured from it.

"Yes," he admitted quietly.

Watching his face as he handled the torch, she knew that if she could read what was in his mind in that second, she would have the answer to everything about him. She could not, however, and he said nothing, but led the way across the room to the dark corridor.

He was silent all the way back to the broken steps.

They stood halfway up, letting their eyes adjust to the daylight which poured down on them, and he said, "You didn't even try the torch to see if it would work, after you took out that egg."

"I knew it would work." She looked at him, amazed. "You're angry."

"Yes," he said.

He took her torch and his and put them away in a niche in the ruined stairwell, and they climbed up into the noon light. It was all but intolerable, as the two suns were all but in syzygy, the blue-white midget shining through the great pale gaseous mass of the giant, so that together they cast only a single shadow.

"It will be hot this afternoon," she said, but he was silent, steeped in some bitterness of his own, so she followed him quietly without attempting conversation.

Old Oyva stirred sleepily in her basking chair, and suddenly sat upright.

Jubilith approached her, pale and straight. "Is it Oyva?"

"It is, Jubilith," said the old woman. "I knew you would be back, my dear. I'm sore in my heart with you."

"Is he here?"

"He is. He has been on a journey. You'll find him tired."

"He should have been here, with all that has happened," said Jubilith.

"He should have done exactly as he has done," Oyva stated bluntly.

Jubilith recognized the enormity of her rudeness, and the taste of it was bad in her mouth. One did not criticize Wrenn's comings and goings.

She faced Oyva and closed her eyes humbly.

Oyva touched her. "It's all right, child. You are distressed. Wrenn!" she called. "She is here!"

"Come, Jubilith," Wrenn's voice called from the house.

"He knows? *No* one knew I was coming here!"

"He knows," said Oyva. "Go to him, child."

Jubilith entered the house. Wrenn sat in his corner. The musical instrument was nowhere in sight. Aside from his cushions, there was nothing in the room.

Wrenn gave her his wise, sweet smile. "Jubilith," he said. "Come close." He looked drawn and pale, but quite untroubled. He put a cushion by him and she crossed slowly and sank down on it.

He was quiet, and when she was sure it was because he waited for her to speak, she said, "Some things may not be understood."

"True," he agreed.

She kneaded her hands. "Is there never a change?"

"Always," he said, "when it's time."

"Osser—"

"Everyone will understand Osser very soon now."

She screwed up her courage. "Soon is not soon enough. I must know him now."

"Before anyone else?" he inquired mildly.

"Let everyone know now," she suggested.

He shook his head and there was no appeal in it.

"Then let me. I shall be a part of you and speak of it only to you."

"Why must you understand?"

She shuddered. It was not cold, or fear, but simply the surgings of a great emotion.

"I love him," she said. "And to love is to guard and protect. He needs me."

"Go to him then." But she sat where she was, her long eyes cast down, weeping. Wrenn said, "There is more, then?"

"I love ..." She threw out an arm in a gesture which enfolded Wrenn, the house, the village. "I love the people, too, the gardens, the little houses; the way we go and come, and sing, and make music, and make our own tools and clothes. To love is to guard and protect ... and I love these things, and I love Osser. I can destroy Osser, because he would not expect it of me; and, if I did, I would protect all of you. But if I protect him, he will destroy you. There is no answer to such a problem, Wrenn; it is a road," she cried, "with a precipice at each end, and no standing still!"

"And understanding him would be an answer?"

"There's no other!" She turned her face up to him, imploring. "Osser is strong, Wrenn, with a—new thing about him, a thing none of the rest of us have. He has told me of it. It is a thing that can change us, make us part of him. He will build cities with our hands, on our broken bodies if we resist him. He wants us to be a great people again—he says we were, once, and have lost it all."

"And do you regard that as greatness, Jubilith—the towers, the bird-machines?"

"How did you know of them? ... Greatness? I don't know, I don't know," she said, and wept. "I love him, and he wants to build a city with a wanting greater than anything I have ever known or heard of before. Could he do it, Wrenn? Could he?"

"He might," said Wrenn calmly.

"He is in the village now. He has about him the ones who built his tower for him. They cringe around him, hating to be near and afraid to leave. He sent them one by one to tell all the people to come out to the foothills tomorrow, to begin work on his city. He wants enough building done in one hundred days to shelter everyone, because then, he says, he is going to burn this village to the ground. Why, Wrenn—why?"

"Perhaps," said Wrenn, "so that we may all face his strength and yield to it. A man who could move a whole village in a hundred days just to show his strength would be a strong man indeed."

"What shall we do?"

38

"I think we shall go out to the foothills in the morning and begin to build."

She rose and went to the door.

"I know what to do now," she whispered. "I won't try to understand any more. I shall just go and help him."

"Yes, go," said Wrenn. "He will need you."

Jubilith stood with Osser on the parapet, and with him stared into the dappled dawn. The whole sky flamed with the loom of the red sun's light, but the white one preceded it up the sky, laying sharp shadows in the soft blunt ones. Birds called and chattered in the Skytree Grove, and deep in the thickets the seven-foot bats grunted as they settled in to sleep.

"Suppose they don't come?" she asked.

"They'll come," he said grimly. "Jubilith, why are you here?"

She said, "I don't know what you are doing, Osser. I don't know whether it's right or whether you will keep on succeeding. I do know there will be pain and difficulty and I—I came to keep you safe, if I could . . . I love you."

He looked down at her, as thick and dark over her as his tower was over the foothills. One side of his mouth twitched.

"Little butterfly," he said softly, "do you think *you* can guard *me?*"

Everything beautiful about her poured out to him through her beautiful face, and for a moment his world had three suns instead of two. He put his arms around her. Then his great voice exploded with two syllables of a mighty laugh. He lifted her and swung her behind him, and leaped to the parapet.

Deeply shaken, she came to follow his gaze.

The red sun's foggy limb was above the townward horizon, and silhouetted against it came the van of a procession. On they came and on, the young men of the village, the fathers. Women were with them, too, and everything on wheels that the village possessed—flatbed wagons, two-wheeled rickshaw carts, children's and vendors' and pleasure vehicles. A snorting team of four tiger-oxen clawed along before a heavily laden stone-boat, and men shared packs that swung in the center of long poles.

Osser curled his lip. "You see them," he said, as if to himself, "doing the only thing they can think of. Push them, they yield. The clods!" he spat. "Well, one day, one will push back. And when he does, I'll break him, and after that I'll use him. Meantime—I have a thousand hands and a single mind. We'll see building now," he crooned. "When they've built, they'll know what they don't know now—that they're men."

"They've all come," breathed Jubilith. "All of them. Osser—"

"Be quiet," he said, leaning into the wind to watch, gloating. With the feel of his hard hands still on her back, she discovered with a crushing impact that there was no room in his heart for her when he thought of his building. And she knew that there never would be, except perhaps for a stolen moment, a touch in passing. With the pain of that realization came the certainty that she would stay with him always, even for so little.

The procession dipped out of sight, then slowly rose over and down the near hill and approached the tower. It spread and thickened at the foot of the slope, as men cast about, testing the ground with their picks, eying the land for its color and vegetation and drainage ... or was that what they were doing?

Osser leaned his elbows on the parapet and shook his head pityingly at their inefficiency. Look at the way they went about laying out houses! And their own houses. Well, he'd let them mill about until they were completely confused, and then he'd go down and make them do it his way. Confused men are soft men; men working against their inner selves are easy to divert from outside.

Beside him, Jubilith gasped.

"What is it?"

She pointed. "There—sending the men to this side, that side. See, by the stone-boat? It's Wrenn!"

"Nonsense!" said Osser. "He'd never leave his house. Not to walk around among people who are sweating. He deals only with people who tell him he's right before he speaks."

"It's Wrenn, it is, it is!" cried Jubilith. She clutched his arm. "Osser, I'm afraid!"

"Afraid? Afraid of what? . . . By the dying Red One, it *is* Wrenn, telling men what to do as if this was *his* city." He laughed. "There are few enough here who are strong, Juby, but he's the strongest there is. And look at him scurry around for me!"

"I'm afraid," Jubilith whimpered.

"They jump when he tells them," said Osser reflectively, shading his eyes. "Perhaps I was wrong to let them tire themselves out before I help them do things right. With a man like him to push them . . . Hm. I think we'll get it done right the first time."

He pushed himself away from the parapet and swung to the stairway.

"Osser, don't, please don't!" she begged.

He stopped just long enough to give her a glance like a stone thrown. "You'll never change my mind, Juby, and you'll be hurt if you try too often." He dropped into the opening, went down three steps, five steps . . .

He grunted, stopped.

Jubilith came slowly over to the stairwell. Osser stood on the sixth step, on tiptoe. Impossibly on tiptoe: the points of his sandals barely touched the step at all.

He set his jaw and placed his massive hands one on each side of the curved wall. He pressed them out and up, forcing himself downward. His sandals touched more firmly; his toes bent, his heels made contact. His face became deep red, and the cords at the sides of his neck ridged like a weathered fallow-field.

A strained crackle came from his shoulders, and then the pent breath burst from him. His hands slipped, and he came up again just the height of the single stair-riser, to bob ludicrously like a boat at anchor, his pointed toe touching and lifting from the sixth step.

He gave an inarticulate roar, bent double, and plunged his hands downward as if to dive head-first down the stairs. His wrists turned under and he yelped with the pain. More cautiously he felt around and down, from wall to wall. It was as if the air in the stairway had solidified, become at once viscous and resilient. Whatever was there was invisible and completely impassable.

He backed slowly up the steps. On his face there was fury and frustration, hurt and a shaking reaction.

Jubilith wrung her hands. "Please, please, Osser, be care—"

The sound of her voice gave him something to strike out at, and he spun about, raising his great bludgeon of a fist. Jubilith stood frozen, too shocked to dodge the blow.

"*Osser!*"

Osser stopped, tensed high, fist up, like some terrifying monument to vengeance. The voice had been Wrenn's—Wrenn speaking quietly, even conversationally, but magnified beyond belief. The echoes of it rolled off and were lost in the hills.

"*Come watch men building, Osser!*"

Dazed, Osser lowered his arm and went to the parapet.

Far below, near the base of the hill, Wrenn stood, looking up at the tower. When Osser appeared, Wrenn turned his back and signaled the men by the stone-boat. They twitched away the tarpaulin that covered its load.

Osser's hands gripped the stone as if they would powder it. His eyes slowly widened and his jaw slowly dropped.

At first it seemed like a mound of silver on the rude platform of the ox-drawn stone-boat. Gradually he perceived that it was a machine, a machine so finished, so clean-lined and so businesslike that the pictures he had shown Jubilith were clumsy toys in comparison.

It was Sussten, a man Osser had crushed to the ground with two heavy blows, who sprang lightly up on the machine and settled into it. It backed off the platform, and Osser could hear the faintest of whines from it. The machine rolled and yet it stepped; it kept itself horizon-level as it ran, its long endless treads dipping and rising with the terrain, its sleek body moving smooth as a swan. It stopped and then went forward, out to the first of a field of stakes that a crew had been driving.

The flat, gleaming sides of the machine opened away and forward and locked, and became a single blade twice the width of the machine. It dropped until its sharp lower edge just touched the ground, checked for a moment, and then sank into the soil.

Dirt mounded up before it until flakes fell back over the wide moldboard. The machine slid ahead, and dirt ran off the sides of the blade to make two straight windrows. And behind the machine as it labored, the ground was flat and smooth; and it was done as easily as a smoothing hand in a sandbox. Here it was cut and there it was filled, but everywhere the swath was like planed wood, all done just as fast as a man can run.

Osser made a sick noise far back in his tight throat.

Guided by the stakes, the machine wheeled and returned, one end of the blade now curved forward to catch up the windrow and carry it across the new parallel cut. And now the planed soil was twice as wide.

As it worked, men worked, and Osser saw that, shockingly, they moved with no less efficiency and certainty than the machine. For Osser, these men had plodded and sweated, drudged, each a single, obstinate unit to be flogged and pressed. But now they sprinted, sprang; they held, drove, measured and carried as if to swift and intricate music.

A cart clattered up and from it men took metal spikes, as thick as a leg, twice as tall as a man. Four men to a spike, they ran with them to staked positions on the new-cut ground, set them upright. A man flung a metal clamp around the spike. Two men, one on each side, drove down on the clamp with heavy sledges until the spike would stand alone. And already those four were back with another spike.

Twenty-six such spikes were set, but long before they were all out of the wagon, Sussten spun the machine in its own length and stopped. The moldboard rose, hinged, folded back to become the silver sides of the machine again. Sussten drove forward, nosed the machine into the first of the spikes, which fitted into a slot at the front of the machine. There was the sound of a frantic giant ringing a metal triangle, and the spike sank as if the ground had turned to bread.

Leaving perhaps two hand's-breadths of the spike showing, the machine slid to the next and the next, sinking the spikes so quickly that it had almost a whole minute to wait while the spike crew set the very last one. At that a sound rolled out of the crowd, a sound utterly unlike any that had ever been heard during the building of the tower—a friendly, jeering roar of laughter at the crew who had made the machine wait.

Men unrolled heavy cable along the lines of spikes; others followed right behind them, one with a tool which stretched the cable taut, two with a tool that in two swift motions connected the cable to the tops of the sunken spikes. And by the time the cable was connected, two flatbeds, a buckboard and a hay wagon had unloaded a cluster of glistening machine parts. Men and women swarmed over them, wrenches, pliers and special tools in hand, bolting, fitting, clamping, connecting. Three heavy leads from the great ground cable were connected; a great parabolic wire basket was raised and guyed.

Wrenn ran to the structure and pulled a lever. A high-pitched scream of force dropped sickeningly in pitch to a jarring subsonic, and rose immediately high out of the audible range.

A rosy haze enveloped the end of the new machine, opposite the ground array and under the basket. It thickened, shimmered, and steadied, until it was a stable glowing sphere with an off-focus muzziness barely showing all around its profile.

The crowd—not a group now, but a line—cheered and the line moved forward. Every conceivable village conveyance moved in single file toward the shining sphere, and, as each stopped, heavy metal was unloaded. Cast-iron stove legs could be recognized, and long strips of tinning solder, a bell, a kettle, the framing of a bench. The blacksmith's anvil was there, and parts of his forge. Pots and skillets. A ratchet and pawl from the gristmill. The weights and pendulum from the big village clock.

As each scrap was unloaded, exactly the number of hands demanded by its weight were waiting to catch it, swing it from its conveyance into the strange sphere. They went in without resistance and without sound, and they did not come out. Wagon after wagon, pack after handsack were unloaded, and still the sphere took and took.

It took heavy metal of more mass than its own dimensions. Had the metal been melted down into a sphere, it would have been a third again, half again, twice as large as the sphere, and still it took.

But its color was changing. The orange went to burned sienna and then to a strident brown. Imperceptibly this darkened until at last it was black. For a moment, it was a black of impossible glossiness, but this softened. Blacker and blacker it became, and at length it was not a good thing to look into—the blackness seemed to be hungry for something more intimate than metal. And still the metals came and the sphere took.

A great roar came from the crowd; men fell back to look upward. High in the west was a glowing golden spark which showed a long blue tail. It raced across the sky and was gone, and moments later the human roar was answered by thunder from above.

If the work had been swift before, it now became a blur. Men no longer waited for the line of wagons to move, but ran back along it to snatch metal and stagger forward again to the sphere. Women ripped off bracelets and hammered earrings and threw them to the implacable melanosphere. Men threw in their knives, even their buttons. A rain of metal was sucked silently into the dazzling black.

Another cry from the crowd, and now there was hurried anguish in it; again the craning necks, the quick gasp. The golden spark was a speed-blurred ovoid now, the blue tail a banner half a horizon long. The roar, when it came, was a smashing thunder, and the blue band hung where it was long after the thing had gone.

A moan of urgency, caught and maintained by one exhausted throat after another, rose and fell and would not leave. Then it was a happy shout as Sussten drove in, shouldering the beautiful cutting machine through the scattering crowd. Its blade unfolded as it ran, latched high and stayed there like a shining forearm flung across the machine's silver face.

As the last scrambling people dove for safety, Sussten brought the huge blade slashing downward and at the same time threw the machine into its highest speed. It leaped forward as Sussten leaped back. Unmanned, it rushed at the sphere as if to sweep it away, crash the structure that contained it. But at the last microsecond, the blade struck the ground; the nose of the machine snapped upward, and the whole gleaming thing literally vaulted into the sphere.

No words exist for such a black. Some people fell to their knees, their faces covered. Some turned blindly away, unsteady on their feet. Some stood trembling, fixed on it, until friendly hands took and turned them and coaxed them back to reality.

And at last a man staggered close, squinting, and threw in the heavy wrought-iron support for an inn sign—

And the sphere refused it.

Such a cry of joy rose from the village that the sleeping bats in the thickets of Sky-Tree Grove, two miles away, stirred and added their porcine grunting to the noise.

A woman ran to Wrenn, screaming, elbowing, unnoticed and unheard in the bedlam. She caught his shoulder roughly, spun him half around, pointed. Pointed up at the tower, at Osser.

Wrenn thumbed a small disc out of a socket in his belt and held it near his lips.

"*Osser!*" The great voice rang and echoed, crushing the ecstatic noises of the people by its sheer weight. "*Osser, come down or you're a dead man!*"

The people, suddenly silent, all stared at the tower. One or two cried, "Yes, come down, come down ..." but the puniness of their voices was ludicrous after Wrenn's magnified tones, and few tried again.

Osser stood holding the parapet, legs wide apart, eyes wide— too wide—open. His hands curled over the edge, and blood dripped slowly from under the cuticles.

"*Come down, come down ...*"

He did not move. His eyeballs were nearly dry, and unnoticed saliva lay in a drying streak from one corner of his mouth.

"*Jubilith, bring him down!*"

She was whimpering, begging, murmuring little urgencies to him. His biceps were as hard as the parapet, his face as changeless as the stone.

"*Jubilith, leave him! Leave him and come!*" Wrenn, wise Wrenn, sure, unshakable, imperturbable Wrenn had a sob in his voice; and under such amplification the sob was almost big enough to be voice for the sobs that twisted through Jubilith's tight throat.

She dropped to one knee and put one slim firm shoulder under Osser's wrist. She drove upward against it with all the lithe strength of her panicked body. It came free, leaving a clot of fingertip on the stone. Down she went again, and up again at the other wrist; but this was suddenly flaccid, and her tremendous effort turned to a leap. She clutched at Osser, who tottered forward.

For one endless second they hung there, while their mutual center of gravity made a slow deliberation, and then Jubilith kicked frantically at the parapet, abrading her legs, mingling her blood with his on the masonry. They went together back to the roof. Jubilith twisted like a falling cat and got her feet down, holding Osser's great weight up.

They spun across the roof in an insane staggering dance; then there was the stairway (with its invisible barrier gone) and darkness (with his hand in hers now, holding and leading) and a sprint into daylight and the shattering roar of Wrenn's giant voice: *"Everybody down, down flat!"*

And there was a time of running, pulling Osser after her, and Osser pounding along behind her, docile and wide-eyed as a cat-ox. And then the rebellion and failure of her legs, and the will that refused to let them fail, and the failure of that will; the stunning agony of a cracked patella as she went down on the rocks, and the swift sense of infinite loss as Osser's hand pulled free of hers and he went lumbering blindly along, the only man on his feet in the wide meadow of the fallen.

Jubilith screamed and someone stood up—she thought it was old Oyva—and cried out.

Then the mighty voice again, *"Osser! Down, man!"* Blearily, then, she saw Osser stagger to a halt and peer around him.

"Osser, lie down!"

And then Osser, mad, drooling, turning toward her. His eyes protruded and he slashed about with his heavy fists. He came closer, unseeing, battling some horror he believed in with great cuts and slashes that threatened elbow and shoulder joints by the wrenching of their unimpeded force.

His voice—but not his, rather the voice of an old, wretched crone—squeaking out in a shrill falsetto, "Not down, never down, but up. I'll build, build, build, break to build, kill to build, and all

47

the ones who can do everything, anything, everything, they will build everything for me. I'm strong!" he shrieked, soprano. "All the people who can do anything are less than one strong man ..."

He jabbered and fought, and suddenly Wrenn rose, quite close by, his left hand enclosed in a round flat box. He moved something on its surface and then waved it at Osser, in a gesture precisely like the command to a guest to be seated.

Down went Osser, close to Jubilith, with his face in the dirt and his eyes open, uncaring. On him and on Jubilith lay the invisible weight of the force that had awaited him in the stairway.

The breath hissed out of Jubilith. Had she not been lying on her side with her face turned skyward in a single convulsive effort toward air, she would never have seen what happened. The golden shape appeared in the west, seen a fraction of a second, but blazoned forever in tangled memories of this day. And simultaneously the earth-shaking cough of the machine as its sphere disappeared. She could not see it move, but such a blackness is indelible, and she sensed it when it appeared in the high distances as its trajectory and that of the golden flyer intersected.

Then there was—*Nothing.*

The broad blue trail swept from the western horizon to the zenith, and sharply ended. There was no sound, no concussion, no blaze of light. The sphere met the ship and both ceased to exist.

Then there was the wind, from nowhere, from everywhere, all the wind that ever was, tearing in agony from everywhere in the world to the place where the sphere had been, trying to fill the strange space that had contained exactly as much matter as the dead golden ship. Wagons, oxen, trees and stones scraped and flew and crashed together in the center of that monstrous implosion.

The weight Wrenn had laid on Jubilith disappeared, but her sucking lungs could find nothing to draw in. There was air aplenty, but none of it would serve her.

Finally she realized that there was unconsciousness waiting for her if she wanted it. She embraced it, sank into it, and left the world to its wailing winds.

Ages later, there was weeping.

She stirred and raised her head.

The sphere machine was gone. There was a heap of something down there, but it supported such a tall and heavy pillar of roiling dust that she could not see what it was. There, and there, and over yonder, in twos and threes, silent, shaken people sat up, some staring about them, some just sitting, waiting for the shock-stopped currents of life to flow back in.

But the weeping . . .

She put her palm on the ground and inched it, heel first, in a weak series of little hops, until she was half sitting.

Osser was weeping.

He sat upright, his feet together and his knees wide apart, like a little child. He rocked. He lifted his hands and let them fall, lifted them and punctuated his crying with weak poundings on the ground. His mouth was an O, his eyes were single squeezed lines, his face was wet, and his crying was the most heartrending sound she had ever heard.

She thought to speak to him, but knew he would not hear. She thought to go to him, but the first shift of weight sent such agony through her broken kneecap that she almost fainted.

Osser wept.

She turned away from him—suppose, later, he should remember that she had seen this?—and then she knew why he was crying. He was crying because his tower was gone. Tower of strength, tower of defiance, tower of hope, tower of rebellion and hatred and an ambition big enough for a whole race of city-builders, gone without a fight, gone without the triumph of taking him with it, gone in an instant, literally in a puff of wind.

"Where does it hurt?"

It was Wrenn, who had approached unseen through the blinding, sick compassion that filled her.

"It hurts there." She pointed briefly at Osser.

"I know," said Wrenn gently. He checked what she was about to say with a gesture. "No, we won't stop him. When he was a little boy, he never cried. He has been hurt more than most people, and nothing ever made him cry, ever. We all have a cup for tears and a reservoir. No childhood is finished until all the tears flow from the reservoir into the cup. Let him cry; perhaps he is going to be a man. It's your knee, isn't it?"

"Yes. Oh, but I can't stand to hear it, my heart will burst!" she cried.

"Hear him out," said Wrenn softly, taking medication from a flat box at his waist. He ran feather-fingers over her knee and nodded. "You have taken Osser as your own. Keep this weeping with you, all of it. It will fit you to him better through the healing time."

"May I understand now?"

"Yes, oh yes . . . and since he has taught you about hate, you will hate me for it."

"I couldn't hate you, Wrenn."

Something stirred within his placid eyes—a smile, a pointed shard of knowledge—she was not sure. "Perhaps you could."

He kept his eyes on his careful bandaging, and as he worked, he spoke.

"Stop a man in his work to tell him that each of his fingers bears a pattern of loops and whorls, and you waste his time. It is a thing he knows, a thing he has seen for himself, a thing which can be checked on the instant—in short, an obvious, unremarkable thing. Yet, if his attention is not called to it, it is impossible to teach him that these patterns are exclusive, original with him, unduplicated anywhere. Sparing him the truism may cost him the fact.

"It is that kind of truism through which I shall pass to reach the things you must understand. So be patient with me through the familiar paths; I promise you a most remarkable turning.

"We are an ancient and resourceful species, and among the many things we have—our happiness, our simplicity, our harmony with each other and with ourselves—some are the products of intelligence, per se, but most of the good things spring from a quality which we possess in greater degree than any other species yet known. That is—logic.

"Now, there is the obvious logic: you may never have broken your knee before, but you knew, in advance, that if you did it would cause you pain. If I hold this pebble so, you may correctly predict that it will drop when I release it, though you have never seen this stone before. This obvious logic strikes deeper levels as well; for example, if I release the stone and it does not fall, logic tells you not only that some unpredicted force is now acting on it, but a great many things about that force: that it equals gravity in the case of this particular pebble; that it is in stasis; that it is phenomenal, since it is out of the statistical order of things.

"The quality of logic, which we (so far as is known) uniquely possess, is this: any of us can do literally anything that anyone else can do. You need ask no one to solve the problems that you face every day, providing they are problems common to all. To cut material so that a sleeve will fit a shoulder, you pause, you close your eyes; the way to cut the material then comes to you, and you proceed. You never need do anything twice, because the first way is the most logical. You may finish the garment and put it away without trying it on for fit, because you know you have done it right and it is perfect.

"If I put you before a machine which you had never seen before, which had a function unknown to you, and which operated on principles you had never heard of, and if I told you it was broken and needed repairing, you would look at it carefully, inside, outside, top and bottom, and you would close your eyes, and suddenly you would understand the principles. With these and the machine, function would explain itself. The step from that point to the location of a faulty part is self-evident.

"Now I lay before you parts which are identical in appearance, and ask you to install the correct one. Since you thoroughly understand the requirements now, the specifications for the correct part are self-evident. Logic dictates the correct tests for the parts. You will rapidly reject the tight one, the heavy one, the too soft one, and the too resilient one, and you will repair my machine. And you will walk away without testing it, since you now know it will operate."

Wrenn continued, "You—all of us—live in this way. We build no cities because we don't need cities. We stay in groups because some things need more than two hands, more than one head, or voice, or mood. We eat exactly what we require, we use only what we need.

"And that is the end of the truism, wherein I so meticulously describe to you what you know about how you live. The turning: Whence this familiar phenomenon, this closing of the eyes and mysterious appearance of the answer? There have been many engrossing theories about it, but the truth is the most fascinating of all.

"We have all spoken of telepathy, and many of us have experienced it. We cannot explain it, as yet. But most of us insist on a limited consideration of it; that is, we judge its success or failure by the amount of detail sent and received. We expect *facts* to be transmitted, *words*, idea sequences—or perhaps pictures; the clearer the picture, the better the telepathy.

"Perhaps one day we will learn to do this; it would be diverting. But what we actually *do* is infinitely more useful.

"You see, we *are* telepathic, not in the way of conveying details, but in the much more useful way of conveying *a manner of thinking*.

"Let us try to envisage a man who lacks this quality. Faced with your broken machine, he would be utterly at a loss, unless he had been specially trained in this particular field. Do not overlook the fact that he lacks the conditioning of a whole life of the kind of sequence thinking which is possible to us. He would probably bumble through the whole chore in an interminable time, trying one thing and then another and going forward from whatever seems to work. You can see the tragic series of pitfalls possible for him in a situation in which an alternate three or four or five consecutive steps are possible, forcing step six, which is wrong in terms of the problem.

"Now, take the same man and train him in this one job. Add a talent, so that he learns quickly and well. Add years of experience —terrible, drudging thought!—to his skill. Face him with the repair problem and it is obvious that he will repair it with a minimum of motion.

"Finally, take this skilled man and equip him with a device which constantly sends out the habit-patterns of his thinking. Long practice has made him efficient in the matter; in terms of machine function he knows better than to question whether a part turns this way or that, whether a rod or tube larger than x diameter is to be considered. Furthermore, imagine a receiving device which absorbs these sendings whenever the receiver is faced with an identical problem. The skilled sender controls the unskilled receiver as long as the receiver is engaged in the problem. Anything the receiver does which is counter to the basic patterns of the sender is automatically rejected as illogical.

"And now I have described our species. We have an unmatchable unitary existence. Each of us with a natural bent—the poets, the musicians, the mechanics, the philosophers—each gives of his basic thinking method every time anyone has an application for it. The expert is unaware of being tapped—which is why it has taken hundreds of centuries to recognize the method. Yet, in spite of what amounts to a veritable race intellect, we are all very much individuals. Because each field has many experts, and each of those experts has his individual approach, only that which is closest both to the receiver *and* his problem comes in. The ones without special talents live fully and richly with all the skills of the gifted. The creative ones share with others in their field as soon as it occurs to any expert to review what he knows; the one step forward then instantly presents itself.

"So much for the bulk of our kind. There remain a few specializing *non*-specialists. When you are faced with a problem to which no logical solution presents itself, you come to one of these few for help. The reason no solution presents itself is that this is a new line of thinking, or (which is very likely) the last expert in it has died. The non-specialist hears your problem and applies simple logic to it. Immediately, others of his kind do the same. But, since they come from widely divergent backgrounds and use a vast variety of methods, one of them is almost certain to find the logical solution. This is your answer—and through you, it is available to anyone who ever faces this particular problem.

"In exceptional cases, the non-specializing specialist encounters a problem which, for good reason, is better left out of the racial 'pool'—as, for example, a physical or psychological experiment within the culture, of long duration, which general knowledge might alter. In such cases, a highly specialized hypnotic technique is used on the investigators, which has the effect of cloaking thought on this particular matter.

"And if you began to fear that I was never coming to Osser's unhappy history, you must understand, my dear, I have just given it to you. Osser was just such an experiment.

"It became desirable to study the probable habit patterns of a species like us in every respect except for our unique attribute. The problem was attacked from many angles, but I must confess that using a live specimen was my idea.

"By deep hypnosis, the telepathic receptors in Osser were severed from the rest of his mind. He was then allowed to grow up among us in real and complete freedom.

"You saw the result. Since few people recognize the nature of this unique talent, and even fewer regard it as worth discussion, this strong, proud, highly intelligent boy grew up feeling a hopeless inferior, and never knowing exactly why. Others did things, made things, solved problems, as easily as thinking about them, while Osser had to study and sweat and piece and try out. He had to assert his superiority in some way. He did, but in as slipshod a fashion as he did everything else.

"So he was led to the pictures you saw. He was permitted to make what conclusions he wished—they were that we are a backward people, incapable of building a city. He suddenly saw in the dreams of a mechanized, star-reaching species a justification of himself. He could not understand our lack of desire for possessions, not knowing that our whole cultural existence is based on sharing—that it is not only undesirable, but impossible for us to hoard an advanced idea, a new comfort. He would master us through strength.

"He was just starting when you came to me about him. You could get no key to his problem because we know nothing about sick minds, and there was no expert you could tap. I couldn't help you—you, of all people—because you loved him, and because we dared not risk having him know what he was, especially when he was just about to take action.

"Why he chose this particular site for his tower I do not know. And why he chose the method of the tower I don't know either, though I can deduce an excellent reason. First, he had to use his strength once he became convinced that in it lay his superiority. Second, he had to *try out* this build-with-hate idea—the bugaboo of all other man-species, the trial-and-error, the inability to know what will work and what will not.

"And so we learned through Osser precisely what we had learned in other approaches—that a man without our particular ability must not live among us, for, if he does, he will destroy us.

"It is a small step from that to a conclusion about a whole race of them coexisting with us. And now you know what happened here this afternoon."

Jubilith raised her head slowly. "A whole ship full of . . . of what Osser was?"

"Yes. We did the only thing we could. Quick, quite painless. We have been watching them for a long time—years. We saw them start. We computed their orbit—even to the deceleration spiral. We chose a spot to launch our interceptor." He glanced at Osser, who was almost quiet, quite exhausted. "What sheer hell he must have gone through, to see us build like that. How could he know that not one of us needed training, explanation, or any but the simplest orders? How could he rationalize to himself our possession of machines and devices surpassing the wildest dreams of the godlike men he admired so? How could he understand that, having such things, we use them only when we must, and that otherwise we live in ways which will not violate the walking, working animal we are?"

She turned to him a mask so cold, so beautiful, he forgot for a moment to breathe. "Why did you do it? You had other logics, other approaches. Did you have to do *that* to him?"

He studiously avoided a glance at Osser. "I said you might hate me," he murmured. "Jubilith, the men in that ship were so like Osser that the experiment could not be passed by. We had astronomical data, historical, cultural—as far as our observations could go—and ethnological. But only by analogy could we get such a psychological study. And it checked too well. As for having him see this thing, today . . . building, Jubilith, is sometimes begun by tearing down."

He looked at her with deep compassion. "This was not the site chosen for the launching of the interceptor. We uprooted the whole installation, brought it here, rebuilt it, just for Osser; just so that he could stand on his tower and see it happen. He had to be broken, leveled to the earth. Ah-h-h ..." he breathed painfully, "Osser has earned what he will have from now on."

"He can be—well again?"

"With your help."

"So very right, you are," she snarled suddenly. "So sure that this or that species is fit to associate with superiors like us." She leaned toward him and shook a finger in his startled face. The courtly awe habitual to all when speaking to such as Wrenn had completely left her.

"So fine we are, so mighty. And didn't we build cities? Didn't we have giant bird-machines and shiny carts on our streets? Didn't we let our cities be smashed—haven't you seen the ruins in the west? Tell me," she sparked, "did we ruin them ourselves, because one superior city insisted on proving its superiority over another superior city?"

She stopped abruptly to keep herself from growling like an animal, for he was smiling blandly, and his smile got wider as she spoke. She turned furiously, half away from him, cursing the broken knee that held her so helpless.

"Jubilith."

His voice was so warm, so kind and so startling in these surroundings, held such a bubbling overtone of laughter that she couldn't resist it. She turned grudgingly.

In his hand he held a pebble. When her eye fell to it he rolled it, held it between thumb and forefinger, and let it go.

It stayed motionless in mid-air. "Another factor, Jubilith."

She almost smiled. She looked down at his other hand, and saw it aiming the disc-shaped force-field projector at low power.

He lifted it and, with the field, tossed the pebble into the air and batted it away. "We have no written history, Jubilith. We don't need one, but once in a while it would be useful.

"Jubilith, our culture is one of the oldest in the Galaxy. If we ever had such cities, there are not even legends about it."

"But I saw—"

"A ship came here once. We had never seen a humanoid race. We welcomed them and helped them. We gave them land and seeds. Then they called a flotilla, and the ships came by the hundreds.

"They built cities and, at that, we moved away and left them alone, because we don't *need* cities. Then they began to hate us. They couldn't hate us until they had tall buildings to do it in. They hated our quiet; they hated our understanding. They sent missionaries to change our ways. We welcomed the missionaries, fed them and laughed with them, but when they left us glittering tools and humble machines to amuse us, we let them lie where they were until they rotted.

"In time they sent no more missionaries. They joked about us and forgot us. And then they built a city on land we had not given them, and another, and another. They bred well, and their cities became infernally big. And finally they began to build that one city too many, and we turned a river and drowned it. They were pleased. They could now rid themselves of the backward natives."

Jubilith closed her eyes, and saw the tumbled agony of the mounds, radiating outward from a lake with its shores too bare. "All of them?" she asked.

Wrenn nodded. "Even one might be enough to destroy us." He nodded toward Osser, who had begun to cry again.

"They seemed ... good," she said, reflectively. "Too fast, too big ... and it must have been noisy, but—"

"Wait," he said. "You mean the people in the picture Osser showed you?"

"Of course. They were the city-builders you—we—destroyed, weren't they?"

"They were not! The ones who built here were thin, hairy, with backward-slanting faces and webs between their fingers. Beautiful, but they hated us ... The pictures, Jubilith, were made on the third planet of a pale star out near the Rim; a world with one Moon; a world of humans like Osser ... the world where that golden ship came from."

"How?" she gasped.

"If logic is good enough," Wrenn said, "it need not be checked. Once we were so treated by humanoids, we built the investigators.

They are not manned. They draw their power from anything that radiates, and they home on any planet which could conceivably rear humans. They are, as far as we know, indetectible. We've never lost one. They launch tiny flyers to make close searches—one of them made the pictures you saw. The pictures and other data are coded and sent out into space and, where distances warrant it, other investigators catch the signal and add power and send them on.

"Whenever a human or humanoid species builds a ship, we watch it. When they send their ships to this sector, we watch their planet *and* their ship. Unless we are sure that those people have the ability we have, to share all expertness and all creative thinking with all who want it—they don't land here. And no such species ever will land here."

"You're so sure."

"We explore no planets, Jubilith. We like it here. If others like us exist—why should they visit us?"

She thought about it, and slowly she nodded. "I like it here," she breathed.

Wrenn knelt and looked out across the rolling ground. It was late, and most of the villagers had gone home. A few picked at the mound of splinters at the implosion center. Their limbs were straight and their faces clear. They owned little and they shared their souls.

He rose and went to Osser, and sat down beside him, facing him, his back to Jubilith. "M-m-mum, mum, mum, mum, mum-mum-mum," he intoned.

Osser blinked at him. Wrenn lifted his hand and his ring, green and gold and a shimmering oval of purple, caught the late light. Osser looked at the ring. He reached for it. Wrenn moved it slightly. Osser's hand passed it and hit the ground and lay there neglected. Osser gaped at the ring, his jaws working, his teeth not meeting.

"Mum, mum, *mummy,* where's your mummy, Osser?"

"In the house," said Osser, looking at the ring.

Wrenn said, "You're a good little boy. When we say the word, you won't be able to do anything but what *you* can do. When we say the key, you'll be able to do anything *anybody* can do."

58

"All right," Osser said.

"Before I give the word, tell me the key. You must remember the key."

"That ring. And 'last 'n' lost.'"

"Good, Osser. Now listen to me. Can you hear me?"

"Sure." He grabbed at the ring.

"I'm going to change the key. It isn't 'last 'n' lost' any more. 'Last 'n' lost' is no good now. Forget it."

"No good?"

"Forget it. What's the key?"

"I—forgot."

"The key," said Wrenn patiently, "is this." He leaned close and whispered rapidly.

Jubilith was peering out past the implosion center to the town-ward path. Someone was coming, a tiny figure.

"Jubilith," Wrenn said. She looked up at him. "You must understand something." His voice was grave. His hair reached for an awed little twist of wind, come miles to see this place. The wind escaped and ran away down the hill.

Wrenn said, "He's very happy now. He was a happy child when first I heard of him, and how like a space-bound human he could be. Well, he's that child again. He always will be, until the day he dies. I'll see he's cared for. He'll chase the sunbeams, a velvet red one and a needle of blue-white; he'll eat and he'll love and be loved just as is right for him."

They looked at Osser. There was a blue insect on his wrist. He raised it slowly, slowly, close to his eyes, and through its gauze wings he saw the flame-and-silver sunset. He laughed.

"All his life?"

"All his life," said Wrenn. "With the bitterness and the trouble wiped away, and no chance to mature again into the unfinished thing that fought the world with the conviction it had something extra."

Then he dropped the ring into Jubilith's hand. "But if you care to, he said, watching her face, the responsive motion of her sensi-tive nostrils, the most delicate index of her lower lip, "if you care to, you can give him back everything I took away. In a moment, you

59

can give him more than he has now; but how long would it take you to make him as happy?"

She made no attempt to answer him. He was Wrenn, he was old and wise; he was a member of a unique species whose resources were incalculable; and yet he was asking her to do something he could not do himself. Perhaps he was asking her to correct a wrong. She would never know that.

"Just the ring," he said, "and the touch of your hand."

He went away, straight and tall, quickening his pace as, far away, the patient figure she had been watching earlier rose and came to meet him. It was Oyva.

Jubilith thought, "He needs her."

Jubilith had never been needed by anyone.

She looked at her hand and in it she saw all she was, all she could ever be in her own right; and with it, the music of ages; never the words, but all of the pressures of poetry. And she saw the extraordinary privacy of love in a world which looked out through her eyes, placed all of its skills in her hands, to do with as she alone wished.

With a touch of her hand ... what a flood of sensation, what a bursting in of voices and knowledge, for a child!

How long a child?

She closed her eyes, and quietly the answer came, full of pictures; the lute picked up and played; the instant familiarity with the most intricate machine; the stars seen otherwise, and yet again otherwise, and every seeing an honest beauty. A thousand discoveries, and manhood with a rush.

She slipped the ring on her finger, and dragged herself over to him. She put her arms around him and his cheek came down to the hollow of her throat and burrowed there.

He said, sleepily, "Is it nighttime, Mummy?"

"For just a little while," said Jubilith.

The World Well Lost

ALL THE WORLD KNEW THEM AS LOVERBIRDS, though they were certainly not birds, but humans. Well, say humanoids. Featherless bipeds. Their stay on Earth was brief, a nine-day wonder. Any wonder that lasts nine days on an Earth of orgasmic trideo shows; time-freezing pills; synapse-inverter fields which make it possible for a man to turn a sunset to perfumes, a masochist to a fur-feeler; and a thousand other euphorics—why, on such an Earth, a nine-day wonder is a wonder indeed.

Like a sudden bloom across the face of the world came the peculiar magic of the loverbirds. There were loverbird songs and loverbird trinkets, loverbird hats and pins, bangles and baubles, coins and quaffs and tidbits. For there was that about the loverbirds which made a deep enchantment. No one can be told about a loverbird and feel this curious delight. Many are immune even to a solidograph. But watch loverbirds, only for a moment, and see what happens. It's the feeling you had when you were twelve, and summer-drenched, and you kissed a girl for the very first time and knew a breathlessness you were sure could never happen again. And indeed it never could—unless you watched loverbirds. Then you are spellbound for four quiet seconds, and suddenly your very heart twists, and incredulous tears sting and stay; and the very first move you make afterward, you make on tiptoe, and your first word is a whisper.

This magic came over very well on trideo, and everyone had trideo; so for a brief while the Earth was enchanted.

There were only two loverbirds. They came down out of the sky in a single brassy flash, and stepped out of their ship, hand in hand. Their eyes were full of wonder, each at the other, and together at the world. They seemed frozen in a full-to-bursting moment of discovery; they made way for one another gravely and with courtesy, they

looked about them and in the very looking gave each other gifts—
the color of the sky, the taste of the air, the pressures of things growing and meeting and changing. They never spoke. They simply *were*
together. To watch them was to know of their awestruck mounting
of staircases of bird notes, of how each knew the warmth of the other
as their flesh supped silently on sunlight.

They stepped from their ship, and the tall one threw a yellow
powder back to it. The ship fell in upon itself and became a pile of
rubble, which collapsed into a pile of gleaming sand, which slumped
compactly down to dust and then to an airblown emulsion so fine
that Brownian movement itself hammered it up and out and away.
Anyone could see that they intended to stay. Anyone could know by
simply watching them that next to their wondrous delight in each
other came their delighted wonder at Earth itself, everything and
everybody about it.

Now, if terrestrial culture were a pyramid, at the apex (where the
power is) would sit a blind man, for so constituted are we that only
by blinding ourselves, bit by bit, may we rise above our fellows. The
man at the apex has an immense preoccupation with the welfare of
the whole, because he regards it as the source and structure of his
elevation, which it is, and as an extension of himself, which it is not.
It was such a man who, in the face of immeasurable evidence, chose
to find a defense against loverbirds, and fed the matrices and coordinates of the loverbird image into the most marvelous calculator
that had ever been built.

The machine sucked in symbols and raced them about, compared
and waited and matched and sat still while its bulging memory, cell
by cell, was silent, was silent—and suddenly, in a far corner, res-
onated. It grasped this resonance in forceps made of mathematics,
snatched it out (translating furiously as it snatched) and put out a
fevered tongue of paper on which was typed:

DIRBANU

Now this utterly changed the complexion of things. For Earth
ships had ranged the cosmos far and wide, with few hindrances. Of

these hindrances, all could be understood but one, and that one was Dirbanu, a transgalactic planet which shrouded itself in impenetrable fields of force whenever an Earth ship approached. There were other worlds which could do this, but in each case the crews knew why it was done. Dirbanu, upon discovery, had prohibited landings from the very first until an ambassador could be sent to Terra. In due time one did arrive (so reported the calculator, which was the only entity that remembered the episode) and it was obvious that Earth and Dirbanu had much in common. The ambassador, however, showed a most uncommon disdain of Earth and all its work, curled his lip and went wordlessly home, and ever since then Dirbanu had locked itself tight away from the questing Terrans.

Dirbanu thereby became of value, and fair game, but we could do nothing to ripple the bland face of her defenses. As this impregnability repeatedly proved itself, Dirbanu evolved in our group mind through the usual stages of being: the Curiosity, the Mystery, the Challenge, the Enemy, the Enemy, the Enemy, the Mystery, the Curiosity, and finally That-which-is-too-far-away-to-bother-with, or the Forgotten.

And suddenly, after all this time, Earth had two genuine natives of Dirbanu aboard, entrancing the populace and giving no information. This intolerable circumstance began to make itself felt throughout the world—but slowly, for this time the blind men's din was cushioned and soaked by the magic of the loverbirds. It might have taken a very long time to convince the people of the menace in their midst had there not been a truly startling development:

A direct message was received from Dirbanu.

The collective impact of loverbird material emanating from transmitters on Earth had attracted the attention of Dirbanu, which promptly informed us that the loverbirds were indeed their nationals, that in addition they were fugitives, that Dirbanu would take it ill if Earth should regard itself as a sanctuary for the criminals of Dirbanu but would, on the other hand, find it in its heart to be very pleased if Earth saw fit to return them.

So from the depths of its enchantment, Terra was able to calculate a course of action. Here at last was an opportunity to consort with Dirbanu on a friendly basis—great Dirbanu which, since it had force fields which Earth could not duplicate, must of necessity have many other things Earth could use; mighty Dirbanu before whom we could kneel in supplication (with purely-for-defense bombs hidden in our pockets) with lowered heads (making invisible the knife in our teeth) and ask for crumbs from their table (in order to extrapolate the location of their kitchens).

Thus the loverbird episode became another item in the weary procession of proofs that Terra's most reasonable intolerance can conquer practically anything, even magic.

Especially magic.

So it was that the loverbirds were arrested, that the *Starmite 439* was fitted out as a prison ship, that a most carefully screened crew was chosen for her, and that she struck starward with the cargo that would gain us a world.

Two men were the crew—a colorful little rooster of a man and a great dun bull of a man. They were, respectively, Rootes, who was Captain and staff, and Grunty, who was midship and inboard corps. Rootes was cocky, springy, white and crisp. His hair was auburn and so were his eyes, and the eyes were hard. Grunty was a shambler with big gentle hands and heavy shoulders half as wide as Rootes was high. He should have worn a cowl and rope-belted habit. He should, perhaps, have worn a burnoose. He did neither, but the effect was there. Known only to him was the fact that words and pictures, concepts and comparisons were an endless swirling blizzard inside him. Known only to him and Rootes was the fact that he had books, and books, and books, and Rootes did not care if he had or not. Grunty he had been called since he first learned to talk, and Grunty was name enough for him. For the words in his head would not leave him except one or two at a time, with long moments between. So he had learned to condense his verbal messages to breathy grunts, and when they wouldn't condense, he said nothing.

They were primitives, both of them, which is to say that they were doers, while Modern Man is a thinker and/or a feeler. The thinkers compose new variations and permutations of euphoria, and the feelers repay the thinkers by responding to their inventions. The ships had no place for Modern Man, and Modern Man had only the most casual use for the ships.

Doers can cooperate like cam and pushrod, like ratchet and pawl, and such linkage creates a powerful bond. But Rootes and Grunty were unique among crews in that these machine parts were not interchangeable. Any good captain can command any good crew, surroundings being equivalent. But Rootes would not and could not ship out with anyone but Grunty, and Grunty was just that dependent. Grunty understood this bond, and the fact that the only way it could conceivably be broken would be to explain it to Rootes. Rootes did not understand it because it never occurred to him to try, and had he tried, he would have failed, since he was inherently nonequipped for the task. Grunty knew that their unique bond was, for him, a survival matter. Rootes did not know this, and would have rejected the idea with violence.

So Rootes regarded Grunty with tolerance and a modified amusement. The modification was an inarticulate realization of Grunty's complete dependability. Grunty regarded Rootes with ... well, with the ceaseless, silent flurry of words in his mind.

There was, besides the harmony of functions and the other link, understood only by Grunty, a third adjunct to their phenomenal efficiency as a crew. It was organic, and it had to do with the stellar drive.

Reaction engines were long forgotten. The so-called "warp" drive was used only experimentally and on certain crash-priority war-craft where operating costs were not a factor. The *Starmite* 439 was, like most interstellar craft, powered by an RS plant. Like the transistor, the Referential Stasis generator is extremely simple to construct and very difficult indeed to explain. Its mathematics approaches mysticism and its theory contains certain impossibilities which are ignored in practice. Its effect is to shift the area of stasis of the ship and everything in it from one point of reference to another. For example, the ship at rest on the Earth's surface is in stasis in reference to the ground on which it rests. Throwing the ship into stasis in reference to the center of the Earth gives it instantly an effective speed equal to the surface velocity of the planet around its core—some one thousand miles per hour. Stasis referential to the sun moves the Earth out from under the ship at the Earth's orbital velocity. GH stasis "moves" the ship at the angular velocity of the sun about the Galactic Hub. The galactic drift can be used, as can any simple or complex mass center in this expanding universe. There are resultants and there are multipliers, and effective velocities can be enormous. Yet the ship is constantly in stasis, so that there is never an inertia factor.

The one inconvenience of the RS drive is that shifts from one referent to another invariably black the crew out, for psychoneural reasons. The blackout period varies slightly between individuals from one to two and a half hours. But some anomaly in Grunty's gigantic frame kept his blackout periods down to thirty or forty minutes, while Rootes was always out for two hours or more. There was that about Grunty which made moments of isolation a vital necessity, for a man must occasionally be himself, which in anyone's company Grunty was not. But after stasis shifts Grunty had an hour or so to himself while his commander lay numbly spread-eagled on the blackout couch, and he spent these in communions of his own devising. Sometimes this meant only a good book.

This, then, was the crew picked to man the prison ship. It had been together longer than any other crew in the Space Service. Its record showed a metrical efficiency and a resistance to physical and psychic debilitations previously unheard of in a trade where close confinements on long voyages had come to be regarded as hazards. In space, shift followed shift uneventfully, and planetfall was made on schedule and without incident. In port Rootes would roar off to the fleshpots, in which he would wallow noisily until an hour before takeoff, while Grunty found, first, the business office, and next, a bookstore.

They were pleased to be chosen for the Dirbanu trip. Rootes felt no remorse at taking away Earth's new delight, since he was one of the very few who was immune to it. ("Pretty," he said at his first encounter.) Grunty simply grunted, but then, so did everyone else. Rootes did not notice, and Grunty did not remark upon, the obvious fact that though the loverbirds' expression of awestruck wonderment in each other's presence had, if anything, intensified, their extreme pleasure in Earth and the things of Earth had vanished. They were locked, securely but comfortably, in the after cabin behind a new transparent door, so that their every move could be watched from the main cabin and control console. They sat close, with their arms about one another, and though their radiant joy in the contact never lessened, it was a shadowed pleasure, a lachrymose beauty like the wrenching music of the wailing wall.

The RS drive laid its hand on the moon and they vaulted away. Grunty came up from blackout to find it very quiet. The loverbirds lay still in each other's arms, looking very human except for the high joining of their closed eyelids, which nictated upward rather than downward like a Terran's. Rootes sprawled limply on the other couch, and Grunty nodded at the sight. He deeply appreciated the silence, since Rootes had filled the small cabin with earthy chatter about his conquests in port, detail by hairy detail, for two solid hours preceding their departure. It was a routine which Grunty found particularly wearing, partly for its content, which interested him not at all, but mostly for its inevitability. Grunty had long ago noted that these recitations, for all their detail, carried the tones of thirst rather than of satiety. He had his own conclusions about it, and, characteristically, kept them to himself. But inside, his spinning gusts of words could shape themselves well to it, and they did. "And man, she moaned!" Rootes would chant. "And take money? She *gave* me money. And what did I do with it? Why, I bought up some more of the same." *And what you could buy with a shekel's worth of tenderness, my prince!* his silent words sang. " . . . across the floor and around the rug until, by damn, I thought we're about to climb the wall. Loaded, Grunty-boy, I tell you, I was loaded!" *Poor little one* ran the hushed susurrus, *thy poverty is as great as thy joy and a tenth as great as thine empty noise.* One of Grunty's greatest pleasures was taken in the fact that this kind of chuntering was limited to the first day out, with barely another word on the varied theme until the next departure, no matter how many months away that might be. *Squeak to me of love, dear mouse,* his words would chuckle. *Stand up on your cheese and nibble away at your dream.* Then, wearily, *But oh, this treasure I carry is too heavy a burden, in all its fullness, to be so tugged at by your clattering vacuum!*

Grunty left the couch and went to the controls. The preset courses checked against the indicators. He logged them and fixed the finder control to locate a certain mass-nexus in the Crab Nebula. It would chime when it was ready. He set the switch for final closing by the push-button beside his couch, and went aft to wait.

He stood watching the loverbirds because there was nothing else for him to do.

They lay quite still, but love so permeated them that their very poses expressed it. Their lax bodies yearned each to each, and the tall one's hand seemed to stream toward the fingers of his beloved, and then back again, like the riven tatters of a torn fabric straining toward oneness again. And as their mood was a sadness too, so their pose, each and both, together and singly, expressed it, and singly each through the other silently spoke of the loss they had suffered, and how it ensured greater losses to come. Slowly the picture suffused Grunty's thinking, and his words picked and pierced and smoothed it down and murmured finally, *Brush away the dusting of sadness from the future, bright ones. You've sadness enough for now. Grief should live only after it is truly born, and not before.*

His words sang,

> *Come fill the cup and in the fire of spring*
> *Your winter garment of repentance fling.*
> *The bird of time has but a little way*
> *To flutter—and the bird is on the wing.*

and added *Omar Khayyam, born circa 1073,* for this, too, was one of the words' functions.

And then he stiffened in horror; his great hands came up convulsively and clawed the imprisoning glass . . .

They were smiling at him.

They were smiling, and on their faces and on and about their bodies there was no sadness.

They had *heard* him!

He glanced convulsively around at the Captain's unconscious form, then back to the loverbirds.

That they should recover so swiftly from blackout was, to say the least, an intrusion; for his moments of aloneness were precious and more than precious to Grunty, and would be useless to him under the scrutiny of those jeweled eyes. But that was a minor matter compared to this other thing, this terrible fact that they *heard*.

Telepathic races were not common, but they did exist. And what he was now experiencing was what invariably happened when humans encountered one. He could only send; the loverbirds could only receive. And they *must not* receive him! No one must. No one must know what he was, what he thought. If anyone did, it would be a disaster beyond bearing. It would mean no more flights with Rootes. Which, of course, meant no flights with anyone. And how could he live—where could he go?

He turned back to the loverbirds. His lips were white and drawn back in a snarl of panic and fury. For a blood-thick moment he held their eyes. They drew closer to one another, and together sent him a radiant, anxious, friendly look that made him grind his teeth.

Then, at the console, the finder chimed.

Grunty turned slowly from the transparent door and went to his couch. He lay down and poised his thumb over the push-button.

He *hated* the loverbirds, and there was no joy in him. He pressed the button, the ship slid into a new stasis, and he blacked out.

The time passed.

"Grunty!"

"?"

"You feed them this shift?"

"Nuh."

"Last shift?"

"Nuh."

"What the hell's matter with you, y'big dumb bastich? What you expect them to live on?"

Grunty sent a look of roiling hatred aft. "Love," he said.

"Feed 'em," snapped Rootes.

69

Wordlessly Grunty went about preparing a meal for the prisoners. Rootes stood in the middle of the cabin, his hard small fists on his hips, his gleaming auburn head tilted to one side, and watched every move. "I didn't used to have to tell you anything," he growled, half pugnaciously, half worriedly. "You sick?"

Grunty shook his head. He twisted the tops of two cans and set them aside to heat themselves, and took down the water suckers.

"You got it in for those honeymooners or something?"

Grunty averted his face.

"We get them to Dirbanu alive and healthy, hear me? They get sick, you get sick, by God. I'll see to that. Don't give me trouble, Grunty. I'll take it out on you. I never whipped you yet, but I will."

Grunty carried the tray aft. "You hear me?" Rootes yelled.

Grunty nodded without looking at him. He touched the control and a small communication window slid open in the glass wall. He slid the tray through. The taller loverbird stepped forward and took it eagerly, gracefully, and gave him a dazzling smile of thanks. Grunty growled low in his throat like a carnivore. The loverbird carried the food back to the couch and they began to eat, feeding each other little morsels.

A new stasis, and Grunty came fighting up out of blackness. He sat up abruptly, glanced around the ship. The Captain was sprawled out across the cushions, his compact body and outflung arm forming the poured-out, spring-steel laxness usually seen only in sleeping cats. The loverbirds, even in deep unconsciousness, lay like hardly separate parts of something whole, the small one on the couch, the tall one on the deck, prone, reaching, supplicating.

Grunty snorted and hove to his feet. He crossed the cabin and stood looking down on Rootes.

The hummingbird is a yellowjacket, said his words, *Buzz and dart, hiss and flash away. Swift and hurtful, hurtful . . .*

He stood for a moment, his great shoulder muscles working one against the other, and his mouth trembled.

He looked at the loverbirds, who were still motionless. His eyes slowly narrowed.

His words tumbled and climbed, and ordered themselves:

I through love have learned three things,
Sorrow, sin and death it brings.
Yet day by day my heart within
Dares shame and sorrow, death and sin. . . .

And dutifully he added *Samuel Ferguson, born 1810.* He glared
at the loverbirds and brought his fist into his palm with a sound like
a club on an anthill. They had heard him again, and this time they
did not smile, but looked into each other's eyes and then turned
together to regard him, nodding gravely.

Rootes went through Grunty's books, leafing and casting aside.
He had never touched them before. "Buncha crap," he jeered. "*Garden of the Plynck. Wind in the Willows. Worm Ouroborous.* Kid
stuff."

Grunty lumbered across and patiently gathered up the books the
Captain had flung aside, putting them one by one back into their
places, stroking them as if they had been bruised.

"Isn't there nothing in here with pictures?"

Grunty regarded him silently for a moment and then took down
a tall volume. The Captain snatched it, leafed through it. "Moun-
tains," he growled. "Old houses." He leafed. "Damn boats." He
smashed the book to the deck. "Haven't you got *any* of what I want?"

Grunty waited attentively.

"Do I have to draw a diagram?" the Captain roared. "Got that
ol' itch, Grunty. You wouldn't know. I feel like looking at pictures,
get what I mean?"

Grunty stared at him, utterly without expression, but deep within
him a panic squirmed. The Captain never, *never* behaved like this
in mid-voyage. It was going to get worse, he realized. Much worse.
And quickly.

He shot the loverbirds a vicious, hate-filled glance. If they weren't
aboard . . .

There could be no waiting. Not now. Something had to be done.
Something . . .

"Come on, come on," said Rootes. "Goddlemighty Godfrey, even
a deadbutt like you must have *something* for kicks."

Grunty turned away from him, squeezed his eyes closed for a tortured second, then pulled himself together. He ran his hand over the books, hesitated, and finally brought out a large, heavy one. He handed it to the Captain and went forward to the console. He slumped down there over the file of computer tapes, pretending to be busy.

The Captain sprawled onto Grunty's couch and opened the book. "Michelangelo, what the hell," he growled. He grunted, almost like his shipmate. "Statues," he half-whispered, in withering scorn. But he ogled and leafed at last, and was quiet.

The loverbirds looked at him with a sad tenderness, and then together sent beseeching glances at Grunty's angry back.

The matrix-pattern for Terra slipped through Grunty's fingers, and he suddenly tore the tape across, and across again. A filthy place, Terra. *There is nothing*, he thought, *like the conservatism of license*. Given a culture of sybaritics, with an endless choice of mechanical titillations, and you have a people of unbreakable and hidebound formality, a people with few but massive taboos, a shockable, narrow, prissy people obeying the rules—even the rules of their calculated depravities—and protecting their treasured, specialized pruderies. In such a group there are words one may not use for fear of their fanged laughter, colors one may not wear, gestures and intonations one must forego, on pain of being torn to pieces. The rules are complex and absolute, and in such a place one's heart may not sing lest, through its warm free joyousness, it betray one.

And if you must have joy of such a nature, if you must be free to be your pressured self, then off to space . . . off to the glittering black loneliness. And let the days go by, and let the time pass, and huddle beneath your impenetrable integument, and wait, and wait, and every once in a long while you will have that moment of lonely consciousness when there is no one around to see; and then it may burst from you and you may dance, or cry, or twist the hair on your head till your eyeballs blaze, or do any of the other things your so unfashionable nature thirstily demands.

It took Grunty half a lifetime to find this freedom: No price would be too great to keep it. Not lives, nor interplanetary diplomacy, nor Earth itself were worth such a frightful loss.

He would lose it if anyone knew, and the loverbirds knew.

He pressed his heavy hands together until the knuckles crackled. Dirbanu, reading it all from the ardent minds of the loverbirds; Dirbanu flashing the news across the stars; the roar of reaction, and then Rootes, Rootes, when the huge and ugly impact washed over him . . .

So let Dirbanu be offended. Let Terra accuse this ship of fumbling, even of treachery—anything but the withering news the loverbirds had stolen.

Another new stasis, and Grunty's first thought as he came alive in the silent ship was *It has to be soon.*

He rolled off the couch and glared at the unconscious loverbirds. The helpless loverbirds.

Smash their heads in.

Then Rootes . . . what to tell Rootes?

The loverbirds attacked him, tried to seize the ship?

He shook his head like a bear in a beehive. Rootes would never believe that. Even if the loverbirds could open the door, which they could not, it was more than ridiculous to imagine those two bright and slender things attacking anyone—especially so rugged and massive an opponent.

Poison? No—there was nothing in the efficient, unfailingly beneficial food stores that might help.

His glance strayed to the Captain, and he stopped breathing. Of *course!*

He ran to the Captain's personal lockers. He should have known that such a cocky little hound as Rootes could not live, could not strut and prance as he did, unless he had a weapon. And if it was the kind of weapon that such a man would characteristically choose—

A movement caught his eye as he searched.

The loverbirds were awake.

That wouldn't matter.

He laughed at them, a flashing, ugly laugh. They cowered close together and their eyes grew very bright.

They knew.

He was aware that they were suddenly very busy, as busy as he. And then he found the gun.

It was a snug little thing, smooth and intimate in his hand. It was exactly what he had guessed, what he had hoped for—just what he needed. It was silent. It would leave no mark. It need not even be aimed carefully. Just a touch of its feral radiation and throughout the body the axones suddenly refuse to propagate nerve impulses. No thought leaves the brain, no slightest contraction of heart or lung occurs again, ever. And afterward, no sign remains that a weapon has been used.

He went to the serving window with the gun in his hand. *When he wakes, you will be dead,* he thought. *Couldn't recover from stasis blackout. Too bad. But no one's to blame, hm? We never had Dirbanu passengers before. So how could we know?*

The loverbirds, instead of flinching, were crowding close to the window, their faces beseeching, their delicate hands signing and signaling, frantically trying to convey something.

He touched the control, and the panel slid back.

The taller loverbird held up something as if it would shield him. The other pointed at it, nodded urgently, and gave him one of those accursed, hauntingly sweet smiles.

Grunty put up his hand to sweep the thing aside, and then checked himself.

It was only a piece of paper.

All of the cruelty of humanity rose up in Grunty. *A species that can't protect itself doesn't deserve to live.* He raised the gun.

And then he saw the pictures.

Economical and accurate, and for all their subject, done with the ineffable grace of the loverbirds themselves, the pictures showed three figures:

Grunty himself, hulking, impassive, the eyes glowing, the tree-trunk legs and hunched shoulders.

Rootes, in a pose so characteristic and so cleverly done that Grunty gasped. Crisp and clean, Rootes' image had one foot up on a chair, both elbows on the high knee, the head half turned. The eyes fairly sparkled from the paper.

And a girl.

She was beautiful. She stood with her arms behind her, her feet slightly apart, her face down a little. She was deep-eyed, pensive, and to see her was to be silent, to wait for those downcast lids to lift and break the spell.

Grunty frowned and faltered. He lifted a puzzled gaze from these exquisite renderings to the loverbirds, and met the appeal, the earnest, eager, hopeful faces.

The loverbird put a second paper against the glass.

There were the same three figures, identical in every respect to the previous ones, except for one detail: they were all naked.

He wondered how they knew human anatomy so meticulously.

Before he could react, still another sheet went up.

The loverbirds, this time—the tall one, the shorter one, hand in hand. And next to them a third figure, somewhat similar, but tiny, very round, and with grotesquely short arms.

Grunty stared at the three sheets, one after the other. There was something . . . something . . .

And then the loverbird put up the fourth sketch, and slowly, slowly, Grunty began to understand. In the last picture, the loverbirds were shown exactly as before, except that they were naked, and so was the small creature beside them. He had never seen loverbirds naked before. Possibly no one had.

Slowly he lowered the gun. He began to laugh. He reached through the window and took both the loverbirds' hands in one of his, and they laughed with him.

Rootes stretched easily with his eyes closed, pressed his face down into the couch, and rolled over. He dropped his feet to the deck, held his head in his hands and yawned. Only then did he realize Grunty was standing just before him.

"What's the matter with you?"

He followed Grunty's grim gaze.

The glass door stood open.

Rootes bounced to his feet as if the couch had turned white-hot. "Where—what—"

75

Grunty's crag of a face was turned to the starboard bulkhead. Rootes spun to it, balanced on the balls of his feet as if he were boxing. His smooth face gleamed in the red glow of the light over the airlock.

"The lifeboat . . . you mean they took the lifeboat? They got away?"

Grunty nodded.

Rootes held his head. "Oh, fine," he moaned. He whipped around to Grunty. "And where the hell were you when this happened?"

"Here."

"Well, what in God's name happened?" Rootes was on the trembling edge of foaming hysteria.

Grunty thumped his chest.

"You're not trying to tell me you let them go?"

Grunty nodded, and waited—not for very long.

"I'm going to burn you down," Rootes raged. "I'm going to break you so low you'll have to climb for twelve years before you get a barracks to sweep. And after I get done with you I'll turn you over to the Service. What do you think they'll do to you? What do you think they're going to do to *me?*"

He leapt at Grunty and struck him a hard, cutting blow to the cheek. Grunty kept his hands down and made no attempt to avoid the fist. He stood immovable, and waited.

"Maybe those were criminals, but they were Dirbanu nationals," Rootes roared when he could get his breath. "How are we going to explain this to Dirbanu? Do you realize this could mean war?"

Grunty shook his head.

"What do you mean? You know something. You better talk while you can. Come on, bright boy—what are we going to tell Dirbanu?"

Grunty pointed at the empty cell. "Dead," he said.

"What good will it do us to say they're dead? They're not. They'll show up again some day, and—"

Grunty shook his head. He pointed to the star chart. Dirbanu showed as the nearest body. There was no livable planet within thousands of parsecs.

"They didn't go to Dirbanu!"

"Nuh."

"Damn it, it's like pulling rivets to get anything out of you. In that lifeboat they go to Dirbanu—which they won't—or they head out, maybe for years, to the Rim stars. That's all they can do!"

Grunty nodded.

"And you think Dirbanu won't track them, won't bring 'em down?"

"No ships."

"They have ships!"

"Nuh."

"The loverbirds told you?"

Grunty agreed.

"You mean their own ship that they destroyed and the one the ambassador used were all they had?"

"Yuh."

Rootes strode up and back. "I don't get it. I don't begin to get it. What did you do it for, Grunty?"

Grunty stood for a moment, watching Rootes' face. Then he went to the computing desk. Rootes had no choice but to follow. Grunty spread out the four drawings.

"What's this? Who drew these? *Them?* What do you know. *Damn!* Who is the chick?"

Grunty patiently indicated all of the pictures in one sweep. Rootes looked at him, puzzled, looked at one of Grunty's eyes, then the other, shook his head, and applied himself to the pictures again. "This is more like it," he murmured. "Wish I'd a' known they could draw like this." Again Grunty drew his attention to all the pictures and away from the single drawing that fascinated him.

"There's you, there's me. Right? Then this chick. Now, here we are again, all buff naked. Damn, what a carcass. All right, all right, I'm going on. Now, this is the prisoners, right? And who's the little fat one?"

Grunty pushed the fourth sheet over. "Oh," said Rootes. "Here everybody's naked too. Hm."

He yelped suddenly and bent close. Then he rapidly eyed all four sheets in sequence. His face began to get red. He gave the fourth picture a long, close scrutiny. Finally he put his finger on the sketch of the round little alien. "This is . . . a . . . a Dirbanu—"

Grunty nodded. "Female."

"Then those two—they were—"

Grunty nodded.

"So that's it!" Rootes fairly shrieked in fury. "You mean we been shipped out all this time with a coupla God damned *fairies*? Why, if I'd a' known that I'd a' killed 'em!"

"Yuh."

Rootes looked up at him with a growing respect and considerable amusement. "So you got rid of 'em so's I wouldn't kill 'em, and mess everything up?" He scratched his head. "Well, I'll be billy-bedamned. You got a think-tank on you after all. Anything I can't stand, it's a fruit."

Grunty nodded.

"God," said Rootes, "it figures. It really figures. Their females don't look anything like the males. Compared with them, our females are practically identical to us. So the ambassador comes, and sees what looks like a planet full of queers. He knows better but he can't stand the sight. So back he goes to Dirbanu, and Earth gets brushed off."

Grunty nodded.

"Then these pansies here run off to Earth, figuring they'll be at home. They damn near made it, too. But Dirbanu calls 'em back, not wanting the likes of them representing their planet. I don't blame 'em a bit. How would you feel if the only Terran on Dirbanu was a fluff? Wouldn't you want him out of there, but quick?"

Grunty said nothing.

"And now," said Rootes, "we better give Dirbanu the good news." He went forward to the communicator.

It took a surprisingly short time to contact the shrouded planet. Dirbanu acknowledged and coded out a greeting. The decoder over the console printed the message for them:

GREETINGS STARMITE 439. ESYABLISH ORBIT. CAN YOU DROP PRISONERS TO DIRBANU? NEVER MIND PARACHUTE.

"Whew," said Rootes. "Nice people. Hey, you notice they don't say come on in. They never expected to let us land. Well, what'll we tell 'em about their lavender lads?"

78

"Dead," said Grunty.

"Yeah," said Rootes. "That's what they want anyway." He sent rapidly.

In a few minutes the response clattered out of the decoder.

STAND BY FOR TELEPATH SWEEP. WE MUST CHECK. PRISONERS MAY BE PRETENDING DEATH.

"Oh-oh," said the Captain. "This is where the bottom drops out."

"Nuh," said Grunty, calmly.

"But their detector will locate—oh—I see what you're driving at. No life, no signal. Same as if they weren't here at all."

"Yuh."

The decoder clattered.

DIRBANU GRATEFUL. CONSIDER MISSION COMPLETE. DO NOT WANT BODIES. YOU MAY EAT THEM.

Rootes retched. Grunty said, "Custom."

The decoder kept clattering.

NOW READY FOR RECIPROCAL AGREEMENT WITH TERRA.

"We go home in a blaze of glory," Rootes exulted. He sent,

TERRA ALSO READY. WHAT DO YOU SUGGEST?

The decoder paused, then:

TERRA STAY AWAY FROM DIRBANU AND DIRBANU WILL STAY AWAY FROM TERRA. THIS IS NOT A SUGGESTION. TAKES EFFECT IMMEDIATELY.

"Why that bunch of bastards!"

Rootes pounded his codewriter, and although they circled the planet at a respectful distance for nearly four days, they received no further response.

The last thing Rootes had said before they established the first stasis on the way home was: "Well, anyway—it does me good to think of those two queens crawling away in that lifeboat. Why, they can't even starve to death. They'll be cooped up there for *years* before they get anywhere they can sit down."

It still rang in Grunty's mind as he shook off the blackout. He glanced aft to the glass partition and smiled reminiscently. "For years," he murmured. His words curled up and spun, and said,

... Yes; love requires the focal space
Of recollection or of hope,
Ere it can measure its own scope.
Too soon, too soon comes death to show
We love more deeply than we know!

Dutifully, then, came the words: *Coventry Patmore, born 1823.*
He rose slowly and stretched, revelling in his precious privacy.
He crossed to the other couch and sat down on the edge of it.
For a time he watched the Captain's unconscious face, reading it
with great tenderness and utmost attention, like a mother with an
infant.

His words said, *Why must we love where the lightning strikes,*
and not where we choose?

And they said, *But I'm glad it's you, little prince. I'm glad it's*
you.

He put out his huge hand and, with a feather touch, stroked the
sleeping lips.

... And My Fear Is Great ...

HE HEFTED ONE CORNER OF THE BOX high enough for him to get his knuckle on the buzzer, then let it sag. He stood waiting, wheezing. The door opened.

"Oh! You *didn't* carry it up five flights!"

"No, huh?" he grunted, and pushed inside. He set the groceries down on the sink top in the kitchenette and looked at her. She was sixty-something and could have walked upright under his armpit with her shoes on.

"That old elevator ..." she said. "Wait. Here's something."

He wiped sweat out of his eyes and sensed her approach. He put out his hand for the coin but it wasn't a coin. It was a glass. He looked at it, mildly startled. He wished it were beer. He tasted it, then gulped it down. Lemonade.

"Slow-ly, slow-ly," she said, too late. "You'll get heat cramps. What's your name?" Her voice seemed to come from a distance. She seemed, in an odd way, to stand at a distance as well. She was small as a tower is small on the horizon.

"Don," he grunted.

"Well, Donny," she said, "sit down and rest."

He had said, "Don," not "Donny." When he was in rompers he was "Donny." He turned to the door. "I got to go."

"Wait a bit."

He stopped without turning.

"That's a beautiful watch for a boy like you."

"I like it."

"May I see it?"

Breath whistled briefly in his nostrils. She had her fingers lightly on the heel of his hand before he could express any more annoyance than that. Grudgingly, he raised his arm and let her look.

"Beautiful. Where did you get it?"

He looked at her, surlily. "In a store."

Blandly she asked, "Did you buy it?"

He snatched his hand away. He swiped nervously, twice, with a hooked index finger at his upper lip. His eyes were slits. "What's it to you?"

"Well, did you?"

"Look, lady. I brought your groceries and I got my lemonade. It's all right about the watch, see? Don't worry about the watch. I got to go now."

"You stole it."

"Whaddaya—crazy? I didn't steal no watch."

"You stole that one."

"I'm gettin' outa here." He reached for the knob.

"Not until you tell me about the watch."

He uttered a syllable and turned the knob. The door stayed closed. He twisted, pulled, pushed, twisted again. Then he whirled, his back thudding against the door. His gangly limbs seemed to compact. His elbows came out, his head down. His teeth bared like an animal's. "Hey, what is this?"

She stood, small and chunky and straight, and said in her faraway voice, "Are you going to tell me?" Her eyes were a milky blue, slightly protruding, and unreadable.

"You lemme out, hear?"

She shook her head.

"You better lemme out," he growled. He took two steps toward her. "Open that door."

"You needn't be frightened. I won't hurt you."

"Somebuddy's goin' to get hurt," he said.

"Not—another—step," she said without raising her voice.

He released an ugly bark of nervous laughter and took the other step. His feet came forward and upward and his back slammed down on the floor. For a moment he lay still, then his eyelids moved slowly, up and down and up again while for a moment he gave himself over to the purest astonishment. He moved his head forward so that he could see the woman. She had not moved.

He sat up, clenching his jaw against pain, and scuttled backward to the door. He helped himself rise with the doorpost, never taking his eyes off her. "Jesus, I slipped."

"Don't curse in this house," she said—just as mild, just as firm.

"I'll say what I damn please!"

Wham! His shoulders hit the floor again. His eyes were closed, his lips drawn back. He lifted one shoulder and arched his spine. One long agonized wheeze escaped through his teeth like an extrusion.

"You see, you didn't slip," said the woman. "Poor child. Let me help you."

She put her strong, small hand on his left biceps and another between his shoulder blades. She would have led him to a chair but he pulled away. "I'm awright," he said. He said it again, as if unconvinced, and, "What'd you . . . do?"

"Sit down," she said solicitously. He cowered where he was. "Sit down," she said again, no more sharply, but there was a difference.

He went to the chair. He sidled along the wall, watching her, and he did not go very fast, but he went. He sank down into it. It was a very low chair. His long legs doubled and his knees thrust up sharply. He looked like a squashed grasshopper. He panted.

"About the watch," she prompted him.

He panted twice as fast for three breaths and whimpered, "I don't want no trouble, lady, just lemme go, huh?"

She pointed at his wrist.

"Awright, you want the watch?" Hysterically he stripped it off and dangled it toward her. "Okay? Take it." His eyes were round and frightened and wary. When she made no move he put the watch on her ancient gateleg table. He put his palms on the seat of the chair and his feet walked two paces doorward, though he did not rise, but swiveled around, keeping his face to her, eager, terrified.

"Where did you get it?"

He whimpered, wordless. He cast one quick, hungry look at the door, tensed his muscles, met her gaze again, and slumped. "You gonna turn me in?"

"Of course not!" she said with more force than she had used so far.

"You're goin' to, all the same."

She simply shook her head, and waited.

He turned, finally, picked up the watch, snapped the flexible gold band. "I swiped it—off Eckhart," he whispered.

"Who?"

"Eckhart on Summit Av-noo. He lives behind the store. It was just laying there, on the counter. I put a box of groceries on it and snagged it out from under. You gonna tell?"

"Well, Donny! Don't you feel better, now you've confessed?"

He looked up at her through his eyebrows, hesitated. "Yeah."

"Is that the truth, Donny?"

"Uh-huh." Then, meeting those calm, imponderable eyes, he said, "Well, no. I dunno, lady. I dunno. You got me all mixed up. Can I go now?"

"What about the watch?"

"I don't want it no more."

"I want you to take it back where you got it."

"*What?*" He recoiled, primarily because in shock he had raised his voice and the sound of it frightened him. "Je—shucks, lady, you want him to put me in the can?"

"My name is Miss Phoebe, not 'lady.' No, Donny, I think you'll do it. Just a moment."

She sat at a shaky escritoire and wrote for a moment, while he watched. Presently, "Here," she said. She handed him the sheet. He looked at her and then at the paper.

> Dear Mr. Eckhart,
>
> Inside the clasp of this watch your name and address is stamped.
>
> Would you be good enough to see that it gets to its rightful owner?
>
> Yours very truly,
> (Miss) Phoebe Watkins

She took it out of his hand, folded it. She put the watch in an envelope, folded that neatly into a square, dropped it in a second envelope with the note, sealed it and handed it to Don.

"You—you're givin' it right back to me!"

"Am I?"

He lowered his eyes, pinched the top edge of the envelope, pulled it through his fingers to crease the top edge sharply. "I know. You're gonna phone him. You're gonna get me picked up."

"You would be no good to me in the reformatory, Donny."

He looked quickly at her eyes, one, then the other. "I'm gonna be some good to you?"

"Tomorrow at four, I want you to come to tea," she said abruptly.

"To what?"

"To tea. That means wash your face and hands and put on a tie and don't be late."

Wash your face and hands. Nobody had dared to order him around like that for years. And yet, instead of resentment, something sharp and choking rose up in his throat. It was not anger. It was something which, when swallowed, made his eyes wet. He frowned and blinked hard.

"You'd better go," she said, before he could accept or refuse, "before the stores close." She didn't even say which stores.

He rose. He pulled his shoulder blades together and his back cracked audibly. He winced, and shambled to the door. He stood waiting, not touching it, head down, patient, like a farm horse before a closed gate.

"What is it, Donny?"

"Ain'tcha gonna unlock it?"

"It was never locked."

For a long moment he stood frozen, his back to her, his eyes down. Then he put a slow hand to the knob, turned it. The door opened. He went out, almost but not quite pausing at the threshold, almost but not quite turning to look back. He closed the door quietly and was gone.

Miss Phoebe began to put her groceries away.

He did not come at four o'clock.

He came at four minutes before the hour, and he was breathing hard.

"Come in, Donny!" She held the door for him. He looked over his shoulder, down the corridor, at the elevator gates and the big window where feathery trees and wide sky showed, and then he came into the room. He stood just inside, watching her as she moved to the kitchenette. He looked around the room, looking for policemen, perhaps, for bars on the windows.

There was nothing in the room but its old-not-antique furniture, the bow-legged occasional chair with the new upholstery which surely looked as old as it had before it was redone; there was the gateleg table, now bearing a silver tea-service with a bit of brass showing at the shoulder of the hot water pot, and a sugar bowl with delicate tongs which did not match the rest of the set. There was the thin rug with its nap quite swept off, and the dustless books; there was the low chair where he had sat before with its tasseled antimacassars on back and arms.

"Make yourself at home," said her quiet voice, barely competing but competing easily with the susurrus of steam that rose from the kettle.

He moved a little further in and stopped awkwardly. His Adam's apple loomed mightily over the straining button of his collar. His tie was blue and red, and he wore a horrendous sports jacket, much too small, with a violent yellow-and-gray tweed weave. His trousers were the color of baked earth, and had as much crease as his shoes had shine, and their soles had more polish than the uppers. But he'd scrubbed his face till his pimples bled, and his hair was raked back so hard that his forehead gleamed like scoured porcelain.

When she faced him he stood his ground and said abruptly, before she could tell him to sit down, "I din' wanna come."

"Didn't you?"

"Well, I did, but I wasn't gonna."

"Why did you come, then?"

"I was scared not to."

She crossed the room with a large platter of little sandwiches. There were cheese and Spam and egg salad and liverwurst. They were not delicacies; they were food. She put it down next to a small store-bought chocolate cake and two bowls of olives, one ripe, one green, neither stuffed. She said, "You had nothing to be afraid of."

"No, huh?" He wet his lips, took a deep breath. The rehearsed antagonism blurted out. "You done something to me yesterday I don't know what it was. How I know I ain't gonna drop dead if I don't show up or somep'n like that?"

"I did nothing to you, child!"

"Somebuddy sure as h—sure did."

"You did it to yourself."

"*What?*"

She looked at him. "Angry people don't live very long, Donny, did you know? But sometimes—" Her eyes fell to her hand on the table, and his followed. With one small age-mottled finger she traced around the table's edge, from the far side around one end. "—sometimes it takes a long time to hurt them. But the hurt can come short and quickly, like *this!*" and she drew her finger straight across from side to side.

Don looked at the table as if something were written on it in a strange language. "All right, but you made it do that."

"Come and sit down," she said

But he hadn't finished. "I took the watch back."

"I knew you would."

"Well, okay then. Thass what I come to tell you. That's what you wanted me for, isn't it?"

"I asked you to *tea*. I didn't want to bully you and I didn't want to discuss that silly watch—the matter is closed. It was closed yesterday. Now *do* come and sit down."

"Oh," he said. "I get it. You mean sit down or *else*."

She fixed her eyes on his and looked at him without speaking and without any expression at all until his gaze dropped. "Donny, go and open the door."

He backed away, felt behind him for the knob. He paused there, tense. When she nodded he opened it.

"You're free to go whenever you like. But before you do, I want you to understand that there are a lot of people I could have tea with. I haven't asked anyone but you. I haven't asked the grocery boy or the thief or any of the other people you seem to be sometimes. Just *you*."

He pulled the door to and stood yanking at his bony knuckles. "I don't know about none of that," he said confusedly. He glanced down between his ribs and his elbow at the doorknob. "I just din' want you to think you hadda put on no feedbag to fin' out did I take the watch back."

"I could have telephoned to Mr. Eckhart."

"Well, din't you?"

"Certainly not. There was no need. Was there?"

He came and sat down.

"Sugar?"

"Huh? Yeah—yeah."

"Lemon, or cream?"

"You mean I can have whichever?"

"Of course."

"Then both."

"Both? I think perhaps the cream would curdle."

"In lemon ice cream it don't."

She gave him cream. He drank seven cups of tea, ate all the sandwiches and most of the cake. He ate quickly, not quite glancing over his shoulder to drive away enemies who might snatch the food. He ate with a hunger that was not of hours or days, but the hunger of years. Miss Phoebe patiently passed and refilled and stoked and served until he was done. He loosened his belt, spread out his long legs, wiped his mouth with one sleeve and his brow with the other, closed his eyes and sighed.

"Donny," she said when his jaws had stopped moving, "have you ever had syphilis?"

The boy literally and immediately fell out of his chair. In this atmosphere of doilies and rectitude he could not have been more jolted by a batted ball on his mountainous Adam's apple. He floundered on the carpet, bumped the table, slopped her tea, and crawled back into his seat with his face flaming.

"No," he said, in a strangled voice.

She began then to talk to him quite calmly about social ills of many kinds. She laid out the grub and smut and greed and struggle of his own neighborhood streets as neatly and as competently as she

88

had laid the tea table. She spoke without any particular emphasis of the bawdy house she had personally closed up after three reports to the police had no effect. (She had called the desk sergeant, stated her name and intentions, and had asked to be met at the house in twenty minutes. When the police got there she had the girls lined up and two-thirds of their case histories already written.) She spoke of playgrounds and civil defense, of pool rooms, dope pushers, candy stores with beer taps in the soda fountain and the visiting nurse service.

Don listened, fairly humming with reaction. He had seen all the things she mentioned, good and bad. Some he had not understood, some he had not thought about, some he wouldn't dream of discussing in mixed company. He knew vaguely that things were better than they had been twenty, fifty, a hundred years ago, but he had never before been face to face with one of those who integrate, correlate, extrapolate this progress, who dirty their hands on this person or that in order to work for people. Sometimes he bit the insides of his cheeks to keep from laughing at her bluntness and efficiency—he wished he could have seen that desk sergeant's *face!*—or to keep from sniggering self-consciously at the way unmentionables rolled off her precise tongue. Sometimes he was puzzled and lost in the complexities of the organizations with which she was so familiar. And sometimes he was slack-jawed with fear for her, thinking of the retribution she must surely be in the way of, breaking up rackets like that. But then his own aching back would remind him that she had ways of taking care of herself, and a childlike awe would rise up in him until he forgot to breathe.

There was no direct instruction in anything she said. It was purely description. And yet he began to feel that in this complex lay duties for him to perform. Exactly what they might be did not emerge. It was simply that he felt, as never before, a functioning part, rather than an excrescence, of his own environment.

He was never to remember all the details of that extraordinary communion, nor the one which immediately followed; for somehow she had stopped speaking and there was a long quiet between them. His mind was so busy with itself that there seemed no break in this milling and chewing of masses of previously unregarded ideas. For a time she had been talking, for a time she did not talk, and in it all he was completely submerged.

At length she said, "Donny, tell me something ugly."

"What do you mean ugly?" The question and its answer had flowed through him almost without contact; had she not insisted, he would have lapsed into his busy silence again.

"Donny, something that you know about that you've done. Anything at all. Something you've seen."

It was easy to turn from introspection to deep recalls. "Went to one of those summer camps that there paper runs for kids. I's about seven, I guess."

"Donny," she said after what may have been a long time, "go on."

"Wasps," he said, negotiating the divided sibilant with some difficulty. "The ones that make paper nests." Suddenly he turned quite pale. "They stung me, it was on the big porch. The nurse, she came out an' hugged me and went away and came back with a bottle, ammonia it was, and put it on where I's stung." He coughed. "Stuff stunk, but it felt fine. Then a counselor, a big kid from up the street, he came with a long stick. There was a ol' rag tied on the end, it had kerosene on it. He lit it up with a match, it burned all yellow and smoky. He put it up high by them paper nests. The wasps, they come out howlin', they flew right into the fire. When they stopped comin' he pushed at the nest and down it come.

"He gone on to the next one, and down the line, twelve, fifteen of them. Every time he come to a new one, the wasps they flew into the fire. You could see the wings go, not like burning, not like melting, sort of *fzzz!* they gone. They fall. They fall all over the floor, they wiggle around, some run like ants, some with they legs burned off they just go around in one place like a phonograph.

"Kids come from all over, watching bug-eyed, runnin' around the porch, stampin' on them wasps with their wings gone, they can't sting nobody. Stamp on 'em and squeal and run away an' run back and stamp some more. I'm back near the door, I'm bawlin'. The nurse is squeezin' me, watchin' the wasps, wipin' the ammonia on me any old place, she's not watchin' what she's doin'. An' all the time the fire goes an' goes, the wasps fly at it, never once a dumb damn wasp goes to see who's at the other end of the stick. An' I'm there with the nurse, bawlin'. *Why am I bawlin'?*" It came out a deep, basic demand.

"You must have been stung quite badly," said Miss Phoebe. She was leaning forward, her strange unlovely eyes fixed on him. Her lower lip was wet.

"Nah! Three times, four . . ." He struggled hard to fit rich sensation to a poverty of words. "It was me, see. I guess if I got stung every wasp done it should get killed. Maybe burned even. But them wasps in the nest-es, they din't sting nobody, an' here they are all . . . all *brave*, that's what, brave, comin' and fallin' and comin' and fallin' and gettin' squashed. Why? Fer *me*, thass why! Me, it was me, I hadda go an' holler because I got stung an' make all that happen." He screwed his eyes tight shut and breathed as if he had been running. Abruptly his eyes opened very wide and he pressed himself upward in his chair, stretching his long bony neck as if he sat in rising water up to his chin. "What am I talkin' about, wasps? We wasn't talkin' about no wasps. How'd we get talkin' like this?"

She said, "It's all part of the same thing."

She waited for him to quiet down. He seemed to, at last. "I asked you to tell me something ugly, and you did. Did it make you feel better?"

He looked at her strangely. *Wasn't there something—oh, yes. Yesterday, about the watch. She made him tell and then asked if he didn't feel better. Was she getting back to that damn watch? I guess not,* he thought, and for some reason felt very ashamed. "Yeah, I feel some better." He looked into himself, found that what he had just said was true, and started in surprise. "Why should that be?" he asked, and it was the first time in his whole life he had asked such a question.

"There's two of us carrying it now," she explained.

He thought, and then protested, "There was twenty people there."

"Not one of them knew why you were crying."

Understanding flashed in him, bloomed almost to revelation. "God damn," he said softly.

This time she made no comment. Instead she said, "You learned something about bravery that day, didn't you?"

"Not until . . . now."

She shrugged. "That doesn't matter. As long as you understand, it doesn't matter how long it takes. Now, if all that happened just to make you understand something about bravery, it isn't an ugly thing at all, is it?"

He did not answer, but his very silence was a response.

"Perhaps one day you will fly into the fire and burn your wings and die, because it's all you can do to save something dear to you," she said softly. She let him think about that for a moment and then said, "Perhaps you will be a flame yourself, and see the brave ones fly at you and lose their wings and die. Either way, you'd know a little better what you were doing, because of the wasps, wouldn't you?"

He nodded.

"The playgrounds," she said, "the medicines, the air-raid watching, the boys' clubs, everything we were discussing . . . each single one of them kills something to do its work, and sometimes what is killed is very brave. It isn't easy to know good from evil."

"You know," he blurted.

"Ah," she said, "but there's a reason for that. You'd better go now, Donny."

Everything she had said to him flew to him as she spoke it, rested lightly on him, soaked in while he waited, and in time found a response. This was no exception. When he understood what she had said he jumped up guiltily covering the thoughtful and receptive self with self-consciousness like a towel snatched up to cover nakedness.

"Yeah I got to, what time is it?" he muttered. "Well," he said, "yeah. I guess I should." He looked about him as if he had forgotten some indefinable thing, turned and gave her a vacillating smile and went to the door. He opened it and turned. Silently and with great difficulty his mouth moved. He pressed the lips together.

"Good-bye, Donny."

"Yeah. Take it easy," he said.

As he spoke he saw himself in the full-length mirror fixed to the closet door. His eyes widened. It was himself he saw there—there was no doubt of that. But there was no sharp-cut seam-strained sports jacket, no dull and tattered shoes, no slicked-down hair smooth in front and down-pointing shag at the nape. In the reflection he was dressed in a dark suit. The coat matched the trousers. The tie was a solid color, maroon, and was held by a clasp so low down that it could barely be seen in the V of the jacket. The shoes gleamed, not like enamel but like the sheen of a new black-iron frying pan.

He gasped and blinked, and in that second the reflection told him only that he was what he was, flashy and clumsy and very much out of place here. He turned one long scared glance on Miss Phoebe and bolted through the door.

Don quit his job at the market. He quit jobs often, and usually needed no reason, but he had one this time. The idea of delivering another package to Miss Phoebe made him sweat, and the sweat was copious and cold. He did not know if it was fear or awe or shame, because he did not investigate the revulsion. He acknowledged it and acted upon it and otherwise locked the broad category labeled "Miss Phoebe" in the most guarded passages of his mind.

He was, unquestionably, haunted. Although he refused to acknowledge its source, he could not escape what can only be described as a sense of function. When he sharked around the pool halls to pick up some change—he carried ordinary seaman's papers, so could get a forty-cent bed at the Seaman's Institute—he was of the nonproductive froth on the brackish edges of a backwater, and he knew it acutely. When he worked as helper in a dockside shop, refurbishing outdated streetcars to be shipped to South America, his hand was unavoidably a link in a chain of vision and enterprise starting with an idea and ending with a peasant who, at this very moment, walked, but who would inevitably ride. Between that idea and that shambling peasant were months and miles and dollars, but the process passed through Don's hands every time they lifted a wrench, and he would watch them with mingled wonder and resentment.

He was a piece of nerve-tissue becoming aware of the proximity of a ganglion, and dimly conscious of the existence, somewhere, of a brain. His resentment stemmed from a nagging sense of loss. In ignorance he had possessed a kind of freedom—he'd have called it loneliness while he had it—which in retrospect filled him with nostalgia. He carried his inescapable sense of *belonging* like a bundle of thorns, light but most irritating. It was with him in drunkenness and the fights, the movies and the statistical shoutings of the baseball season. He never slept, but was among those who slept. He could not laugh without the realization that he was among the laughers. He no longer moved in a static universe, or rested while the world went by, for his every action had too obvious a reaction. Unbidden, his mind made analogies to remind him of this, inverting everything to illuminate this unwanted duality. The street, he found, pressed upward to his feet with a force equal to his weight. A new job and he approached one another with an equal magnetism, and he lost it or claimed it not by his effort or lack of it, but by an intricate resultant compounded of all the forces working with him matched against those opposed. On going to bed he would remove one shoe, and wake from a reverie ten minutes later to find with annoyance that he had sat motionless all that time to contemplate the weight of the shoe versus the upward force of the hand that held it. No birth is painless, and the stirrings of departure from a reactive existence are most troubling, since habit opposes it and there is no equipment to define the motivating ambition.

His own perceptions began to plague him. There had been a time when he was capable of tuning out that which did not concern him. But whatever it was that was growing within him extended its implacable sense of kinship to more areas than those of human endeavor. *Why*, he would ask himself insistently, *is the wet end of a towel darker than the dry end? What do spiders do with their silk when they climb up a single strand? What makes the brows of so many big executives tilt downward from the center?*

He was not a reader, and though he liked to talk, his wharf-rat survival instinct inhibited him from talking "different" talk, which is what his "different" questions would be, for one does not expose oneself to the sharp teeth of raillery.

He found an all-night cafe where the talk was as different as the talkers could make it; where girls who were unsure of their difference walked about with cropped hair and made their voices boom, and seedy little polyglots surreptitiously ate catsup and sugar with their single interminable cup of coffee; where a lost man could exchange his broken compass for a broken oar. He went there night after night, sitting alone and listening, held by the fact that many of these minds were genuinely questing. Armed with his strange understanding of opposites, he readily recognized those on one side or the other of forces which most naturally oppose one another, but since he could admire neither phrasing nor intensity for their own sakes, he could only wonder at the misery of these children perched so lonesomely on their dialectical seesaws, mourning the fact that they did not get off the ground while refusing to let anyone get on the other end. Once he listened raptly to a man with a bleeding ear who seemed to understand the things he felt, but instead of believing many things, this man believed in nothing. Don went away, sad, wondering if there were anyone, anywhere who cared importantly that when you yawn, an Italian will ask you if you're hungry while a Swede will think you need sleep; or that only six parallel cuts on a half-loaf of bread will always get you seven slices.

So for many months he worked steadily so that his hands could drain off tensions and let him think. When he had worked through every combination and permutation of which he was capable, he could cast back and discover that all his thoughts had stemmed from Miss Phoebe. His awe and fear of her ceased to exist when he decided to go back, not to see her, but to get more material.

A measure of awe returned, however, when he phoned. He heard her lift the receiver, but she did not say, "Hello." She said, "Why, Don! How are you?"

He swallowed hard and said, "Good, Miss Phoebe."

"Four o'clock tomorrow," she said, and hung up.

He put the receiver back carefully and stood looking at the telephone. He worked the tip of the finger-stop under his thumbnail and stood for a long time in the booth, carefully cleaning away the thin parenthesis of oily grime which had defied his brush that morning. When it was gone, so was his fright, but it took a long time. *I've forgotten it all right*, he thought, *but oh, my aching back!*

Belatedly he thought, *Why, she called me Don, not Donny.*

He went back to the cafe that night, feeling a fine new sense of insulation. He had so much to look forward to that searches could wait. And like many a searcher before him, he found what he was looking for as soon as he stopped looking. It was a face that could not have drawn him more if it had been luminous, or leaf-green. It was a face with strong and definite lines, with good pads of laughter-muscles under the cheekbones, and eye-sockets shaped to catch and hold laughter early and long. Her hair was long and seemed black, but its highlights were not blue but red. She sat with six other people around a large table, her eyes open and sleeping, her good mouth lax and miserable.

He made no attempt to attract her attention, or to join the group. He simply watched her until she left, which was some three or four hours later. He followed her and so did another man. When she turned up the steps of a brownstone a few blocks away the man followed her, and was halfway up the steps when she was at the top, fumbling for a key. When Don stopped, looking up, the man saw him and whirled. He blocked Don's view of the girl. To Don he was not a person at all, but something in the way. Don made an impatient, get-out-of-the-way gesture with his head, and only then realized that the man was at bay, terrified, caught red-handed. His eyes were round and he drooled. Don stood looking upward, quite astonished, as the man sidled down, glaring, panting, and suddenly leapt past him and pelted off down the street.

Don looked from the shadowed, dwindling figure to the lighted doorway. The girl had both hands on the side of the outer, open doorway and was staring down at him with bright unbelief in her face. "Oh, dear God," she said.

Don saw that she was frightened, so he said, "It's all right." He stayed where he was.

She glanced down the street where the man had gone and found it empty. Slowly she came toward Don and stopped on the third step above him. "Are you an angel?" she asked. In her voice was a childlike eagerness and the shadow of the laughter that her face was made for.

96

Don made a small, abashed sound. "Me? Not me."

She looked down the street and shuddered. "I thought I didn't care any more *what* happened," she said, as if she were not speaking to him at all. Then she looked at him. "Anyway, thanks. Thanks. I don't know what he might've ... if you ..."

Don writhed under her clear, sincere eyes. "I didn't do nothing." He backed off a pace. "What do you mean, am I a angel?"

"Didn't you ever hear about a guardian angel?"

He had, but he couldn't find it in himself to pursue such a line of talk. He had never met anyone who talked like this. "Who was that guy?"

"He's crazy. They had him locked up for a long time, he hurt a little girl once. He gets like that once in a while."

"Well, you want to watch out," he said.

She nodded gravely. "I guess I care after all," she said. "I'll watch out."

"Well, take it easy;" he said.

She looked quickly at his face. His words had far more dismissal in them than he had intended, and he suddenly felt miserable. She turned and slowly climbed the steps. He began to move away because he could think of nothing else to do. He looked back over his shoulder and saw her in the doorway, facing him. He thought she was going to call out, and stopped. She went inside without speaking again, and he suddenly felt very foolish. He went home and thought about her all night and all the next day. He wondered what her name was.

When he pressed the buzzer, Miss Phoebe did not come to the door immediately. He stood there wondering if he should buzz again or go away or what. Then the door opened. "Come in, Don."

He stepped inside, and though he thought he had forgotten about the strange mirror, he found himself looking for it even before he saw Miss Phoebe's face. It was still there, and in it he saw himself as before, with the dark suit, the quiet tie, the dull, clean-buffed shoes. He saw it with an odd sense of disappointment, for it had given him such a wondrous shock before, but now reflected only what a normal mirror would, since he was wearing such a suit and tie and shoes—but wait; the figure in the reflection carried something and he did not. A paper parcel ... a wrapped bunch of flowers; not a florist's elaboration, but tissue-wrapped jonquils from a subway peddler. He blinked, and the reflection was now quite accurate again.

All this took place in something over three seconds. He now became aware of a change in the room, *it's—oh, the light.* It had been almost glary with its jewel-clean windows and scrubbed white woodwork, but now it was filled with mellow orange light. Part of this was sunlight struggling through the inexpensive blinds, which were drawn all the way down. Part was something else he did not see until he stepped fully into the room and into the range of light from the near corner. He gasped and stared, and, furiously, he felt tears rush into his eyes so that the light wavered and ran.

"Happy birthday, Don," said Miss Phoebe severely.

Don said, "Aw." He blinked hard and looked at the little round cake with its eighteen five-and-dime candles. "Aw."

"Blow them out quickly," she said. "They run."

He bent over the cake.

"Every one, mind," she said. "In one breath."

He blew. All the candles went out but one. He had no air left in his lungs, and he looked at the candle in purple panic. In a childlike way, he could not bring himself to break the rules she had set up. His mouth yawped open and closed like that of a beached fish. He puffed his cheeks out by pushing his tongue up and forward, leaned very close to the candle, and released the air in his mouth with a tiny explosive pop. The candle went out.

"Splendid. Open the blinds for me like a good boy."

He did as he was asked without resentment. As she plucked the little sugar candleholders out of the cake, he said, "How'd you know it was my birthday?"

"Here's the knife. You must cut it first, you know."

He came forward. "It's real pretty. I never had no birthday cake before."

"I'm glad you like it. Hurry now. The tea's just right."

He busied himself, serving and handing and receiving and setting down, moving chairs, taking sugar. He was too happy to speak.

"Now then," she said when they were settled. "Tell me what you've been up to."

He assumed she knew, but if she wanted him to say, why, he would. "I'm a typewriter mechanic now," he said. "I like it fine. I work nights in big offices and nobody bothers me none. How've you been?"

She did not answer him directly, but her serene expression said that nothing bad could ever happen to her. "And is that all? Just work and sleep?"

"I been thinkin'," he said. He looked at her curiously. "I thought a lot about what you said." She did not respond. "I mean about everything working on everything else, an' the wasps and all." Again she was silent, but now there was response in it.

He said, "I was all mixed up for a long time. Part of the time I was mad. I mean, like you're working for a boss who won't let up on you, thinks he owns you just because you work there. Used to be I thought about whatever I wanted to, I could stop thinkin' like turnin' a light off."

"Very apt," she remarked. "It was exactly that."

He waited while this was absorbed. "After I was here I couldn't turn off the light; the switch was busted. The more I worked on things, the more mixed-up they got." In a moment he added, "For a while."

"What things?" she asked.

"Hard to say," he answered honestly. "I never had nobody to tell me much, but I had some things pretty straight. It's wrong to swipe stuff. It's right to do what they tell you. It's wrong to play with yourself. It's right to go to church."

"It's right to worship," she interjected. "If you can worship in a church, that's the best place to do it. If you can worship better in another place, then that's where you should go instead."

"*That's* what I mean!" he barked, pointing a bony finger like a revolver. "You say something like that, so sure and easy, an' all the— the fences go down. Everything's all in the right box, see, an' you come along and shake everything together. You don't back off from nothing. You say what you want about anything, an' you let me say anything I want to you. Everything I ever thought was right or wrong could be wrong or right. Like those wasps dyin' because of me, and you say they maybe died *for* me, so's I could learn something. Like you sayin' I could be a wasp or a fire, an' still know what was what … I'll get mixed up again if I go on talkin' about it."

"I think not," she said, and he felt very pleased. She said, "It's in the nature of things to be 'shaken all together,' as you put it. A bird brings death to a worm and a wildcat brings death to the bird. Can we say that what struck the worm and the bird was evil, when the wildcat's kittens took so much good from it? Or if the murder of the worm is good, can we call the wildcat evil?"

"There isn't no … no *altogether* good or bad, huh."

"Now, that is a very wrong thing to say," she said with soft-voiced asperity.

"You gone an' done it again!" he exclaimed.

She did not smile with him. "There is an absolute good and an absolute evil. They cannot be confused with right and wrong, or building and destroying as we know them, because, like the cat and the worm, those things depend on whose side you take. Don, I'm going to show you something very strange and wonderful."

She went to her little desk and got pencil and paper. She drew a circle, and within it she sketched in an S-shaped line. One side of this line she filled in with quick short strokes of her pencil:

"This," she said, as Don pored over it, "is the most ancient symbol known to man. It's called 'yin and Yang.' 'Yin' is the Chinese term for darkness and earth. 'Yang' means light and sky. Together they form the complete circle—the universe, the cosmos—everything. Nothing under heaven can be altogether one of these things or the other. The symbol means light and dark. It means birth and death. It is everything which holds together and draws down, with everything that pours out and disperses. It is male and female, hope and history, love and hate. It's—everything there is or could be. It's why you can't say the murder of a worm by a bird is good or evil."

"This here yin an' Yang's in everything we do, huh."

"Yes."

"It's God an' the Devil then."

"*Good* and the devil." She placed her hand over the entire symbol. "God is all of it."

"Well, all right!" he exclaimed. "So it's like I said. There ain't a 'altogether good' and a 'altogether bad'. Miss Phoebe, how you know you're right when you bust up some pusher's business or close a house?"

"There's a very good way of knowing, Don. I'm very glad you asked me that question." She all but beamed at him—she, who hardly ever even smiled. "Now listen carefully. I am going to tell you something which it took me many years to find out. I am going to tell you because I do not see why the young shouldn't use it.

"Good and evil are active forces—almost like living things. I said that nothing under heaven can be completely one of these things or the other, and it's true. But, Don—good and evil come to us from *somewhere*. They reach this cosmos as living forces, constantly replenished—from *somewhere*. It follows that there is a Source of good and a Source of evil . . . or call them light and dark, or birth and death if you like."

She put her finger on the symbol. "Human beings, at least with their conscious wills, try to live here, in the Yang part. Many find themselves on the dark side; some cross and recross the borderline. Some set a course for themselves and drive it straight and true, and never understand that the border itself turns and twists and will have them on one side and then the other.

"In any case, these forces are in balance, and they must remain so. But as they are living, vital forces, there must be those who willingly and purposefully work with them."

With his thumbnail he flicked the paper. "From this, everything's so even-steven you'd never know who you're working for."

"Not true, Don. There are ways of knowing."

He opened his lips and closed them, turned away, shaking his head.

"You may ask me, Don," she said.

"Well, okay. You're one of 'em. Right?"

"Perhaps so."

"Perhaps nothing. You knocked me flat on my noggin twice in a row an' never touched me. You're—you're somethin' special, that's for sure. You even knew about my birthday. You know who's callin' when the phone rings."

"There are advantages."

"All right then, here's what I'm gettin' to, and I don't want you to get mad at me. What I want to know is, why ain't you rich?"

"What do you mean by rich?"

He kicked the table leg gently. "Junk," he said. He waved at the windows. "Everybody's got venetian blinds now. Look there, cracks in the ceiling 'n you'll get a rent rise if you complain, long as it ain't leakin'. You know, if I could do the things you do, I'd have me a big house an' a car. I'd have flunkies to wash dishes an' all like that."

"I wouldn't be rich if I had all those things, Don."

He looked at her guardedly. He knew she was capable of a preachment, though he had been lucky so far. "Miss Phoebe," he said respectfully, "You ain't goin' to tell me the—uh—inner riches is better'n a fishtail Cadillac."

"I'll ask *you*," she said patiently. "Would you want a big house and servants and all those things?"

"Well, *sure!*"

"Why?"

"Why? Well, because, because—well, that's the way to live, that's all."

"Why is it the way to live?"

"Well, anyone can see why."

"Don, answer the question. Why is that the way to live?"

"Well," he said. He made a circular gesture and put his hand down limply. He wet his lips. "Well, because you'd have what you wanted." He looked at her hopefully and realized he'd have to try again. "You could make anyone do what you wanted."

"Ah," she said. "Why would you want to do that?"

"So you wouldn't have to do your own work."

"Aside from personal comfort—why would you want to be able to tell other people what to do?"

"You tell me," he said with some warmth.

"The answers are in you if you'll only look, Don. Tell me: Why?"

He considered. "I guess it'd make me feel good."

"Feel good?"

"The boss. The Man. You know. I say jump, they jump."

"Power?"

"Yeah, that's it, power."

"Then you want riches so you'll have a sense of power."

"You're in."

"And you wonder why I don't want riches. Don, I've *got* power. Moreover, it was given me and it's mine. I needn't buy it for the rest of my life."

"Well, now ..." he breathed.

"You can't imagine power in any other terms than cars and swimming pools, can you?"

"Yes I can," he said instantly. Then he grinned and added, "But not yet."

"I think that's more true than you know," she said, giving him her sparse smile. "You'll come to understand it."

They sat in companionable silence. He picked up a crumb of cake icing and looked at it. "Real good cake," he murmured, and ate it. Almost without change of inflection, he said, "I got a real ugly one to tell you."

She waited, in the responsive silence he was coming to know so well.

"Met a girl last night."

He was not looking at her and so did not see her eyes click open, round and moist. He hooked his heel in the chair rung and put his fist on the raised knee, thumb up. He lowered his head until the thumb fitted into the hollow at the bridge of his nose. Resting his head precariously there, rolling it slightly from time to time as if he perversely enjoyed the pressure and the ache, he began to speak. And if Miss Phoebe found surprising the leaps from power to birthday cake to a girl to what happened in the sewer, she said nothing.

"Big sewer outlet down under the docks at Twenny-Seventh," he said. "Was about nine or ten, playing there. Kid called Renzo. We were inside the pipe, it was about five feet high, and knee-deep in storm water. Saw somethin' bobbin' in the water, got close enough to look. It was the hind feet off a dead rat, a great big one, and *real* dead. Renzo, he was over by the outlet tryin' to see if he could get up on a towboat out there, and I thought it might be fine if I could throw the rat on his back on account he didn't have no shirt on. I took hold of the rat's feet and pulled but that rat, he had his head stuck in a side-pipe somehow, an' I guess he swole some too. I guess I said something and Renzo he come over, so there was nothin' for it then but haul the rat out anyway. I got a good hold and yanked, an' something popped an' up he came. I pulled 'im right out of his skin. There he was wet an' red an' bare an' smellin' a good deal. Renzo, he lets out a big holler, laughin', I can still hear it in that echoey pipe. I'm standin' there like a goofball, starin' at this rat. Renzo says, 'Hit'm quick, Doc, or he'll never start breathin'!' I just barely got the idea when the legs come off the rat an' it fell in the water with me still holdin' the feet."

It was very quiet for a while. Don rocked his head, digging his thumb into the bridge of his nose. "Renzo and me we had a big fight after. He tol' everybody I had a baby in the sewer. He tol' 'em I's a first-class stork. They all started to call me Stork. I hadda fight five of 'em in two days before they cut it out.

"Kid stuff," he said suddenly, too loudly, and sat upright, wide-eyed, startled at the sound. "I know it was kid stuff, I can forget it. But it won't ... it won't forget."

Miss Phoebe stirred, but said nothing. Don said, "Girls. I never had nothing much to do with girls, kidded 'em some if there was somebody with me started it, and like that. Never by myself. I tell you how it is, it's—" He was quiet for a long moment. His lips moved as if he were speaking silently, words after words until he found the words he wanted. He went on in precisely the same tone, like an interrupted tape recorder. "—like this, I get so I like a girl a whole lot, I want to get close to her, I think about her like any fellow does. So before I can think much about it, let alone *do* anything, zing! I'm standin' in that stinkin' sewer, Renzo's yellin' 'Hit'm quick, Doc,' an' all the rest of it." He blew sharply from his nostrils. "The better a girl smells," he said hoarsely, "the worse it is. So I think about girls, I think about babies; I think about babies, it's Renzo and me and that echo. Laughin'," he mumbled, "him laughin'.

"I met a girl last night," he said clearly, "I don't want ever to think about like that. I walked away. I don't know what her name is. I want to see her some more. I'm afraid. So that's why."

After a while he said, "That's why I told you."

And later, "You were a big help before, the wasps." As he spoke he realized that there was no point in hurrying her; she had heard him the first time and would wait until she was ready. He picked up another piece of icing, crushed it, tossed the pieces back on the plate.

"You never asked me," said Miss Phoebe, "about the power I have, and how it came to me."

"Din't think you'd say. I wouldn't, if I had it. This girl was—"

"Study," said Miss Phoebe. "More of it than you realize. Training and discipline and, I suppose, a certain natural talent which," she said, fixing him sternly with her eyes as he was about to interrupt, "I am sure you also have. To a rather amazing degree. I have come a long way, a long hard way, and it isn't so many years ago that I first began to feel this power ... I like to think of you with it, young and strong and ... and good, growing greater year by year. Don, would you like the power? Would you work hard and patiently for it?"

He was very quiet. Suddenly he looked up at her. "What?"

She said—and for once the control showed—"I thought you might want to answer a question like that."

He scratched his head and grinned. "Gee, I'm sorry, Miss Phoebe, but for that one second I was thinkin' about ... something else, I guess. Now," he said brightly, "what was it you wanted to know?" "What was this matter you found so captivating?" she asked heavily. "I must say I'm not used to talking to myself, Don."

"Ah, don't jump salty, Miss Phoebe," he said contritely. "I'll pay attention, honest. It's just that I—you din't say word *one* about what I told you. I guess I was tryin' to figure it out by myself if you wasn't goin' to help."

"Perhaps you didn't wait long enough."

"Oh." He looked at her and his eyes widened. "*Oh!* I never thought of that. Hey, go ahead, will you?" He drew his knees together and clasped them, turned to face her fully.

She nodded with a slightly injured satisfaction. "I asked you, Don, if you'd like the kind of power I have, for yourself."

"*Me?*" he demanded, incredulously.

"You. And I also asked you if you would work hard and patiently to get it."

"Would I! Look, you don't really think, I mean, I'm just a—"

"We'll see," she said.

She glanced out the window. Dusk was not far away. The curtains hung limp and straight in the still air. She rose and went to the windows, drew the blinds down. The severe velour drapes were on cranes. She swung them over the windows. They were not cut full enough to cover completely; each window admitted a four-inch slit of light. But that side of the building was in shadow, and she turned back to find Don blinking in deep obscurity. She went back to her chair.

"Come closer," she said. "No, not that way—facing me. That's it. Your back to the window. Now, I'm going to cover my face. That's because otherwise the light would be on it; I don't want you to look at me or at anything but what you find inside yourself." She took a dark silk scarf from the small drawer in the end of the gateleg table. "Put your hands out. Palms down. So." She dropped the scarf over her face and hair, and felt for his hands. She slipped hers under his, palms upward, and leaned forward until she could grasp his wrists. "Hold mine that way too. Good.

"Be absolutely quiet."

He was. She said, "There's something the matter. You're all tightened up. And you're not close enough. Don't move! I mean, in your mind ... ah, I see. You'll have your questions answered. Just trust me." A moment later she said, "That's *much* better. There's something on your mind, though, a little something. Say it, whatever it is."

"I was thinkin', this is a trapeze grip, like in the circus."

"So it is! Well, it's a good contact. Now, don't think of anything at all. If you want to speak, well, do; but nothing will be accomplished until you no longer feel like talking.

"There is a school of discipline called Yoga," she said quietly. "For years I have studied and practiced it. It's a lifetime's work in itself, and still it's only the first part of what I've done. It has to do with the harmony of the body and the mind, and the complete control of both. My breathing will sound strange to you. Don't be frightened; it's perfectly all right."

His hands lay heavily in hers. He opened his eyes and looked at her but there was nothing to see, just the black mass of her silk-shrouded head and shoulders in the dim light. Her breathing deepened. As he became more and more aware of other silences, her breathing became more and more central in his attention. He began to wonder where she was putting it all; an inhalation couldn't possibly continue for so long, like the distant hiss of escaping steam. And when it dwindled, the silence was almost too complete, for too long; no one could hold such a deep breath for as long as that! And when at last the breath began to come out again, it seemed as if the slow hiss went on longer even than the inhalation. If he had wondered where she was putting it, he now wondered where she was getting it.

And at last he realized that the breathing was not deep at all, but shallow in the extreme; it was just that the silence was deeper and her control greater than he had imagined.

His hands—

"It tingles. Like electric," he said aloud.

His voice did not disturb her in the least. She made no answer in any area. The silence deepened, the darkness deepened, the tingling

107

continued and grew . . . not grew; it spread. When he first felt it, it had lived in a spot on each wrist, where it contacted hers. Now it uncoiled, sending a thin line of sensation up into his forearms and down into his hands. He followed its growth, fascinated. Around the center of each palm the tingling drew a circle, and sent a fine twig of feeling growing into his fingers, and at the same time he could feel it negotiating the turn of his elbows.

He thought it had stopped growing, and then realized that it had simply checked its twig-like creeping, and was broadening; the line in his arms and fingers was becoming a band, a bar of feeling. It crossed his mind that if this bothered him at all he could pull his hands away and break the contact, and that if he did that Miss Phoebe would not resent it in any way. And, since he knew he was free to do it, knew it without question, he was not tempted. He sat quietly, wonder-struck, tasting the experience.

With a small silent explosion there were the tingling, hair-thin lines of sensation falling like distant fireworks through his chest and abdomen, infusing his loins and thighs and the calves of his legs. At the same time more of them crept upward through his neck and head, flared into and around his ears, settled and boiled and shimmered through his lobes and cheeks, curled and clasped the roots of his eyelids. And again there was the feeling of the lines broadening, fusing one with the other as they swelled. Distantly he recognized their ultimate; they would grow inward and outward until they were a complete thing, bounded exactly by everything he was, every hair, every contour, every thought and function.

He opened his eyes, and the growth was not affected. The dark mass of Miss Phoebe's head was where it had been, friendly and near and reassuring. He half-smiled, and the sparkling delicate little lines of feeling on his lips yielded to the smile, played in it like infinitesimal dolphins, gave happy news of it to all the other threads, and they all sang to his half-smile and gave him joy. He closed his eyes comfortably, and cheerful filaments reached for one another between his upper and lower lashes.

An uncountable time passed. Time now was like no time he knew of, drilling as it always had through event after event, predictable and obedient to rust, springtime, and the scissoring hands of clocks. This was a new thing . . . not a suspension, for it was too alive for that. It was different, that's all, different the way this feeling was, and now the lines and bands and bars were fused and grown, and he was filled, he was, himself, of a piece with what had once been the tingling of a spot on his wrist.

It was a feeling, still a feeling, but it was a substance too, Don-sized, Don-shaped. A color . . . no, it wasn't a color, but if it had been a color it was beginning to glow and change. It was glowing as steel glows in the soaking pits, a color impossible to call black because it is red inside; and now you can see the red; and now the red has orange in it, and now in the orange is yellow, and when white shows in the yellow you may no longer look, but still the radiation beats through you, intensifying . . . not a color, no; this thing had no color and no light, but if it had been a color, this would have been its spectral growth.

And this was the structure, this the unnamable *something* which now found itself alive and joyous. It was from such a peak that the living thing rose as if from sleep, became conscious of its own balance and strength, and leapt heavenward with a single cry like all the satisfying, terminal resolving chords of all music, all uttered in a wingbeat of time.

Then it was over not because it was finished, like music or a meal, but because it was perfect, like foam or a flower caught in the infrangible amber of memory. Don left the experience without surfeit, without tension, without exhaustion. He sat peacefully with his hands in Miss Phoebe's, not dazzled, not numb, replenished in some luxurious volume within him which kept what it gained for all of life, and which had an infinite capacity. But for the cloth over her face and the odd fact that their hands were dripping with perspiration, they might just that second have begun. It may even have been that second.

Miss Phoebe disengaged her hands and plucked away the cloth. She was smiling—really smiling, and Don understood why she so seldom smiled, if this were the expression she used for such experiences.

He answered the smile, and said nothing, because about perfect things nothing can be said. He went and dried his hands and then pulled back the drapes and raised the blinds while she straightened the chairs.

"The ancients," said Miss Phoebe, "recognized four elements: earth, air, fire and water. This power can do anything those four elements can do." She put down the clean cups, and went to get her crumb brush. "To start with," she added.

He placed the remark where it would soak in, and picked up a piece of icing from the cake plate. This time he ate it. "Why is a wet towel darker than a dry one?"

"I—why, I hadn't thought," she said. "It is, now that you mention it. I'm sure I don't know why, though."

"Well, maybe you know this," he said. "Why I been worrying about it so much?"

"Worrying?"

"You know what I mean. That and why most motors that use heat for power got to have a cooling system, and why do paper towels tear where they ain't perf'rated, and a zillion things like that. I never used to."

"Perhaps it's . . . yes, I know. Of *course!*" she said happily. "You're getting a—call it a kinship with things. A sense of interrelationship."

"Is that good?"

"I think it is. It means I was right in feeling that you have a natural talent for what I'm going to teach you."

"It takes up a lot of my time," he grumbled.

"It's good to be alive all the time," she said. She poured. "Don, do you know what a revelation is?"

"I heard of it."

"It's a sudden glimpse of the real truth. You had one about the wasps."

"I had it awful late."

That doesn't matter. You had it, that's the important thing. You had one with the rat, too."

"I did?"

"With the wasps you had a revelation of sacrifice and courage. With the rat—well, you know yourself what effect it has had on you."

"I'm the only one I know has no girl," he said.

"That is exactly it."

"Don't tell me it's s'posed to be that way!"

"For you, I—I'd say so."

"Miss Phoebe, I don't think l know what you're talkin' about." She looked at her teacup. "I've never been married."

"Me too," he said somberly. "Wait, is that what you—"

"Why do people get married?"

"Kids."

"Oh, that isn't all."

He said, with his mouth full, "They wanna be together, I guess. Team up, like. One pays the bills, the other runs the joint."

"That's about it. Sharing. They want to share. You know the things they share."

"I heard," he said shortly.

She leaned forward. "Do you think they can share anything like what we've had this afternoon?"

"*That* I never heard," he said pensively.

"I don't wonder. Don, your revelation with the rat is as basic a picture of what is called 'original sin' as anything I have ever heard."

"Original sin," he said thoughtfully. "That's about Adam an'—no, wait. I remember. Everybody's supposed to be sinful to start with because it takes a sin to get'm started."

"Once in a while," she said, "it seems as if you know so few words because you don't need them. That was beautifully put. Don, I think that awful thing that happened to you in the sewer was a blessing. I think it's a good thing, not a bad one. It might be bad for someone else, but not for you. It's kept you as you are so far. I don't think you should try to forget it. It's a warning and a defense. It's a weapon against the 'yin' forces. You are a very special person, Don. You were made for better things than—than others."

"About the wasps," he said. "As soon as you started to talk I begun to feel better. About this, I don't feel better." He looked up to the point where the wall met the ceiling and seemed to be listening to his own last phrase. He nodded definitely. "I don't feel better. I feel worse."

She touched his arm. It was the only time she had made such a gesture. "You're strong and growing and you're just eighteen." Her voice was very kind. "It would be a strange thing indeed if a young man your age didn't have his problems and struggles and tempta— I mean, battles. I'm sorry I can't resolve it for you, Don. I wish I could. But I know what's right. Don't I, Don, don't I?"

"Every time," he said glumly. "But I . . ." His gaze became abstracted.

She watched him anxiously. "Don't think about her," she whispered. "Don't. You don't have to. Don, do you know that what we did this afternoon was only the very beginning, like the first day of kindergarten?"

His eyes came back to her, bright. "Yeah, huh. Hey, how about that."

"When would you like to do some more?"

"Now?"

"Bless you, no! We both have things to do. And besides, you have to think. You know it takes time to think."

"Yeah, okay. When?"

"A week."

"Don't worry about me, I'll be here. Hey, I'm gonna be late for work."

He went to the door. "Take it easy," he said.

He went out and closed the door but before the latch clicked he pushed it open again. He crossed the room to her.

He said, "Hey, thanks for the birthday cake. It was . . ." His mouth moved as he searched. "It was a good birthday cake." He took her hand and shook it heartily. Then he was gone.

Miss Phoebe was just as pink as the birthday cake. To the closed door she murmured, "Take it easy."

Don was in a subway station two nights later, waiting for an express. The dirty concrete shaft is atypical and mysterious at half-past four in the morning. The platforms are unlittered and deserted, and there is a complete absence of the shattering roar and babble and bustle for which these urban entrails are built. An approaching train can be heard starting and running and stopping sometimes ten or twelve minutes before it pulls in, and a single set of footfalls on the mezzanine above will outlast it. The few passengers waiting seem always to huddle together near one of the wooden benches, and there seems to be a kind of inverse square law in operation, for the closer they approach one another the greater the casual unnoticing manners they affect, though they will all turn to watch someone walking toward them from two hundred feet away. And when angry voices bark out, the effect is more shattering than it would be in a cathedral.

A tattered man slept uneasily on the bench. Two women buzz-buzzed ceaselessly at the other end. A black-browed man in gray tweed strode the platform, glowering, looking as if he were expected to decide on the recall of the Ambassador to the Court of St. James by morning.

Don happened to be looking at the tattered man, and the way the old brown hat was pulled down over the face (it could have been a headless corpse, and no one would have been the wiser), when the body shuddered and stirred. A strip of stubbled skin emerged between the hat and the collar, and developed a mouth into which was stuffed a soggy collection of leaf-mold which may have been a cigar butt yesterday. The man's hand came up and fumbled around, coming away with most of the soggy thing. The jaws worked, the lips smacked distastefully. The hand pushed the hat brim up only enough to expose a red eye, which glared at the butt. The hat fell again, and the hand pitched the butt away.

At this point the black-browed man hove to, straddle-legged in front of the bench. He opened his coat and hooked his thumbs in the armholes of his waistcoat. He tilted his head back, half-closed his eyes, and sighted through the cleft on his chin at the huddled creature on the bench. "You!" he grated, and everyone swung around to stare at him. He thumped the sleeping man's ankle with the side of his foot. "You!" Everyone looked at the bench.

The tattered man said "Whuh-wuh-wuh-wuh," and smacked his lips. Suddenly he was bolt upright, staring.

"You!" barked the black-browed man. He pointed to the butt. "Pick that up!"

The tattered man looked at him and down at the butt. His hand strayed to his mouth, felt blindly on and around it. He looked down again at the butt and dull recognition began to filter into his face. "Oh sure boss, sure," he whined. He cringed low, beginning to stoop down off the bench but afraid to stop talking, afraid to turn his gaze away from the danger point. "I don't make no trouble for anybody, mister, not me, honest I don't," he wheedled. "A feller gets down on his luck, you know how it is, but I never make trouble, mister . . ."

"Pick it up!"

"Oh sure, sure, right away, boss."

At this point Don, to his own intense amazement, felt himself approaching the black-browed man. He tapped him on the shoulder. "Mister," he said. He prayed that his tight voice would not break. "Mister, make *me* pick it up, huh?"

"*What?*"

Don waved at the tattered man. "A two-year-old kid could push him around. So what are you proving, you're a big man or something? Make *me* pick up the butt, you're such a big man."

"Get away from me," said the black-browed man. He took two quick paces backwards. "I know what you are, you're one of those subway hoodlums."

Don caught a movement from the corner of his eye. The tattered man had one knee on the platform, and was leaning forward to pick up the butt. "Get away from that," he snapped, and kicked the butt onto the local tracks.

"Sure, boss, sure, I don't want no . . ."

"Get away from me, both of you," said the black-browed man. He was preparing for flight. Don suddenly realized that he was afraid—afraid that he and the tattered man might join forces, or perhaps even that they had set the whole thing up in advance. He laughed. The black-browed man backed into a pillar. And just then a train roared in, settling the matter.

Something touched Don between the shoulder blades and he leaped as if it had been an ice pick. But it was one of the women. "I just had to tell you, that was very brave. You're a fine young man," she said. She sniffed in the direction of the distant tweed-clad figure and marched to the train. It was a local. Don watched it go, and smiled. He felt good.

"Mister, you like to save my life, you did. I don't want no trouble, you unnerstan', I never do. Feller gets down on his luck once in a wh—"

"Shaddup!" said Don. He turned away and froze. Then he went back to the man and snatched off the old hat. The man cringed.

"I know who you are. You just got back from the can. You got sent up for attackin' a girl."

"I ain't done a *thing*," whispered the man. "Gimme back my hat, please, mister?"

Don looked down at him. He should walk away, he ought to leave this hulk to rot, but his questing mind was against him. He threw the hat on the man's lap and wiped his fingers on the side of his jacket. "I saw you stayin' out of trouble three nights ago on Mulberry Street. Followin' a girl into a house there."

"It was you chased me," said the man. "Oh God." He tucked himself up on the bench in a uterine position and began to weep.

"Cut that out," Don snarled. "I ain't hit you. If I wanted I coulda thrown you in front of that train, right?"

"Yeah, instead you saved me f'm that killer," said the man brokenly. "Y'r a prince, mister. Y'r a real prince, that's what you are."

"You goin' to stay away from that girl?"

"*Your* girl? Look, I'll never even walk past her house no more. I'll kill anybody looks at her."

"Never mind that. Just *you* stay away from her."

The express roared in. Don rose and so did the man. Don shoved him back to the bench. "Take the next one."

"Yeah, sure, anything you say. Just you say the word."

Don thought, *I'll ask him what it is that makes it worth the risk, chance getting sent up for life just for a thing like that.* Then, *No,* he thought. *I think I know why.* He got on the train.

He sat down and stared dully ahead. *A man will give up anything, his freedom, his life even, for a sense of power.*

Q. *How much am I giving up?*

A. *How should I know?*

He looked at the advertisements. "Kulkies are better." "The better skin cream." He wondered if anyone ever wanted to know what these things were better *than.* "For that richer, creamier, safer lather." "Try Miss Phoebe for that better, more powerful power."

He wondered, and wondered . . .

Summer dusk, all the offices closed, the traffic gone, no one and nothing in a hurry for a little while. Don put his back against a board fence where he could see the entrance, and took out a toothpick. She might be going out, she might be coming home, she might be home and not go out, she might be out and not come home. He'd stick around.

He never even got the toothpick wet.

She stood at the top of the steps, looking across at him. He simply looked back. There were many things he might have done. Rushed across. Waved. Done a time-step. Looked away. Run. Fallen down.

But he did nothing, and the single fact that filled his perceptions at that moment was that as long as she stood there with russet gleaming in her black hair, with her sad, sad cups-for-laughter eyes turned to him, with the thin summer cloak whipping up and falling to her clean straight body, why there was nothing he could do.

She came straight across to him. He broke the toothpick and dropped it, and waited. She crossed the sidewalk and stopped in front of him, looking at his eyes, his mouth, his eyes. "You don't even remember me."

"I remember you all right."

She leaned closer. The whites of her eyes showed under her pupils when she did that, like the high crescent moon in the tropics that floats startlingly on its back. These two crescents were twice as startling. "I don't think you do."

"Over there." With his chin he indicated her steps. "The other night."

It was then, at last, that she smiled, and the eyes held what they were made for. "I saw him again."

"He try anything?"

She laughed. "He *ran!* He was afraid of me. I don't think anybody was ever afraid of me."

"I am."

"Oh, that's the silliest—" She stopped, and again leaned toward him. "You mean it, don't you?"

He nodded. "Don't ever be afraid of me," she said gravely, "not *ever*. What did you do to that man?"

"Nothin'. Talked to him."

"You didn't hurt him?"

He shook his head.

"I'm glad," she said. "He's sick and he's ugly and he's bad, too, I guess, but I think he's been hurt enough. What's your name?"

"Don."

She counted on her fingers. "Don is a Spanish grandee. Don is putting on clothes. Don is the sun coming up in the morning. Don is . . . is the opposite of up. You're a whole lot of things, Don." Her eyes widened. "You laughed!"

"Was that wrong?"

"Oh, *no!* But I didn't know you ever laughed."

"I watched you for three hours the other night and you didn't laugh. You didn't even talk."

"I would've talked if I'd known you were there. Where were you?"

"That all-night joint. I followed you."

"Why?"

He looked at his shoeshine. With his other foot, he carefully stepped on it. "Why did you follow me? Were you going to talk to me?"

"No!" he said. "No, by God, I wasn't. I wouldn'ta."

"Then why did you follow me?"

"I liked looking at you. I liked seeing you walk." He glanced across at the brownstone steps. "I didn't want anything to happen to you, all alone like that."

"Oh, I didn't care."

"That's what you said that night."

The shadow that crossed her face crossed swiftly, and she laughed. "It's all right now."

"Yeah, but what was it?"

"Oh," she said. Her head moved in an impatient gesture, but she smiled at the sky. "There was nothing and nobody. I left school. Daddy was mad at me. Kids from school acted sorry for me. Other kids, the ones you saw, they made me tired. I was tired because they were the same way all the time about the same things all the time, and I was tired because they kept me up so late."

"What did you leave school for?"

"I found out what it was for."

"It's for learning stuff."

"It isn't," she said positively. "It's for learning how to learn. And I know that already. I can learn anything. Why did you come here today?"

"I wanted to see you. Where were you going when you came out?"

"Here," she said, tapping her foot. "I saw you from the window. I was waiting for you. I was waiting for you yesterday too. What's the matter?"

He grunted.

"Tell me, tell me!"

"I never had a girl talk to me like you do."

"Don't you like the way I talk?" she asked anxiously.

"Oh for Pete's sake it ain't that!" he exploded. Then he half-smiled at her. "It's just I had a crazy idea. I had the idea you always talk like this. I mean, to anybody."

"I don't, I don't!" she breathed. "Honestly, you've got to believe that. Only you. I've always talked to you like this."

"What do you mean always?"

"Well, everybody's got somebody to talk to, all their life. You know what they like to talk about and when they like to be quiet, and when you can be just silly and when they'd rather be serious and important. The only thing you don't know is their face. For that you wait. And then one day you see the face, and then you have it all."

"You ain't talkin' about *me!*"

"Yes I am."

"Look," he said. He had to speak between heartbeats. He had

never felt like this in his whole life before. "You could be—takin' a—*awful* chance."

She shook her head happily.

"Did you ever think maybe everybody ain't like that?"

"It doesn't matter. I am."

His face pinched up. "Suppose I just walked away now and never saw you again."

"You wouldn't."

"But suppose."

"Why then I—I'd've had this. Talking to you."

"Hey, you're crying!"

"Well," she said, "there you were, walking away."

"You'd've called me back though."

She turned on him so quickly a tear flew clear of her face and fell sparkling to the back of his hand. Her eyes blazed. "Never that!" she said between her teeth. "I want you to stay, but if you want to go, you go, that's all. All *I* want to do is make you want to stay. I've managed so far . . ."

"How many minutes?" he teased.

"Minutes? Years," she said seriously.

"The—somebody you talked to, you kind of made him up, huh?"

"I suppose."

"How could he ever walk away?"

"Easiest thing in the world," she said. "Somebody like that, they're somebody to live up to. It isn't always easy. You've been very patient," she said. She reached out and touched his cheek.

He snatched her wrist and held it, hard. "You know what I think," he said in a rough whisper, because it was all he had. "I think you're out of your goddam head."

She stood very straight with her eyes closed. She was trembling.

"What's your name, anyway?"

"Joyce."

"I love you too, Joyce. Come on, I want you to meet a friend of mine. It's a long ride on the subway and I'll tell you all about it."

He tried hard but he couldn't tell her all of it. For some of it there were no words at all. For some of it there were no words he could use. She was attentive and puzzled. He bought flowers from a cart, just a few—red and yellow rosebuds.

"Why flowers?"

He remembered the mirror. That was one of the things he hadn't been able to talk about. "It's just what you do," he said, "bring flowers."

"I bet she loves you."

"Whaddaya mean, she's pushin' sixty!"

"All the same," said Joyce, "if she does she's not going to like me."

They went up in the elevator. In the elevator he kissed her.

"What's the matter, Don?"

"If you want to crawl around an' whimper like a puppy-dog," he whispered, "if you feel useful as a busted broom-handle and worth about two wet sneezes in a hailstorm—this is a sense of power?"

"I don't understand."

"Never mind."

In the corridor he stopped. He rubbed a smudge off her nose with his thumb. "She's sorta funny," he said. "Just give her a little time. She's quite a gal. She looks like Sunday school and talks the same way but she knows the score. Joyce, she's the best friend I ever had."

"All right all right all *right!* I'll be good."

He kissed where the smudge had been. "Come on."

One of Miss Phoebe's envelopes was stuck to the door by its flap. On it was his name.

They looked at one another and then he took the envelope down and got the note from it.

> Don:
> I am not at home. Please phone me this evening.
> P. W.

"Don, I'm *sorry!*"

"I shoulda phoned. I wanted to surprise her."

"Surprise her? She knew you were coming."

"She didn't know you were coming. Damn it anyway."

"Oh it's all right," she said. She took his hand. "There'll be other times. Come on. What'll you do with those?"

"The flowers? I dunno. Want 'em?"

"They're hers," said Joyce.

He gave her a puzzled look. "I got a lot of things to get used to. What do you mean when you say somethin' that way?"

"Almost exactly what I say."

He put the flowers against the door and they went away.

The phone rang four times before Miss Phoebe picked it up.

"It is far too late," she said frigidly, "for telephone calls. You should have called earlier, Don. However, it's just as well. I want you to know that I am *very* displeased with you. I have given you certain privileges, young man, but among them is not that of calling on me unexpectedly."

"Miss—"

"Don't interrupt. In addition, I have never indicated to you that you were free to—"

"But Miss Ph—"

"—to bring to my home any casual acquaintance you happen to have scraped up in heaven knows where—"

"Miss *Phoebe*! Please! I'm in jail."

"—and invade my—you are *what*?"

"Jail, Miss Phoebe, I got arrested."

"Where are you now?"

"County. But you don't need—"

"I'm coming right down," said Miss Phoebe.

"No, Miss Phoebe, I didn't call you for that. You go back to b—"

Miss Phoebe hung up.

Miss Phoebe strode into the County Jail with grim familiarity, and before her red tape disappeared like confetti in a blast-furnace. Twelve minutes after she arrived she had Don out of his cell and into a private room, his crisp new jail-record card before her, and was regarding him with a strange expression of wooden ferocity. "Sit there," she said, as the door clicked shut behind an awed and reverberating policeman.

Don sat. He was rumpled and sleepy, angry and hurt. But he smiled when he said, "I never thought you'd come. I never expected that, Miss Phoebe."

She did not respond. Instead she said coldly, "Indeed? Well, young man, the matters I have to discuss will not wait." She sat down opposite him and picked up the card.

"Miss Phoebe," he said, "could you be wrong about what you said about me and girls . . . that original sin business, and all? I'm all mixed up, Miss Phoebe. I'm all mixed up!" In his face was a desperate appeal.

"Be quiet," she said sternly. She was studying the card. "This," she said, putting the card down on the table with a dry snap, "tells a great deal but says nothing. Public nuisance, indecent exposure, suspicion of rape, impairing the morals of a minor, resisting an officer, and destruction of city property. Would you care to explain this—this catalogue to me?"

"What you mean, tell you what happened?"

"That is what I mean."

"Miss Phoebe, where is she? What they done with her?"

"With whom? You mean the girl? I do not know; moreover, it doesn't concern me and it should no longer concern you. Didn't she get you into this?"

"I got her into it. Look, could you find out, Miss Phoebe?"

"I do not know what I will do. You'd better explain to me what happened."

Again the look of appeal, while she coldly waited. He scratched his head hard with both hands at once. "Well, we went to your house."

"I am aware of that."

"Well, you wasn't home so we went out. She said take her father's car. I got a license; it was all right. So we went an' got the car and rode around. Well, we went to a place an' she showed me how to dance some. We went somewheres else an' ate. Then we parked over by the lake. Then, well, a cop come over and poked around an' made some trouble an' I got mad an' next thing you know here we are."

"I asked you," said Miss Phoebe evenly, "what happened?"

"Aw-w . . ." It was a long-drawn sound, an admixture of shame and irritation. "We were in the car an' this cop came pussy-footin' up. He had a big flashlight *this* long. I seen him comin'. When he got to the car we was all right. I mean, I had my arm around Joyce, but that's all."

"What *had* you been doing?"

"Talkin', that's all, just talkin', and . . ."

"And what?"

"Miss Phoebe," he blurted, "I always been able to say anything to you I wanted, about anything. Listen, I *got* to tell you about this. That thing that happened, the way it is with me and girls because of the rat, well, it just wasn't there with Joyce, it was nothin', it was like it never happened. Look, you and me, we had that thing with the hands; it was . . . I can't say it, you know how good it was. Well, with Joyce it was somepin' different. It was like I could fly. I never felt like that before. Miss Phoebe, I had too much these last few days, I don't know what goes on . . . you was right, you was always right, but this I had with Joyce, that was right too, and they can't both be right." He reached across the table, not quite far enough to touch her. The reaching was in his eyes and his voice.

Miss Phoebe stiffened a spine already straight as a bowstring. "I have asked you a simple question and all you can do is gibber at me. *What happened in that car?*"

Slowly he came back to the room, the hard chair, the bright light, Miss Phoebe's implacable face. "That cop," he said. "He claimed he seen us. Said he was goin' to run us in, I said what for, he said carryin' on like that in a public place. There was a lot of argument. Next thing you know he told Joyce to open her dress, he said when it was the way he seen it before he'd let me know. Joyce she begun to cry an' I tol' her not to do it, an' the cop said if I was goin' to act like that he would run us in for *sure*. You know, I got the idea if she'd done it he'da left us alone after?

"So I got real mad, I climbed out of the car, I tol' him we ain't

123

done nothin', he pushes me one side, he shines the light in on Joyce. She squinchin' down in the seat, cryin', he says, 'Come on, you, you know what to do.' I hit the flashlight. I on'y meant to get the light off her, but I guess I hit it kind of hard. It come up and clonked him in the teeth. Busted the flashlight too. That's the city property I destroyed. He started to cuss and I tol' him not to. He hit me and opened the car door an' shoved me in. He got in the back an' took out his gun and tol' me to drive to the station house." He shrugged. "So I had to. That's all."

"It is not all. You have not told me what you did before the policeman came."

He looked at her, startled. "Why, I—we . . ." His face flamed, "I love her," he said, with difficulty, as if he spoke words in a new and troublesome tongue. "I mean I . . . do, that's all."

"What did you do?"

"I kissed her."

"What else did you do?"

"I—" He brought up one hand, made a vague circular gesture, dropped the hand. He met her gaze. "Like when you love somebody, that's all."

"Are you going to tell me exactly what you did, or are you not?"

"Miss Phoebe . . ." he whispered, "I ain't never seen you look like that."

"I want the whole filthy story," she said. She leaned forward so far that her chin was only a couple of inches from the table top. Her protruding, milky eyes seemed to whirl, then it was as if a curtain over them had been twitched aside, and they blazed.

Don stood up. "Miss Phoebe," he said. "Miss Phoebe . . ." It was the voice of terror itself.

Then a strange thing happened.

It may have been the mere fact of his rising, of being able, for a moment, to stand over her, look down on her. "Miss Phoebe," he said "there—ain't—no—filthy—story."

She got up and without another word, marched to the door. As she opened it the boy raised his fists. His wrists and forearms corded and writhed. His head went back, his lungs filled, and with all his strength he shouted the filthiest word he knew. It had one syllable, it was sibilant and explosive, it was immensely satisfying.

Miss Phoebe stopped, barely in balance between one pace and the next, momentarily paralyzed. It was like the breaking of the drive-coil on a motion picture projector.

"They locked her up," said Don hoarsely. "They took her away with two floozies an' a ole woman with DT's. She ain't never goin' to see me again. Her ole man'll kill me if he ever sets eyes on me. You were all I had left. Get the hell out of here . . ."

She reached the door as it was opened from the other side by a policeman, who said, "What's goin' on here?"

"Incorrigible," Miss Phoebe spat, and went out. They took Don back to his cell.

The courtroom was dark and its pew-like seats were almost empty. Outside it was raining, and the statue of Justice had a broken nose. Don sat with his head in his hands, not caring about the case being heard, not caring about his own, not caring about people or things or feelings. For five days he had not cared about the whitewashed cell he had shared with the bicycle thief; the two prunes and weak coffee for breakfast, the blare of the radio in the inner court; the day in, day out screaming of the man on the third tier who hoarsely "din't do it I din't do it I din't do . . ."

His name was called and he was led or shoved—he didn't care which —before the bench. A man took his hand and put it on a book held by another man who said something rapidly. "I do," said Don. And then Joyce was there, led up by a tired kindly old fellow with eyes like hers and an unhappy mouth. Don looked at her once and was sure she wasn't even trying to recognize his existence. If she had left her hands at her sides, she was close enough for him to have touched one of them secretly, for they stood side by side, facing the judge. But she kept her hands in front of her and stood with her eyes closed, with her whole face closed, her lashes down on her cheeks like little barred gates.

The cop, the lousy cop was there too, and he reeled off things about Don and things about Joyce that were things they hadn't done, couldn't have done, wouldn't do ... he cared about that for a moment, but as he listened it seemed very clear that what the cop was saying was about two other people who knew a lot about flesh and nothing about love; and after that he stopped caring again.

When the cop was finished, the kindly tired man came forward and said that he would press no charges against this young man if he promised he would not see his daughter again until she was twenty-one. The judge pushed down his glasses and looked over them at Don. "Will you make that promise?"

Don looked at the tired man, who turned away. He looked at Joyce, whose eyes were closed. "Sure," he told the judge.

There was some talk about respecting the laws of society which were there to protect innocence, and how things would be pretty bad if Don ever appeared before that bench again, and next thing he knew he was being led through the corridors back to the jail, where they returned the wallet and fountain pen they had taken away from him, made him sign a book, unlocked three sets of doors and turned him loose. He stood in the rain and saw, half a block away, Joyce and her father getting into a cab.

About two hours later one of the jail guards came out and saw him. "Hey, boy. You like it here?"

Don pulled the wet hair out of his eyes and looked at the man, and turned and walked off without saying anything.

"Well, he*llo!*"

"Now you get away from me, girl. You're just going to get me in trouble and I don't want no trouble."

"I won't make any trouble for you, really I won't. Don't you want to talk to me?"

"Look, you know me, you heard 'bout me. Hey, you been sick?"

"No."

"You look like you been sick. I was sick a whole lot. Fellow down on his luck, everything happens. Here comes the old lady from the delicatessen. She'll see us."

"That's all right."

"She'll see you, she knows you, she'll see you talkin' to me. I don't want no trouble."

"There won't be any trouble. Please don't be afraid. I'm not afraid of you."

"I ain't scared of you either but one night that young fellow of yours, that tall skinny one, he said he'll throw me under a train if I talk to you."

"I have no fellow."

"Yes you have, that tall skin—"

"Not any more. Not any more . . . talk to me for a while. Please talk to me."

"You sure? You sure he ain't . . . you ain't . . ."

"I'm sure. He's gone, he doesn't write, he doesn't care."

"You been sick."

"No, no, no, no! . . . I want to tell you something: if ever you eat your heart out over something, hoping and wishing for it, dreaming and wanting it, doing everything you can to make yourself fit for it; and then that something comes along, know what to do?"

"I do' wan' no trouble . . . yeah, grab it!"

"No. *Run!* Close your eyes and turn your back and run away. Because wanting something you've never had hurts, sometimes, but not like having it and then losing it."

"I never had *nothing.*"

"You did so. And you were locked up for years."

"I didn't have it, girl. I used it. It wasn't mine."

"You didn't lose it, then; ah, I *see!*"

"If a cop comes along he'll pinch me just because I'm talkin' to you. I'm just a bum, I'm down on my luck, we can't stand out here like this."

"Over there, then. Coffee."

"I ain't got but four cents."

"Come on. I have enough."

"What'sa matter with you, you want to talk to a bum like me!"

"Come on, come on . . . listen, listen to this:

"'It is late last night the dog was speaking of you; the snipe was speaking of you in her deep marsh. It is you are

127

*the lonely bird throughout the woods; and that you may
be without a mate until you find me.*

*"'You promised me and you said a lie to me, that you
would be before me where the sheep are flocked. I gave a
whistle and three hundred cries to you; and I found nothing there but a bleating lamb.*

*"'You promised me a thing that was hard for you, a
ship of gold under a silver mast; twelve towns and a market in all of them, and a fine white court by the side of the
sea.*

*"'You promised me a thing that is not possible; that
you would give me gloves of the skin of a fish; that you
would give me shoes of the skin of a bird, and a suit of
the dearest silk in Ireland.*

*"'My mother said to me not to be talking with you,
today or tomorrow or on Sunday. It was a bad time she
took for telling me that, it was shutting the door after the
house was robbed. . . .*

*"'You have taken the east from me, you have taken the
west from me, you have taken what is before me and what
is behind me; you have taken the moon, you have taken
the sun from me, and my fear is great you have taken God
from me.'"*

"... That's something I remembered. I remember, I remember everything."

"That's a lonesome thing to remember."

"Yes ... and no one knows who she was. A man called Yeats
heard this Irish girl lamenting, and took it down."

"I don't know, I seen you around, I never saw you like this, you
been sick."

"Drink your coffee and we'll have another cup."

Dear Miss Phoebe:

Well dont fall over with surprise to get a letter from
me I am not much at letter writing to any body and I never

thot I would wind up writing to you.

I know you was mad at me and I guess I was mad at you too. Why I am writing this is I am trying to figure out what it was all about. I know why I was mad I was mad because you said there was something dirty about what I did. Mentioning no names. I did not do nothing dirty and so thats why I was mad.

But all I know about you Miss Phoebe is you was mad I dont know why. I never done nothing to you I was ascared to in the first place and anyway I thot you was my freind. I thot anytime there was something on my mind I could not figure it out, all I had to do was to tell you. This one time I was in more trouble then I ever had in my entire. All you did you got mad at me.

Now if you want to stay mad at me thats your busnis but I wish you would tell me why. I wish we was freinds again but okay if you dont want to.

Well write to me if you feel like it at the Seamans Institute thats where I am picking up my mail these days I took a ride on a tank ship and was sick most of the time but thats life.

I am going to get a new fountan pen this one wont spell right (joke). So take it easy yours truly Don.

Don came out of the Seaman's Institute and stood looking at the square. A breeze lifted and dropped, carrying smells of fish and gasoline, spices, sea-salt, and a slight chill. Don buttoned up his peajacket and pushed his hands down into the pockets. Miss Phoebe's letter was there, straight markings on inexpensive, efficient paper, the envelope torn almost in two because of the way he had opened it. He could see it in his mind's eye without effort.

My Dear Don:

Your letter came as something of a surprise to me. I thought you might write, but not that you would claim unawareness of the reasons for my feelings toward you.

You will remember that I spent a good deal of time and energy in acquainting you with the nature of Good and the nature of Evil. I went even further and familiarized you with a kind of union between souls which, without me, would have been impossible to you. And I feel I made quite clear to you the fact that a certain state of grace is necessary to the achievement of these higher levels of being.

Far from attempting to prove to me that you were a worthy pupil of the teachings I might have given you, you plunged immediately into actions which indicate that there is a complete confusion in your mind as to Good and Evil. You have grossly defiled yourself, almost as if you insisted upon being unfit. You engaged in foul and carnal practices which make a mockery of the pure meetings of the higher selves which once were possible to you.

You should understand that the Sources of the power I once offered you are ancient and sacred and not to be taken lightly. Your complete lack of reverence for these antique matters is to me the most unforgivable part of your inexcusable conduct. The Great Thinkers who developed these powers in ancient times surely meant a better end for them than that they be given to young animals.

Perhaps one day you will become capable of understanding the meaning of reverence, obedience, and honor to ancient mysteries. At that time I would be interested to hear from you again.

Yours very truly,
(Miss) Phoebe Watkins.

Don growled deep in his throat. Subsequent readings would serve to stew all the juices from the letter; one reading was sufficient for him to realize that in the note was no affection and no forgiveness. He remembered the birthday cake with a pang. He remembered the painful hot lump in his throat when she had ordered him to wash his face; she had *cared* whether he washed his face or not.

He went slowly down to the street. He looked older; he felt older.

He had used his seaman's papers for something else besides entree to a clean and inexpensive dormitory. Twice he had thought he was near that strange, blazing loss of self he had experienced with Miss Phoebe, just in staring at the living might of the sea. Once, lying on his back on deck in a clear moonless night, he had been sure of it. There had been a sensation of having been *chosen* for something, of having been fingertip-close to some simple huge fact, some great normal coalescence of time and distance, a fusion and balance, like yin and Yang, in all things. But it had escaped him, and now it was of little assistance to him to know that his sole authority in such things considered him as disqualified.

"Foul an' carnal practices," he said under his breath. *Miss Phoebe,* he thought, *I bet I could tell you a thing or two about 'reverence, obedience an' honor to ancient mysteries.'* In a flash of deep understanding, he saw that those who hold themselves aloof from the flesh are incapable of comprehending this single fact about those who do not: only he who is free to take it is truly conscious of what he does when he leaves it alone.

Someone was in his way. He stepped aside and the man was still in the way. He snapped out of his introspection and brought his sight back to earth, clothed in an angry scowl.

For a moment he did not recognize the man. He was still tattered, but he was clean and straight, and his eyes were clear. It was obvious that he felt the impact of Don's scowl; he retreated a short pace, and with the step were the beginnings of old reflexes: to cringe, to flee. But then he held hard, and Don had to stop.

"Y'own the sidewalk?" Don demanded. "Oh—it's you."

"I got to talk to you," the man said in a strained voice.

"I got nothin' to talk to you about," said Don. "Get back underground where you belong. Go root for cigar butts in the subway."

"It's about Joyce," said the man.

Don reached and gathered together the lapels of the man's old jacket. "I told you once to stay away from her. That means don't even talk about her."

"Get your hands off me," said the man evenly.

Don grunted in surprise, and let him go. The man said, "I had somepin' to tell you, but now you can go to hell."

Don laughed. "What do you know! What are you—full of hash or somethin'?"

The man tugged at the lapels and moved to pass Don. Don caught his arm. "Wait. What did you want to tell me?"

The man looked into his face. "Remember you said you was going to kill me, I get near her?"

"I remember."

"I seen her this morning. I seen her yesterday an' four nights last week."

"The hell you did!"

"You got to get that through your head 'fore I tell you anything."

Don shook his head slowly. "This beats anything I ever seen. What happened to you?"

As if he had not heard, the man said, "I found out what ship you was on. I watched the papers. I figured you'd go to the Institoot for mail. I been waitin' three hours."

Don grabbed the thin biceps. "Hey. Is somethin' wrong with Joyce?"

"You give a damn?"

"Listen," said Don, "I can still break your damn neck."

The man simply shrugged. Baffled, Don said, between his teeth, "Talk. You said you wanted to talk—go ahead."

"Why ain't you wrote to her?"

"What's that to you?"

"It's a whole lot to her."

"You seem to know a hell of a lot."

"I told you I see her all the time," the man pointed out.

"She must talk a lot."

"To me," said the man, closing his eyes, "a whole lot."

"She wouldn't want to hear from me," Don said. Then he barked, "What are you tryin' to tell me? You and her—what are you to her? You're not messin' with her, comin' braggin' to me about it?"

The man put a hand on Don's chest and pushed him away. There was disgust on his face, and a strange dignity. "Cut it out," he said. "Look, I don't like you. I don't like doin' what I'm doin' but I got to. Joyce, she's been half crazy, see. I don't know why she started to talk to me; maybe she just didn't care any more, maybe she felt so bad she wanted to dive in a swamp an' I was the nearest thing to it. She been talkin' to me, she . . . smiles when she sees me. She'll eat with me, even."

"You shoulda stayed away from her," Don mumbled uncertainly.

"Yeah, maybe. And suppose I did, what would she do? If she didn't have me to talk to, maybe it would be someone else. Maybe someone else wouldn't . . . be as . . . leave her . . ."

"You mean, take care of her," said Don softly.

"Well, if you want to call it that. Take up her time, anyway, she can't get into any other trouble." He looked at Don beseechingly. "I ain't never laid a hand on her. You believe that?"

Don said, "Yeah, I believe that."

"You going to see her?"

Don shook his head.

The man said in a breathy, shrill voice, "I oughta punch you in the mouth!"

"Shaddup," said Don miserably. "What you want me to see her for?"

Suddenly there were tears in the weak blue eyes. But the voice was still steady. "I ain't got nothin'. I'll never have nothin'. This is all I can do, make you go back. Why won't you go back?"

"She wouldn't want to see me," said Don, "after what I done."

"You better go see her," whispered the man. "She thinks she ain't fit to live, gettin' you in jail and all. She thinks it was her fault. She thinks you feel the same way. She even . . . she even thinks that's right. You dirty rotten no-good lousy—" he cried. He suddenly raised his fists and hit his own temples with them, and made a bleating sound. He ran off toward the waterfront.

Don watched him go, stunned to the marrow. Then he turned blindly and started across the street. There was a screeching of brakes, a flurry of movement, and he found himself standing with one hand on the front fender of a taxi.

"Where the hell you think you're goin'?"

Stupidly, Don said, "What?"

"What's the matter with you?" roared the cabby. Don fumbled his way back to the rear door. "A lot, a whole lot," he said. He got in. "Thirty-Seven Mulberry Street," he said.

It was three days later, in the evening, when he went to see Miss Phoebe.

"Well!" she said when she opened to his ring.

"Can I come in?"

She did not move. "You received my letter?"

"Sure."

"You understood . . ."

"I got the idea."

"There were—ah—certain conditions."

"Yeah," said Don. "I got to be capable of understandin' the meaning of reverence, obedience, an' honor to certain ancient mysteries."

"Have you just memorized it, or do you feel you really are capable?"

"Try me."

"Very well." She moved aside. He came in, shoving a blue knitted cap into his side pocket. He shucked out of the pea-jacket. He was wearing blue slacks and a black sweater with a white shirt and blue tie. He was as different from the scrubbed schoolboy neatness of his previous visit as he was from the ill-fit flashiness of his first one. "How've you been?"

"Well, thank you," she answered coolly. "Sit down."

They sat facing one another. Don was watchful, Miss Phoebe wary. "You've . . . grown," said Miss Phoebe. It was made not so much as a statement but as an admission.

"I did a lot," said Don. "Thought a lot. You're so right about people in the world that work for—call it yin an' Yang— an' know what they're doin', why they're doin' it. All you got to do is look around you. Read the papers.

She nodded. "Do you have any difficulty in determining which side these people are on?"

"No more."

"If that's true," she said, "it's wonderful." She cleared her throat. "You've seen that—that girl again."

"I couldn't lie."

"Are you willing to admit that beastliness is no substitute for the true meeting of minds?"

"Absolutely."

"Well!" she said. "This *is* progress!" She leaned forward suddenly. "Oh, Don, that wasn't for you. Not you! You are destined for great things, my boy. You have no idea."

"I think I have."

"And you're willing to accept my teaching?"

"Just as much as you'll teach me."

"I'll make tea," she said, almost gaily. She rose and as she passed him she squeezed his shoulder. He grinned.

When she was in the kitchenette he said, "Fellow in my neighborhood just got back from a long stretch for hurting a little girl."

"Oh?" she said. "What is his name?"

"I don't know."

"Find out," she said. "They have to be watched."

"Why?"

"Animals," she said, "wild animals. They have to be caught and caged."

He nodded. The gesture was his own, out of her range. He said, "I ate already. Don't go to no trouble."

"Very well. Just some cookies." She emerged with the tea service. "It's good to have you back. I'm rather surprised. I'd nearly given you up."

He smiled. "Never do that."

She poured boiling water from the kettle into the teapot and brought it out. "You're almost like a different person."

"How come?"

"Oh, you—you're much more self-assured." She looked at him searchingly. "More complete. I think the word for it is 'integrated'. Actually, I can't seem to . . . to . . . Don, you're not hiding anything from me, are you?"

"Me? Why, how could I do that?"

She seemed troubled. "I don't know." She gave him a quick glance, almost spoke, then shook her head slightly.

"What's the matter? I do something wrong?"

"No, oh no."

They were quiet until the tea was steeped and poured.

"Miss Phoebe . . . ?"

"What is it?"

"Just what did you think went on in that car before we got arrested?"

"Isn't that rather obvious?"

"Well," he said, with a quick smile, "to me, yeah. I was there."

"You can be cleansed," she said confidently.

"Can I now! Miss Phoebe, I just want to get this clear in my mind. I think you got the wrong idea, and I'd like to straighten you out. I didn't go the whole way with that girl."

"You didn't?"

He shook his head. "Oh," she said. "The policeman got there in time after all."

He put down his teacup very carefully. "We had lots of time. What I'm telling you is we just didn't."

"Oh," she said. "Oh!"

"What's the matter, Miss Phoebe?"

"Nothing," she said, tensely. "Nothing. This . . . puts a different complexion on things."

"I sort of thought you'd be glad."

"But of course!" She whirled on him. "You are telling me the truth, Don?"

"You can get in an' out of County," he reminded her. "There's records of her medical examination there that proves it, you don't believe me."

"Oh," she said, "oh dear." Suddenly her face cleared. "Perhaps I've underestimated you. What you're telling me is that you . . . you didn't *want* to, is that it? But you said that the old memory of the rat left you when you were with her. Why didn't you—*why?*"

"Hey—easy, take it easy! You want to know why, it was because it wasn't time. What we had would last, it would keep. We din't have to grab."

"You . . . really felt that way about her?"

He nodded.

"I had no idea," she said in a stunned whisper. "And afterward ... did you ... do you still ..."

"You can find out, can't you? You know ways to find out what I'm thinking."

"I can't," she cried. "I can't! Something has happened to you. I can't get in, it's as if there were a steel plate between us!"

"I'm sorry," he said with grave cheerfulness.

She closed her eyes and made some huge internal effort. When she looked up, she seemed quite composed. "You are willing to work with me?"

"I want to."

"Very well. I don't know what has happened and I must find out, even if I have to use ... drastic measures."

"Anything you say, Miss Phoebe."

"Lie down over there."

"On that? I'm longer than it is!" He went to the little sofa and maneuvered himself so that at least his shoulder blades and head were horizontal. "Like so?"

"That will do. Make yourself just as comfortable as you can." She threw a tablecloth over the lampshade and turned out the light in the kitchenette. Then she drew up a chair near his head, out of his visual range. She sat down.

It got very quiet in the room. "You're sleepy, you're so sleepy," she said softly. "You're sl—"

"No I ain't," he said briskly.

"Please," she said, "fall in with this. Just let your mind go blank and listen to me."

"Okay."

She droned on and on. His eyes half closed, opened, then closed all the way. He began to breathe more slowly, more deeply.

"... And sleep, sleep, but hear my voice, hear what I am saying, can you hear me?"

"Yes," he said heavily.

"Lie there and sleep, and sleep, but answer me truthfully, tell me only the truth, the truth, answer me, whom do you love?"

"Joyce."

"You told me you restrained yourself the night you were arrested. Is this true?"

"Yes."

Miss Phoebe's eyes narrowed. She wet her lips, wrung her hands.

"The union you had with me, that flight of soul, was that important to you?"

"Yes."

"Would you like to do more of it?"

"Yes."

"Don't you realize that it is a greater, more intimate thing than any union of the flesh?"

"Yes."

"Am I not the only one with whom you can do it?"

"No."

Miss Phoebe bit her lip. "Tell the truth, the truth," she said raggedly. "Who else?"

"Joyce."

"Have you ever done it with Joyce?"

"Not yet."

"Are you sure you can?"

"I'm sure."

Miss Phoebe got up and went into the kitchenette. She put her forehead against the cool tiles of the wall beside the refrigerator. She put her fingertips on her cheeks, and her hands contracted suddenly, digging her fingers in, drawing her flesh downward until her scalding, tight-shut eyes were dragged open from underneath. She uttered an almost soundless whimper.

After a moment she straightened up, squared her shoulders and went noiselessly back to her chair. Don slumbered peacefully.

"Don, go on sleeping. Can you hear me?"

"Yes."

"I want you to go down deeper and deeper and deeper, down and down to a place where there is nothing at all, anywhere, anywhere, except my voice, and everything I say is true. Down and down, deep, deep . . ." On and on she went, until at last she reached down and gently rolled back one of his eyelids. She peered at the eye, nodded with satisfaction.

"Stay down there, Don, stay there."

She crouched in the chair and thought, hard. She knew of the difficulty of hypnotically commanding a subject to do anything repugnant to him. She also knew, however, that it is a comparatively simple matter to convince a subject that a certain person is a pillow, and then fix the command that a knife must be thrust into that pillow.

She pieced and fitted, and at last, "Don, can you hear me?"

His voice was a bare whisper, slurred, "Yes ..."

"The forces of evil have done a terrible thing to Joyce, Don. When you see her again she will look as before. She will speak and act as before. But she is different. The real Joyce has been taken away. A substitute has been put in her place. The substitute is dangerous. You will know, when you see her. You will not trust her. You will not touch her. You will share nothing with her. You will put her aside and have nothing to do with her.

"But the real Joyce is alive and well, although she was changed. I saved her. When she was replaced by the substitute, I took the real Joyce and made her a part of me. So now when you talk to Miss Phoebe you are talking to Joyce, when you touch Miss Phoebe you are touching Joyce, when you kiss and hold and love Miss Phoebe you will be loving Joyce. Only through Miss Phoebe can you know Joyce, and they are one and the same. And you will never call Joyce by name again. Do you understand?"

"Miss ... Phoebe is ... Joyce now ..."

"That's right."

Miss Phoebe was breathing hard. Her mouth was wet.

"You will remember none of this deep sleep, except what I have told you. Don," she whispered, "my dear, my dear ..."

Presently she rose and threw the cloth off the lampshade. She felt the teapot; it was still quite hot. She emptied the hot-water pot and filled it again from the kettle. She sat down at the tea table, covered her eyes, and for a moment the only sound in the room was her deep, slow, controlled breathing as she oxygenated her lungs. She sat up, refreshed, and poured tea.

"Don! Don! Wake up, Don!"

He opened his eyes and stared unseeingly at the ceiling. Then he raised his head, sat up, shook himself.

"Goodness!" said Miss Phoebe. "You're getting positively absent-minded. I like to be answered when I speak to you."

"Whuh? Hm?" He shook himself again and rose. "Sorry, Miss Phoebe. Guess I sorta ... did you ask me something?"

"The tea, the tea," she said with pleasant impatience. "I've just poured."

"Oh," he said. "Good."

"Don," she said, "we're going to accomplish so *very* much."

"We sure are. And we'll do it a hell of a lot faster with your help."

"I beg—*what?*"

"Joyce and me," he said patiently. "The things you can do, that planting a reflection in a mirror the way you want it, and knowing who's at the door and on the phone and all ... we can sure use those things."

"I—I'm afraid I don't ..."

"Oh God, Miss Phoebe, don't! I hate to see you cut yourself up like this!"

"You were faking."

"You mean just now, the hypnosis routine? No I wasn't. You had me under all right. It's just that it won't stick with me. Everything worked but the commands."

"That's—impossible!"

"No it ain't. Not if I had a deeper command to remember 'em— and disregard 'em."

"Why didn't I think of that?" she said tautly. "*She* did it!"

He nodded.

"She's evil, Don, can't you see? I was only trying to save—"

"I know what you were tryin' to save," he interrupted, not unkindly. "You're in real good shape for a woman your age, Miss Phoebe. This power of yours, it keeps you going. Keeps your glands going. With you, that's a problem. With us, now, it'll be a blessing. Pity you never thought of that."

"Foul," she said, "how perfectly foul ..."

"No it ain't!" he rapped. "Look, maybe we'll all get a chance to work together after all, and if we do, you'll get an idea what kind of chick Joyce is. I hope that happens. But mind you, if it don't, we'll get along. We'll do all you can do, in time."

"I'd *never* cooperate with evil!"

"You went and got yourself a little mixed up about that, Miss Phoebe. You told me yourself about yin an' Yang, how some folks set a course straight an' true an' never realize the boundary can twist around underneath them. You asked me just tonight was I sure which was which, an' I said yes. It's real simple. When you see somebody with power who is usin' it for what Yang stands for—good, an' light, an' all like that, you'll find he ain't usin' it for himself."

"I wasn't using it for myself!"

"No, huh?" He chuckled. "Who was it I was goin' to kiss an' hold just like it was Joyce?"

She moaned and covered her face. "I just wanted to keep you pure," she said indistinctly.

"Now that's a thing you got to get straightened out on. That's a big thing. Look here." He rose and went to the long bookcase. Through her fingers, she watched him. "Suppose this here's all the time that has passed since there was anything like a human being on earth." He moved his hand from one end of the top shelf to the other. "Maybe way back at the beginning they was no more 'n smart monkeys, but all the same they had whatever it is makes us human beings. These forces you talk about, they were operatin' then just like now. An' the cave men an' the savages an' all, hundreds an' hundreds of years, they kept developing until we got humans like us.

"All right. You talk about ancient mysteries, your Yoga an' all. An' this tie-up with virgins. Look, I'm going to show you somepin. You an' all your studyin' and copyin' the ancient secrets, you know how ancient they were? I'll show you." He put out his big hand and put three fingers side by side on the "modern" end of the shelf. "Those three fingers covers it—down to about fourteen thousand years before Christ. Well, maybe the thing did work better without sex. But only by throwin' sex into study instead of where it was meant to go. Now you want to free yourself from sex in your thinkin', there's a much better way than that. You do it like Joyce an' me. We're a bigger unit together than you ever could be by yourself. An' we're not likely to get pushed around by our glands, like you. No offense, Miss Phoebe . . . so there's your *really* ancient mystery. Male an' female together; there's a power for you. Why you s'pose people in love get to fly so high, get to feel like gods?" He swept his hand the full length of the shelf. "A *real* ancient one."

"Wh—where did you learn all this?" she whispered.

"Joyce. Joyce and me, we figured it out. Look, she's not just any chick. She quit school because she learns too fast. She gets everything right now, this minute, as soon as she sees it. All her life everyone around her seems to be draggin' their feet. An' besides, she's like a kid. I don't mean childish, I don't mean simple; I mean, like she believes in something even when there's no evidence around for it, she keeps on believing until the evidence comes along. There must be a word for that."

"Faith," said Miss Phoebe faintly.

He came and sat down near her. "Don't take it so hard, Miss Phoebe," he said feelingly. "It's just that you got to stand aside for a later model. If anybody's going to do Yang work in a world like this, they got to get rid of a lot of deadwood. I don't mean you're deadwood. I mean a lot of your ideas are. Like that fellow was in jail about the little girl, you say *watch 'im!* one false move an' back in the cage he goes. And all that guy wanted all his life was just to have a couple people around him who give a damn, 'scuse me, Miss Phoebe. He never had that, so he took what he could get from whoever was weaker'n him, and that was only girls. You should see him now, he's goin' to be our best man."

"You're a child. You can't undertake work like this. You don't know the powers you're playing with."

"Right. We're goin' to make mistakes. Some of 'em will be real bloopers, an' a lot of people are goin' to get hurt. But we know what we're doin', we know what we want to do. We see some guy in Congress is featherin' his own nest instead of workin' for all the people—especially the guy who's after power more than anything else—an' we go after him. We fight whoever wants to burn books.

We fight whoever wants to make all the people think a certain way—any certain way. But sure, we'll fumble some of the plays. An' that's where you come in. Are you on?"

"I—don't quite—"

"We want your help," he said, and bluntly added, "but if you can't help, don't hinder."

"You'd want to work with me after I . . . Joyce, Joyce will hate me!"

"Joyce ain't afraid of you."

Her face crumpled. He patted her clumsily on the shoulder. "Come on, Miss Phoebe, what do you say?"

She sniffled, then turned red-rimmed, protruding eyes up to him. "If you want me. I'd have to . . . I'd like to talk to Joyce."

"Okay. JOYCE!"

Miss Phoebe started. "She—she's not—*oh!*" she cried as the doorknob turned. She said, "It's locked."

He grinned. "No it ain't."

Joyce came in. She went straight to Don, her eyes on his face, searching, and did not look around her until her hand was in his. Then she looked down at Miss Phoebe.

"This here, this is Joyce," Don said.

Joyce and Miss Phoebe held each other's eyes for a long moment, tense at first, gradually softening. At last Miss Phoebe made a tremulous smile.

"I'd better make some tea," she said, gathering her feet under her.

"I'll help," said Joyce. She turned her face to the tea tray, which lifted into the air and floated to the kitchenette. She smiled at Miss Phoebe. "You tell me what to do."

The Wages of Synergy

IT WAS THE WAY THEY WERE BREATHING, *she thought in despair and disgust, that was making her mind run on like this. The breathing was open throated in the darkness, consciously quiet though its intensity was almost beyond control. It was quiet because of the thin walls in this awful place, quiet to hide what should have been open and joyful. And as the blind compulsion for openness and joy rose, so rose the necessity for more control, more quiet. And then it was impossible to let her mind rest and ride, to bring in that rare ecstatic sunburst. The walls were growing thinner and thinner, surely— and outside people clustered, listening. More and more people, her mind told her madly. People with more and more ears, until she and Karl were trying to be quiet and secret in the center of a hollow sphere of great attentive ears, a mosaic of lobes and folds and inky orifices, all set together like fish scales....*

Then the catch in his breath, the feeling of welcome, of gratitude ... the wrong gratitude, the wrong relief, for it was based only on the fact that now it was over—but oh, be quiet.

The heaviness now, the stillness ... quiet. Real quiet, this now, and no pretense. She waited.

Anger flicked at her. Enough is enough. This weight, this stillness....

Too much weight. Too much stillness....

"Karl." She moved.

"Karl!" She struggled, but quietly.

Then she knew why he was so quiet and so still. She looked numbly at the simple fact, and for a long moment she breathed no more than he did, and that was not at all, for he was dead. And then the horror. And then the humiliation.

Her impulse to scream died as abruptly as he had died, but the

*sheer muscular spasm of it flung her away from him and out into
the room. She stood cowering away from the cold, the rhythmic flare
of an illuminated sign somewhere outside, and again she opened her
throat so her gulping breath would be silent.*

*She had to escape, and every living cell in her cried for shrieking
flight. But no; somehow she had to get dressed. Somehow she had
to let herself out, travel through corridors where the slightest glimpse
of her would cause an alarm. There were lights, and a great glaring
acreage of lobby to be crossed.*...

*And somehow she did all these things, and got away into the
blessed, noisy, uncaring city streets.*

Killilea sat at yet another bar, holding still another gin and water,
wondering if this were going to be another of those nights.

Probably. When you're looking for someone, and you won't go
to the police, and you know it's no use to advertise in the papers
because she never reads the papers, and you don't know anyone who
might know where she is, but you do know that if she is upset enough,
unhappy enough, she drinks in bars—why then, you go to bars. You
go to good ones and dirty ones, empty and bright and dusty and
dark ones, night after night, never knowing if she's going to pieces
in the one you went to last night, or if she'll be here tomorrow when
you are somewhere else.

Someone sneezed explosively, and Killilea, whose nerves had
always been good and who was, besides, about as detached from
his immediate surroundings as a man can get, astonished himself by
leaping off the bar stool. His drink went *pleup* and shot a little tongue
of gin upwards, to lick the side of his neck coldly. He swore and
wiped it with the back of his hand, and turned to look at the source
of that monstrous human explosion.

He saw a tall young man with bright red ears and what had doubt-
less been a display handkerchief, with which he was scrubbing at
the camel's hair sleeve of a girl in the booth opposite. Killilea's nostrils distended in mild disgust, while his lips spread in amusement
just as mild. Sort of thing that might happen to anybody, he thought,
but my God, that fellow must feel like a goon. And look at the guy

in the booth with the girl. Doesn't know what to say. So what do you say? Don't spit on my chick? Too late. I'm going to punch you in the mouth? That wouldn't help. But if he doesn't do something he can't expect his lady-friend to be happy about it.

Killilea ordered another drink and glanced back to the booth. The tall young man was backing off in a veritable cloud of apologies; the girl was dabbing at her sleeve with a paper napkin, and her friend still sat speechless. He pulled his own handkerchief out, then put it back. He leaned forward to speak, said nothing, straightened up again, miserably.

"Fine Sir Galahad you turned out to be," said the girl.

"I don't think Galahad was ever faced with just this situation," her escort replied reasonably. "I'm sorry. . . ."

"You're sorry," said the girl. "That helps a lot, don't it?"

"I'm sorry," the man said again. Then slightly annoyed, "What did you expect me to do? Sneeze right back at him?"

She curled her lip. "That would've been better than just doing nothing. Nothing, that's you—*nothing*."

"Look," he said, half rising.

"Going someplace?" she asked nastily. "Go on then. I can get along. Beat it."

"I'll take you home," he said.

"Not me you won't."

"Okay," he said. He got out of the booth and looked at her, licking his lips unhappily. "Okay, then," he said. He dropped a dollar bill on the table and walked toward the door. She looked after him, her lower lip protruding wet and sulky. "Thanks for the neighborhood movie," she yelled at him, in a voice that carried all over the room. His shoulders gave a tight, embarrassed shrug. He grasped his lapels and gave his jacket a pathetic, angry little tug downward and left without looking back.

Killilea swung back to the bar and found he could see the booth in the mirror. "Big deal," said the girl, speaking into her open compact as if it were a telephone.

The tall young man who had sneezed approached cautiously. "Miss—"

She looked up at him calculatingly.

"Miss, I couldn't help hearing, and it was really my fault."

"No it wasn't," she said. "Forget it! He didn't mean nothing to me anyway."

"You're real nice about it anyway," said the young man. "I wish I could do something."

She looked at his face, his clothes. "Sit down," she said.

"Waiter!" he said, and sat down.

Now Killilea looked into his drink and smiled. Smiles didn't come easily these days and he welcomed them. He thought about the couple behind him. Suppose they had a great romance now. Suppose they got married and lived for years and years until they were old, and held hands on their golden wedding anniversary, and thought back to this night, this meeting: "First time you saw me, you spit on me. . . ." First time he saw Prue, she'd barged in on him in a men's room. Crazy, crazy, the way things happen.

"The way things happen," said a voice. "Crazy."

"What?" Killilea demanded, startled. He turned to look at the man next to him. He was a small man with pugnacious eyebrows and mild eyes, which became troubled and shy at Killilea's barking tone. He thumbed over his shoulder and said placatingly, "Them."

"Yeah," said Killilea. "I was just thinking the same thing."

The mild eyes looked comforted. The man said, "Crazy."

The door opened. Someone came in. It wasn't Prue. Killilea turned back to the bar.

"Waitin' for somebody?" said his neighbor.

"Yes," said Killilea.

"I'll beat it if your company gets here," said the man with the mild eyes. He breathed deeply, as if about to perform something brave. "Okay if I talk to you in the meantime?"

"Oh hell yes," said Killilea.

"Man needs somebody to talk to," said his neighbor. There was a taut silence as they both strove to find something to talk about, now that the amenities had been satisfied. Suddenly the man said, "Hartog."

"What?" said Killilea. "Oh. Killilea." They shook hands gravely. Killilea grunted, looked down at his hand. It was bleeding from a small cut in the palm. "Now how the hell did I do that?" "Let me see," said the man called Hartog. "Oh, I say ... I don't know what to ... I think it was my fault." He showed his right hand, on the middle finger of which was a huge, gaudily designed ring with the gold plate wearing off the corners of the mounting. The stone was gone, and one of the mounting claws pointed up, sharp and gleaming. "I lost the stone yesterday," said Hartog. "I shouldn't have worn it. Turned it around inside my hand like always when I come to a place like this. But what can I do?" He looked as if he were about to cry. He worried at the ring until he could get it off, and dropped it into his pocket. "I just don't know what to say!"

"Hey, you didn't cut my arm off, you know," Killilea said goodnaturedly. "Don't say anything. Not to me." Killilea pointed at the bartender. "Tell him what you're drinking."

They sipped companionably while the couple behind them laughed and murmured, while the jukebox unwound identical sentiments in assorted keys. "I fix refrigerators," said Hartog.

"Chemist," said Killilea.

"You don't say. Mix prescriptions, and all?"

"That's a pharmacist," said Killilea. He was going to say more, but decided against it. He was going to say that he was a biological chemist specializing in partial synthesis, and that he'd developed one he wished he could forget about, and that it had been so fascinating that Prue had left him, and that that had made him leave chemistry to look for her. But it would have been tiring to go through it all, and he was not used to unburdening himself to people. Even so, as Hartog had said, a man needs someone to talk to. I need Prue to talk to, he thought. I need Prue, oh God, but I do. He said, abruptly, "You're English."

"I was once," said Hartog. "How'd you know?"

"They call a drug store a chemist shop."

"I forgot," said Hartog; and this time, strangely, he seemed to be talking to himself, chidingly. Without understanding, Killilea said, "That's all right."

Hartog said, "I wonder if I spit on some girl she'll pick me up."

"It takes all kinds," said Killilea.

"*All* kinds," said Hartog, and nodded sagely. "All want the same thing. Each one wants to get it a different way. Hell of a thing to know what one wants, not know how she wants it."

"Keeps it interesting," said Killilea.

Hartog fumbled a cigarette out of a pack without removing the pack from his pocket. "One been hanging out at Roby's, where I just was. You just *know* it about her, way she looks at everyone, way she watches." Killilea gave him matches. Hartog used one, blew it out with smoke from his nostrils, and stared for a long time at the charred end. Funny little thing. Skinny. Everything wrong—bony here, flat there, and she got a big nose. Looks hungry. When you look at her you feel hungry too." He looked at Killilea swiftly, as if Killilea might be laughing at him. Killilea was not. "You feel hungry, not for food, see what I mean?"

Killilea nodded.

Hartog said, "I couldn't make it with her. Everything fine until you make *this* much—" he held a thumb and forefinger perhaps a sixteenth of an inch apart—"of a pass. Then she cares."

"A come-on."

"Nup," said Hartog. He closed his eyes to look at something behind them, and shook his head positively. "I mean scared—*real* scared. Show her a snake, shoot off a gun, she wouldn't scare like that." He shrugged. He picked up his glass, saw it was empty, and put it down again. Killilea was aware that it was Hartog's turn to buy. Then he noticed how carefully Hartog was keeping his eyes off Killilea's glass, which was also empty, and he remembered the way the single cigarette had come out. He beckoned the bartender, and Hartog thanked him. "Get up a parade," said Hartog. "Guys with ways to get a woman. Send 'em in one at a time to this funny little thing I'm telling you about. One brings sweet talk. One brings beads 'n' bracelets. One brings troubles to get sympathy. One brings sympathy for her troubles. One brings a fishtail Cadillac an' a four-carat blinker. One brings a hairy chest. All they going to do, all the specialists, they going to scare her, they won't get next to her a-*tall*."

"She doesn't want it then."

"You wouldn't say that, you see her," said Hartog, shaking his head. "Must be some way, some one way. I got a theory, there's a way to get to anything, you can only think of it."

Killilea swirled his drink. Bars are full of philosophers. But just now he wasn't collecting philosophers. "You selling something?" he asked nastily.

"I'm in the refrigerator repair business," said Hartog, apparently unaware of the insult. His ash dropped on his coat, whereupon he tapped his cigarette uselessly on the rim of an ashtray. "And why I keep talking about her, I don't know. Skinny, like I said. Her nose is big."

"All right, you're not selling," said Killilea contritely.

"Got only one ear lobe," said Hartog. "Saw when she pushed her hair back to scratch her neck. What's the matter, Mr. Killdeer?"

"Killilea," said Killilea hoarsely. "Which ear?"

Hartog closed his eyes. "Right one."

"The right one has a lobe, or the right one hasn't?"

"Taken in parts," said Hartog, "that's a real homely woman. Taken altogether, I don't know why she makes a man feel like that, but damn if she—"

Should I explain to this disyllabic solon, thought Killilea, that the day I met Prue in the men's room she charged out and went face-first through the frosted-glass door and lost an earlobe? And that therefore I would like very much to know if this ... what had the idiot said? He'd just come from ... Roark's ...? Rory's? *Roby's!*

Killilea turned and bucketed out.

The bartender blinked as the door crashed open, and then his cold professional gaze swung to Hartog. He advanced. Hartog sipped, licked his lips, sipped again, and put the empty glass down. He met the bartender's eye.

"Your friend forget something?"

Hartog pulled a roll of bills from a jacket pocket, separated a twenty, and dropped it on the bar. "Not a thing. Take it out of this. Build me another. Have one yourself and keep the change." He leaned forward suddenly, and for the first time spoke in a broad Oxford accent. "You know, old chap, I'm extraordinarily pleased with myself."

She didn't see him when he came into Roby's, which wasn't surprising. He remembered how she used to lean close to see his expression when they held hands. The only reason she had been in the men's room the day they met—what was it, four years ago? Five?—was that LADIES is a longer word than MEN, but the sign on this particular one said GENTLEMEN, and since it seemed to have more letters, she headed for it. She had glasses, good ones, but she wouldn't wear them, not without drawing the blinds first.

He moved to a table fifteen feet from hers and sat down. She was facing him almost directly, wearing the old, impenetrable, inturning expression he used to call her fogbound look. He had seen that face that way in happiness and in fright, in calm rumination and in moments of confusion; it was an expression to be read only in context. So he looked at the hands he knew so well, and saw that the left was flat on the table and the right palm upon it, pressing it from wrist to knuckles, over and over in a forceful sliding motion that would leave the back of the right hand hot and red and tender.

That's all I need to know, he said to himself, and rose and went to her. He put his big hand gently down on hers and said "It's going to be all right, Prue."

He pulled a chair close to her and silently patted her shoulder while she cried. When a waiter came near he waved the man away. In due time, he said, "Come home, Prue."

Her strange face whipped up, close to his. It was flogged, flayed, scored with the cicatrices of sheer terror. He had her hands and gripped them tightly as she started to rise. She sank down limply, and again she had the fogbound face. "Oh no, Killy; no. Never. Hear me, Killy? Never."

There was only one thing to say "—why?"—and since he knew that if he said nothing, she must answer the question, he was quiet, waiting.

Prue, Prue . . . in his mind he paraphrased the odd fantasy of Hartog, the barfly he had met this evening: Get up a parade. Ask the specialists, one by one, what do you think of a girl like Prue? (Correction: what do you think of Prue? There were no girls *like* Prue.)

Send in a permanent secretary of the Ladies Auxiliary: *Sniff!* Send in a social worker: *Tsk!* A Broadwayite: *Mmm* ... A roué: Ah ...! The definition for Prue, like beauty, could be found only in the eye of the beholder. Killilea had one, a good one. For Killilea—perhaps because he was a steroid chemist and familiar with complex and subtle matters—saw things from altitudes and in directions which were not usual. Prue lived in ways which, in aggregate, are called sophistication; but Killilea had learned that the only true sophistication lies in exemplary and orthodox behavior. It takes a wise, careful and deeply schooled gait to pace out the complicated and shifting patterns of civilized behavior. It takes a nimble and fleet hypocrisy to step from conflict to paradox among the rules of decency. A moral code is an obstinate anagram indeed. So Prue, thought Killilea, is an innocent.

And never to be with him again? Never? *Why?*

"It would kill you," she explained finally.

He laughed suddenly. "We understand each other better than that, Prue. What awful thing has happened to me, then? Or what wonderful thing has happened to you?"

Then she told him about Karl. She told him all about it. "The men's floor of that silly hotel," she finished. "It seemed a sort of— different thing to do. We conspired ... and it was funny."

"Getting out of there wasn't funny," he conjectured.

"No," she said.

"Poor Prue. I read about it in the papers."

"What? The papers?"

"About Karl's death, Miss Misty. Not about you!... He was quite an important man, you know."

"Was he?"

Killilea had long since ceased to be amazed at Prue's utter inability to be impressed by the things that impress everyone else. "He was a sort of columnist. More like an essayist. Most people read him for his political commentaries. Some people thought he was a poet. He shouldn't have died. We need people like him."

"He liked *The Little Prince* and mango chutney and he would rather look at penguins than baby rabbits," said Prue, stating her qualifications. "I killed him, don't you understand?"

"Prue, that's ridiculous. They had an autopsy and everything. It was heart failure."

She put her left hand flat on the table and with the right pressed and slid cruelly. "Prue," he said. She stopped.

"I did, Killy. I know I did."

"How do you know you did?"

That terror flitted across her face again.

"You can tell me, Prue."

"Because." She looked up into his face, leaning forward in that swift, endearing, myopic way. She so seldom really wanted to look at anything, he thought. The things she knows . . . the way she thinks . . . she doesn't *need* to see. "Killy, I couldn't bear it if you died. And you'd die."

He snorted. Gently, then, he asked her, "That isn't why you went away, is it?"

"No," she said without hesitation. "But it's why I stayed away."

He paused to digest that. "Why did you go away?"

"You weren't you any more."

"Who was I?"

"Someone who didn't look at the snow before it had footprints, someone who read very important papers all the way through the crepe Suzettes, someone who didn't feed the goldfish," she said thoughtfully, and added, "Someone who didn't need me."

"Prue," he began, and cast about for words. He wished devoutly that he could talk to her in terms of ketoprogesterone and the eleventh oxygen in a four-ring synthesis. "Prue, I stumbled on something terribly important. Something that . . . you know those old horror stories, all built on the thesis that there are certain mysteries that man should not know? I always sneered at them. I don't any more. I was interested, and then fascinated, and then I was frightened, Prue."

"I know, Killy," she said. There was deep understanding in her voice. She seemed to be trying as hard as he was to find words. "It was important." The way she used the term included "serious" and "works of the world" and even "pompous."

"Don't you see, Killy," she said earnestly, "that you can have

something important, or you can have me? But you can't have both."
There was a gallant protest to be made at this point, and he knew
better than to make it. If he told her how very important she was,
she would look at him in astonishment—not because she could not
realize her importance to him, but because he would have so badly
misused the term. He understood her completely. There was room
in his life for Prue and his work when he built on his steroid nuclei
as Bach built on a theme, surely and with joy. But when the work
became "important," it excluded Prue and crepe Suzettes and a lov-
ingly bitten toe: music straight from a sunset rather than a sunset
taken through music; the special sting across the sight from tears of
happiness; and all the other brittle riches that give way when that
which is "important" grows greater to a man than that which is
vital. And she was perfectly right in saying that he had not needed
her then.

"I've dropped it now," he said humbly. All of it. No more fractionations. No more retained benzoquinones. No more laboratories,
no more chemistry. Sometimes," he continued in her strange idiom,
"there's a door to a flight of steps down to a long passageway, and
it's magic every way you look. And on you go, down and around
and along, until you find where it all leads, and that's a place as bad
as a place can get. It's so bad you never want to go there again. It's
so bad you never want the corridor again, or the steps. It's so bad
you'll never go through the door. You close it and you lock it and
you never even go near the door again."

"You wouldn't leave chemistry for me," she said factually.

"No, I wouldn't. I didn't. Prue, I'm trying to tell you that I closed
the door eighteen months ago. Not for you. For me."

"Oh, Killy!" She was deeply concerned. "Not you! But whatever
have you been doing instead?"

"Looking for you."

"Oh dear," she whispered.

"It's all right. All those fellowships, the prizes—I don't need chemistry any more. I don't even have to work. Prue, come with me. Come
home."

She closed her eyes and her cheekbones seemed to rise toward them, so tightly were they sealed. She shook her head very slowly, twice, and at last a tear pressed through the lids. "I can't, Killy. Don't ask me, don't ever," she choked.

The inconceivable thought struck him, and the fact that it was inconceivable was the most eloquent thing which could be said about Prue and Killilea. "Don't you *want* to?" he asked painfully.

"Want to? You don't know, you can't. Oh, I want *so* much to." She made a swift, vague gesture which silenced him. "I can't, Killy. You'd *die*."

He thought about Karl and the dreadful thing that had happened to her. To call that experience traumatic would be fabulous understatement. But what peculiar twist made her insist that *he* might be harmed?

"Why are you so sure?" When he saw her face, he said, "You've got to tell me, Prue. I'll ask and ask until you do."

She leaned close to see his eyes. She looked into one, and the other. She touched his hair, a touch like the stirring of a warm wind. "Karl wasn't the first one. I . . . I killed Landey, Roger Landey."

Killilea's eyes widened. Landey, professor extraordinary, whose philosophy courses were booked solid two years in advance, whose deep wisdom and light touch had made legends before he was thirty . . . whose death four months earlier had shocked even the *Evening Graphic* into putting out a black-bordered edition.

"You *can't* really believe that you—"

"And someone else too. His name . . . they told me his name at a party." She wrinkled her brow and shook the wrinkles away impatiently. "I had a name for him that was much better. He was a round little man. He made you want to pick him up and give him a hug. I called him Koala. I used to see him in the park. I gave him some leaves once, that's how I met him."

"Leaves?"

"Koalas look like teddy-bears and all they ever eat is eucalyptus leaves," she explained. "I saw him every day in the park and I began to wonder if he ever had any eucalyptus leaves, he reminded me so much of a Koala, I s'pose I thought he was one. I got some and went to him and gave them to him. He understood right away and laughed like ... he laughed like you, Killy."

Killilea half-smiled through his distress, visualizing the scene; Prue so grave and silent, wordlessly handing the leaves to the man who looked like a koala ... "Prue," he breathed. "Oh Prue ..." "I killed him too. The same way as the others, just the same. Here," she said suddenly. "Look, he gave me this." And from her pocketbook she drew a small cube and dropped it into his hand. It looked like blue glass, until he realized that it was not a cube but a chunk of monoclinic crystal.

"What is it?"

"It's lovely," was her typical answer. "Cup it in your hands, make it dark, and peek."

He put his hands together with the crystal inside, and brought it up to his eye. The crystal phosphoresced ... no, he realized excitedly, it was fluorescing with a beautiful deep-blue glow, which had about it the odd "black-halo" characteristic of ultraviolet. But luminescents don't fluoresce without an energy source of some kind. Unless—"What is it?"

"You mean, what's it made of? I don't know. Isn't it just lovely?"

"Who ... who was this Koala?" he asked faintly.

"Someone very fine," she said. Then she added, in a whisper, "That I killed."

"Don't say that ever again, Prue," he said harshly.

"All right. But it's true no matter what I say."

"What can I do?" he asked in despair. "How can I make you understand that these are crazy coincidences, that you had nothing to do with them?"

"Make me understand that I couldn't kill you, too, the same way. Can you do that?"

"Just take my word for it."

"No."

"Trust me. You used to trust me, Prue."

"You used to tell me things that were so. You used to say things that came true. But if you'd begun to say this table is not a table, that lark isn't singing, it's a noise a cow makes ... then I never could have trusted you at all."

"But—"

"Prove it to me, Killy. Find a way, I mean a real way, not words, not just clever ideas all strung out like a diamond necklace, all dazzly and going right around in a circle. Prove it a real way, like one of the things you did in chemistry. Build it, and show it to me. You can't show me I didn't kill those others, because I did. But show me I can't kill you, and I'll come . . . come home."

He looked at her for a long moment. Then he said, "I'll prove it to you."

"You won't ask me to come with you until you prove it?"

"I won't ask you," he said heavily.

"Oh, good, good," she said thankfully. "Because I can see you, if you'll promise that. I can see you and talk with you. Killy, I've missed you so very much."

They were together for a while longer. They let the waiter serve them. They exchanged addresses and left, and outside they parted.

Killilea thought, I had my work to keep me busy, and then I had Prue to look for. And I used to figure if I couldn't find her, I'd spend the rest of my life looking. If I could find her, I'd spend the rest of my life with her. I never thought what I might do if I found her and she wouldn't come home.

And here that's happened. But instead of a great big empty nothin'-to-do, I've got something to build.

Once I start. But where do I start?

Once home, he thought about that a great deal, while he smoked and paced. Part of the time he thought, this is no job for me. It's a psychopathologist's kick. And part of the time he thought, what can I do? I know I can do it, if I can only find the right thing to do. But I can't. And all this time he felt very bad. Then at last he thought about the one part of the problem you could pick up in your hand, look at, wonder about, find out. . . . The crystal.

He sprang to the phone, scrabbled through his number book, and dialed rapidly. The phone rang and rang at the other end, and Killilea was about to give up when a fast-asleep voice said "Hello," without a question mark.

"Hi. Egg?"

The voice came awake with a roar. "That's not Killilea?"

"Yup."

"Well godslemighty, where you been? What have you been doing for the last year? Hell, it's more than a year."

"Research," said Killilea, as the receiver made a yawning noise at him. "Gosh, Egmont, I just realized what time it is. I wake you?"

"Oh, that's all right. Like the man says, I had to get up to answer the phone anyway! What are you, up late or up early?"

"Egg, I'm racking my brains. Something I read someplace, a crystal with a self-contained energy source that fluoresces."

"There's no such," said Egmont.

"Blue. Right up near the u-v," persisted Killilea.

"Know anything about the lattice?"

"No. It's monoclinic, though."

"Hm. Nup—hey—wait! There is such a thing, but nobody ever gets to see one."

"No?"

"Not for a while yet. High-level blue, you say? I think what you're talking about is stilbene, crystallized after an infusion of tritium."

"Tritium!"

"Like I said, son. You won't find 'em on the toy counters this Christmas. Or next either, now that Pretorio checked out."

"Oh. Was that one of his tricks?" Killilea asked.

"His big trick," said Egmont. "Set up a whole line of constant light sources that way. Bid fair to do for crystallography what Jo-blocks did for the machine shop. Still a lot to do on it, though, and Pretorio was the boy could do it. Why, Killy? What's up?"

"Just got to worrying where I read about it. Egg, did you know Pretorio personally?"

"Had lunch with him one time. He was thirty-eight chairs due north of me. A convention banquet. Speaking of banquets and Pretorio, Killy, remember my offer to take you to the Ethical Science Board dinner one of these years?"

"Gosh yes! That'd be—"

"It wouldn't be," said the telephone. "I'm not going."

"I thought you were—"

"AII het up about it? I was. I still am, about the main idea. But the outfit is but dead."

"I didn't know."

"What you expect?" barked Egmont. "Here's the finest idea of the century, see—to establish a genuine ethic for science, right across the board; to study the possible end effects on humanity of any progress in any science. They had Pretorio to run it, Landey the philosopher to steer it, and Karl Monck to correlate it with politics. And they're all dead. So where do you go when your car's suddenly missing a motor, the steering gear and a driver? I tell you, Killy, if some mastermind had set out to wreck the first real chance this crazy world ever had to get onto itself, he couldn't have done it more efficiently."

"But couldn't someone else—"

The wires sizzled. "Someone else," Egmont inflected it like profanity. "Those three were unique, but not as unique as the fact that they were contemporaries. Where else are we going to find scientists who can buck the trend of anti-science?"

"Huh?"

"Yes, anti-science! Even the politicians are saying we have to turn to higher spiritual accomplishments *because* of what science has created. But their way of doing it will be to stop science from creating anything. It's a little like blaming the gunsmith every time somebody gets shot, but that's what's happening. Hell, four-fifths of the stories in science fiction magazines are anti-scientific." Egmont paused to breathe—at last—and said in more subdued tones, "Looka me. Off on a hobby horse, straight out of a sound sleep. Sorry, Killy. I'm lecturing."

"Gosh no," said Killilea. "Man's got something important to get excited about, he gets excited. Egg—"

"*Mmm?*"

"What did Pretorio look like?"

"Pretorio? Mild little guy. Pudgy." There was a pause while Egmont scanned a mental photograph. "He looked like one of those gentle little tree-climbing bears in Australia, know what I mean?"

"Koala," said Killilea.

"Something the matter, Killy?"

God yes. "No, Egg ... look, go back to bed. Swell talking to you again. I'll give you a buzz for lunch or a beer or something, sometime."

"Great," said Egmont. "Do that. Soon, huh? Right."

Slowly Killilea hung up and went to sit on the edge of his bed. He thought, I quit chemistry because I was about to isolate the most ghastly substance this earth has ever known, and I didn't want it isolated.

But I think someone has finished my work....

Killilea, as anyone who met him could attest, was not an ordinary man. The ways in which he was extraordinary did not include fictional commonplaces like the easy familiarity with phones, cabs and the police methods of a private eye and the adventure-hero's fisty resourcefulness. He was a scientist—or rather, an ex-scientist— rather more sure of things he did not believe in than those in which he did. His personal habits tended toward those of a hermit, though intellectually he recognized no horizons. He was at a serious disadvantage with other people because of a deep conviction that people were good. And though he had found that most were good, the few who were not invariably caught him off-guard. His work in biochemistry had been esoteric in the extreme, and he had worked in it alone. But even if it had been more general an endeavor, he would not comfortably have worked with anyone else.

So now he found himself very much alone; no allies, no confidants. Yet he had always worked this way in the lab; you find a brick that fits a brick, and see what you can build with them. Or you know what to build, and you find the bricks that will do the job.

He called Prue late the next morning, and she was not at home. So he went back to the restaurant where he had found her, not expecting to see her, but simply because he felt he could think better there.

The table they had had was vacant. He sat down and ordered some lunch and a bottle of ale, and stared at the chair she had used. Somewhere, he thought, there is a lowest common denominator in all this. Somewhere the deaths of three great liberal scientists in Prue's arms, and the work I have been doing are tied together. Because what

I almost had was a thing that would make men die that way. And since it was men it would work on, and not women, then Prue isn't the lowest common denominator.

Under the arch which separated the dining room from the bar a man stopped and gasped audibly. Killy looked up into the man's shocked face, then turned around to find out what had so jolted him. A wall, some tables—nothing else. Killy turned back again and now had time to recognize the man—the philosophic barfly, Hartog. "Hi."

Hartog came forward timidly. "Oh. Mr.—uh . . ."

"Killilea. You all right?"

Hartog hesitated, his hand on a chair. "I—I get a twinge now and again," he said. "I don't want to horn in."

"Sit down," said Killilea. The man looked badly shaken.

"Well," he said, and sat down. Killilea beckoned the waiter. "Had lunch?"

Hartog shook his head. Killilea ordered a double sirloin. "Medium rare all right?" and when Hartog agreed gratefully, sent the waiter off.

"Is your hand all right?" Hartog asked. "I'm real sorry about that."

Killilea noticed he had removed the ring. "I told you last night to forget it. Uh—while people are apologizing, I just remembered I belted out of that bar sort of suddenly last night. Did I pay or not?"

"Yes, it's all right," said the other. His fierce brows drew together. "I sort of had the idea you went after that funny little girl I was telling you about."

"You did?"

"Well, I don't want to pry," said Hartog mildly. "Just wondered how you made out, that's all."

Killilea let the subject lie unnoticed until it went away. He finished his ale and waved the bottle at the waiter.

"Women are trouble," Hartog mumbled.

"I heard," said Killilea.

"I like to know where I stand," Hartog said reflectively. "Like if I have a girl, I like to know is she my girl or not."

"When you say *your* girl," asked Killilea, "what do you mean?"

"Well, you know. She's not playing around."

"Do you talk about women all the time?" Killilea demanded with some irritation.

Hartog answered mildly, in his uninsulted way, "I guess I do. Does it make you mad, your girl two-timing you? I mean," he added quickly and apologetically, "say you have a girl and she does play around."

"It wouldn't happen," Killilea said bluntly. "Not to me."

"You mean any woman does that to you, you'll throw her out?"

"That's not what I mean," said Killilea. He pushed back a little and let the waiter set out the steak and the two bottles of ale.

"Fidelity," said Hartog. "What about fidelity? You don't think it's a good thing?"

"I think it's a bad thing," said Killilea.

"Oh," said Hartog.

"What's the matter?"

Hartog, in two senses, addressed his steak. With his mouth full, he said, "I had you figured as a man would stick by a woman, whatever."

"You figured right."

"But you just said—"

"Look," said Killilea, "I don't know what the word 'fidelity' was supposed to mean when people first began to use it, but it's come to mean being faithful, not to a person, but to a set of regulations. It's a kind of obedience. A woman that brags about fidelity to her husband, or a man that's puffed up because he's faithful to his wife— these people are doing what one or two zebras, a few fleas, and millions of dogs do—obey. Point is, they have to be trained to do it. They have to develop a special set of muscles to stay obedient. It's a—a task. I think it's a bad thing."

"Yeah, but you—"

"Me," said Killilea. "If what I have with someone needs no extra set of muscles—if I don't and couldn't want anyone else—then I'll stick with it. Not because I'm obedient. But because I couldn't do anything else. I'd have to have the extra set of muscles to break away."

"Yeah," said Hartog, "but suppose your girl don't feel the same way?"

"Then we wouldn't have anything. See what I'm driving at? If you have to work at it, it isn't worth it."

"So when you don't have that kind of a life with someone, what do you do—play the field, I guess, huh?"

"No," said Killilea. "I have that kind of a life, or none at all."

"Sounds like a lazy man's way to me," said Hartog, the timidity of his eyes taking the sting out of the statement.

Killilea smiled again. "I said I wouldn't work at it," he said softly. "I didn't say I wouldn't work *for* it."

"So you wait for the one woman you can live like that with," said Hartog, "and unless you find that one, you pass 'em all up, and if you do find her, you pass up all the others. Right?"

"Right."

Hartog said, "Those regulations you talked about, don't they call for just that kind of living?"

"I suppose."

"Then what's the difference?"

"I guess," said Killilea, "it's in the way you feel when you do it because you want to and not because you're told to."

"Oh."

"You know, you sound downright disappointed."

Hartog met his eyes. "Do I? Well, maybe . . . I had a chick I thought maybe you should meet. You are alone, aren't you?"

"Yes," said Killilea, and thought of Prue with a pang. Then his eyes narrowed. "You were going on like this last night too. Are you *sure* you're in the refrigerator business?"

"Aw, don't get salty," said Hartog. "It's just I hate to see anybody lonesome when he don't have to be."

"You're very kind," said Killilea sourly. "I wish you hadn't gone to the trouble."

"Shucks," said Hartog. "You're mad. You shouldn't get mad. Just wanted to do what I could, and only found out it was wrong by doing it."

Killilea laughed, relenting.

"Killy. . . ."

He leapt to his feet. Prue had come in so quietly he had not seen her. But then, she always moved like that.

"Hello," said Hartog.

"I'll come back later," said Prue to Killilea.

With that, Hartog forked in a lump of steak as big as his two thumbs, and rose. "I got to go anyhow," he said slushily around it. He looked at Killilea, fumbled toward his pocket.

"Forget it," said Killilea. "I'll pick up the tab."

"Thanks," said Hartog. "Thanks a lot. So long."

"Good-by," said Killilea.

"'By," said Hartog to Prue.

Prue turned to Killilea. "I hadn't hoped to see you so early today."

Hartog hesitated embarrassedly, then went out through the arch "What's the matter, Prue?"

"I don't like him," she said in a low voice.

Killilea remembered, belatedly, Hartog's account of his fruitless efforts to get somewhere with the funny little girl with one ear lobe. He had a moment of fury, and quickly molded it into laughter by application of some objectivity.

"He's harmless," he said. "Forget him, Prue. Sit down. Have you had lunch?"

"I'd like an apple," she said. "And some toast."

He ordered them, deeply pleased in some strange way because it was unnecessary to suggest anything else to her. It was good to know her so well. Soft and strange and so very sure . . . Prue . . . he felt a surge of longing that almost blinded him, and he all but put out his arms hungrily to her. But with the impulse came the thought, I know so well that an apple and some toast is her lunch, the only lunch she wants; and I know just as well that she was just that sure when she said she wouldn't come home.

He took her hands and put his face close to hers so she could see how serious he was. "Prue, I need help. You'll help me, won't you, Prue?"

"Oh yes. . . ."

"I'll have to talk about 'important' things."

"I don't know if I can help with those," she half-smiled.

"I'll have to talk about chemistry."

"I won't understand."

"I'll have to talk about Koala and the others. . . ."

"Oh. . . ."

"You'll help me, won't you?"

"Killy, I'll try."

"Thank you, Prue."

"Why don't you ever call me 'darling' and 'sweetheart'?"

"Because 'Prue' means all those things and says them better."

Prue nodded gravely at his explanation, not flattered, not amused, having asked and received information. She waited.

"I have a lot of pieces, but not enough," he began. "I can put some together, but not enough. They make some sense, but not enough." He lifted his glass and stared at the fine lacework of foam that clung to the inside surface. With one finger he wiped away a little semicircle of it, and then another, until he had the words he needed.

"Chemistry is a strange country where sometimes the whole is greater than the sum of its parts, if you put the right parts on top. When one reaction finishes with *blue,* and another reaction finishes with *hot,* and you put the end products together and the result is bluer and hotter than the blue one and the hot one before, that's synergy."

"Synergy," Prue repeated dutifully.

"The thing that made me leave chemistry was something so fascinating that I followed it too far, and so complicated that it would take me most of the day to explain it to somebody who knew my branch as well as I do. It's up a broad highway and sharp left down a little road that no one knows is there, and across a sticky place to a pathway, and then out where no one's ever been before.

"That's an analogy, and so was what I was doing. I was trying to understand what happens chemically throughout the whole sexual process. That's an orchestration, you know, with more pieces in its music than any conductor ever used. There are subtle and tiny parts to be played by finely made and exquisitely measured chemicals—so much from the strings, so much from the brasses. And there are cues to be followed, so that the flutes are silent until they can pick up the theme the horns give them.

"And that's an analogy of an analogy, the music that sweeps on to its climax and is scored from beginning to end. But there are even chemical motifs that aren't scored, for they happen before the music and after it, in silence. In a man's head, nestled deep down below and between the halves of his brain, lies a little nubbin which has a strange and wonderful power, for it can take a thought, or the very shadow of a thought, and with it sound an A that can send the whole orchestra rustling and trembling, tuning up. And there are chemical workers who let the curtain down, send the musicians away to do other work—they're all very talented and can do many things—and pack away the chairs and music stands.

"In my chemical analogy I made a working model of that process; if the real thing was music, mine was poetry that strove to create the same feelings; if the real thing was the course of a hunting swallow, mine was the trajectory of a hungry stingray.

"I did it, and it worked, and I should have left it alone. Because through it I found a substance which did to the music what you do when you turn off your phono-amplifier. This substance killed, and it did it just at that great final resolving crescendo. I isolated it because it made the experiment fail and it had to be removed. The experiment then succeeded—but I had found this terrible substance. . . . I left chemistry."

His hands, twined together, crackled suddenly. She touched them to cool them. "Killy, that was just an analogy, though. It wouldn't work on a person."

He looked away from the hands to her face. "The analogy was too clear, too close. Anyone who understood it could follow it through, and apply it. You don't need a Manhattan Project to make any but the first bomb. All you need after that is a factory. You don't need scientists—engineers will do. And when they're done with it, all you need is mechanics.

"Prue, Prue . . . it's synergy, you see? All the products of all the ductless glands, tempered and measured to build the climax, and then the tiny triggering, and the synergistic reaction flooding into the medulla, where a marvelous being lives, telling the heart when to beat, the lungs to expand, even instructing the microscopic fingers of the cilia which nudge the nutrients through the yards of digestive tract. The medulla simply stops, and everything stops. Yes, yes, heart failure," he almost sobbed.

"But Killy . . . you didn't make any of it!"

"No, I didn't. But I found out how, and I want no part of it."

"A dream," she said. "A horror. But—it's something in a museum. It can't get out. Poison in a locked cabinet—a guillotine in a picture book—they can't get out to hurt people, Killy."

"You're my true Prue because you could never in a thousand years see how this could get out and hurt people," he said thickly. "Because you have your world and you live in it your way, and it doesn't touch this other, where three billions teem and plan and ferment evil. Let me tell you the ugly thing then." He wet his lips. "Do you know what would happen with this substance in a world where men can soberly plan the use of such a thing as an H-bomb? I'll tell you. It would be snatched up. It would be synthesized by the bucket, by the thousand-gallon tank. It would be sprayed out as a mist over human beings and their cities and their land. And then the ghastly thing that has happened to you three times already would happen to thousands, to millions of women. *Leibestod*—love-death."

Her face was chalky. "It was me, then. It's been done to me. . . ."

"No!" he roared. Heads turned all over the restaurant, and that was a blessing, because it brought him into the present where he had to remember appearances and modes and manners, and, remembering, relieve the awful pressure of what he was saying. "This synergy is purely a complex of male functions. The synergic factor would be absorbed painlessly and without warning, through the lungs, through any tiny break in the skin. Then it would lie in wait until just the proper impulse of just the mixture of hormones and enzymes, and all their fractions, set it free. And that is. . . ."

"*Liebestod,*" she whispered.

"You still don't realize how devilish this is. Being you, you can't. You see, it would do more than kill men and put their women through the hell you already know. It would throw a city, a whole nation, a culture, into an unthinkable madness. You know the number of pitiful sicknesses that are traced to frustration. Who would dare to relieve frustration with a ghostly killer like that loose in the land? What of the conflicts within each man, once the thing was defined for him? (And defined it must be, because the people must be warned!) Do you know of the old psychology-class joke, 'Don't think of a white horse'? What else could a man think of? He'd be afraid to read, he'd be afraid to sleep, he'd be afraid to be alone, and he'd be afraid to be with others. In a week there would be suicides and mutilations; in two they would start to murder their women to get them out of sight. And all the while no man would truly know whether the sleeping devil lay within him or not. He'd feel it stir and murmur whether it was there or not.

"And their women would watch this, and slowly understand it. And the little children would watch, and they would never understand it, and perhaps that is the worst thing of all.

"And this is my accomplishment."

Nothing, nothing at all could be said at that time. But she could be with him. She could sit there and let him know she was close, while he lost himself for a long moment in the terrible pictures that flashed and burned across the inner surface of his closed eyelids. . . .

At last he could see again. He tried to smile at her, the kind of tortured effort that a woman remembers all her life. "So you can come home with me," he said shakily.

"No, Killy."

All he did was to close his eyes again.

"Don't, Killy, please don't," she wept. "Listen to me. Understand me. You didn't make the factor—but someone has. You say there's no way of knowing whether it's within you or not. Well, it was there in three men who died, and it may be in you."

"And it may not," said Killilea hoarsely. "If not—good. And if it is—do you think I've wanted to live, this last year and a half?"

"It doesn't matter what you want!" she snapped. "Think of me. Think of me, think of yourself dying that way, with me . . . and each time might be the last, and it would all be a hell where every love-word was a threat. . . . No, Killy!"

"What, then? What else?"

"You have to stop it. There's got to be a way to stop it. You have a clue—Landey and Karl and Koala. Think, Killy! What had they in common?"

"You," he said cruelly.

Any other woman on earth would have killed him for that. But not Prue. She didn't even notice it, except as part of the subject in hand. "Yes," she said eagerly. "Why, then? Why me?"

"I wouldn't know that." Almost in spite of himself, his brain began to search, to piece, to discard and rematch. "They were all scientists. Well, not Karl Monck. I don't know—maybe he was a sort of thought-scientist. A human engineer."

"They were all—good," she said. "Gentle and thoughtful. They truly cared about people."

"They were all members of the Ethical Science Board. Pretorio founded it. It's going to die without them, too."

"What was it supposed to do?"

"Synthesize. Make people understand science—not what it is, but what it's for. Make scientists in one branch understand scientists in another—keep them working toward the same ends, with the same sense of responsibility. A wonderful thing, but there's no one left who has both science and ethics to such a degree that the Board can be anything but a social club."

Her eyes glowed. This was a thing she could really understand. "Killy, would anyone want to stop work like that?"

"Only a madman. Why, such a Board could—"

"I think I know what it could do. What kind of a madman, Killy?"

He thought about it. "Perhaps the old-time 'robber-baron'—the international munitions-maker, if he still existed, which he doesn't, since governments took over the munitions trade."

"Or someone who might try to sell it to the highest bidder?"

"I wouldn't think so, Prue. A man can get terribly twisted, but I can't believe a mind capable of reasoning a series of reactions as complex as this one could fail to see consequences. And one very likely consequence is the end of an environment where his riches would mean anything."

"Every pathway has a big 'NO' sign," she murmured.

"That's what I've been living with," he said bitterly.

They were silent until Prue said, "They were all like you."

"What? Oh—those three ... whatever do you mean, Prue? Karl with his deep socio-political insights, me with nothing but bewilderment in the everyday world. Landey, that philosophy of his ... oh, Prue! He was a scholar and a humorist; that isn't me! And Pretorio, your koala—him and his ENIAC brain! No, you couldn't be more wrong."

"I'm right," she said. "They were like you. I couldn't have been with them if they weren't."

"Thank you," he said ardently, "But how?"

"None of them were ... pretty men," she said slowly. "They all respected *Homo sapiens,* and themselves for being members of it, for all they feared it. They all feared it the way a good sailor fears a hurricane; they feared it competently. They all laughed the way you do, from deep down. And they all still knew how to wonder like children."

"I don't quite know what to say to that."

"You can believe me. You can believe *me,* Killy."

"I do, then; but that doesn't help." Again he plunged into thought, seeking, turning, testing. "There's only one single hypothesis so far. It's crazy. But—here goes. Someone was gunning for those three, maybe because of the Ethical Science Board. He discovered my fractionations and synthesis, maybe independently, maybe not. Maybe not," he repeated, and filed the question in his mental 'pending' folder.

"Anyway, he succeeds—I don't know how; he injects the factor into those three men without their knowing it; he divines that all three would find you deeply appealing; he sees to it that each in turn meets you. He must have kept a pretty close watch on things, all the time—" Prue shuddered—"and so he kills them."

Prue said, in a dead voice, "You can add to that." She took his hand. "There were not three, but four men he was after, and he wants you to take me back home. If that doesn't work he will try something else. Killy, be careful, careful!"

"Why?" he asked, and cracked his knuckles against the side of his head. "Why? What would anyone gain that way?"

"You said it yourself. It would cripple the Board, maybe kill it. Oh, and another thing! If he knows about the factor, how to make it, how to use it, he probably knows that you know it, too. He wouldn't want that, don't you see? He wouldn't want someone like you around, alert, watching for some sign of that hellish thing, ready to tell the authorities, the Government, the Board about it. He'd want that secret kept until it was too late to stop it.

"You'll have to find him and kill him."

"I'm not a killer," he said.

"There isn't any other way. I'll help you."

"There are always other ways." He was shocked.

"You're so ... damn ... wonderful," she said suddenly.

Again he was shocked. It was the first time he had ever heard her say "damn."

"I had a think," she said detachedly. The phrase thrilled the part of him that was always so nerve-alive to her; so many rich moments had begun with her sudden, "Killy, had a think...."

"Tell me your think," he said.

"It was after I went away," she said, "and I was alone, and I had the think, and you weren't there. I made a special promise to save it for you. Here is the think: There is a difference between morals and ethics, and I know what it is."

"Tell me your think," he said again.

"An act can be both moral and ethical. But under some circumstances a moral act can be counter to ethics, and an ethical act can be immoral."

"I'm with you so far," he said.

"Morals and ethics are survival urges, both of them. But look: an individual must survive within his group. The patterns of survival within the group are morals."

"Gotcha. And ethics?"

"Well, the group itself must survive, as a unit. The patterns of an individual within the group, toward the end of group survival, are ethics."

Cautiously, he said, "You'd better go on a bit."

"You'll see it in a minute. Now, morals can dictate a pattern to a man such that he survives within the group, but the group itself may have no survival value. For example, in some societies it is immoral *not* to eat human flesh. But to refrain from it would be ethical, because that would be toward group survival. See?"

"Hey." His eyes glowed. "You're pretty damn wonderful yourself. Lessee. It was 'moral' to kill Jews under Hitler, but unethical in terms of the survival of Humanity."

"It was even against the survival of Germany."

He looked at her in fond amazement. "Did you bring all this out because of what I said—I'm not a killer?"

"Partly," said Prue. "Even if I agreed that killing that hypothetical devil of ours was immoral—which I wouldn't— what about the ethics of it?"

He grinned. "Check, comma; mate. I'll kill him." The grin faded. "You said 'partly.' Why else do I get this study in pragmatism?"

"I'll tell you when you're uncluttered a bit. That is, if you don't think of it yourself first. Now then: how do we find him?"

"We might wait until he goes after me."

"Don't even think that way!" she said, paling.

"I'm serious. If that's the only way, then we'll do it. But I admit I'd rather think of another. Good gosh, Prue, he has an identity. He's been around, watching—he *must* have been. He's someone we know."

"Start with the fractionations. Did you keep notes that anyone might have seen?"

"Not after I began to suspect what I was getting to, and that was comparatively early. Up to that point it was fairly routine. I told you it went off into a side-road no one knew about."

"Could anyone have studied your apparatus—what was left in the stills and thingummies?"

"The stills and thingummies were cleaned enough and dismantled enough to bewilder anyone, every day when I was through with them," he said positively. "You do just so much classified and secret work and you get into habits like that. Of course, some of that apparatus was—no," he said, and shook his head. "It wouldn't tell anyone anything unless they knew the exact order in which the pieces were set up."

"You weren't a Board member at all," she mused.

"Me? I was a hermit—remember? Oh sure, I knew I'd join it some time. Matter of fact, I had a date for their banquet next month, which was cancelled. Fellow who was taking me is dropping out because of those deaths. Says the Board is dying or dead already." Prue seemed to be waiting for something, so he said "Why?" He thought he detected the smallest slump of disappointment in her shoulders.

"Could there have been anything the Board was about to do that would be undesirable or dangerous to anyone?"

"Now, that I wouldn't know." He scratched his ear. "I think I can find out, though. Hold on. Don't go away." He sprang to his feet, stopped, and turned back. "Prue," he said softly, "you're not going to go away again, are you?"

"Not now," she said, her eyes bright.

He went to the telephone, dropped in a coin and dialed Egmont's number. "Hello—Egg? Hiya. Killy here."

"What is it you want, Killilea?"

Killilea had already started to talk by the time he realized how formal and frigid Egmont's voice was. A small frown appeared, but he went right on. "Look, you were pretty much in on the Ethical Science Board doings until recently, weren't you?"

There was a pause. Then "Suppose I was?"

"Cut the rib, Egghead," said Killilea. "This is serious. What I want to find out is, do you know if Pretorio or Monck or Landey, singly or in combination, had anything up their sleeves before they were killed? Some bombshell, or very important announcement that they were about to spring at a meeting?"

"Whatever I know, Killilea, I most certainly am not passing on to you. I want to make that absolutely clear to you."

Killilea's jaw dropped. Like most men who genuinely liked people, he was extraordinarily vulnerable to this sort of thing. "*Egg!* he gasped, then, almost timidly, "This *is* Egmont . . . Richard Egmont?"

"This is Egmont, and I have no information for you, not now or ever."

Click!

Killilea walked slowly back to the table, rubbing his ear, which was still stinging.

Prue looked up, and started. "Killy! What happened?"

He told her. "Egg," he said. "Hell, I've known him for ... what do you suppose is eating ... why, I never—"

Prue patted his arm. "I hate it when something hurts you. Why didn't you ask him what was wrong?"

"I didn't have time," said Killilea miserably. "Hey!" he barked. "Somebody's been working on him. If we can find out who—"

"That's it, that's it," said Prue. "Call him again!"

Back in the booth, Killilea set his jaw and waited for the first sound of Egmont's voice. Being struck under his guard was one thing: going after something he urgently wanted was something else again.

"Hello?"

"Listen, you," growled Killilea. "Hang up on me and so help me I'll come over there to that office of yours, gag your secretary and kick your door down. The only way you can get rid of me is over the phone."

He could hear Egmont's furious breathing. Finally, "I don't care what you do, you're not getting any Board information out of me."

"Hold it!" snapped Killilea as he sensed the other receiver coming down. Egmont said "Well?"

"All I want to know is what's gotten into you since last night. You sound like I'd punched your grandmother, and I haven't even seen her."

"You're a pandering little scut," growled Egmont.

Killilea squeezed his eyes tight and bit back the rage that had begun to churn inside him. "Egmont," he said somberly, "we were friends for a long time. If you did something I didn't like I might write you off, but damn it I'd tell you why first. At least you owe me that. Come on—tell me what's with you. I honest-to-God don't know."

"All right," said Egmont, his voice shaking. "You asked for it. I'm going to tell you a thing or two about your buddy that you don't know."

"Buddy? What buddy?"

"Just shut up and listen," hissed Egmont. "You make me madder every time you open your mouth. Jules Croy, that's what buddy. You and your bright and cheerful questions about the Board. This is the guy that's taking over what's left of the Board and making a marching and chowder society out of it—a damned jackal, a corpse-eater."

"But I don't—"

"More money than he knows what to do with, and nothing to do with his time but hack up what's left of the finest damn. . . ." He subsided to a splutter, and then growled, "And you. Spying around, seeing what you can pick up. You're just right for it, too, the hermit with the big name in science, back in circulation again, picking up loose ends. Well, anybody I can get to won't have any ends to give you. You louse!"

"Now you hold it right there," flared Killilea. "That's damn well enough, Egmont. I've heard of this Croy—who hasn't? But I wouldn't know him if he was in this phone booth with me. I've never had a single damned word with him!"

Egmont's voice was suddenly all disdainful amazement. "If I didn't know you were a rat by now, this would clinch it. Who'd you have lunch with today?"

"Lunch? Oh—some character. A barfly I met last night. Name's Hartog. What's that got to do with—"

"Lie to the end, won't you? Well, it'll amaze you to know that I ducked into the bar at Roby's for a standup lunch today at one-thirty and saw you with my own eyes."

"You better get those eyes retreaded," snarled Killilea. "Why didn't you take the trouble to walk over and make sure?"

"If I ever got close enough to Jules Croy to talk to him, I'd tear his head off. And from now on the same goes for you. And if I hear one syllable from you on this phone again, I'll slam this thing down so hard I'll shunt it clear down to your end."

This time Killilea was ready, and had the receiver away from his ear when the crash came.

"It seems," he told Prue tiredly, "that I was seen having lunch with an arch-villain, who has tainted me. I didn't have lunch with anyone but the man you saw. Hartog."

"I don't like him," Prue said, for the second time that day.

"Who was the villain?"

"Name's Croy, Jules Croy," said Killilea. Prue shook her head vaguely. "I've heard of him. One of those business octopi, finger in this, fifty thousand shares in that. Always buying up educators and research people with bequests. Egmont says he's trying to make a sort of glorified Parent-Teacher's Association out of what's left of the Ethical Science Board. Egg's always been real passionate about the Board, and it was like losing an arm to him when it folded. I guess he needed something to be real mad at, and the idea of me spying for this Croy supplied it."

"What about this man you had lunch with, this Hartog?"

"Oh, he's harmless. Interesting sometimes, the way one of those medical museums that feature replicas of skin diseases in life-size wax models is interesting. Did he give you a bad time?'

"Who—that little man?"

"I gather he made a series of passes...."

"Oh," she said. "That. That never bothers me, Killy. You know that."

He knew it. When anyone irritated or bored her, she could leave the room without stirring from her chair. Her fogbound mood was absolutely impervious. "Oh," he said. "I thought ... but you say he annoyed you."

"I didn't. I said I didn't like him. He ... was the one who introduced me to Landey. And Koala—Dr. Pretorio—he knew him too. Koala and I once went to a party where he was. Compared to them, Hartog is such a little snipe."

"Knew Pretorio ... hmm. Prue, did he know Karl Monck too?"

"I don't know. I don't think so. Killy, what is it?"

"Let me think ... let me think." Suddenly he brought his hand down on the table, hard. "Prue! Hartog is the one who found you for me. He introduced himself to me at a bar down the street ... let me see if I can remember exactly how ... he questioned me in that funny way of his, I remember. He made sure of my name—yes, and—"

He looked down at his right palm. "What is it?" asked Prue, terror in her voice at the expression on his face.

"When we shook hands," he said evenly, "he scratched me. Look. With a ring he wore. A big cheap ring, the stone was missing, but the mounting had an edge."

Anger and terror mingled and mounted in the look they exchanged.

"I was right," she whispered. "You see ... if I'd come home last night—oh, Killy!"

He looked at the hand. He felt as if he had been kicked in the stomach.

"Is there a—an antidote?"

He shook his head. "It's not the sort of thing that has an antidote. I mean, an acid poison can be counteracted by a base chemical of equal strength and opposite action. But things like this—hormones, for example. Progesterone and testosterone have opposite end effects, but a very similar way of bringing them about. I've never made any of this stuff, you know. I can't tell exactly how it acts or how long it lasts unless I do. It would surely have an active period, and then get absorbed and excreted like any hormone. How long that would be, I don't really know. I've got to develop a test for it. Another test for it," he said, giving her a painful grin.

"Well, at least we know. Now—this nasty little Hartog. Do you suppose Egmont was right? Could he really be this Jules Croy?"

"I guess he could. I'm trying to recall what happened today, at lunch. He came in—yes, that's right, he saw me and stopped dead, and I never saw a more astonished man."

"He sent you to me last night, didn't he? He must have known you were looking for me. He cut you with his ring, and he told you where I was, and he must have been sure that—no wonder he was astonished! You shouldn't have been alive today! Well—what did he say?"

"An involved sort of philosophic conversation. As usual with him, it was about sex." He thought back. "What it amounted to, was an attempt to pump me for information about you, and when that drew a blank, an effort to find some other woman for me, and then some delving into why I wasn't at all interested. It all fits," he said, almost awed. "The warped, wealthy little misfit, trying to buy his way into the high levels of science, trying to get control of the Ethical Science Board, removing the men who would have no use for his kind. He'll run it, Prue—it'll still attract every real scientist who has more humanity than a milling machine—and the men he can't control he'll eliminate. He has my factor as a weapon, and if that ever doesn't work, he can certainly think of other ways."

"The factor—how did he get it?"

"That's the one thing I can't figure," Killilea said grimly.

"We'll ask him." He looked at his watch. "Come on. We have things to do. I need a laboratory."

The first part was easy.

It was two nights later. Prue sat alone pale and unhappy-looking, at a table at Roby's. A cigarette burned to a long ash in the ashtray. An untouched drink stood warming in front of her. And—

"Well, hello," said Hartog.

"Oh," she said. She gave him a fleeting smile. He sat down quickly, opportunistically. "Expecting anyone?"

"No," she said.

"Oh," he said, in his ferocious, timid way. "Dined yet?"

"Not yet," she said. She took out a cigarette and waited. He fumbled in his pockets, and she glanced at the silver lighter lying next to her cigarettes. He mumbled an apology, picked it up, used it. When he put it down he looked puzzedly at his thumb. "I'm glad you came," she said.

He was surprised and showed it. "I guess I'm glad too," he said. He circled his thumb with his other hand and might have pressed it, but she reached out impulsively and took one of his hands in hers. "You haven't ever really talked to me," she said softly. "You've never given me a chance to really know you."

He talked, then, and when the conversation edged over to his preoccupation, it found her unperturbed. They dined. Afterward he said he felt strange. She said she had a little apartment nearby. Perhaps he'd be more comfortable there. . . .

She took him home.

She took his hat and coat and made him a drink and softly asked permission to change, and slipped into the bedroom. Hartog sat and sipped his drink and when he heard a sound behind him he said, "Come sit by me."

"All right," said Killilea.

Hartog came up on the couch as if it had contained a spark coil. Killilea circled the couch and pushed his chest. Hartog sat down again.

"Wh-what is this? The old badger game?"

"A much better game than that, Croy," said Killilea.

"Croy?"

"You're not going to deny it," said Killilea flatly. "Can you use a jeweler's loupe?"

"Use a what? What are you talking about? What is all this?"

"Here," said Killilea. Hartog took the loupe hesitatingly.

"I want to show you something." Killilea scooped the silver lighter off the end table and sat down close to Hartog. He raised the snuffer-lid of the lighter and held it close to Hartog's face. "Look through the loupe. Look right there, at the spark wheel."

Hartog stared at him then screwed the loupe into his eye Killilea took out a mechanical pencil and pointed with it. "Watch right there." With the tip of his finger on the side—not the rim—of the spark wheel, he turned it. "See it, Croy?"

"No. Yes I do. A little hair."

"Not a hair. A needle."

"It worked fine, Killy," said Prue from the bedroom doorway. She had not changed. "He barely felt it."

"A little more refined than cutting someone with a finger ring," said Killilea.

"What have you done to me? Let me out of here!"

"What did you do to him?" Prue asked coldly of Hartog, pointing at Killilea.

"Is this some sort of a joke? I told you I was sorry about cutting you. What sort of childish—"

"Shut up, Croy," said Killilea tiredly. "I know who you are and what you're up to."

"I don't know what you mean. Why are you calling me Croy? What do you want from me?"

"Not a thing. Not a thing in the world." Killilea crossed to the door and locked it. "Just sit there and take it easy."

"You know your biochemistry," said Prue. "You're going to have heart failure, poor man."

Hartog looked at his thumb. "You mean you . . . that this is going to—why, you idiot, that won't work unless I—" he stopped.

Killilea grinned coldly. "Unless you what?" When Hartog didn't answer, Killilea said, "Hospitality has its limits, after all. Much as we enjoy company . . ." The bantering dropped out of his voice. "You have the wrong idea. You're going to die, Croy. In a half hour or so. I didn't have the time or the apparatus to make up the factor you used on me. You've got a dose of nice, simple, undetectable hormone poison."

"No!" gasped Hartog. "You *can't*! You mustn't! You've got this all wrong, Killilea. I swear it! I'm not what you think I am. . . ."

"Yes you are," said Killilea blackly. "I think you're a megalomaniac name of Jules Croy. I think you got on to my research in hormone-complex analogies. I think you used it to make some of the deadliest, most hellish extract that ever appeared on this Earth. I'm sure that besides myself no one but you knows about it, and inside the hour no one but I will have it. It will be safe with me."

"What are you going to do with it?" Hartog asked faintly.

"Forget it. Pretend it never existed. . . . I see you're not denying anything any more."

"I'm Croy," said the man, with his eyes closed. "You're doing the right thing with the factor. But you're wrong about me. Believe me, you are. And you're wrong about no one else knowing."

Killilea caught his breath "Who else knows?" he demanded.

"I can't tell you that."

"He's lying," said Killilea. "Croy, we have thirty minutes or so to kill, and there's nothing that can save you now. Why go out full of lies? Why not tell the truth?"

"There's nothing you could do if I did . . . it's too late now. I'm the only one who could help." He looked up at them piteously. "Am

I going to die? Am I really going to die?"

Killilea nodded.

"It's a hard idea to get used to," Croy said, as if to himself.

"Tough," said Killilea. He wiped his forehead. "If you think we're enjoying this, we're not."

"I know that," said Croy surprisingly.

"You're taking this better than I thought you would."

"Am I? I hate the idea of dying—no, I don't. It's the idea of being dead I hate."

"Still the barroom philosopher," Killilea sneered.

"Don't," said Prue. "We don't have to hurt him, Killy. We just want him dead."

"Thanks," said Croy. He looked at Killilea. "I'm going to tell you everything. I don't expect you to believe it. You will, though. That won't help me, of course; I'll be dead several weeks by that time. But as you say, I have a few minutes to kill . . ."

He lay back. Sweat glistened on his upper lip. "You give me too much credit. I'm no scientist. I wouldn't know a ketosteroid from castor oil. I'm just a little man with a big bank account. I s'pose everyone has his poses. My analyst once told me I had a Haroun-al-Raschid pattern. Dressing up in cheap clothes and pretending to be something less than I was . . . giving sums of money secretly to this one and that one, not to help, just to *affect* people. Intrigues, secrets . . . the breath of life to me. Breath of life . . . I feel awful. Is that symptomatic or psychosomatic?"

"Symptomatic," said Killilea. "Go on. If you want to."

"It was Pretorio who got on to what you were doing. One of the few real all-around scientists in this century. Immense ability to extrapolate. He saw the directions your researches were taking you, and he got alarmed when you quit reporting progress but kept on working."

"But how did he *know*?"

"Through me. I own Zwing & Rockwood."

Killilea clapped a hand to his head. "I *never* thought of that!"

"What, Killy? Who's Zwing and Rockwood?"

"Glassblowers! Work like mine calls for very special custom apparatus. And step by step, as I ordered apparatus—"

"That's it," nodded Croy. "For Pretorio it wasn't too tough. He was working right along with you the whole time. Sometimes he was ahead. Sometimes he would call and tell me exactly what piece of glass you'd order next."

"I *thought* I was getting fantastically good service."

"You were."

"What on earth was Pretorio after? Why didn't he come to me? How did you happen to be working with him?"

"What was he after? What he told me was that he was afraid you didn't know the possibilities of what you were doing. He was so afraid of it that he didn't want to tip you off by asking you. After all, he was the great extrapolator, you know. As for me, I was flattered. He had me completely spellbound. You just don't know what a tremendous man he was, what an—an aura he had."

"I do," said Prue.

"I did absolutely everything he told me to do. Some of it I couldn't understand, but I trusted him completely."

"And then he died."

"I went sort of crazy after that, I guess. Didn't know what to do with myself. It was pretty bad. Then one day I got a call from a man with a husky voice. He said Pretorio had left him instructions. I didn't believe him at first, but when he started giving me details that no one but Pretorio could have told him, I had to believe."

"Who was he?"

"He never told me. I never met him. He said it had to be that way because he hadn't Pretorio's great reputation. But Pretorio's work had to go on. Well, I followed orders. You know about Landey, and then Monck. I was blind, stupid, I guess. You'll have to take my word for it that I injected both of them and introduced them to her—" he indicated Prue with his chin—"without knowing why they were dying. I thought it was heart failure, just like everyone else. I didn't even know she was with them when they died."

"What about Pretorio? You infected him, didn't you?"

"No, damn it, I didn't!" shouted Croy, his voice angry for the first time since he had started his narrative. "That must have been an accident—the one crazy accident that fell in line with the things I arranged. Or maybe he injected himself by accident. It doesn't take much, you know."

"I know," said Killilea grimly.

"Well, the day came when I got orders to do the same for you. I didn't know until then who she was. When I found that out I got some thinking done. It was like coming up out of a dream. I'd never doubted this man's word any more than I had Pretorio's, but now I did. I saw then what these deaths meant; I connected them with the Ethical Science Board that I was supposed to take over and run for this man; I saw suddenly how you four—Pretorio, Landey, Monck and yourself—would have stood in his way. I called him back and refused to go on with him.

"He told me then what he was after. He told me what the factor was, what it could do, how the world had to be protected from it. He told me that you developed it, that unless you were stopped it would slip out of your hands and plunge the world into ruin. And about the Board, he said the world wasn't ready for a group that would efficiently cross-fertilize scientific specialties. We haven't caught up, as a culture, with the science we already have.

"I agreed with him and promised to go on."

"Why—the man is crazy! And so are you, for swallowing that drivel!"

"Who swallowed it? I knew then he was crazy, that he was responsible for the death of one of the finest men since Leonardo, that he'd made a murderer out of me and put you two through hell . . . so I made up my mind to play along with him until I could find out who he was. I was ready to kill him, but how do you kill a man unless you can find him, and how do you find him when you don't know his name or what he looks like?" He spread his hands, dropped them. "And that's all. I know it looks bad for me, and I guess I've earned what I'm getting. But—like I said . . . no one but me can find him, and by the time you get proof of that I'll be dead. He's going to kill you, you know. He's got to. He can't afford to have anyone else know about the factor." Killilea strode across to the sofa and lifted a heavy fist.

"Killy!" cried Prue.

With difficulty Killilea lowered the fist. "You're a liar," he said thickly. "If that ingenious story is true, why did you cut my hand with the ring?"

"I told you. I had to play it his way. But I didn't inject the factor! It was something else—something that may have saved your life. Progesterone."

"Why on earth progesterone?"

"Orders were to tell you where *she* was, see to it you went to her. You were looking for her; you wanted her back. It was a wonderful setup for his plan. I didn't know too much about hormones, but I did what I could. I had the stuff compounded; progesterone and a large charge of SF—hyaluronidase, I think it was—to make it spread."

"What on earth is that?" asked Prue.

"An enzyme. SF means 'spreading factor,'" said Killilea. "Lectures later, Prue. Go on, Croy."

"You had enough progesterone in you to bank your fire for a week," said Croy. "By that time I hoped to have the whole thing cracked."

"You sure were upset when you found me alive the next day."

"I was upset when I found you were there. I wanted to get you out of my sight. I didn't know when my—my would-be boss might see you."

"Then why all the talk about finding me another chick?"

"I wanted to see if the hormone was working. I wanted to find out where you stood with *her*. But when she came in, there was nothing I could do. It was all right, anyway. As long as you were together, he could assume only that you were taking your time in making peace."

"An answer for everything," said Killilea. "How much of this do you believe, Prue?"

"I don't know," she said, troubled. To Croy she said, "Why didn't you tell us this before? Why didn't you tell me tonight at dinner? Or even after you found Killy here?"

"Do you know of a scientist worth his salt that would even speak to me?" Croy said wistfully. "The first chance I ever had to do something really fine for science—I wasn't going to jeopardize that by getting slapped down when you found out who I was. Don't you see that's why I was so pleased to be able to work with Pretorio?"

"I remember what Egmont said about him," mused Killilea.

"Egmont," said Croy. "The crystallographer? Yes; a good case in point. He can't stand the sight of me. When he found out I was behind the scenes in the Board membership, I thought he would explode."

"He did explode," said Killilea. "Prue, we've got quite a story to tell the Egg."

"There'll be time for that later. Killy, suppose he's right? Suppose there really is someone else who knows about your factor—someone as dangerous as Croy says?"

"We'll hear from him," said Killilea.

"He won't be as clumsy as I was," said Croy. "I tell you you'll be dead before you know who killed you."

"I guess I'll have to chance it," said Killilea. "You said if you lived you could find him for us. At least you can tell us how, so we can try."

"There would be only one way—to trace him when he calls me. He won't call me after I'm dead."

Killilea watched Croy narrowly. "If you had a chance to catch him now, would you do it?"

"Would I! If I only could!"

"We've killed you," Prue pointed out.

"You did what you could; you were right as far as you knew. And I suppose I have to pay for what I've done . . . I'm not angry at you two."

"All right then. Either you're the cleverest liar or one of the bravest men I've ever met," said Killilea. "Now I'm going to remind you of something. You said that when he ordered you to inject me with the factor, you balked. *You called him back*. Give us that phone number and you've proved your point."

"The phone number," Croy breathed. "It hadn't occurred to me, because he always said it was useless to call except in the afternoon; he wouldn't be there at any other time."

"Ever try it?"

"No."

Killilea pointed to the phone. "Try it."

"What shall I say?"

There was a heavy silence. "Get him here."

"He wouldn't come here."

"He would if his whole plan depended on it," said Killilea. "Come on, Croy. You're the boy for intrigue."

Croy put his head in his hands.

"I knew he'd balk," snarled Killilea.

"Shut up," said Croy, startlingly. "Let me think."

He crouched there. He covered his eyes, then suddenly raised his head. "Give me the phone."

"Better tell us first what you're going to say."

"Oh, Killy," said Prue, "stop acting like a big bad private detective! Let him do it his way!"

"No," said Killilea. "He's dying, Prue. And if he isn't half-cracked just now, we know he has been. How do we know he isn't going to pull us in the hole after him?"

"Phone him," said Prue evenly.

Croy looked from one to the other, then took the phone from the end table. From his wallet he took a piece of paper and dialed. "You better be right," Killilea whispered to Prue. He went to Croy and took the paper out of his hand and put it in his own pocket. Through the silent room the sound of the ringing signal rasped at them. At the sixth unanswered ring Killilea said, "Even if he's there now, Prue, it might be just a trick...."

Croy covered the transmitter. "I haven't time for tricks," he said. And just then the receiver clicked, and a hoarse voice said, "Well?"

Prue gripped Killilea's biceps so hard that he all but grunted. Croy, pale but steady, said, "I'm in trouble."

"It better be bad trouble," said the voice. "I told you not to call me this late."

"It's bad, right enough," said Croy. The reversion to an English accent under strain was quite noticeable. "She took me to her apartment. Killilea was here."

"Alive?"

"I should say so. Alive and very much aware of what's happening. I hit him with the poker."

"Go hit him again."

"I can't—I can't do that. Besides, he told her everything. She knows, now, too."

"Where is she?"

"Tied up. What shall I do?"

A long pause. No one breathed. "I'll come over. Where is it?" Croy gave the address and apartment number. "And hurry. I don't know how long he'll stay under. Take you long?"

"Fifteen minutes." *Click*. Croy looked up at them. "Have I got fifteen minutes?" he asked. His face was wet.

Killilea looked at his watch. "How do you feel?"

"Not good."

Killilea went into the bedroom and came out a moment later with a hypodermic in his hand. "Lie down," he said.

"Relax. Relax," he said again, touching the side of Croy's neck, "completely. Better." He slid the left sleeve up, squirted a drop of fluid upward from the needle, and buried the gleaming point in the large vein inside the elbow. "Just take it easy until he gets here. You'll last."

"What is it?"

"Adrenalin."

Croy closed his eyes. His lips were slightly cyanotic and his breathing was shallow.

"Are you sure he'll last?" asked Prue.

"Sure." Killilea smiled tightly. "Believe him?"

"Mostly, I think."

"Me too. Mostly. We could be making an awful mistake, Prue."

"Mmm. Either way."

He took a turn up and down the room. "Morals and ethics," he said. "You never really know, do you?"

"You do the best you can," she said. "Killy, you do very well indeed."

"Do I?"

"You react ethically much oftener than morally. You react ethically as much as other people do morally."

"What are you thinking about?"

"Killy, you never said a word to me about what I did. With those men, Karl and the Koala...."

"What word should I say?"

She looked at her hands. "You've read books. Insane jealousies and bitterness and distrust...."

"Oh," he said. He thought hard for a moment. "The things you did were ... just little, unimportant, corroborative details. The big thing was that you had gone. I didn't like your going. But I didn't feel that a part of me was doing those things; which is the feeling jealous people have. You didn't stray when you were with me. You won't when you come back."

"No," she said almost inaudibly. "I won't. But, Killy, that's what I mean when I say you don't react morally. Morals, per se, would have killed what we have together. Ethics—and here it's just another name for our respect for one another—have saved it. Another argument for the higher survival value of ethics."

They sat quietly then, together in the easy chair that was built for one, and were quiet, until Killilea looked at his watch, extricated himself from the chair, and went to Croy.

"It's almost time, Croy," he said levelly. "Go into your act. You feel up to it?"

Croy swung his feet down and shook his head violently. "My face is made of rubber and my heart thinks I'm running the three hundred meter," he said. "I'll make it, though."

"Come on, Prue."

They went into the bedroom, turned out the light, and closed the door until just a finger's breadth of golden light showed from the living room lamp.

They waited.

The doorbell rang. Croy started for the door. "That's downstairs," Killilea murmured. "Push the button in the kitchenette. And don't forget the door here is locked when you try to open it. Speak fairly loud so he will too. I'll take your cues. And Croy, God help you if—"

Prue's hand slid up and covered his mouth. "Good luck, Mr. Croy," she said.

The buzzer hissed like a snake. Croy drew a deep breath, crossed the room, unlocked the door and opened it. "Where are they?" said a hoarse voice.

"In there," said Croy, "but wait ... what are you going to do?"

"What do you expect?" said the newcomer. Killilea could see him now—short, heavy, almost chinless; wide forehead, low hairline.

"You're going to kill them," said Croy.

"Do you have a better idea?"

"Have you thought about the details—what happens when the bodies are found, what will the police do?"

The stranger opened his overcoat and from what must have been a special pocket drew out a leather-covered wooden case. He set it on the table, opened it, and took out a hypodermic. He grinned briefly. "Heart failure. So common nowadays."

"Two cases at once?"

"Hmm. You have something there. Well ... I can take one of them away in my car."

"I was wondering," Croy said tightly, "if you'd expect me to do it."

The man regarded him without expression. "It's a possibility."

"It would mean I'd have to leave here alive. You wouldn't want that, would you?"

The man laughed. "Oh, I see! My dear fellow, you needn't fear for yourself. Aside from considerations of friendship—even admiration—I couldn't possibly complete my plans for the Board without you."

Killilea, his eye fixed to the crack of the door, felt an urgent tugging at his shoulder. Killilea backed away and let her work her way silently around him so that she could see as well.

The man started toward the bedroom. Croy said evenly, "Where have I seen you before?"

The man stopped without turning. The needle glinted in his hand. "I have no idea. I doubt that you ever have."

"I have, though. I have—someplace...."

Prue gasped suddenly. Killilea took her shoulders and with one easy motion flung her through the air. She landed on the middle of the bed. The gasp alerted their visitor who dove for the door. Killilea stepped aside and let it crash open. Light from the living room flooded the man's broad back as he stopped, blinking, in the darkness, peering from one side to the other. Killilea stood up on tiptoe and with all his strength brought the edge of his right hand down on the nape of the man's neck. He went down flat with no sound but his falling, and lay still.

Killilea was gasping as if he had run up steps. He bent and lifted the man's shoulder. It fell back loosely. "Out, all right," said Killilea. "Prue, what got into you? You almost gave us away by making that silly—Prue! What—"

She sat on the edge of the bed, her hands over her face, shuddering. He put his arms around her. "It's Koala," she said. "Oh, Killy, it's Koala...."

Croy was standing white-faced in the doorway. "What's she say? What's koala mean?"

"It means a great deal. Turn him over and look at him, Croy. Maybe you'll remember where you saw him."

Croy bent down and rolled the heavy body over. "He's dead!"

Killilea left the bed and ran to Croy, knelt down. "Yeah," he said. "Yeah." He picked up a broken tube of glass, looked at it, laid it down on the carpet. Then he began running his fingers lightly over the front of the man's coat.

"Careful," said Croy.

"Oh, but yes. Here it is." Slowly and cautiously he unbuttoned jacket, vest and shirt. The undershirt showed a small blood spot, just a drop. From its center extended the needle. Using his handkerchief folded twice, Killilea grasped it and pulled it out. It had penetrated only a fraction of an inch. "Far enough," said Killilea and Croy gave an understanding grunt.

"Heart trouble," said Killilea.

Croy said, "You're still going to have ... two bodies ... to explain. And you don't even know who this one is."

"Yes I do," said Killilea. "You do too, if you'll only look at him."
He bent close. "Brown-tinted contact lenses," he said. "I think his
eyes are blue. Right, Prue?"

She gave a long, shuddering sigh. "Yes," she whispered. "And he
had a beard to hide that little chin."

"Beard," said Croy, and then dropped to his knees. "*Dr. Pretorio!*"

"It had to be. Now I feel like the boys at that dinner table where
Columbus demonstrated how to stand an egg on end."

"But he's . . . he was dead!"

"When we get his coffin dug up—if we bother—we'll find out
who really was buried at Pretorio's funeral," said Killilea. "If anyone."

"Why?" moaned Croy.

Killilea stood up and dusted off his hands. "Thought a lot of him,
didn't you, Croy? Why did he do it? I guess we'll never know in
detail. But I'd say his mind snapped. He got afraid of the Board,
really his own creation, when he discovered my factor, and wanted
it for himself. The Board needed wrecking, and he threw his own
supposed death on the wreckage, along with his great reputation. A
mind like that, working against society instead of for it, would be
happier operating underground. I wonder what he would have done
with the factor?"

"He told me last week that the reorganized Board could run the
world," said Croy in a small voice. "I thought he was flattering me.
I thought it was a figure of speech. Oh, God. Pretorio." Tears ran
down his face.

"You'll have to give me a hand," said Killilea. "We'll get him
down to his car and leave him in it. And that will be that."

"All right . . . do I have time?" asked Croy.

Killilea came to him. "Let's see your tongue. Mmmm-hm!" He
lifted Croy's damp wrist and looked thoughtful. "In your condition,
I'd give you about forty more years."

Croy simply looked at him blankly. Killilea slapped him on the
shoulder. "Maybe it's morals, and maybe it's ethics," he said kindly,
"but neither Prue nor I could sit and talk while we watched a man
die. You got an injection of dilute caffeine citrate to sweat you up,
and some adrenaline to make you tingle."

Croy's jaw opened and closed ludicrously. At last he said, "But I'm supposed to ... I have to pay for...."

Killilea laughed. "Listen, philosopher. If you really feel nice and guilty and want to get punished—live with it, don't die for it just so you can escape all those sleepless nights."

Then Croy began to laugh....

Together they got the heavy body downstairs while Prue scouted ahead. They saw no one, though they had a drunken-friend story ready. They arranged the corpse carefully behind the wheel and left it.

Back in the foyer of the apartment house, Killilea asked, "Which way do you go?"

"Bilville."

"You can't go all the way out there this late!" Prue cried. "Go back upstairs. You can make yourself quite comfortable there. There's orange juice in the refrigerator, and the clean towels are—"

"But won't you—"

"No," said Killilea flatly, "she won't. I'm taking my wife home."

The Dark Room

THE WORLD ENDED AT THAT DAMN PARTY OF BECK'S.

At least if it had fallen into the sun, or if it had collided with a comet, it would have been all right with me. I mean, I'd have been able to look at that fellow in the barber chair, and that girl on the TV screen, and somebody fresh from Tasmania, and I'd have been able to say, "Ain't it hell, neighbor?" and he would've looked at me with sick eyes, feeling what I felt about it.

But this was much worse. Where you sit and look around, that's the center of the whole universe. Everything you see from there circles around you, and you're the center. Other people share a lot of it, but they're circling around out there too. The only one who comes right in and sits with you, looking out from the same place, is the one you love. That's your world. Then one night you're at a party and the one you love disappears with a smooth-talking mudhead; you look around and they're gone; you worry and keep up the bright talk; they come back and the mudhead calls you "old man" and is too briskly polite to you, and she—she won't look you in the eye. So the center of the universe is suddenly one great big aching nothing, nothing at all—it's the end of your world. The whole universe gets a little shaky then, with nothing at its center.

Of course, I told myself, this is all a crazy suspicion, and you, Tom Conway, ought to hang your head and apologize. This sort of thing happens to people, but not to us. Women do this to their husbands, but Opie doesn't do this to me—does she, *does she?*

We got out of there as soon as I could manage it without actually pushing Opie out like a wheelbarrow. We left party noises behind us, and I remember one deep guttural laugh especially that I took extremely personally, though I knew better. It was black dark outside, and we had to feel the margins of the path through our soles before our eyes got accustomed to the night. Neither of us said anything. I could almost sense the boiling, bottled-up surging agony in Opie, and I knew she felt it in me, because we always felt things in each other that way.

Then we were through the arched gateway in the hedge and there was concrete sidewalk under us instead of gravel. We turned north toward where the car was parked and I glanced quickly at her. All I could see was the turn of her throat, curved a bit more abruptly than usual because of the stiff, controlled way she was holding her head.

I said to myself, something's happened here and it's bad. Well, I'll have to ask her. I know, I thought, with a wild surge of hope, I'll ask her what happened; I'll ask her if it was the worst possible thing, and she'll say no, and then I'll ask her if it's the next worse, and so on, until when I get to it I'll be able to say things aren't so bad after all.

So I said, "You and that guy, did you—" and all the rest of it, in words of one syllable. The thing I'm grateful to her about is that she didn't let one full second of silence go by before she answered me.

She said, "Yes."

And that was the end of the world.

The end of the world is too big a thing to describe in detail. It's too big a thing to remember clearly. The next thing that happened, as far as I can recall, is that there was gravel under my feet again and party noises ahead of me, and Opie sprinting past me and butting me in the chest to make me stop. "Where are you going?" she gasped.

I pushed her but she bounded right back against me. "Get out of the way," I said, and the sound of my voice surprised me.

"Where are you going?" she said again.

"Back there," I said. "I'm going to kill him."

"Why?"

I didn't answer that because there wasn't room inside me for such a question, but she said, "He didn't do it by himself, Tom. I was . . . I probably did more than he did. Kill me."

I looked down at the faint moon-glimmer that told where her face was. I whispered, because my voice wouldn't do anything else, "I don't want to kill you, Opie."

She said, with an infinite weariness, "There's less reason to kill him. Come on. Let's go—" I thought she was going to say "home," and winced, but she realized as much as I did that the word didn't mean anything anymore. "Let's go," she said.

When the world ends it doesn't do it once and finish with the business. It rises up and happens again, sometimes two or three times in a minute, sometimes months apart but for days at a time. It did it to me again then, because the next thing I can remember is driving the car. Next to me where Opie used to sit was just a stretch of seat-cushion. Where there used to be a stretch of seat-cushion, over next to the right-hand door, Opie sat.

Back there in the path Opie had asked me a one-word question, and in me there was no room for it. Now, suddenly, there was no room in me for anything else. The word burst out of me, pressed out by itself.

"Why?"

Opie sat silently. I waited until I couldn't stand it any longer and then looked over at her. A streetlight fled past and the pale gold wash of it raced across her face. She seemed utterly composed, but her eyes were too wide, and I sensed that she'd held them that way long enough for the eyeballs to dry and hurt her. "I asked you why," I snarled.

"I heard you," she said gently. "I'm just trying to think."

"You don't know why?"

She shook her head.

I looked straight through the windshield again and wrenched the wheel. I'd damned near climbed a bank. I was going too fast, too. I knew she'd seen it coming, and she hadn't moved a muscle to stop it. I honestly don't think she cared just then.

I got the car squared away and slowed down a little. "You've got to know why. A person doesn't just—just go ahead and—and do something without a reason."

"I did," she said in that too-tired voice.

I'd already said that people don't just do things that way, so there was no point in going over it again. Which left me nothing further to say. Since she offered nothing more, we left it like that.

A couple of days later Hank blew into my office. He shut the door, which people don't usually do, and came over and half-sat on the desk, swinging one long leg. "What happened?" he said.

Hank is my boss, a fine guy, and Opie's brother.

"What happened to who?" I asked him. I was as casual as a guy can be who is rudely being forced to think about something he's trying to wall up.

He wagged his big head. "No games, Tom. What happened?"

I quit pretending. "So that's where she is. Home to mother, huh?"

"Have you been really interested in where she is?"

"Cut it out, Hank. This 'have you hurt my little sister, you swine' routine isn't like you."

He had big amber eyes like Opie's, and it was just as hard to tell what flexed and curled behind them. Finally he said, "You know better than that. You and Opie are grownups and usually behave like grownups."

"We're not now?"

"I don't know. Tom, I'm not trying to protect Opie. Not from you. I know you both too well."

"So what *are* you trying to do?"

"I just want to know what happened."

"Why?" I rapped. There it was again: why, why, why.

He scratched his head. "Not to get sloppy about it, I want to know because I think that you and Opie are the two finest bipeds that ever got together to make a fine combo. I have one of these logical minds. A fact plus a fact plus a force gives a result. If you know all the facts, you can figure the result. I've been thinking for a lot of years that I know all the facts about both of you, everything that matters. And this—this just doesn't figure. Tom, what happened?"

He was beginning to annoy me. "Ask Opie," I spat. It sounded ugly. Why not? It was ugly.

Hank swung the foot and looked at me. I suddenly realized that this guy was miserable. "I did ask her," he said in a choked voice.

I waited.

"She told me."

That rocked me. "She told you what?"

"What happened. Saturday night, at Beck's party."

"She told you?" I couldn't get over that. "What in time made her tell you?"

"I made her. She held out for a long while and then let me have it, in words of one syllable. I guess it was to shut me up."

I put my head in my hands. It made a difference to have someone else in on it. I didn't know whether I cared for the difference or not.

I jumped up then and yelled at him. "So you know what happened and you came bleating in here what happened, what happened! Why ask me, if you know?"

"You got me wrong, Tom," he said. His voice was so soft against my yelling that it stopped me like a cut throat. "Yeah, I know what she did. What I want to know is what happened to make her do it."

I didn't say anything.

"Have you talked to anyone about it?" he wanted to know.

I shook my head.

He spread his hands. "Talk to me about it."

When I didn't move, he leaned closer. "What do you say, Tom?"

"I say," I breathed, "that I got work to do. We have a magazine to get out. This is company time, remember?"

He got up off the desk right away. Did you ever listen to someone walk away from you when you weren't looking at him, and know by his footsteps that he was hurt and angry?

He opened the door and hesitated. "Tom ..."

"What?"

"If you've got nothing to do this evening ... call me. I'll come over."

I glared at him. "Fat chance."

He didn't say anything else. Just went away. I sat there staring at the open door. Here was a guy bragging how much he knew about me. Thinking I'd want to call him, talk to him.

Fat chance.

I didn't call him, either. Not until after eight o'clock. His phone didn't get through the first ring. He must have been sitting with his hand on it. "Hank?" I said.

He said, "I'll be right over," and hung up.

I had drinks ready when he got there. He came in saying, the stupid way people do, "How are you?"

"I'm dead," I said. I was, too. No sleep for two nights; dead tired. No Opie in the house. Dead. Dead inside.

He sat down and had sense enough to say nothing. When I could think of something to say, it was, "Hank, I'm not going to say anything about Opie that sounds lousy. But I have to check, I have to be sure. Just what did she tell you?"

He sighed and said what Opie had done. What she had done to me, to a marriage. She'd told him, all right. He said it and, "Better drink your drink, Tom."

I drank it. I needed to. Then I looked at him. "Now that's on the record, what do you do about it?"

Hank didn't say anything. I covered my face and rocked back and forth. "I guess this happens to lots of guys, their wives making it with someone else. Sometimes it breaks them up, sometimes it doesn't. How do they live when it doesn't?"

Hank just fiddled with a table lighter. I picked up my empty glass and looked at it and all of a sudden the stem broke in two. Red blood began welling out. Hank yelped and came to me with his handkerchief. He tied it around my wrist and pulled it so tight it hurt. "Why is it so important that Opie and I get back together, Hank? To you, I mean?"

He gave me a strange look and went into the bathroom. I heard him rummaging around in the medicine chest. "There's more in it than you and Opie, Tom," he called out. He came back in with bandages. "I guess you're so full of this that it's around you every way you look, but there are other things going on in the world, honest."

"I guess there are, but they don't seem to matter."

"Hold still," he said. "This'll hurt." He stuck the iodine on my cut. It hurt like hell and I wished all hurts were as easy to take. He said, "Something awful funny is going on at Beck's."

"What happened to me is funny?" I said.

"Shut up. You know what I mean." He finished the bandage and went to the bar. "Well, maybe you don't. Look, how long have you known Beck?"

"Years."

"How well?"

"As well as you can know a guy you went to school with, roomed with, lent money to and had lunch with four times a week for eight-nine years."

"Ever notice anything odd about him?"

"No. Not Beck. The original predictable boy. Right-wing Republican, solid-color tie, independent income, thinks 'Rustle of Spring' is opera, drinks vermouth-and-soda in hot weather and never touches a martini until 4 P.M. Likes to have people around, all kinds of people. The wackier the better. But he never did, said, or thought a wacky thing in his life."

"Never? You did say never?"

"Never. Except—"

"Except?"

I looked at the bandage he had made. Very neat. "That rumpus room of his. What got into him to fix it up that way I'll never know. I almost dropped dead when I saw it."

"Why?"

"Have you been there?"

He nodded. Something uncoiled back of his eyes, and it reminded me so much of Opie that I grunted the way a man does when he walks into a wagon-tongue in the dark. I took a good pull at the glass he'd brought and hung on to the subject, hard. "So you've been there. Does that look like the setup of a man who's surrounded himself all his life with nothing more modern than Dutch Queen Anne?"

He didn't say anything.

"I tell you I *know*. I think Beck would ride around in a Victorian brougham if it wouldn't make him conspicuous. He hates to be conspicuous as much as he hates modern furniture."

"A room can't get more 'modern' than that one," said Hank.

"Foam rubber and chromium," I said reminiscently. "Fireplace of black marble; high-gloss black Formica on the table-tops. Wall-to-wall broad-looms and freeform scatter-rugs. Fluorescents, all in coves, yet. The bookcase looks like a bar; the bar looks like a legitimate flight of steps."

"Maybe he's a masochist, making himself unhappy in a house furnished the way he hates it."

"He's no masochist, unless you figure the painful company of some of the weirdies he invites to his parties. And he doesn't live in a *house* furnished in Science Fiction Modern. He lives in a house with alternate Chinese Chippendale and that Dutch Queen Anne I was talking about. Only that room, that one rumpus room, is modern; and what he did it for I'll never know. It must have cost him a young fortune."

"It cost him what you might call a middle-aged fortune," Hank said bluntly. "I got the figures."

I snapped out of the mild reminiscences. "Have you now! Hank, what's the burning interest in Beck and his decor?"

Hank got up, stretched, sat down again and leaned forward with such earnestness and urgency that I drew back. "Tom, suppose I could prove that it wasn't her fault at all?"

I thought about it. Finally, between my teeth, I said, "If you could really prove that, I know one mudhead that would get thoroughly killed."

"There'll be none of that talk," he rapped. I squinted up at him and decided not to protest. He really meant it. He went on, "You have *got* to understand exactly what I mean." He paused to chew words before he let them out, then said, "I don't want you to get up any wild hopes. I'm not going to be able to prove Opie didn't . . . didn't do what she said she did Saturday night. She did it, and that's that. Shut up, now, Tom—don't say it! Not to me. She's my sister; do you think I'm enjoying this?" When I simmered down a bit, Hank said, "All I think I can prove is that what happened was completely beyond her control, and that she's completely innocent in terms of intention, even if she is guilty in terms of action."

"I'd like that," I said, with all my heart. "I'd like that just fine. Only it's hardly the kind of thing you can really prove." I double-took it. "What are you talking about?" I demanded angrily. "You mean she was hypnotized?"

"I do not," he said positively. "No amount of hypnotism would make her do something she didn't want to do, and I'm working on the premise that she didn't want to."

"Dope, then?"

"I don't think so. Did she look doped to you?"

"No." I thought back carefully. "Besides, I never heard of a drug that could do that to a woman that quickly and leave no after-effects."

"There is none, and if there were it wasn't used on her."

"Cut out the guessing games then, and tell me what it was!"

He looked at me and his face changed. "Sorry," he said softly. "I can't. I don't know. But I mean to find out."

"You better say more," I said, dazed. "You lost me back there some place."

"You know where Klaus was picked up?"

I started. "The atom spy? No. What's that got to do with it?"

"Maybe a lot," said Hank. "Just a hunch I've got. Anyway, they got him at one of Beck's parties."

"I'll be damned," I breathed. "I didn't know that."

"Most people don't. It was one-two-three-hush. There was a Central Intelligence agent there and Klaus walked over to him and spilled the whole thing. The agent got him out of there and arrested him, then checked his story. It checked all right. Do you know *Cry for Clara?*"

"Do I know it? I wish I'd never heard it. Seventeen weeks on the 'Hit Parade,' and squalling out of every radio and every record store and juke-box in creation. Do I know it?"

"Know who wrote it?"

"No."

"Guy called Willy Simms. Never wrote a song before, never wrote one since."

"So?"

"He did the first draft at one of Beck's parties."

"I don't see what that has to do with—"

He interrupted me. "The hen fight that put two nice deep fingernail gouges across Marie Munro's million-dollar face happened at Beck's. A schoolteacher did it—an otherwise harmless old biddy who'd never even seen a Munro picture and hadn't even spoken to The Face that evening. The man who—"

"Wait a minute, wait a min—" I started, but he wouldn't wait.

"The man who killed that preacher on Webb Street two weeks ago—remember?—did it with Beck's poker, which he threw out of Beck's rumpus room window like a damn javelin. That hilarious story—I heard you telling it yourself—about the pansy breeder at the Flower Show."

"Don't tell me that one came from Beck's." I grinned in spite of myself.

"It did. Because of someone's remark that nobody knows where dirty stories originate. And *bing*, that one was originated on the spot." He paused. "By Lila Falsehaven."

"Lila? You mean the white-haired old granny who writes children's books?" I drank on that. That was too fine. "Hank, what are you getting at with all this?"

Hank pulled on an earlobe. "All these things I mentioned—all different, all happening to different kinds of people. I think there's a lowest common denominator."

"You've already told me that; they all happened at Beck's parties."

"The thing I'm talking about *makes* things happen at Beck's parties."

"Aw, for Pete's sake. Coincidence...."

"Coincidence hell!" he rumbled. "Can't you understand that I've known about this thing for a long time now? I'm not telling you all these things occurred to me just since Opie ... uh ... since last Saturday night. I'm telling you that what Opie did is another one of those things."

I grunted thoughtfully. "Lowest common denominator.... Heck, the main thing all those people have in common is that they have nothing in common."

"That's right," Hank nodded. "That seems to be Beck's rule-of-thumb: always mix them up. A rich and a talented one, a weird one, a dull one."

"Makes for a good party," I said stupidly.

He had the good sense not to pick that one up. Good party. Swell party. Opie. ... No, I wouldn't think about it. I said, "What's this all about, anyway? Why worry so much about Beck? It's his business who he invites. Strange things happen—sure, they'd happen at your house if you filled it up with characters."

"Here's what it's about. I want you to go back there and find out what that lowest common denominator is."

"Why?"

"For the magazine, maybe. It depends. Anyhow, kid, that's an assignment."

"Stick it," I said. "I'm not going back there."

"Why not?"

"That's the stupidest question yet!"

"Tom," he said gently. "Getting riled up won't help. I really want to know why you don't want to go back. Is it the place you can't stand, or the idea of seeing Opie there?"

"I don't mind the place," I said sullenly.

He was so pleased I was astonished. "Then you can go back. She will never go there again."

"You sound real positive."

"I am. Things happen at Beck's parties. But if they happen to you, you don't go back."

"I don't get it."

"Neither do I. But that's one of the things I want you to find out about."

"Hank, this is crazy!"

"Sure it's crazy. And you're just the man for the job."

"Why, especially?"

"Because you know Beck better than most people. Because you have something personal at stake. Because you're a good reporter. And—well, because you're so damn normal."

I didn't feel normal. I said, "If you're so interested in Beck and his shindigs, why don't you chase the story down yourself? You seem to know what to look for."

When he didn't answer, I looked up. He had turned his back. After a while he said, "I'm one of the ones who can't go back."

I thought that over. "You mean something happened to you?"

"Yes, something happened to me," he snarled in angry mimicry. "And that part of it you can skip."

For the first time I felt that little nubbin of intrigue that bites me when I'm near a really hot story. "So you've taken care of my Saturday nights. What am I supposed to do the rest of the week?"

"You've been around the magazine long enough not to ask me how to do your work. I just mentioned a lot of people. Go find out why they did the things they did." And all of a sudden he stalked to the door, scooped up his hat, growled a noise that was probably "Goodnight," and left.

I went to see Lila Falsehaven. It was no trouble at all to get her address from Kiddy-Joy Books, Inc. She invited me to tea when I called her up. Tea, no less. Me. Tom Conway.

She was a real greeting-card grandma. Steel-rimmed specs with the thickest part at the lower edges. Gleaming, perfect, even false teeth. A voice that reminded you of a silver plate full of warm spice cookies. And on the table between us, a silver plate full of warm spice cookies. "Cream?" she said. "Or lemon?"

"Straight."—"I mean, neither, thank you. This place looks just like the place where the Lila Falsehaven books are written."

"Thank you," she said, inclining her neat little head. She passed me tea in a convoluted bone-china cup I could have sneezed off a mantel at forty paces. "I've been told before that my books and my home and my appearance are those of the perfect grandmother. I've never had a child, you know. But I believe I've more grandchildren than anyone who ever lived." She delivered up an intricate old laugh like intricate old lace.

I tasted the tea. People should drink more tea. I put down the little cup and leaned back and smiled at her. "I like it here."

She blushed like a kid and smiled back. "And now—what can I do for you? Surely that wicked magazine of yours doesn't want a story by me. Or even about me."

"It's not a wicked magazine," I said loyally. "Just true-to-life. We call them as we see them."

"Some truths," she said gently, "are better left uncalled."

"You really believe that?"

"I really do," she said.

"But the world isn't what your grandchildren read about in your books."

"My world is," she said with conviction.

I had come here for something, and now was the time to get it. I shook my head. "Not completely. Some of your world has flower shows with pansies in them."

She didn't make a sound. She closed her eyes, and I watched her smooth old skin turn to ivory and then to paper. I waited. At last her eyes opened again. She looked straight at me, lifted one hand, then the other, spread them apart and placed each on the carven chair-arms. I looked at the hands, and saw each in turn relax as if by a deep effort of will. Her eyes drew me right up out of my chair. Deep in them was a spark, as hot, as bright, and quite as clean as a welding arc. The whole sweet room held its breath.

"Mr. Conway," she said in a voice that was very faint and very distinct, "I believe in truth as I believe in innocence and in beauty, so I shall not lie to you. I understand now that you came here to find out if I was really the one who contrived that filthy anecdote. I was. But if you came to find out why I did it, or what is in me that made it possible, I cannot help you. I'm sorry. If I knew, if I only knew, perhaps I'd tell you. Now you'd better go."

"But—"

Then I found out that the clean bright fire so deep in her eyes could repel as well as attract, and I was in the doorway with my hat in my hand. I said, "I'm sor—" but the way she looked, the way she sat there looking at me without moving, made it impossible for me to speak or bow, or do anything but just get out. I knew I'd never be back, too, and that was a shame. She's a nice person. She lives in a nice place.

The whole thing was spoiled, and I felt lousy. Lousy.

My press card got me as far as Col. Briggs, and the memory of the time I got Briggs out of a raided stag party just after the war got me the rest of the way. If it hadn't been for those two items, I'd never have seen Klaus. The death house was damn near as hard to get into as it was to get out of.

They gave me ten minutes and left me alone with him, though there was a guard standing where he could see in. Klaus did not look as if he'd have brought out the silver tea service even if he had one.

All he did when I came in was to say the name of the magazine under his breath, and said that way it sounds pretty dirty. I sat down on the bunk beside him and he got right up off it. I didn't say anything, and after a while that bothered him. I don't suppose anyone did that to him, ever.

"Well, what is it? What do you want?" he snarled finally.

"You'd never guess," I said.

"Am I guilty? Yes. Did I know what I was doing? Yes. Is it true that I just want to see this crummy human race blown off this crummy planet as soon as possible? Yes. Am I sorry? Yes—that I got caught. Otherwise—no." He shrugged. "That's my whole story, you know it, everybody knows it. I've been scooped dry and the bottom scraped. Why can't you guys leave me alone?"

"There's still something I'd like to know, though."

"Don't you read the papers?" he asked. "Once I got nabbed I had no secrets."

"Look," I said, "this guy Stevens—" Stevens was the Central Intelligence man who had dragged him in.

"Yeah, Stevens," Klaus snorted. "Our hero. I not only put him on page one—he's on boxes of breakfast cereal. You *really* got to be a hero to get on corn flakes."

"He wasn't a hero," I said. "He didn't know you from Adam and didn't care until you spilled to him."

Klaus stopped his pacing and slowly turned toward me. "Do you believe that?"

"Why not? That's what happened."

He came and sat beside me, looking at me as if I had turned into a two-headed giraffe. "You know, I've told that to six million different people and you're the first one who ever believed it. What did you say your name was? If you don't mind my asking."

"Conway," I said.

"I'm glad you came," he said. For him, that was really something.

He shoved back so he could lean against the wall and gave me a cigarette. "What do you want to know?"

"Why you did it."

He looked at me angrily, and I added quickly, "Not about the atom secrets. About the spill."

The angry look went away, but he didn't say anything. I pushed a bit. "You never made another mistake. Nobody in history ever operated as quietly and cleverly as you did. No one in the world suspected you, and as far as I've been able to discover no one was even about to. So you suddenly find yourself at a party with a C.I.A. man, walk over, and sing. Why?"

He thought about it. "It was a good party," he said, after a bit. Then, "I guess I figured the game had gone on long enough, that's all."

I snorted.

"What's that for?" he wanted to know.

"You don't really believe that."

"I don't?"

"You don't," I said positively. "That's just something you figured out after it happened. What I want to know is what went on in your head before it happened."

"You know a hell of a lot about how I think," he said sneeringly.

"Sure I do," I said, and when he was quiet, I added, "Don't I?"

"Yeah," he growled. "Yeah." He closed his eyes to think about it, and then said, "You just asked me the one thing I don't know. One second I was sitting there enjoying myself, and the next I was backing that goonboy into the corner and telling him about my life of sin. It just seemed a good idea at the time."

The guard came then to let me out. "Thanks for coming," Klaus said.

"That's all right. You're sure you can't tell me?"

"Yes, I'm sure."

"Shall I come back? Maybe after you think about it for a while...."

He shook his head. "Wouldn't do no good," he said positively. "I know, because I haven't thought about anything else much since it happened. But I'm glad somebody believes it, anyway."

"So long. Drop me a note if you figure it out."

I don't know if he ever did. They burned him a few days later. I never got a note.

209

I grabbed another name from the list I'd run up. Willy Simms. Song writer.

I went into a music shop and asked the man if he had a record of *Cry for Clara*. He looked as if he'd found root beer in a bock bottle. "Still?" he breathed with a sort of weary amazement, and went and got the record.

"Look," I told him, "I think this platter is the most awful piece of candy corn that ever rolled out of the Alley." I don't often explain myself to people, but I couldn't have even a total stranger think I liked it.

He leaned across the counter. "Did you know," he said in a much friendlier tone of voice, "that Guy Lombardo is cutting it this week?"

I shared his tired wonder for a long moment, and then got out of there.

One and three-quarter million copies sold and still moving, and yet Willy Simms still lived in a place with four flights of stairs up to it. I found the door and leaned against the frame for a while, blowing hard. When the spots went away from my eyes, I knocked. A wrinkled little man opened the door.

"Is Willy Simms here?"

He looked at me and down at the flat record envelope I held. "What's that?"

"*Cry for Clara,*" I said. He took it out of my hand and asked me how much I paid for it. I told him. He held the door open with his foot, scooped up a handful of change from an otherwise empty bookshelf, and counted out the price into my hand. Then he broke the record in two on his thigh, put the pieces together and broke them again, and slung them into the fireplace at his right. "I'm Willy Simms," he said. "Come on in."

I went in and stood just inside. I didn't know what this little prune would do next. I said, "My name's Tom—"

"Drop your hat there," he said. He crossed the room.

"I just dropped in to—"

"Drink?" he asked.

Since I never say no to that, and didn't have to say yes because he was already pouring, I just waited.

He came smiling with a glass. He had good teeth.

"Bourbon," he said. "A man's drink. Knew the minute I saw you you were a bourbon man."

I very much prefer rye. I said, "Once in a while—"

"Sure," he said. "Nothing like Bourbon. Sit down."

"Mr. Simms," I said.

"Willy. Nobody ever called me mister. Used to be I wasn't worth a 'mister.' Now I'm too good for it." He salvaged his modesty as he said this with a warm grin. "Maybe you think I shouldn't of busted your record."

"Well," I smiled, "I thought it a bit strange."

"I don't have a copy here and I won't let one in. Two reasons," he barked, making a V with shiny-dry, bony fingers. "First, I don't like it. What I specially don't like is the way people try to make me sit and listen to it and tell me how good this part is and that part, and where did I ever get the idea of going from the sub-dominant into an unrelated minor. Yeah, that's what one of them wanted to know."

"I remember that part," I said. "It's—"

"Second," said Willy Simms, "every time I bust one of those records it reminds me I can afford to do it, and I like to be reminded."

"Yeah," I said. "That's—"

"Besides," he said, "any time I bust one, the party walks out of here and buys another. It ain't the royalty, you understand. It's the score I'm running up. They tell me it'll sell two and a quarter million."

"Two and a—"

"You've finished your drink," he said. He took it out of my hand and filled it again. I wished it was rye, raised it to him and then sipped. "Willy," I began.

"I never wrote a song before," Willy said.

"Yes," I answered. "So I—"

"And I'm going to tell you something I ain't told nobody else. I'm going to tell it to you, and from now on, I just decided, I'm going to tell everybody."

He leaned toward me excitedly. I realized that he was boiled. I knew instinctively that it hadn't made any difference in him; he was probably this way cold sober too. He was obviously waiting for me to say something, but by this time I didn't want to spoil anything.

"So I'll tell you first, and it's this: I'm never going to write another song, either."

"But you've just begun to—"

"There's a good reason for it," he said. "Since you ask me, I'll tell you. I ain't going to write another song because I can't. It ain't that I don't read or write music. They say Leadbelly couldn't read music either. And it ain't that I don't want to. I want to, all right. But did you ever hear the old saying lightning never strikes twice in the same place?"

That I could match. "Sure, and they say it's always darkest before the dawn, too, but that doesn't—"

"The real reason," said Willy Simms, "is this." He paused dramatically. "I'm tone deaf. I couldn't carry a chord in a keyster. Do you see a piano here, or even a harmonica?"

"Listen," I said, "no one who was tone deaf could have—"

"Lightning," he said gravely. "It struck, that's all. Way down inside me was one little crumb called *Cry for Clara*, and the lightning struck and drove it out. But there was just the one little crumb there, and now there is no more."

"Shucks," I said. "Maybe—"

"And I could be wrong even about that," he said morosely. "I don't really believe even the little crumb was there. What I actually did just can't be done, not by me, anyway. Like a lobster writing a book. Like a phonograph playing a pizza pie. Like us not having another drink."

He demonstrated the impossibility of his last remark. I said, "There are certain things a man can do and certain things—"

"Like a trip back to one of Beck's parties," he said. "Some things just can't happen." He glowered at me suddenly. "You don't happen to be a friend of this Beck? This is the guy made me hate myself."

"Me? Why, I—"

"If you were, I'd throw you right down those stairs out there, big as you are." He half rose, and for a split second I was genuinely alarmed. He was one of those people who, in speaking of anger, acts it out, pulsing temples, narrowed eyes and all. But he sank back and recovered his disarming smile. "I been doing all the talking. What was it you came to see me about?"

I opened my mouth, and hesitated. To my amazement, he waited. "I just dropped up to sort of. . . ." I paused. He nodded encouragingly. "To find out about—" I began, then stopped.

"I see everybody," he confided. "Some people, now, they pick and choose who comes in. Not me."

I was at the door with my hat, which I'd picked up on the way. "Thanks for the dr—"

"Well, don't rush off."

I searched valiantly for the one word which might serve me, and found it. "Goodbye," I said, and whipped through the door. I could hear Willy Simms' muffled voice through the panel: "All right, I'll finish your drink if you're in such a damn hurry."

All the way down the stairs I could hear him, though I could no longer distinguish his words. Once he laughed. I got to the sidewalk and turned left. There was a man standing by a tree a few yards down the street, curbing a dog. "Hey," I said.

He turned toward me, raising his eyebrows. "Who—me?"

I tapped his shoulder with my left index finger. "New York would have the largest telephone book in the world," I said, "if they didn't have to break it into five sections."

He said, "Huh?"

"Don't mind me," I told him, "I just wanted to see if I could say a whole sentence all the way through." I tipped my hat and walked on. At the corner I looked back. He was still standing there, staring at me. When he saw me turn he called, "Whaddaya—wise?" I just waved at him and went home.

"Beck," I said into the phone, "I want to see you." "Sure," he said. "You're coming over Saturday, aren't you?"

"Uh . . . yes. But I want to see you before that."

"It'll wait," he said easily.

"No, it won't," I said. There must have been something special in my voice because he asked me if anything was the matter.

"I don't know, Beck," I said honestly. "I mean, something is, but I don't know what." I had an idea suddenly. "Beck, can I bring someone to the party?"

"You know you can, Tom. Anyone you like."

"My brother-in-law Hank."

There was a long silence at the other end. Then, in a slightly strained voice, Beck said, "Why him?"

"Why not?"

The silence again. Then, as if he had had a brainwave, Beck said easily, "No reason. If he wants to come, bring him."

"Thanks. Now, about seeing you before. How about tonight?"

"Tom, I'd love to, but I'm tied up. It'll wait till Saturday, won't it?"

"No," I said. "Tomorrow?"

"I'm out of town tomorrow. I'm really very sorry, Tom."

Abruptly, I said, "It's about the lowest common denominator."

"What?"

"Your parties," I said patiently. "The people who go to them."

He laughed suddenly. "The one thing they have in common is that they have nothing in common."

"That I know," I said. "I meant the people who used to go to your parties and don't any more."

The silence, but much shorter this time. "I'm looking at my book," he said. "Maybe I could squeeze in a few minutes with you tomorrow."

"What time?" I said, keeping the humorless grin out of my voice.

"Two o'clock. Kelly's all right?"

"At the bar. I'll be there, Beck, and thanks."

I hung up and scratched my chin. Lowest common denominator?

Hank's phrase, that was. Hank. The guy who'd put me on to this weird business. The guy who'd told me that if things happened to you at Beck's parties, you didn't go back. The guy who said *he* was never going back.

And wouldn't say why.

Well, if I had anything to do with it he'd be back.

Opie, Lila Falsehaven, Klaus, Willy Simms, Hank. Each had done something they shouldn't—maybe *couldn't* was the word—have done. Each would not—could not?—go back. Sometimes the thing was just silly, like Lila Falsehaven's dirty story. Sometimes it was deadly, like Klaus's crazy break.

Well, I told myself, keep plugging at it. Get enough case histories and a basic law will show itself. Avogadro worked up a fine theory about the behavior of gas molecules because he had enough molecules to work with. Sociologists struggle toward theories without enough numbers to work with, and they make some sort of progress. If I worked hard enough and lived long enough, maybe I could pile up a couple hundred million case histories of people who didn't go to Beck's parties any more, and come out with an answer.

Meanwhile, I'd better talk to Hank.

This time I went to his office and closed the door. He picked up the phone and said, "Sue, don't ring this thing until I tell you. . . . I know, I *know*. I don't care. Tell him to wait." Then he just lounged back and looked at me.

"Hank," I said, "about this assignment. How much are you willing to help me?"

"All the way."

"Okay," I said. "Saturday night you have a date."

"I have? Where?"

"Beck's."

He sat upright, his eyes still on my face. "No."

"That's what you mean by 'all the way'?" I asked quietly.

"I said I'd help you. Me going there—that wouldn't help anything. Besides, Beck wouldn't hold still for it."

"Beck told me to bring you."

"The hell he did!"

"Look, Hank, when I tell you—"

"Okay, okay, cool down, will you? I'm not calling you a liar." He pulled at his lip. "Tell me exactly what you said about it and what he said. As near as you can remember it."

I thought back. "I asked him if I could bring someone and he said sure. Then I mentioned your name and he—well, sort of hesitated. So I wanted to know why not, and he came off it right away. Said 'If he wants to come, bring him.'"

"The foxy little louse!" Hank said from between clenched teeth.

"What's the matter?"

Hank got up, smacked his fist into his palm. "He meant exactly what he said, Tom. Bring me—*if* I want to come. Conversely, if I don't want to come, don't bring me. I don't want to, Tom."

"Not even in the process of 'going all the way' to help me?" I asked sarcastically.

He said tightly. "That's right." I must have looked pretty grim, because he tried to explain. "If I could be sure it would break the case, Tom, I'd do it no matter what. If you can convince me that that one single act on my part is all you need, why, I'm your boy. Can you do that?"

"No," I said in all honesty. "It might help like crazy, though. All right," I conceded reluctantly. "If you don't want to go, you won't, and that's that. Now—short of that, will you help?"

"Absolutely," he said relievedly.

Then I aimed a forefinger at him and barked "Okay. Then you'll tell me what happened to you there, and why you won't go back. You'll tell me now, and you won't even try to wriggle out of it."

It got real quiet in the office then. Hank's eyes half-closed, and I had seen that sleepy look before. Every time I had, somebody had gotten himself rather badly hurt.

"I should have known better," he said after a while, "than to put a real reporter on something that concerned me. You really want that information?"

I nodded.

"Tom," he said, and his voice was almost a lazy yawn, "I'm going to punch you right in the middle of your big fat mouth."

"For asking you a businesslike question that you made my business?"

"Not exactly," Hank said. "I'm going to tell you, and you're going to laugh, and when you laugh I'm going to let you have it."

"I haven't laughed at any of this yet," I said.

"And you still want to know."

I just waited.

"All right," he said. He came around his desk, balled up his fist, and eyed my face carefully. "I went to one of Beck's parties, and right in the middle of the proceedings I wet my pants."

I bit down hard on the insides of my cheeks, but I couldn't hold it. I let out a joyful whoop. Then I caromed off the water cooler, slid eight feet on the side of my head, and brought up against the wall. A great cloud of luminous fog rolled in, swirled, then gradually began to clear. I sat up. There was blood on my mouth and chin. Hank was standing over me, looking very sad. He dropped a clean handkerchief where I could reach it. I used it, then got my feet under me.

"Damn it, Tom, I'm sorry," he said. The way he said it I believed him. "But you shouldn't've laughed. I told you you shouldn't."

I went to the desk-side chair and sat down. Hank drew me some water and brought it over. "Dip the handkerchief," he ordered. "Tom, this'll make more sense to you when you have a chance to think it over. Why don't you cut out?"

"I don't have to, I guess," I said with difficulty. "I guess if a thing like that happened to. . . ."

"If it happened," Hank said soberly, "it wouldn't be funny, and God help the man who laughed at it. It would shake your confidence like nothing else could. You'd think of it suddenly in a bus, at a board meeting, in the composing room. You'd think of it when you were tramping up and down the office dictating. You'd remember that when it happened it came without warning and there was nothing you could do about it until it was over. It would be the kind of thing that just couldn't happen—and forever after you'd be afraid of its happening again."

"And the last place in the world you'd go back to is the place where it happened."

"I'd go through hell first," he said, his voice thick, like taking a vow. "And . . . just to cap it, that damned Beck—"

"He laughed?"

"He did not," said Hank viciously. "All he did was meet me at the door when I was escaping, and tell me I'd do just as well not to come again. He was polite enough, I guess, but he meant it."

I dunked the handkerchief again and leaned over the glass desktop, where I could see my reflection. I mopped at my chin. "This Beck," I said. "He certainly makes sure. Hank, all the other people who used to go to Beck's and don't any more . . . do you suppose Beck told them all not to come back?"

"I never thought of it. Probably so. Except maybe Klaus. He wasn't going anywhere after what he did."

"I saw Willy Simms," I told him. "He acted mad at Beck, and said something about going there again being as impossible as writing another song. He's tone deaf, you know."

"I didn't know. What about Miss Falsehaven? Did you see her?"

"She wouldn't be seen dead in the place. She's half crazy with the memory of what she did. To you or me, that would be nothing. To her it was the end of the world."

The end of the world. The end of the world. "Hank, I'm just dimly beginning to understand what you meant about . . . Opie. That what she did wasn't her doing." Suddenly, shockingly—I believe I was more startled than Hank—I bellowed, "But it was in her to do it! There had to be that one grain of—of whatever it took!"

"Maybe, maybe . . . ," he said gently. "I'd like to think not, though. I'd like to think there is something there at Beck's that puts the bee in people's bonnets. An alien bee, one that couldn't under any other circumstances exist with that person." He blushed. "I'd feel better if I could prove that."

"I got to get out of here. I'm meeting Beck," I said, after a glance at his desk clock.

"Are you now?" He sat down again. "Give him my regards."

I started out. "Tom—"

"Well?"

"I'm sorry I had to hit you. I had to. See?"

"Sure I see," I said, and when I grinned it hurt. "If I didn't see, they'd be mixing a cast for your busted back by now." I went out.

Beck was waiting for me when I rushed into Kelly's. I picked up his drink and started back to the corner.

"Not a table," he bleated, following me. "I have a train to catch, Tom. I told you that."

"Come on," I said. "This won't take but a minute." He came, grumbling, and he let me maneuver him into the upholstered corner of a booth. I sat down where he'd have to climb over me if the conversation should make him too impulsive.

"Sorry I'm late, Beck. But I'm glad you're in a hurry. I won't have to beat about the bush."

"What's on your mind?" he said, irritatingly looking at his watch and, for a moment, closing his eyes as he calculated the minutes.

"Where's your money come from?" I asked bluntly.

"Why, it—well, really, Tom. You've never—I mean—" He shifted gears and began to get stuffy. "I'm not used to being catechized about my personal affairs, old man. We are old friends, yes, but after all—"

"Shove it," I said. "I'm the boy who knew you when, remember? We roomed together in college, and unless my memory fails me it was State College, as near to being a public school as you can find these days. We had three neckties and one good blanket between us for more than two years, and skipped forty-cent lunches for date money. That wasn't so long ago, Beck. You graduated into pushing a pen for an insurance company—right? And when you left it you never took another job. But here you are with a big ugly house full of big ugly furniture, a rumpus room by Hilton out of Tropics, and a passion for throwing big noisy parties every week."

"May I ask," he said between his protruding front teeth, "why you are so suddenly interested?"

"You look more than ever like a gopher," I said detachedly, figuring it wouldn't hurt to make him mad. He always blurts things when he's mad enough. "Now, Beck—working around a magazine like ours, we get a lot of advance stuff about things that are about to break. I'm just trying to do you a favor, son."

"I don't see—"

"How would you make out," I asked, "if they dragged out your income tax returns for the last four years and balanced them against your real property?"

"I'd make out nicely," he said smugly. "If you must know, my income comes from investments. I've done very well indeed."

"What did you use for capital in the first place?"

"That's really none of your business, Tom," he said briskly, and I almost admired him for the way he stood up to me. "But I might remind you that you need very little capital to enter the market, and if you can buy low and sell high just a few times in a row, you don't have to worry about capital."

"You're not a speculator, Beck," I snorted, "Not *you!* Why I never figured you had the sense to pour pith out of a helmet. Who's your tipster?"

For some reason, that hit him harder than anything else I'd said. "You're being very annoying," he said prissily, "and you're going to make me miss my train. I'll have to leave now. I don't know what's gotten into you, Tom. I don't much care for this kind of thing, and I'm sure I don't know what this is all about."

"I'll go with you," I said, "and explain the whole thing."

"You needn't bother," he snapped. He got up, and so did I. I let him out from behind the table and followed him to the door. The hat check girl rummaged around and found a pigskin suitcase for him. I took it from her before he could get a hand on it. "Give me that!" he yelled.

"Don't stand here and argue," I said urgently. "You'll be late." I barreled on out to the curb and whistled. I whistle pretty well. Cabs stopped three blocks in every direction. I shoved him into the nearest one and climbed in after him. "You know you could never catch a cab like I can," I said. "I just want to help."

"Central Depot," Beck said to the driver. "Tom, what are you after? I've never seen you like this."

"Just trying to help," I said. "A lot of people starting to talk about you, Beck."

He paled. "Really?"

"Oh, yes. What do you expect: hidden income, big parties that anyone can come to, and all?"

"Lot of people have parties."

"Nobody talks about them afterward the way they do about yours."

"What are they saying, Tom?" He hated to be conspicuous.

"Why did you tell Willy Simms never to show his face at your house again?" It was a shot in the dark, but the bell rang.

"I think I was quite reasonable with him," Beck protested. "He talks all the time, and he bored me. He bored everybody, every time he came."

"He still talks all the time," I said mysteriously, and dropped that part of it. Beck began to squirm. "Personally, I think you get something from the people who come to those brawls. And once you've gotten it, you drop them."

Beck leaned forward to speak to the driver, but for some reason his voice wouldn't work. He coughed and tried again. "Faster, driver."

"So what I want to know is, what do you get from those people, and how do you get it?"

"I don't know what you mean, and I don't see how any of this concerns you."

"Something happened to my wife last Saturday."

"Oh," he said. "Oh, dear." Then, "Well, what do you suppose I got from her?"

I put my hands behind me, lifted up, and sat on them. "I know you awful well," I grated, "which fact just saved your life. You don't mean what you just said, old man, do you?"

He went quite white. "Oh, good heavens, Tom, no! No! It was what you said before—that I got something out of every one of these people. I'm more sorry than I can say about—about Opie—I couldn't help it, you know, I was busy, there was a lot to do, there always is. . . . No, Tom, I didn't mean that the way you thought. "

He didn't, either. Not Beck. There were some things that were just not in Beck's department. I took a deep, head-clearing breath and asked, "Why did you tell Hank not to come back?"

"I'd rather not say exactly," he said, pleading and sincere. "It was for his own benefit, though. He . . . er . . . made rather a fool of himself. I thought it would be a kindness if he could be angry at me instead of at himself."

I gave him a long careful look. He had never been very smart, but he had always been as glib as floor wax. The cab turned into the station ramp just then, so I came up with the big question. "Beck, does everybody who goes to your parties sooner or later make a fool of himself?"

"Oh dear no," he said, and I think if he had not been looking at his watch and worrying, he would never have said what came out. "Some people are immune."

The cab stopped and he got out. "I'll take it," I said when his hand went for his pocket. "You better run." I hung my head out the window, watching him, waiting, wondering if it would come, even after all this. And it came.

From fifty feet away he called over his shoulder, "See you Saturday, Tom!"

"Kelly's," I told the cabbie, and settled back.

So. I couldn't make Beck so mad he'd exclude me from one of his parties—and somehow or other the rich and dumb and smart and stupid and ugly and big and famous and nowhere people who came there became prone to making fools of themselves—and Beck got something out of it when they did—and what did he want out of me? And what did he mean by "some people are immune"? Immune . . . that was a peculiar word to use. Immune. There was something in that house—in that room—that made people do things that—Wait a minute. Hank and Miss Falsehaven and, if you wanted to be broad about it, Opie—they had indeed made fools of themselves. But the guy who killed the preacher with Beck's poker—and Klaus the spy—that wasn't what you'd call foolishness. And then Willy Simms. Is the creation of a hit song foolishness?

Lowest common denominator . . .

I paid off the cab and went in to Kelly's to double the drink I'd missed because Beck had been in such a hurry. I was drinking the second one when some simple facts fell into place.

The next best thing to knowing what the answer is is to know where it is. Beck was on his way out of town.

There was only one single thing that connected all these crazy facts: Beck's rumpus room.

A good thing I have credit at Kelly's. I flew out of there so fast I forgot to leave anything on the bar. Except a half shot of rye.

It wasn't quite dark when I reached Beck's, but that didn't matter. The house was set well back in its mid-city three acres. High board fences guarded the sides, and a thick English privet hid it from the street. Once I'd slipped through the gate and onto the lawn, I might as well have been underground. The house was one of those turn-of-the-century horrors, not quite chalet, not quite manse, with a little more gingerbread than the moderns like and a little less than the Victorians drooled about. It had gables and turrets and rooms scattered on slightly different levels, so that the windows looked like the holes on an IBM card.

I hefted the package I'd picked up at the hardware store on the way and, sticking close to the north hedge, worked my way cautiously around to the back.

One glance told me I couldn't do business there. The house was built at the very back of its property, and behind it ran a small street or a large alley, whichever you like. The back of the house hung over it like a cliff, and there was traffic and neighbors across the way. No, it would have to be a side. I cursed, because I knew the rumpus room faced the back with its huge picture windows of one-way glass; then I remembered that the room was air-conditioned; the windows wouldn't open and couldn't be cut because they were certainly double-pane jobs.

I tried two ground-floor windows, but they were locked. Another was open, but barred. Then nothing but a bare, windowless stretch. On a hunch I approached it, through the flowerbed at its base. And sure enough, just at chest-height, hidden behind a phalanx of hollyhocks, was a small window.

I got out the pen-lite flash I'd just bought and peered in. The window was locked with one of those burglarproof cast-steel locks that screws a rubber ferrule up against the frame. I was pleased. I got out the can of aquarium cement and worked the stuff into a cone, which I placed against the glass. Then I got out the glass cutter and scribed around the cone. I rapped the cut circle once, and with a snap it broke out, with the cone of putty holding it. I reached down and laid putty and glass on the window sill, unscrewed the burglarproof lock, opened the window and climbed in. With my putty-knife I carefully removed the broken pane, and cracked it and the circle into small enough pieces to wrap up in the brown paper from the parcel I carried. I measured the frame and cut the one spare piece of window glass I'd brought along, and installed it using the aquarium cement. The stuff's black and doesn't glare at you the way clean, new putty does. I cleaned the new pane inside and out, shut and locked the window, and carefully swept the sill and the floor under it. I dumped the sweepings into my jacket pocket and stowed the tools here and there in my jacket and pants. So now nobody ever had to know I'd been here.

I was in a large storage closet which turned out to belong to the butler's pantry. That led to the kitchen, and that to the dining room, and now I knew where I was. I went into the front hall and down toward the back of the house. The door to the rumpus room was closed. On this side it was all crudded up with carven wainscoting; golden oak and Ionic columns. It was a sliding door; I rolled it back and on the other side it was a flat slab of birch to match the shocking modern of the rumpus room. Again I had that strange feeling of wonderment about Beck and his single peculiarity.

I shut the door and crossed the dim room to the picture windows. There I touched the button that closed the heavy drapes. There was a faint hum and they began to move. As they did, all but sourceless light began to grow in the room, until when they met the room was filled with a pervasive golden glow.

And standing in the middle of the rug which I had just crossed, standing yards away from any door and a long way from any furniture, was a girl.

The shock of it was almost physical. And for a split second I thought my eyes registered a dazzle, like the subjective afterglow of a lightning flash. Then I got hold of myself and met her long, level, green-eyed gaze.

If a woman can be strong and elfin at once, she was. Her hair was blue-black with a strange reddish light in it. Her skin was too flawless, like something in a wax museum, but for all that it was real and warm-looking. She was smiling, and I could see how her teeth met edge to edge in that rarity, the perfect bite. Her low-cut dress was of a heavy gold and purple brocade, and she must have had a dozen petticoats under it. Sixteenth century—seventeenth century? In *this* room?

"That was nice," she said.

"It was?" I said stupidly.

"Yes, but it didn't last. I suppose you're immune."

"Depends," I said, looking at the neckline of her dress. Then I remembered Beck's strange remark.

She said, "You're not supposed to be here. Not all alone."

"I could say the same for you. But since we're both here, we're not alone."

"I'm not," she said. "But you are." And she laughed. "You're Conway."

"Oh. He told you about me, did he? Well, he never said a word about you."

"Of course not. He wouldn't dare."

"Do you live here?"

She nodded. "I've always lived here."

"What do you mean always? Beck's been here three—yes, it's four years now. And you've been here all this time?"

She nodded. "Since before that."

"I'll be damned," I said. "Good for Beck. I thought he didn't like women."

"He doesn't need to." I saw her gaze stray over my shoulder and fix on something behind me. I whirled. Clinging to the drape was a spider as big as a Stetson hat. I didn't know whether it was going to jump or what. With the same motion which began when I turned, I snatched up a heavy ash stand made of links of chain welded together. Before I could heave it the girl was beside me, holding it with both hands. "Don't," she said. "You'll break the window and people will come. I want you to stay here for a while."

"But the—"

"It isn't real," she said. I looked and the spider was gone. I turned back to her. "What the hell goes on here?"

She sighed. "That wasn't so good," she said. "You were supposed to be frightened. But you just got angry at it. Why weren't you frightened?"

"I am now," I said, glancing at the drapes. "I guess I get mad first and scared later. What's the idea? You put that thing there, didn't you?"

She nodded.

"What for?"

"I was hungry."

"I don't get you."

"I know."

She moved to the divan, rustling wonderfully as she walked. She subsided into the foam rubber, patted the seat next to her. I crossed slowly. You don't have to know what a thing's all about to like it. I sat beside her.

She cast her eyes down and smoothed her skirt. It was as if she were waiting for something.

I didn't give her long to wait. I pulled her to me and clawed at the back of her dress. It slipped downward easily just as my cheek encountered the heavy stubble on hers.

The heavy—

With a shout I sprang back, goggle-eyed. There on the couch sprawled a heavy-set man with bad teeth and a four-day beard. He roared with rich baritone laughter.

You don't have to understand a situation to dislike it. I stepped forward and let loose with my Sunday punch. It travels from my lower rib to straight ahead, and by the time it gets where it's going it has all of me behind it. But this time it didn't get anywhere. My elbow crackled from the strain as my fist connected with nothing at all. But from the seat of the divan came a large black cat. It leaped to the floor and streaked across the room. I fell heavily onto the divan, bounced off, and rushed the animal. It doubled back at the end of the room, eluded my grasping fingers easily, and the next thing I knew it was climbing the drapes, hand over hand.

Yes, hands; the cat had three-fingered hands and an opposed thumb.

When it got up about fifteen feet it tucked itself into a round ball and—I think *spun* is the word for it. I shook my head to clear it and looked again. There was no sign of the animal; there was only a speaker baffle I had not noticed before.

Speaker baffle?

Anyone who knows ultramodern knows there's a convention against speakers or lights showing. Everything has to be concealed or to look like something else.

"That," said the speaker in a sexless, toneless voice, "was more like it."

I backed away and sank down on the divan, where I could watch the baffle.

"Even if you are immune, I can get something out of you."

I said, "How do you mean immune?"

"There is nothing you wouldn't do," said the impersonal voice. "Now, when I make somebody do something he *can't* do—then I feed. All I can do with you is make you mad. Even then, you're not mad at yourself at all. Just the girl or the spider or whatever else."

I suddenly realized the speaker wasn't there any more. However, a large spotted snake was on the rug near my feet. I dived on it, found in my hand the ankle of the girl I had seen before. I backed off and sat down again. "See?" she said in her velvet voice. "You don't even scare much now."

"I won't scare at all," I said positively.

"I suppose not," she said regretfully. Then she brightened. "But it's almost Saturday. *Then* I'll feed."

"What are you, anyhow?"

She shrugged. "You haven't a name for it. How could a thing like me have a name anyhow? I can be anything I like."

"Stay this way for a while." I looked her up and down. "I like you fine this way. Why don't you come over here and be friendly?"

She stepped back a pace, shaking her head.

"Why not? It wouldn't matter to you."

"That's right. I won't though. You see, it wouldn't matter to you."

"I don't get you."

She said patiently, "In your position, some men wouldn't want me. Some would in spite of themselves, and when they found out what I was—or what I *wasn't*—they'd hate themselves for it. That I could use," she crooned, and licked her full lips. "But you—you want me the way I am right now, and it doesn't matter in the least to you that I might be reptile, insect, or just plain hypocrite, as long as you got what you want."

"Wait a minute—this feeding. You feed on—hate?"

"Oh, no. Look, when a human being does something he's incapable of, like—oh, that old biddy who clawed the pretty actress—there's a glandular reaction set up that's unlike any other. All humans have a drive to live and a drive to die—a drive to build and a drive to destroy. In most people they're shaken down pretty well. But what I do is to give them a big charge of one or the other, so the two parts are thrown into conflict. That conflict creates a—call it a field, an aura. That's what feeds me. Now do you see?"

"Sort of like the way a mosquito injects a dilutant into the blood." I looked at her. "You're a parasite."

"If you like," she said detachedly. "So are you, if you define parasitism as sustaining oneself from other life-forms."

"Now tell me about the immunity."

"Oh, that. Very annoying. Like being hungry and finding you have nothing but canned food and no opener. You know it's there but you can't get to it. It's quite simple. You're immune because you're capable of anything—anything at all."

"Like Superman?"

She curled her lip. "You? No, I'm sorry."

"What then?"

She was thoughtful. "Do you remember asking me what I was? Well, down through your history there have been a lot of names for such as I. All wrong, of course. But the one that's used most often is *conscience*. A man's natural conscience tells him when he's done wrong. But any time you see a case of a man's conscience working on him, trying to destroy him—you can bet one of us has been around. Any time you see a man doing something utterly outside all his background and conditioning—you can be sure one of us is there with him."

I was beginning to understand a whole lot of things. "Why are you telling me all this?"

"Why not? I like to talk, same as you do. It can't do any harm. No one would believe you. After a while you yourself won't believe anything I've told you. Humans *can't* believe in things that have no set size or shape or weight or behavior. If an extra fly buzzes around your table; if your morning-glory vine has a new shoot it lacked ten minutes ago—you wouldn't believe it. These things happen around all humans all the time, and they never notice. They explain everything in terms of what they already believe. Since they never believe in anything remotely resembling us, we are free to pass and repass in front of their silly eyes, feeding when and where we want...."

"You can't get away with it. Humans will catch up with you," I blurted. "Humans are learning to think in new ways. Did you ever hear of non-Euclidean geometry? Do you know anything about non-Aristotelian systems?"

She laughed. "We know about them. But by the time they are generally accepted, we'll no longer be parasites. We'll be symbiotes. Some of us already are. I am."

"Symbiotes? You mean you depend on another life-form?"

"And it depends on me."

"What does?"

She indicated the incongruous room. "Your silly friend Beck, of course. Some of the people who are attracted to the feeding-grounds here are operators—very shrewd. The last thing in the world they would ever do is to pass on investment secrets to anyone. I see to it that they tell Beck. And oh, *how* they regret it! How *foolish* they feel! And how I feed! In exchange, Beck brings them here."

"I *knew* he couldn't do it by himself!" I said. "Now tell me— why does he have me hanging around here all the time?"

"My doing." She looked at me coolly. "One day I'm going to eat you. One day I'll find that can-opener. I'll learn how to slam a door on you, or pound you with a flatiron, and I'll eat you like candy."

I laughed at her. "You'll have to find something I'll regret doing first."

"There has to be something." She yawned. "I have to work up a new edge to my appetite," she said lazily. "Go away."

"She's wrong," Hank said, when I'd finished telling him the story. He'd galloped over to my place when I called and just let me talk. "Wrong how?"

"She said it was impossible for a human to believe this. Well, by God I do."

"I think I do myself," I said. Then, "Why?"

"Why?" Hank repeated. He gave a thoughtful pull to his lower lip. "Maybe it's just because I want to believe in any theory that keeps Opie clean—that makes what she did really out of character."

"Opie," I said. "Yes."

He gave me a swift look. "Something I've been thinking about, Tom. That night it happened—with Opie, I mean...."

"Spill it if it bothers you," I said, recognizing the expression.

"Thanks, Tom. Well ... no matter what Opie was suffering from, no matter how ... uh ... willing she might have been—these things take time. You can see them happening."

"So?"

"*Where were you when that guy started making passes at her?*"

I thought. I started to smile, cut it off. Then I got mad. "I don't remember."

"Yes you do. Where were you, Tom?"

"Around. "

"You weren't even in the room."

"I wasn't?"

"No."

"Who told you?"

"You did," he said. He began to get that sleepy look. "You're a lousy liar, Tom. When you duck a question, you're saying yes. Who was the babe, Tom?"

"I don't know."

"*What?*"

"I said I don't know," I said sullenly. "Just a babe."

"Oh. You didn't ask her her name."

"Guess not."

"And you raised all that fuss about Opie."

"You leave Opie out of this!" I blazed. "There's a big difference."

"You ought to be hung by your thumbs," he said pityingly. "But I guess it isn't your fault." He snorted. "No wonder that parasite of Beck's can't reach you. You don't do anything you regret because you never regret anything you do. Not one thing!"

"Well, why not?" I jumped to my feet. "Listen, Hank, I'm alive, see. I'm alive all over. Everybody I know is killing off this part of themselves, that part of themselves—parts that get hungry get starved, they die. Don't drink this, don't look at that, don't eat the other, when all the time something in you is hungry for these things. It's easily fed—and once it's fed it's quiet. I'm alive, damn it, and I mean to stay alive!"

Hank went to the door. "I'm getting out of here," he said in a shaking voice. "I got to think of my sister. I don't want you to get hurt. She might not forgive me."

He slammed the door. I kicked the end-table and busted a leg off it. The door opened again. Hank said, "I'm going with you to Beck's Saturday night. I'll pick you up here. Don't leave until I get here."

The front door at Beck's stood wide, as it always did on Saturdays. There was nothing to stop Hank or any other "graduate" from walking right in. Unless the something was inside those people. Hank sure felt it; I could tell by the way he jammed his hands in his pockets and sauntered through the door. He looked so relaxed, but he radiated tension.

It was the usual unusual type of party. Beck self-effacingly rode herd on about nineteen of the goofiest assortment of people ever collected—since last week. A famous lady economist. An alderman. A pimply Leftist. A brace of German tourists, binoculars and all. A dazed-looking farmer in store clothes. Somebody playing piano. Somebody looking adoringly at the piano player—she obviously didn't play. Somebody else looking disgustedly at the piano player. He obviously did play.

When we came in, Beck hurried over, chortling greetings, which dried up completely when he recognized Hank. "Hank," he gasped. "Really, old man, I think—"

"Hiya, Beck," Hank said. "Been quite a while." He walked out into the room and to the bar in the far corner. Beck gawped like a beached haddock. "Tom," Beck said, "you shouldn't have taken a chance like—"

"I'm just as thirsty as he is," I told him, and followed Hank. I got a rye. "Hank."

"What?" His eyes were on the crowd.

"When are you going to quit the silent treatment and tell me what you have in mind?"

He looked at me, and the strain he was under must have been painful. "Hey," I said, "take it easy. Nothing's going to happen to you. Our hungry little friend here is an epicure. I don't think she's interested in anything but the first rush of anguish she kicks up. You're old stuff."

"I know," he muttered. "I know . . . I guess." He wiped his forehead. "Do you see her?"

"No," I said. "But then, how would I know her if I did see her? Maybe she's not in the room."

"I think she is," he said. "I think she's stuck here."

"That's a thought. Hey! Her specialty is the incongruous—right? The out-of-character. Well, that's what this room is all about."

He nodded. "That's what I mean. And that's what I'm going to check on, but for sure. Here."

He moved close to the bar and to me, and quickly and secretly passed me something chunky and flat. "Hank!" I whispered. "A gun! What—"

"Take it. I have one too. Follow my cue when the time comes."

I don't like guns. But it was in my pocket before I could make any more talk. I wondered if Hank had gone off his rocker. "Bullets wouldn't make no nevermind to her."

"They aren't for her," he said, watching the crowd again.

"But—"

"Shut up. Tom," he asked abruptly, "does somebody always do something crazy at these shindigs? Every time?"

I remembered about the "investment" tips, the number of quiet, unnoticed times people must have done things in this room that caused them humiliation, regret. "Maybe so, Hank."

"Early or late in the proceedings?"

"That I don't know, Hank. I really don't."

"I can't wait," he muttered. "I can't risk it. Maybe it only feeds once. Here I go," he said clearly.

I called to him, but he put his chin down between his collarbones and went to the piano. I flashed a look around. I remember Beck's face watching Hank was white and strained.

Hank climbed right up on the piano, one foot on the bench, one foot on the keys, both big feet on the exquisite finish of the top. The pianist faltered and stopped. The ardent girl watching him squeaked. People looked. People rushed to finish a sentence while they turned. Others didn't even notice. After all—those parties of Beck's. . . .

"Parasite!" Hank bellowed. And do you know, four-fifths of that crowd practically snapped to attention.

"He's not immune," Hank said. He was talking, apparently, to the place where the wall met the ceiling. "Here's your can-opener, parasite. Listen to me."

He paused, and in the sudden embarrassed silence Beck's voice came shakingly, stretched and gasping. "Get off there, you hear? Get—"

Hank pulled out his gun. "Shut up, Beck." Beck sat right down on the floor. Hank lifted his big head. "All he wants to do is live. He'd hate to die. But how do you suppose he'd feel if he killed himself?"

There shouldn't be silences like that. But it didn't last long. Somebody whimpered. Somebody shuffled. And then, in that voice I had heard here before, on the crazy day I saw the spider and the cat with hands, I heard a single syllable.

Starve a man for a day and a half, then put a piece of charcoal-crusted, juicy-pink steak in his mouth. Set out glasses of a rough red wine, and secretly substitute a vintage burgundy in one man's glass. Drop a silky mink over the shoulders of a shabby girl as she stands in front of a mirror. Do any of these things and you'll hear that sound, starting suddenly, falling in pitch, turning to a sigh, then a breath.

"M-m-m-m-m... !"

"You won't have long to take it, but it doesn't take long, does it?" asked Hank.

I thought, what the hell is he talking about? Who?

And then I pulled the gun out of my pocket.

233

Now I've got to talk about how much can run through a man's mind, how fast. In the time it took to raise the gun and aim it and pull the trigger, I thought:

It's Tom Conway he's been talking about to the parasite.

Hank wants the parasite to take me.

It's the parasite, not Hank, not I, who is raising this gun, aiming it.

This is Hank's way to avenge himself on me. And why vengeance? Only because I think differently from him. Doesn't Hank know that to me my thinking is right and needs no excuse?

And it's a stupid vengeance, because it's on Opie's behalf, and surely Opie wouldn't want it; certainly it can't benefit her.

The gun was aimed at my temple and I pulled the trigger.

I'm alive, I'm alive all over. Everybody has to die sometime, but oh, the stupid, stupid, sick realization that you did it to yourself! That you let yourself be killed, that you let your own finger tighten on the trigger.

A gunshot is staccato, sharp, short. This was different. This was a sound that started with a gunshot but sustained itself; it was a roar, it filled the world. It roared and roared while the room hazed over, spun, turned on its side as my cheek thumped the carpet. The roar went on and on while the light faded, and through it I could hear their screams, and Hank's voice, distant but clear. "Everybody out! This place is going to blow sky-high." "Fire!" he shouted a second later "Fire!" And, *"Beck, damn you, help me with Tom."*

Nothing then but a sense of time passing, then cool air, darkness, and a moment of lucidity I saw too clearly, heard too well. Everything hurt. The roar was still going on as a background, I heard the gunshot, tasted it bitterly, saw it as a flickering aurora in and of everything around me, smelled it acrid and sharp and felt it. I was on the gravel path, and frightened people poured out of the house.

"Stay with him!" Hank roared, and my head was cradled on Beck's trembling knees.

"But there is no fire—no fire," Beck quavered.

And Hank was a black bulk in blackness, and his voice was distant as he raced to the bushes. "Wait," he said. "Wait." He stooped back there, and there was a dull explosion inside the house, and another, and white light showed in the downstairs windows, turned to yellow, flickered and grew.

Hank came back. "There's a fire," he said.

Beck screamed. "You'll kill it!" He tried to rise. Hank caught his shirt and held him down.

"Yes, I'll kill it, you Judas!"

"You don't understand," Beck cried, "I can't live without it."

"Go back to your insurance company job. Make your own way, and don't harvest better people than yourself to feed monsters." Flames shot from the second-story windows. "But if you really can't live without it—die," said Hank, and then he shouted, "Is everybody out?"

"All accounted for," called a voice. I remember thinking then that if they had counted heads and all were safe—who was that screaming in the fire?

After that even the roar stopped.

First pain, and then enough light to filter through my closed lids. I tried to move my right hand and failed. I opened my eyes and saw the cast on my right forearm. I turned my head.

"Tom?"

I looked up at the speaking blur. Then it wasn't a blur, it was Hank.

"You're all right now, Tom. You're home. My house."

I turned from him and looked at the ceiling, the window, then back to him. "You tried to kill me," I said.

He shook his head. "I used you for bait. I had to know if it was in that room. I had to know if it would feed. I had to know what it could do, what it would do. I tried to shoot the gun out of your hand. I missed, and hit your forearm. It's broken. Your bullet creased your scalp. It was awful close, Tom."

"Suppose I'd killed myself?"

He said, "Bait is expendable."

"You booby-trapped the house, didn't you?"

"After your blow-by-blow instruction in burglary, it was no trouble."

"You tried to kill me," I said.

"I didn't," he said with finality.

I wondered—I really wondered—why what I had done was that important. And it was as if Hank read my mind. "It's because of the difference between you and Opie," he said. "Superficially, you and Opie did exactly the same thing that night.

"But Opie's own feelings about it will cost her something for the rest of her life. And you didn't even remember who you were with."

I lay there like a block of wood. Hank went away. Maybe I slept. Next thing I knew, Opie was there, kneeling by the bed.

"Tom," she said brokenly. "Oh, Tom. I wish I were dead. Tom," she said, "I'll spend the rest of my life making it up to you. . . ."

I thought, I wish that thing, whatever it was, hadn't died in the fire. I know what I am now, I thought. I'm immune. And knowing that gives me enough anguish to feed the likes of you for a thousand years.

Talent

MRS. BRENT AND PRECIOUS WERE SITTING on the farmhouse porch when little Jokey sidled out from behind the barn and came cat-footing up to them. Precious, who had ringlets and was seven years old and very clean, stopped swinging on the glider and watched him. Mrs. Brent was reading a magazine. Jokey stopped at the foot of the steps.

"MOM!" he rasped.

Mrs. Brent started violently, rocked too far back, bumped her knobby hairdo against the clapboards, and said, "Good heavens, you little br—darling, you frightened me!"

Jokey smiled.

Precious said, "Snaggletooth."

"If you want your mother," said Mrs. Brent reasonably, "why don't you go inside and speak to her?"

Disgustedly, Jokey vetoed the suggestion with "Ah-h-h ..." He faced the house. "MOM!" he shrieked, in a tone that spoke of death and disaster.

There was a crash from the kitchen, and light footsteps. Jokey's mother, whose name was Mrs. Purney, came out, pushing back a wisp of hair from frightened eyes.

"Oh, the sweet," she cooed. She flew out and fell on her knees beside Jokey. "Did it hurt its little, then? Aw, did it was ..."

Jokey said, "Gimme a nickel!"

"Please," suggested Precious.

"Of course, darling," fluttered Mrs. Purney. "My word, yes. Just as soon as ever we go into town, you shall have a nickel. Two, if you're good."

"Gimme a nickel," said Jokey ominously.

"But, darling, what for? What will you do with a nickel out here?"

Jokey thrust out his hand. "I'll hold my breath."

Mrs. Purney rose, panicked. "Oh, dear, don't. Oh, please don't. Where's my reticule?"

"On top of the bookcase, out of my reach," said Precious, without rancor.

"Oh, yes, so it is. Now, Jokey, you wait right here and I'll just . . ." and her twittering faded into the house.

Mrs. Brent cast her eyes upward and said nothing.

"You're a little stinker," said Precious.

Jokey looked at her with dignity. "Mom," he called imperiously.

Mrs. Purney came to heel on the instant, bearing a nickel.

Jokey, pointing with the same movement with which he acquired the coin, reported, "She called me a little stinker."

"Really!" breathed Mrs. Purney, bridling. "I think, Mrs. Brent, that your child could have better manners."

"She has, Mrs. Purney, and uses them when they seem called for."

Mrs. Purney looked at her curiously, decided, apparently, that Mrs. Brent meant nothing by the statement (in which she was wrong) and turned to her son, who was walking briskly back to the barn.

"Don't hurt yourself, Puddles," she called.

She elicited no response whatever and, smiling vaguely at Mrs. Brent and daughter, went back to her kitchen.

"Puddles," said Precious ruminatively. "I bet I know why she calls him that. Remember Gladys's puppy that—"

"Precious," said Mrs. Brent, "you shouldn't have called Joachim a word like that."

"I s'pose not," Precious agreed thoughtfully. "He's really a—"

Mrs. Brent, watching the carven pink lips, said warningly, "Precious!" She shook her head. "I've asked you not to say that."

"Daddy—"

"Daddy caught his thumb in the hinge of the car trunk. That was different."

"Oh, no," corrected Precious. "You're thinking of the time he opened on'y the bottom half of the Dutch door in the dark. When he pinched his thumb, he said—"

"Would you like to see my magazine?"

238

Precious rose and stretched delicately. "No, thank you, Mummy. I'm going out to the barn to see what Jokey's going to do with that nickel."

"Precious ..."

"Yes, Mummy."

"Oh—nothing. I suppose it's all right. Don't quarrel with Jokey, now."

"Not 'less he quarrels with me," she replied, smiling charmingly.

Precious had new patent leather shoes with hard heels and broad ankle-straps. They looked neat and very shiny against her yellow socks. She walked carefully in the path, avoiding the moist grasses that nodded over the edges, stepping sedately over a small muddy patch.

Jokey was not in the barn. Precious walked through, smelling with pleasure the mixed, warm smells of chaff-dust, dry hay and manure. Just outside, by the wagon door, was the pigpen. Jokey was standing by the rail fence. At his feet was a small pile of green apples. He picked one up and hurled it with all his might at the brown sow. It went *putt!* on her withers, and she went *ergh!*

"Hey!" said Precious.

Putt-ergh! Then he looked up at Precious, snarled silently, and picked up another apple. *Putt-ergh!*

"Why are you doing that for?"

Putt-ergh!

"Hear that? My mom done just like that when I hit her in the stummick."

"She did?"

"Now this," said Jokey, holding up an apple, "is a stone. Listen." He hurled it. *Thunk-e-e-e-ergh!*

Precious was impressed. Her eyes widened, and she stepped back a pace.

"Hey, look out where you're goin', stoopid!"

He ran to her and grasped her left biceps roughly, throwing her up against the railings. She yelped and stood rubbing her arm—rubbing off grime, and far deeper in indignation than she was in fright.

Jokey paid her no attention. "You an' your shiny feet," he growled. He was down on one knee, feeling for two twigs stuck in the ground about eight inches apart. "Y'might've squashed 'em!

Precious, her attention brought to her new shoes, stood turning one of them, glancing light from the toe-caps, from the burnished sides, while complacency flowed back into her.

"What?"

With the sticks, Jokey scratched aside the loose earth and, one by one, uncovered the five tiny, naked, blind creatures which lay buried there. They were only about three-quarters of an inch long, with little withered limbs and twitching noses. They writhed. There were ants, too. Very busy ants.

"What are they?"

"Mice, stoopid," said Jokey. "Baby mice. I found 'em in the barn."

"How did they get there?"

"I put 'em there."

"How long have they been there?"

"'Bout four days," said Jokey, covering them up again. "They last a long time."

"Does your mother know those mice are out here?"

"No, and you better not say nothin', ya hear?"

"Would your mother whip you?"

"*Her?*" The syllable came out as an incredulous jeer.

"What about your father?"

"Aw, I guess he'd like to lick me. But he ain't got a chance. Mom'd have a fit."

"You mean she'd get mad at him?"

"No, stoopid. A fit. You know, scrabbles at the air and get suds on her mouth, and all. Falls down and twitches." He chuckled.

"But—why?"

"Well, it's about the on'y way she can handle Pop, I guess. He's always wanting to do something about me. She won't let 'um, so I c'n do anything I want."

"What do you do?"

"I'm talunted. Mom says so."

"Well, what do you do?"

"You're sorta nosy."

"I don't believe you can do anything, stinky."

"Oh, I can't?" Jokey's face was reddening.

"No, you can't! You talk a lot, but you can't really do anything."

Jokey walked up close to her and breathed in her face the way the man with the grizzly beard does to the clean-cut cowboy who is tied up to the dynamite kegs in the movies on Saturday.

"I can't, huh?"

She stood her ground. "All right, if you're so smart, let's see what you were going to do with that nickel!"

Surprisingly, he looked abashed. "You'd laugh," he said.

"No, I wouldn't," she said guilelessly. She stepped forward, opened her eyes very wide, shook her head so that her gold ringlets swayed, and said very gently, "Truly I wouldn't, Jokey ..."

"Well—" he said, and turned to the pigpen. The brindled sow was rubbing her shoulder against the railing, grunting softly to herself. She vouchsafed them one small red-rimmed glance, and returned to her thoughts.

Jokey and Precious stood up on the lower rail and looked down on the pig's broad back.

"You're not goin' to tell anybody?" he asked.

"'Course not."

"Well, awright. Now lookit. You ever see a china piggy bank?"

"Sure I have," said Precious.

"How big?"

"Well, I got one about this big."

"Aw, that's nothin'."

"And my girl-friend Gladys has one *this* big."

"Phooey."

"Well," said Precious, "in town, in a big drugstore, I saw one THIS big," and she put out her hands about thirty inches apart.

"That's pretty big," admitted Jokey. "Now I'll show you *something.*" To the brindled sow, he said sternly, "You are a piggy bank."

The sow stopped rubbing herself against the rails. She stood quite still. Her bristles merged into her hide. She was hard and shiny—as shiny as the little girl's hard shoes. In the middle of the broad back, a slot appeared—or had been there all along, as far as Precious could tell. Jokey produced a warm sweaty nickel and dropped it into the slot.

There was a distant, vitreous, hollow bouncing click from inside the sow.

Mrs. Purney came out on the porch and creaked into a wicker chair with a tired sigh.

"They are a handful, aren't they?" said Mrs. Brent.

"You just don't know," moaned Mrs. Purney.

Mrs. Brent's eyebrows went up. "Precious is a model. Her teacher says so. That wasn't too easy to do."

"Yes, she's a very good little girl. But my Joachim is—talented, you know. That makes it very hard."

"How is he talented? What can he do?"

"He can do anything," said Mrs. Purney after a slight hesitation.

Mrs. Brent glanced at her, saw that her tired eyes were closed, and shrugged. It made her feel better. Why must mothers always insist that their children are better than all others?"

"Now, my Precious," she said, "—and mind you, I'm not saying this because she's my child—my Precious plays the piano very well for a child her age. Why, she's already in her third book and she's not eight yet."

Mrs. Purney said, without opening her eyes, "Jokey doesn't play. I'm sure he could if he wanted to."

Mrs. Brent saw what an inclusive boast this might be, and wisely refrained from further itemization. She took another tack. "Don't you find, Mrs. Purney, that it is easy to make a child obedient and polite by being firm?"

Mrs. Purney opened her eyes at last, and looked troubledly at Mrs. Brent. "A child should love its parents."

"Oh, of course!" smiled Mrs. Brent. "But these modern ideas of surrounding a child with love and freedom to an extent where it becomes a little tyrant—well! I just can't see that! Of course I don't mean Joachim," she added quickly, sweetly. "He's a *dear* child, really . . ."

"He's got to be given everything he wants," murmured Mrs. Purney in a strange tone. It was fierce and it was by rote. "He's *got* to be kept happy."

"You must love him very much," snapped Mrs. Brent viciously, suddenly determined to get some reaction out of this weak, indulgent creature. She got it.

"I hate him," said Mrs. Purney.

Her eyes were closed again, and now she almost smiled, as if the release of those words had been a yearned-for thing. Then she sat abruptly erect, her pale eyes round, and she grasped her lower lip and pulled it absurdly down and to the side.

"I didn't mean that," she gasped. She flung herself down before Mrs. Brent, and gabbled. "I didn't mean it! Don't tell him! He'll do things to us. He'll loosen the house-beams when we're sleeping. He'll turn the breakfast to snakes and frogs, and make that big toothy mouth again out of the oven door. Don't tell him! Don't tell him!"

Mrs. Brent, profoundly shocked, and not comprehending a word of this, instinctively put out her arms and gathered the other woman close.

"I can do lots of things," Jokey said. "I can do anything."

"Gee," breathed Precious, looking at the china pig. "What are you going to do with it now?"

"I dunno. I'll let it be a pig again, I guess."

"Can you change it back into a pig?"

"I don't hafta, stoopid. It'll be a pig by itself. Soon's I forget about it."

"Does that always happen?"

"No. If I busted that ol' china pig, it'd take longer, an' the pig would be all busted up when it changed back. All guts and blood," he added, sniggering. "I done that with a calf once."

"Gee," said Precious, still wide-eyed. "When you grow up you'll be able to do anything you want."

"Yeah." Jokey looked pleased. "But I can do anything I want now." He frowned. "I just sometimes don't know what to do next."

"You'll know when you grow up," she said confidently.

"Oh, sure. I'll live in a big house in town and look out of the windows, and bust up people and change 'em to ducks and snakes and things. I'll make flies as big as chicken hawks, or maybe as big as horses, and put 'em in the schools. I'll knock down the big buildings an' squash people."

He picked up a green apple and hurled it accurately at the brown sow.

"Gosh, and you won't have to practice piano, or listen to any old teachers," said Precious, warming to the possibilities. "Why, you won't even have to—*oh!*"

"What'sa matter?"

"That beetle. I hate them."

"Thass just a stag beetle," said Jokey with superiority. "Lookit here. I'll show you something."

He took out a book of matches and struck one. He held the beetle down with a dirty forefinger, and put the flame in its head. Precious watched attentively until the creature stopped scrabbling.

"Those things scare me," she said when he stood up.

"You're a sissy."

"I am not."

"Yes you are. *All* girls are sissies."

"You're dirty and you're a stinker," said Precious.

He promptly went to the pigpen and, from beside the trough, scooped up a heavy handful of filth. From his crouch, Jokey hurled it at her with a wide overhand sweep, so that it splattered her from the shoulder down, across the front of her dress, with a great wet gob for the toe of her left shiny shoe.

"Now who's dirty? Now who stinks?" he sang.

Precious lifted her skirt and looked at it in horror and loathing. Her eyes filled with angry tears. Sobbing, she rushed at him. She slapped him with little-girl clumsiness, hand-over-shoulder fashion. She slapped him again.

"Hey! Who are you hitting?" he cried in amazement. He backed off and suddenly grinned. "I'll fix you," he said, and disappeared without another word.

Whimpering with fury and revulsion, Precious pulled a handful of grass and began wiping her shoe.

Something moved into her field of vision. She glanced at it, squealed, and moved back. It was an enormous stag beetle, three times life-size, and it was scuttling toward her.

Another beetle—or the same one—met her at the corner.

With her hard black shiny shoes, she stepped on this one, so hard that the calf of her leg ached and tingled for the next half-hour.

The men were back when she returned to the house. Mr. Brent had been surveying Mr. Purney's fence lines. Jokey was not missed before they left. Mrs. Purney looked drawn and frightened, and seemed glad that Mrs. Brent was leaving before Jokey came in for his supper.

Precious said nothing when asked about the dirt on her dress, and, under the circumstances, Mrs. Brent thought better of questioning her too closely.

In the car, Mrs. Brent told her husband that she thought Jokey was driving Mrs. Purney crazy.

It was her turn to be driven very nearly mad, the next morning, when Jokey turned up. Most of him.

Surprising, really, how much beetle had stuck to the hard black shoe, and, when it was time, turned into what they found under their daughter's bed.

A Way of Thinking

I'LL HAVE TO START WITH AN ANECDOTE or two that you may have
heard from me before, but they'll bear repeating, since it's Kelley
we're talking about.

I shipped out with Kelley when I was a kid. Tankships, mostly
coastwise: load somewhere in the oil country—New Orleans, Aransas
Pass, Port Arthur, or some such—and unload at ports north of Hat-
teras. Eight days out, eighteen hours in, give or take a day or six
hours. Kelley was ordinary seaman on my watch, which was a laugh;
he knew more about the sea than anyone aft of the galley. But he
never ribbed me, stumbling around the place with my blue A.B.
ticket. He had a sense of humor in his peculiar quiet way, but he
never gratified it by proofs of the obvious—that he was twice the
seaman I could ever be.

There were a lot of unusual things about Kelley, the way he looked,
the way he moved; but most unusual was the way he thought. He
was like one of those extraterrestrials you read about who can think
as well as a human being but not *like* a human being.

Just for example, there was that night in Port Arthur. I was sitting in a honky-tonk up over a bar with a red-headed girl called Red,
trying to mind my own business while watching a chick known as
Boots, who sat alone over by the jukebox. This girl Boots was watching the door and grinding her teeth, and I knew why, and I was worried. See, Kelley had been seeing her pretty regularly, but this trip
he'd made the break and word was around that he was romancing
a girl in Pete's place—a very unpopular kind of rumor for Boots to
be chewing on. I also knew that Kelley would be along any minute
because he'd promised to meet me here.

And in he came, running up that long straight flight of steps easy
as a cat, and when he got in the door everybody just hushed, except

the jukebox, and it sounded scared.

Now, just above Boots' shoulder on a little shelf was an electric fan. It had sixteen-inch blades and no guard. The very second Kelley's face showed in the doorway, Boots rose up like a snake out of a basket, reached behind her, snatched that fan off the shelf and threw it.

It might as well have been done with a slow-motion camera as far as Kelley was concerned. He didn't move his feet at all. He bent sideways, just a little, from the waist, and turned his wide shoulders. Very clearly I heard three of those whining blade-tips touch a button on his shirt *bip-bip-bip!* and then the fan hit the doorpost.

Even the jukebox shut up then. It was *so* quiet. Kelley didn't say anything and neither did anyone else.

Now, if you believe in do-as-you-get-done-to, and someone heaves an infernal machine at you, you'll pick it right up and heave it back. But Kelley doesn't think like you. He didn't look at the fan. He just watched Boots, and she was white and crazed-looking, waiting for whatever he might have in mind.

He went across the room to her, fast but not really hurrying, and he picked her out from behind that table, and he threw her.

He threw her at the fan.

She hit the floor and slid, sweeping up the fan where it lay, hitting the doorjamb with her head, spinning out into the stairway. Kelley walked after her, stepped over her, went on downstairs and back to the ship.

And there was the time we shipped a new main spur gear for the starboard winch. The deck engineer used up the whole morning watch trying to get the old gear-wheel off its shaft. He heated the hub. He pounded it. He put in wedges. He hooked on with a handy-billy—that's a four-sheave block-and-tackle to you—and all he did with that was break a U-bolt.

Then Kelley came on deck, rubbing sleep out of his eyes, and took one brief look. He walked over to the winch, snatched up a crescent wrench, and relieved the four bolts that held the housing tight around the shaft. He then picked up a twelve-pound maul, hefted it, and swung it just once. The maul hit the end of the shaft and the shaft shot out of the other side of the machine like a torpedo out of its tube. The gearwheel fell down on the deck. Kelley went forward to take the helm and thought no more about it, while the deck crew stared after him, wall-eyed. You see what I mean! Problem: Get a wheel off a shaft. But in Kelly's book it's: Get the shaft out of the wheel.

I kibitzed him at poker one time and saw him discard two pair and draw a winning straight flush. Why that discard? Because he'd just realized the deck was stacked. Why the flush? God knows. All Kelley did was pick up the pot—a big one—grin at the sharper, and leave.

I have plenty more yarns like that, but you get the idea. The guy had a special way of thinking, that's all, and it never failed him.

I lost track of Kelley. I came to regret that now and then; he made a huge impression on me, and sometimes I used to think about him when I had a tough problem to solve. What would Kelley do? And sometimes it helped, and sometimes it didn't; and when it didn't, I guess it was because I'm not Kelley.

I came ashore and got married and did all sorts of other things, and the years went by, and a war came and went, and one warm spring evening I went into a place I know on West 48th St. because I felt like drinking tequila and I can always get it there. And who should be sitting in a booth finishing up a big Mexican dinner but—no, not Kelley.

It was Milton. He looks like a college sophomore with money. His suits are always cut just so, but quiet; and when he's relaxed he looks as if he's just been tagged for a fraternity and it matters to him, and when he's worried you want to ask him has he been cutting classes again. It happens he's a damn good doctor.

He was worried, but he gave me a good hello and waved me into the booth while he finished up. We had small talk and I tried to buy him a drink. He looked real wistful and then shook his head. "Patient in ten minutes," he said, looking at his watch.

"Then it's nearby. Come back afterward."

"Better yet," he said, getting up, "come with me. This might interest you, come to think of it."

He got his hat and paid Rudy, and I said, "Luego," and Rudy grinned and slapped the tequila bottle. Nice place, Rudy's.

"What about the patient?" I asked as we turned up the avenue. I thought for a while he hadn't heard me, but at last he said, "Four busted ribs and a compound femoral. Minor internal hemorrhage which might or might not be a ruptured spleen. Necrosis of the oral frenum—or was while there was any frenum left."

"What's a frenum?"

"That little strip of tissue under your tongue."

"Ongk," I said, trying to reach it with the tip of my tongue. "What a healthy fellow."

"Pulmonary adhesions," Milton ruminated. "Not serious, certainly not tubercular. But they hurt and they bleed and I don't like 'em. And acne rosacea."

"That's the nose like a stoplight, isn't it?"

"It isn't as funny as that to the guy that has it."

I was quelled. "What was it—a goon-squad?"

He shook his head.

"A truck?"

"No."

"He fell off something."

Milton stopped and turned and looked me straight in the eye. "No," he said. "Nothing like anything. Nothing," he said, walking again, "at all."

I said nothing to that because there was nothing to say.

"He just went to bed," said Milton thoughtfully, "because he felt off his oats. And one by one these things happened to him."

"In *bed?*"

"Well," said Milton, in a to-be-absolutely-accurate tone, "when the ribs broke he was on his way back from the bathroom."

"You're kidding."

"No I'm not."

"He's lying."

Milton said, "I believe him."

I know Milton. There's no doubt that he believed the man. I said, "I keep reading things about psychosomatic disorders. But a broken—what did you say it was?"

"Femur. Thigh, that is. Compound. Oh, it's rare, all right. But it can happen, has happened. These muscles are pretty powerful, you know. They deliver two-fifty, three-hundred-pound thrusts every time you walk up stairs. In certain spastic hysteriae, they'll break bones easily enough."

"What about all those other things?"

"Functional disorders, every one of 'em. No germ disease."

"Now this boy," I said, "*really* has something on his mind."

"Yes, he has."

But I didn't ask what. I could hear the discussion closing as if it had a spring latch on it.

We went into a door tucked between storefronts and climbed three flights. Milton put out his hand to a bell-push and then dropped it without ringing. There was a paper tacked to the door.

DOC I WENT FOR SHOTS COME ON IN.

It was unsigned. Milton turned the knob and we went in.

The first thing that hit me was the smell. Not too strong, but not the kind of thing you ever forget if you ever had to dig a slit trench through last week's burial pit. "That's the necrosis," muttered Milton. "Damn it." He gestured. "Hang your hat over there. Sit down. I'll be out soon." He went into an inner room, saying, "Hi, Hal," at the doorway. From inside came an answering rumble, and something twisted in my throat to hear it, for no voice which is that tired should sound that cheerful.

I sat watching the wallpaper and laboriously un-listening to those clinical grunts and the gay-weary responses in the other room. The wallpaper was awful. I remember a nightclub act where Reginald Gardiner used to give sound-effect renditions of wallpaper designs. This one, I decided, would run "Body to *weep* ... yawp, yawp; body to weep ... yawp, yawp," very faintly, with the final syllable a straining retch. I had just reached a particularly clumsy join where the paper utterly demolished its own rhythm and went "Yawp yawp body to *weep*" when the outer door opened and I leaped to my feet with the rush of utter guilt one feels when caught in an unlikely place with no curt and lucid explanation.

He was two long strides into the room, tall and soft-footed, his face and long green eyes quite at rest, when he saw me. He stopped as if on leaf springs and shock absorbers, not suddenly, completely controlled, and asked, "Who are you?"

"I'll be damned," I answered. "Kelley!"

He peered at me with precisely the expression I had seen so many times when he watched the little square windows on the one-armed bandits we used to play together. I could almost hear the tumblers, see the drums; not lemon . . . cherry . . . cherry . . . and *click!* this time but tankship . . . Texas . . . him! . . . and *click!* "I be *god*dam," he drawled, to indicate that he was even more surprised than I was. He transferred the small package he carried from his right hand to his left and shook hands. His hand went once and a half times around mine with enough left over to tie a half-hitch. "Where in time you been keepin' yourse'f? How'd you smoke me out?"

"I never," I said. (Saying it, I was aware that I always fell into the idiom of people who impressed me, to the exact degree of that impression. So I always found myself talking more like Kelley than Kelley's shaving mirror.) I was grinning so wide my face hurt. "I'm glad to see you." I shook hands with him again, foolishly. "I came with the doctor."

"You a doctor now?" he said, his tone prepared for wonders.

"I'm a writer," I said deprecatingly.

"Yeah, I heard," he reminded himself. His eyes narrowed; as of old, it had the effect of sharp-focusing a searchlight beam. "I heard!" he repeated, with deeper interest. "Stories. Gremlins and flyin' saucers an' all like that." I nodded. He said, without insult, "Hell of a way to make a living."

"What about you?"

"Ships. Some dry-dock. Tank cleaning. Compass adjustin'. For a while had a job holdin' a insurance inspector's head. You know."

I glanced at the big hands that could weld or steer or compute certainly with the excellence I used to know, and marveled that he found himself so unremarkable. I pulled myself back to here and now and nodded toward the inner room. "I'm holding you up."

"No you ain't. Milton, he knows what he's doin'. He wants me, he'll holler."

"Who's sick?"

His face darkened like the sea in scud-weather, abruptly and deep down. "My brother." He looked at me searchingly. "He's ..." Then he seemed to check himself. "He's sick," he said unnecessarily, and added quickly, "He's going to be all right, though."

"Sure," I said quickly.

I had the feeling that we were both lying and that neither of us knew why.

Milton came out, laughing a laugh that cut off as soon as he was out of range of the sick man. Kelley turned to him slowly, as if slowness were the only alternative to leaping on the doctor, pounding the news out of him. "Hello, Kelley. Heard you come in."

"How is he, Doc?"

Milton looked up quickly, his bright round eyes clashing with Kelley's slitted fierce ones. "You got to take it easy, Kelley. What'll happen to him if you crack up?"

"Nobody's cracking up. What do you want me to do?"

Milton saw the package on the table. He picked it up and opened it. There was a leather case and two phials. "Ever use one of these before?"

"He was a pre-med before he went to sea," I said suddenly.

Milton stared at me. "You two know each other?"

I looked at Kelley. "Sometimes I think I invented him."

Kelley snorted and thumped my shoulder. Happily I had one hand on a built-in china shelf. His big hand continued the motion and took the hypodermic case from the doctor. "Sterilize the shaft and needle," he said sleepily, as if reading. "Assemble without touching needle with fingers. To fill, puncture diaphragm and withdraw plunger. Squirt upward to remove air an' prevent embolism. Locate major vein in—"

Milton laughed. "Okay, okay. But forget the vein. Any place will do—it's subcutaneous, that's all. I've written the exact amounts to be used for exactly the symptoms you can expect. Don't jump the gun, Kelley. And remember how you salt your stew. Just because a little is good, it doesn't figure that a lot has to be better."

Kelley was wearing that sleepy inattention which, I remembered, meant only that he was taking in every single word like a tape recorder. He tossed the leather case gently, caught it. "Now?" he said.

"Not now," the doctor said positively. "Only when you have to."

Kelley seemed frustrated. I suddenly understood that he wanted to do something, build something, fight something. Anything but sit and wait for therapy to bring results. I said, "Kelley, any brother of yours is a—well, you know. I'd like to say hello, if it's all—"

Immediately and together Kelley and the doctor said loudly, "Sure, when he's on his feet," and "Better not just now, I've just given him a sedat—" And together they stopped awkwardly.

"Let's go get that drink," I said before they could flounder any more.

"Now you're talking. You too, Kelley. It'll do you good."

"Not me," said Kelley. "Hal—"

"I knocked him out," said the doctor bluntly. "You'll cluck around scratching for worms and looking for hawks till you wake him up, and he needs his sleep. Come on."

Painfully I had to add to my many mental images of Kelley the very first one in which he was indecisive. I hated it.

"Well," said Kelley, "let me go see."

He disappeared. I looked at Milton's face, and turned quickly away. I was sure he wouldn't want me to see that expression of sick pity and bafflement.

Kelley came out, moving silently as always. "Yeah, asleep," he said. "For how long?"

"I'd say four hours at least."

"Well all right." From the old-fashioned clothes tree he took a battered black engineer's cap with a shiny, crazed patent leather visor. I laughed. Both men turned to me, with annoyance, I thought.

On the landing outside I explained. "The hat," I said. "Remember? Tampico?"

"Oh," he grunted. He thwacked it against his forearm.

"He left it on the bar of this gin mill," I told Milton. "We got back to the gangplank and he missed it. Nothing would do but he has to go back for it, so I went with him."

"You was wearin' a tequila label on your face," Kelley said. "Kept tryin' to tell the taxi man you was a bottle."

"He didn't speak English."

Kelley flashed something like his old grin. "He got the idea."

"Anyway," I told Milton, "the place was closed when we got there. We tried the front door and the side doors and they were locked like Alcatraz. We made so much racket I guess if anyone was inside they were afraid to open up. We could see Kelley's hat in there on the bar. Nobody's *about* to steal that hat."

"It's a good hat," he said in an injured tone.

"Kelley goes into action," I said. "Kelley don't think like other people, you know, Milt. He squints through the window at the other wall, goes around the building, sets one foot against the corner stud, gets his fingers under the edge of that corrugated iron siding they use. 'I'll pry this out a bit,' he says. 'You slide in and get my hat.'"

"Corrugated was only nailed on one-by-twos," said Kelley.

"He gives one almighty pull," I chuckled, "and the whole damn side falls out of the building, I mean the second floor too. You never heard such a clap-o'-thunder in your life."

"I got my hat," said Kelley. He uttered two syllables of a laugh. "Whole second floor was a cathouse, an' the one single stairway come out with the wall."

"Taxi driver just took off. But he left his taxi. Kelley drove back. I couldn't. I was laughing."

"You was drunk."

"Well, *some,*" I said.

We walked together quietly, happily. Out of Kelley's sight, Milton thumped me gently on the ribs. It was eloquent and it pleased me. It said that it was a long time since Kelley had laughed. It was a long time since he had thought about anything but Hal.

I guess we felt it equally when, with no trace of humor ... more as if he had let my episode just blow itself out until he could be heard ... Kelley said, "Doc, what's with the hand?"

"It'll be all right," Milton said.

"You put splints."

Milton sighed. "All right, all right. Three fractures. Two on the middle finger and one on the ring."

Kelley said, "I saw they were swollen."

I looked at Kelley's face and I looked at Milton's, and I didn't like either, and I wished to God I were somewhere else, in a uranium mine maybe, or making out my income tax. I said, "Here we are. Ever been to Rudy's, Kelley?"

He looked up at the little yellow-and-red marquee. "No."

"Come on," I said. "Tequila."

We went in and got a booth. Kelley ordered beer. I got mad then and started to call him some things I'd picked up on waterfronts from here to Tierra del Fuego. Milton stared wall-eyed at me, and Kelley stared at his hands. After a while Milton began to jot some of it down on a prescription pad he took from his pocket. I was pretty proud.

Kelley gradually got the idea. If I wanted to pick up the tab and he wouldn't let me, his habits were those of *uno puñeto sin cojones* (which a Spanish dictionary will reliably misinform you means "a weakling without eggs"), and his affections for his forebears were powerful but irreverent. I won, and soon he was lapping up a huge combination plate of beef tostadas, chicken enchiladas, and pork tacos. He endeared himself to Rudy by demanding salt and lemon with his tequila and dispatching same with flawless ritual: hold the lemon between left thumb and forefinger, lick the back of the left hand, sprinkle salt on the wet spot, lift the tequila with the right, lick the salt, drink the tequila, bite the lemon. Soon he was imitating the German second mate we shipped out of Puerto Barrios one night, who ate fourteen green bananas and lost them and all his teeth over the side, in gummed gutturals which had us roaring.

But after that question about fractured fingers back there in the street, Milton and I weren't fooled any more, and though everyone tried hard and it was a fine try, none of the laughter went deep enough or stayed long enough, and I wanted to cry.

We all had a huge hunk of the Nesselrode pie made by Rudy's beautiful blond wife—pie you can blow off your plate by flapping a napkin . . . sweet smoke with calories. And then Kelley demanded to know what time it was and cussed and stood up.

"It's only been two hours," Milton said.

"I just as soon head home all the same," said Kelley. "Thanks."

"Wait," I said. I got a scrap of paper out of my wallet and wrote on it. "Here's my phone. I want to see you some more. I'm working for myself these days; my time's my own. I don't sleep much, so call me any time you feel like it."

He took the paper. "You're no good," he said. "You never were no good." The way he said it, I felt fine.

"On the corner is a newsstand," I told him. "There's a magazine called *Amazing* with one of my lousy stories in it."

"They print it on a roll?" he demanded. He waved at us, nodded to Rudy, and went out.

I swept up some spilled sugar on the tabletop and pushed it around until it was a perfect square. After a while I shoved in the sides until it was a lozenge. Milton didn't say anything either. Rudy, as is his way, had sense enough to stay away from us.

"Well, that did him some good," Milton said after a while.

"You know better than that," I said bitterly.

Milton said patiently. "Kelley thinks *we* think it did him some good. And thinking that does him good."

I had to smile at that contortion, and after that it was easier to talk. "The kid going to live?"

Milton waited, as if some other answer might spring from somewhere, but it didn't. He said, "No."

"Fine doctor."

"Don't kid like that!" he snapped. He looked up at me. "Look, if this was one of those—well, say pleurisy cases on the critical list, without the will to live, why I'd know what to do. Usually those depressed cases have such a violent desire to be reassured, down deep, that you can snap 'em right out of it if only you can think of the right thing to say. And you usually can. But Hal's not one of those. He wants to live. If he didn't want so much to live he'd've been dead three weeks ago. What's killing him is sheer somatic trauma—one broken bone after another, one failing or inflamed internal organ after another."

"Who's doing it?"

"Damn it, *no*body's doing it!" He caught me biting my lip. "If either one of us should say Kelley's doing it, the other one will punch him in the mouth. Right?"

"Right."

"Just so that doesn't have to happen," said Milton carefully, "I'll tell you what you're bound to ask me in a minute: why isn't he in a hospital?"

"Okay, why?"

"He was. For weeks. And all the time he was there these things kept on happening to him, only worse. More, and more often. I got him home as soon as it was safe to get him out of traction for that broken thigh. He's much better off with Kelley. Kelley keeps him cheered up, cooks for him, medicates him—the works. It's all Kelley does these days."

"I figured. It must be getting tough."

"It is. I wish I had your ability with invective. You can't lend that man anything, give him anything ... proud? God!"

"Don't take this personally, but have you had consultations?"

He shrugged. "Six ways from the middle. And nine-tenths of it behind Kelley's back, which isn't easy. The lies I've told him! Hal's just *got* to have a special kind of Persian melon that someone is receiving in a little store in Yonkers. Out Kelley goes, and in the meantime I have to corral two or three doctors and whip 'em in to see Hal and out again before Kelley gets back. Or Hal has to have a special prescription, and I fix up with the druggist to take a good two hours compounding it. Hal saw Grundage, the osteo man, that way, but poor old Ancelowics the pharmacist got punched in the chops for the delay."

"Milton, you're all right."

He snarled at me, and then went on quietly, "None of it's done any good. I've learned a whole encyclopedia full of wise words and some therapeutic tricks I didn't know existed. But ..." He shook his head. "Do you know why Kelley and I wouldn't let you meet Hal?" He wet his lips and cast about for an example. "Remember the pictures of Mussolini's corpse after the mob got through with it?"

I shuddered. "I saw 'em."

"Well, that's what he looks like, only he's alive, which doesn't make it any prettier. Hal doesn't know how bad it is, and neither Kelley nor I would run the risk of having him see it reflected in someone else's face. I wouldn't send a wooden Indian into that room."

I began to pound the table, barely touching it, hitting it harder and harder until Milton caught my wrist. I froze then, unhappily conscious of the eyes of everyone in the place looking at me. Gradually the normal sound of the restaurant resumed. "Sorry."

"It's all right."

"There's got to be some sort of reason!"

His lips twitched in a small acid smile. "That's what you get down to at last, isn't it? There's always a reason for everything, and if we don't know it, we can find it out. But just one single example of real unreason is enough to shake our belief in everything. And then the fear gets bigger than the case at hand and extends to a whole universe of concepts labeled 'unproven.' Shows you how little we believe in anything, basically."

"That's a miserable piece of philosophy!"

"Sure. If you have another arrival point for a case like this, I'll buy it with a bonus. Meantime I'll just go on worrying at this one, and feeling more scared than I ought to."

"Let's get drunk."

"A wonderful idea."

Neither of us ordered. We just sat there looking at the lozenge of sugar I'd made on the tabletop. After a while I said, "Hasn't Kelley any idea of what's wrong?"

"You know Kelley. If he had an idea he'd be working on it. All he's doing is sitting by watching his brother's body stew and swell like yeast in a vat."

"What about Hal?"

"He isn't lucid much any more. Not if I can help it."

"But maybe he—"

"Look," said Milton, "I don't want to sound cranky or anything, but I can't hold still for a lot of questions like . . ." He stopped, took out his display handkerchief, looked at it, put it away. "I'm sorry. You don't seem to understand that I didn't take this case yesterday afternoon. I've been sweating it out for nearly three months now. I've already thought of everything you're going to think of. Yes, I questioned Hal, back and forth and sideways. Nothing. N-n-nothing." That last word trailed off in such a peculiar way that I looked up abruptly. "Tell me," I demanded.

"Tell you what?" Suddenly he looked at his watch. I covered it with my hand. "Come on, Milt."

"I don't know what you're—damn it, leave me alone, will you? If it was anything important, I'd've chased it down long ago."

"Tell me the unimportant something."

"No."

"Tell me why you won't tell me."

"Damn you, I'll do that. It's because you're a crackpot. You're a nice guy and I like you, but you're a crackpot." He laughed suddenly, and it hit me like the flare of a flashbulb. "I didn't know you could look so astonished!" he said. "Now take it easy and listen to me. A guy comes out of a steak house and steps on a rusty nail, and ups and dies of tetanus. But your crackpot vegetarian will swear up and down that the man would still be alive if he hadn't poisoned his system with meat, and uses the death to prove his point. The perennial Dry will call the same casualty a victim of John Barleycorn if he knows the man had a beer with his steak. This one death can be ardently and wholeheartedly blamed on the man's divorce, his religion, his political affiliations or on a hereditary taint from his great-great-grandfather who worked for Oliver Cromwell. You're a nice guy and I like you," he said again, "and I am not going to sit across from you and watch you do the crackpot act."

"I do not know," I said slowly and distinctly, "what the hell you are talking about. And now you *have* to tell me."

"I suppose so," he said sadly. He drew a deep breath. "You believe what you write. No," he said quickly, "I'm not asking you, I'm telling you. You grind out all this fantasy and horror stuff and you believe every word of it. More basically, you'd rather believe in the *outré* and the so-called 'unknowable' than in what I'd call *real* things. You think I'm talking through my hat."

"I do," I said, "but go ahead."

"If I called you up tomorrow and told you with great joy that they'd isolated a virus for Hal's condition and a serum was on the way, you'd be just as happy about it as I would be, but way down deep you'd wonder if that was what was really wrong with him, or if the serum is what really cured him. If on the other hand I admitted to you that I'd found two small punctures on Hal's throat and a wisp of fog slipping out of the room—by God! see what I mean? You have a gleam in your eye already!"

I covered my eyes. "Don't let me stop you now," I said coldly. "Since you are not going to admit Dracula's punctures, what are you going to admit?"

"A year ago Kelley gave his brother a present. An ugly little brute of a Haitian doll. Hal kept it around to make faces at for a while and then gave it to a girl. He had bad trouble with the girl. She hates him—really hates him. As far as anyone knows she still has the doll. Are you happy now?"

"Happy," I said disgustedly. "But Milt—you're not just ignoring this doll thing. Why, that could easily be the whole basis of . . . hey, sit down! Where are you going?"

"I told you I wouldn't sit across from a damn hobbyist. Enter hobbies, exit reason." He recoiled. "Wait—*you* sit down now."

I gathered up a handful of his well-cut lapels. "We'll both sit down," I said gently, "or I'll prove to your heart's desire that I've reached the end of reason."

"Yessir," he said good-naturedly, and sat down. I felt like a damn fool. The twinkle left his eyes and he leaned forward. "Perhaps now you'll listen instead of riding off like that. I suppose you know that in many cases the voodoo doll does work, and you know why?"

"Well, yes. I didn't think you'd admit it." I got no response from his stony gaze, and at last realized that a fantasist's pose of authority on such matters is bound to sit ill with a serious and progressive physician. A lot less positively, I said, "It comes down to a matter of subjective reality, or what some people call faith. If you believe firmly that the mutilation of a doll with which you identify yourself will result in your own mutilation, well, that's what will happen."

"That, and a lot of things even a horror story writer could find out if he researched anywhere else except in his projective imagination. For example, there are Arabs in North Africa today whom you dare not insult in any way really important to them. If they feel injured, they'll threaten to die, and if you call the bluff they'll sit down, cover their heads, and damn well *die*. There are psychosomatic phenomena like the stigmata, or wounds of the cross, which appear from time to time on the hands, feet and breasts of exceptionally devout people. I know you know a lot of this," he added abruptly, apparently reading something in my expression, "but I'm not going to get my knee out of your chest until you'll admit I'm at least capable of taking a thing like this into consideration and tracking it down."

"I never saw you before in my life," I said, and in an important way I meant it.

"Good," he said, with considerable relief. "Now I'll tell you what I did. I jumped at this doll episode almost as wildly as you did. It came late in the questioning because apparently it *really didn't matter* to Hal."

"Oh, well, but the subconscious—"

"Shaddup!" He stuck a surprisingly sharp forefinger into my collarbone. "I'm telling you; you're not telling me. I won't disallow that a deep belief in voodoo might be hidden in Hal's subconscious, but if it is, it's where sodium amytal and word association and light and profound hypnosis and a half-dozen other therapies give not a smidgin of evidence. I'll take that as proof that he carries no such conviction. I guess from the looks of you I'll have to remind you again that I've dug into this thing in more ways for longer and with more tools than you have—and I doubt that it means any less to me than it does to you."

"You know, I'm just going to shut up," I said plaintively.

"High time," he said, and grinned. "No, in every case of voodoo damage or death, there has to be that element of devout belief in the powers of the witch or wizard, and through it a complete sense of identification with the doll. In addition, it helps if the victim knows what sort of damage the doll is sustaining—crushing, or pins sticking into it, or what. And you can take my word for it that no such news has reached Hal."

"What about the doll? Just to be absolutely sure, shouldn't we get it back?"

"I thought of that. But there's no way I know of getting it back without making it look valuable to the woman. And if she thinks it's valuable to Hal, we'll *never* see it."

"Hm. Who is she, and what's her royal gripe?"

"She's as nasty a piece of fluff as they come. She got involved with Hal for a little while—nothing serious, certainly not on his part. He was ... he's a big good-natured kid who thinks the only evil people around are the ones who get killed at the end of the movie. Kelley was at sea at the time and he blew in to find this little vampire taking Hal for everything she could, first by sympathy, then by threats. The old badger game. Hal was just bewildered. Kelley got his word that nothing had occurred between them, and then forced Hal to lower the boom. She called his bluff and it went to court. They forced a physical examination on her and she got laughed out of court. She wasn't the mother of anyone's unborn child. She never will be. She swore to get even with him. She's without brains or education or resources, but that doesn't stop her from being pathological. She sure can hate."

"Oh. You've seen her."

Milton shuddered. "I've seen her. I tried to get all Hal's gifts back from her. I had to say all because I didn't dare itemize. All I wanted, it might surprise you to know, was that damned doll. Just in case, you know ... although I'm morally convinced that the thing has nothing to do with it. Now do you see what I mean about a single example of unreason?"

"'Fraid I do." I felt upset and quelled and sat upon and I wasn't fond of the feeling. I've read too many stories where the scientist just hasn't the imagination to solve a haunt. It had been great, feeling superior to a bright guy like Milton.

We walked out of there, and for the first time I felt the mood of a night without feeling that an author was ramming it down my throat for story purposes. I looked at the clean-swept, star-reaching cubism of the Radio City area and its living snakes of neon, and I suddenly thought of an Evelyn Smith story the general idea of which was "After they found out the atom bomb was magic, the rest of the magicians who enchanted refrigerators and washing machines and the telephone system came out into the open." I felt a breath of wind and wondered what it was that had breathed. I heard the snoring of the city and for an awesome second felt it would roll over, open its eyes, and ... *speak.*

On the corner I said to Milton, "Thanks. You've given me a thumping around. I guess I needed it." I looked at him. "By the Lord I'd like to find some place where you've been stupid in this thing."

"I'd be happy if you could," he said seriously

I whacked him on the shoulder. "See? You take all the fun out of it."

He got a cab and I started to walk. I walked a whole lot that night, just anywhere. I thought about a lot of things. When I got home, the phone was ringing. It was Kelley.

I'm not going to give you a blow-by-blow of that talk with Kelley. It was in that small front room of his place—an apartment he'd rented after Hal got sick, and not the one Hal used to have—and we talked the night away. All I'm withholding is Kelley's expression of things you already know: that he was deeply attached to his brother, that he had no hope left for him, that he would find who or what was responsible and deal with it his way. It is a strong man's right to break down if he must, with whom and where he chooses, and such an occasion is only an expression of strength. But when it happens in a quiet sick place, where he must keep the command of hope strongly in the air; when a chest heaves and a throat must be held wide open to sob silently so that the dying one shall not know; these things are not pleasant to describe in detail. Whatever my ultimate feeling for Kelley, his emotions and the expressions of them are for him to keep.

He did, however, know the name of the girl and where she was. He did not hold her responsible. I thought he might have a suspicion, but it turned out to be only a certainty that this was no disease, no subjective internal disorder. If a great hate and a great determination could solve the problem, Kelley would solve it. If research and logic could solve it, Milton would do it. If I could do it, I would.

She was checking hats in a sleazy club out where Brooklyn and Queens, in a remote meeting, agree to be known as Long Island. The contact was easy to make. I gave her my spring coat with the label outward. It's a good label. When she turned away with it I called her back and drunkenly asked her for the bill in the right-hand pocket. She found it and handed it to me. It was a hundred. "Damn taxis never got change," I mumbled and took it before her astonishment turned to sleight-of-hand. I got out my wallet, crowded the crumpled note into it clumsily enough to display the two other C-notes there, shoved it into the front of my jacket so that it missed the pocket and fell to the floor, and walked off. I walked back before she could lift the hinged counter and skin out after it. I picked it up and smiled foolishly at her. "Lose more business cards that way," I said. Then I brought her into focus. "Hey, you know, you're cute."

I suppose "cute" is one of the four-letter words that describe her. "What's your name?"

"Charity," she said. "But don't get ideas." She was wearing so much pancake makeup that I couldn't tell what her complexion was. She leaned so far over the counter that I could see lipstick stains on her brassiere.

"I don't have a favorite charity yet," I said. "You work here alla time?"

"I go home once in a while," she said.

"What time?"

"One o'clock."

"Tell you what," I confided, "let's both be in front of this place at a quarter after and see who stands who up, okay?" Without waiting for an answer I stuck the wallet into my back pocket so that my jacket hung on it. All the way into the dining room I could feel her eyes on it like two hot, glistening, broiled mushrooms. I came within an ace of losing it to the head waiter when he collided with me, too.

She was there all right, with a yellowish fur around her neck and heels you could have driven into a pine plank. She was up to the elbows in jangly brass and chrome, and when we got into a cab she threw herself on me with her mouth open. I don't know where I got the reflexes, but I threw my head down and cracked her in the cheekbone with my forehead, and when she squeaked indignantly I said I'd dropped the wallet again and she went about helping me find it quietly as you please. We went to a place and another place and an after-hours place, all her choice. They served her sherry in her whiskeyponies and doubled all my orders, and tilted the checks something outrageous. Once I tipped a waiter eight dollars and she palmed the five. Once she wormed my leather notebook out of my breast pocket thinking it was the wallet, which by this time was safely tucked away in my knit shorts. She did get one enamel cuff link with a rhinestone in it, and my fountain pen. All in all it was quite a duel. I was loaded to the eyeballs with thiamin hydrochloride and caffeine citrate, but a most respectable amount of alcohol soaked through them, and it was all I could do to play it through. I made it, though, and blocked her at every turn until she had no further choice but to take me home. She was furious and made only the barest attempts to hide it.

We got each other up the dim dawn-lit stairs, shushing each other drunkenly, both much soberer than we acted, each promising what we expected not to deliver. She negotiated her lock successfully and waved me inside.

I hadn't expected it to be so neat. Or so cold. "I didn't leave that window open," she said complainingly. She crossed the room and closed it. She pulled her fur around her throat. "This is awful."

It was a long low room with three windows. At one end, covered by a venetian blind was a kitchenette. A door at one side of it was probably a bathroom.

She went to the venetian blind and raised it. "Have it warmed up in a jiffy," she said.

I looked at the kitchenette. "Hey," I said as she lit the little oven, "coffee. How's about coffee?"

"Oh, all right," she said glumly. "But talk quiet, huh?"

"Sh-h-h-h." I pushed my lips around with a forefinger. I circled the room. Cheap phonograph and records. Small-screen TV. A big double studio couch. A bookcase with no books in it, just china dogs.

It occurred to me that her unsubtle approach was probably not successful as often as she might wish.

But where was the thing I was looking for?

"Hey, I wanna powder my nose," I announced.

"In there," she said. "Can't you talk quiet?"

I went into the bathroom. It was tiny. There was a foreshortened tub with a circular frame over it from which hung a horribly cheerful shower curtain, with big red roses. I closed the door behind me and carefully opened the medicine chest. Just the usual. I closed it carefully so it wouldn't click. A built-in shelf held towels.

Must be a closet in the main room, I thought. Hatbox, trunk, suitcase, maybe. Where would I put a devil-doll if I were hexing someone?

I wouldn't hide it away, I answered myself. I don't know why, but I'd sort of have it out in the open somehow . . .

I opened the shower curtain and let it close. Round curtain, square tub.

"Yup!"

I pushed the whole round curtain back, and there in the corner, just at eye level, was a triangular shelf. Grouped on it were four figurines, made apparently from kneaded wax. Three had wisps of hair fastened by candle-droppings. The fourth was hairless, but had slivers of a horny substance pressed into the ends of the arms. Fingernail parings.

I stood for a moment thinking. Then I picked up the hairless doll, turned to the door. I checked myself, flushed the toilet, took a towel, shook it out, dropped it over the edge of the tub. Then I reeled out.

"Hey honey, look what I got, ain't it *cute?*"

"Shh!" she said. "Oh for crying out loud. Put that back, will you?"

"Well, what is it?"

"It's none of your business, that's what it is. Come on, put it back."

I wagged my finger at her. "You're not being nice to me," I complained.

She pulled some shreds of patience together with an obvious

effort. "It's just some sort of toys I have around. Here."

I snatched it away. "All right, you don't wanna be nice!" I whipped my coat together and began to button it clumsily, still holding the figurine.

She sighed, rolled her eyes, and came to me. "Come on, Dadsy. Have a nice cup of coffee and let's not fight." She reached for the doll and I snatched it away again.

"You got to tell me," I pouted.

"It's pers'nal."

"I wanna be personal," I pointed out.

"Oh all right," she said. "I had a roommate one time, she used to make these things. She said you make one, and s'pose I decide I don't like you, I got something of yours, hair or toenails or something. Say your name is George. What is your name?"

"George," I said.

"All right, I call the doll George. Then I stick pins in it. That's all. Give it to me."

"Who's this one?"

"That's Al."

"Hal?"

"Al. I got one called Hal. He's in there. I hate him the most."

"Yeah, huh. Well, what happens to Al and George and all when you stick pins in 'em?"

"They're s'posed to get sick. Even die."

"Do they?"

"Nah," she said with immediate and complete candor. "I told you, it's just a game, sort of. If it worked, believe me old Al would bleed to death. He runs the delicatessen." I handed her the doll, and she looked at it pensively. "I wish it did work, sometimes. Sometimes I almost believe in it. I stick 'em and they *just yell.*"

"Introduce me," I demanded.

"What?"

"Introduce me," I said. I pulled her toward the bathroom. She made a small irritated "oh-h," and came along.

"This is Fritz and this is Bruno and—where's the other one?"

"What other one?"

"Maybe he fell behind the—down back of—" She knelt on the edge of the tub and leaned over to the wall, to peer behind it. She regained her feet, her face red from effort and anger. "What are you trying to pull? You kidding around or something?"

I spread my arms. "What you mean?"

"Come on," she said between her teeth. She felt my coat, my jacket. "You hid it someplace."

"No I didn't. There was only four." I pointed. "Al and Fritz and Bruno and Hal. Which one's Hal?"

"That's Freddie. He give me twenny bucks and took twenny-three out of my purse, the dirty—. But Hal's gone. He was the best one of all. You *sure* you didn't hide him?" Then she thumped her forehead.

"The window!" she said, and ran into the other room. I was on my four bones peering under the tub when I understood what she meant. I took a last good look around and then followed her. She was standing by the window, shading her eyes and peering out. "What do you know. Imagine somebody would swipe a thing like that!"

A sick sense of loss was born in my solar plexus.

"Aw, forget it. I'll make another one for that Hal. But I'll never make another one that ugly," she added wistfully. "Come on, the coffee's—what's the matter? You sick?"

"Yeah," I said, "I'm sick."

"Of all the things to steal," she said from the kitchenette. "Who do you suppose would do such a thing?"

Suddenly I knew who would. I cracked my fist into my palm and laughed.

"What's the matter, you crazy?"

"Yes," I said. "You got a phone?"

"No. Where you going?"

"Out. Goodbye, Charity."

"Hey, now wait, honey. Just when I got coffee for you."

I snatched the door open. She caught my sleeve.

"You can't go away like this! How's about a little something for Charity?"

"You'll get yours when you make the rounds tomorrow, if you don't have a hangover from those sherry highballs," I said cheerfully. "And don't forget the five you swiped from the tip plate. Better watch out for that waiter, by the way. I think he saw you do it."

"You're not drunk'" she gasped.

"You're not a witch," I grinned. I blew her a kiss and ran out.

I shall always remember her like that, round-eyed, a little more astonished than she was resentful, the beloved dollar signs fading from her hot brown eyes, the pathetic, useless little twitch of her hips she summoned up as a last plea.

Ever try to find a phone booth at five A.M.? I half-trotted nine blocks before I found a cab, and I was on the Queens side of the Triboro Bridge before I found a gas station open.

I dialed. The phone said, "Hello?"

"Kelley!" I roared happily. "Why didn't you tell me? You'd 'a saved sixty bucks worth of the most dismal fun I ever—"

"This is Milton," said the telephone. "Hal just died."

My mouth was still open and I guess it just stayed that way. Anyway it was cold inside when I closed it. "I'll be right over."

"Better not," said Milton. His voice was shaking with incomplete control. "Unless you really want to . . . there's nothing you can do, and I'm going to be . . . busy."

"Where's Kelley?" I whispered.

"I don't know."

"Well," I said. "Call me."

I got back into my taxi and went home. I don't remember the trip.

Sometimes I think I dreamed I saw Kelley that morning.

A lot of alcohol and enough emotion to kill it, mixed with no sleep for thirty hours, makes for blackout. I came up out of it reluctantly, feeling that this was no kind of world to be aware of. Not today.

I lay looking at the bookcase. It was very quiet. I closed my eyes, turned over, burrowed into the pillow, opened my eyes again and saw Kelley sitting in the easy chair, poured out in his relaxed feline fashion, legs too long, arms too long, eyes too long and only partly open.

I didn't ask him how he got in because he was already in, and welcome. I didn't say anything because I didn't want to be the one to tell him about Hal. And besides I wasn't awake yet. I just lay there.

"Milton told me," he said. "It's all right."

I nodded.

Kelley said, "I read your story. I found some more and read them too. You got a lot of imagination."

He hung a cigarette on his lower lip and lit it. "Milton, he's got a lot of knowledge. Now, both of you think real good up to a point. Then too much knowledge presses him off to the no'theast. And too much imagination squeezes you off to the no'thwest."

He smoked a while.

"Me, I think straight through but it takes me a while."

I palmed my eyeballs. "I don't know what you're talking about."

"That's okay," he said quietly. "Look, I'm goin' after what killed Hal."

I closed my eyes and saw a vicious, pretty, empty little face. I said, "I was most of the night with Charity."

"Were you now."

"Kelley," I said, "if it's her you're after, forget it. She's a sleazy little tramp but she's also a little kid who never had a chance. She didn't kill Hal."

"I know she didn't. I don't feel about her one way or the other. I know what killed Hal, though, and I'm goin' after it the only way I know for sure."

"All right then," I said. I let my head dig back into the pillow. "What did kill him?"

"Milton told you about that doll Hal give her."

"He told me. There's nothing in that, Kelley. For a man to be a voodoo victim, he's got to believe that—"

"Yeah, yeah, yeah. Milton told me. For hours he told me."

"Well all right."

"You got imagination," Kelley said sleepily. "Now just imagine along with me a while. Milt tell you how some folks, if you point a gun at 'em and go bang, they drop dead, even if there was only blanks in the gun?"

"He didn't, but I read it somewhere. Same general idea."

"Now imagine all the shootings you ever heard of was like that, with blanks."

"Go ahead."

"You got a lot of evidence, a lot of experts, to prove about this believing business, ever' time anyone gets shot."

"Got it."

"Now imagine somebody shows up with live ammunition in his gun. Do you think those bullets going to give a damn who believes what?"

I didn't say anything.

"For a long time people been makin' dolls and stickin' pins in 'em. Wherever somebody believes it can happen, they get it. Now suppose somebody shows up with the doll all those dolls was copied from. The real one."

I lay still.

"You don't have to know nothin' about it," said Kelley lazily. "You don't have to be anybody special. You don't have to understand how it works. Nobody has to believe nothing. All you do, you just point it where you want it to work."

"Point it how?" I whispered.

He shrugged. "Call the doll by a name. Hate it, maybe."

"For God's sake, Kelley, you're crazy! Why, there can't be anything like that!"

"You eat a steak," Kelley said. "How's your gut know what to take and what to pass? Do *you* know?"

"Some people know."

"You don't. But your gut does. So there's lots of natural laws that are goin' to work whether anyone understands 'em or not. Lots of sailors take a trick at the wheel without knowin' how a steering engine works. Well, that's me. I know where I'm goin' and I know I'll get there. What do I care how does it work, or who believes what?"

"Fine, so what are you going to do?"

"Get what got Hal." His tone was just as lazy but his voice was very deep, and I knew when not to ask any more questions. Instead I said, with a certain amount of annoyance, "Why tell me?"

"Want you to do something for me."

"What?"

"Don't tell no one what I just said for a while. And keep something for me."

"What? And for how long?"

"You'll know."

I'd have risen up and roared at him if he had not chosen just that second to get up and drift out of the bedroom. "What gets me," he said quietly from the other room, "is I could have figured this out six months ago."

I fell asleep straining to hear him go out. He moves quieter than any big man I ever saw.

It was afternoon when I awoke. The doll was sitting on the mantelpiece glaring at me. Ugliest thing ever happened.

I saw Kelley at Hal's funeral. He and Milt and I had a somber drink afterward. We didn't talk about dolls. Far as I know Kelley shipped out right afterward. You assume that seamen do, when they drop out of sight. Milton was as busy as a doctor, which is very. I left the doll where it was for a week or two, wondering when Kelley was going to get around to his project. He'd probably call for it when he was ready. Meanwhile I respected his request and told no one about it. One day when some people were coming over I shoved it in the top shelf of the closet, and somehow it just got left there.

About a month afterward I began to notice the smell. I couldn't identify it right away; it was too faint; but whatever it was, I didn't like it. I traced it to the closet, and then to the doll. I took it down and sniffed it. My breath exploded out. It was that same smell a lot of people wish they could forget—what Milton called necrotic flesh. I came within an inch of pitching the filthy thing down the incinerator, but a promise is a promise. I put it down on the table, where it slumped repulsively. One of the legs was broken above the knee. I mean, it seemed to have two knee joints. And it was somehow puffy, sick-looking.

I had an old bell-jar somewhere, that once had a clock in it. I found it and a piece of inlaid linoleum, and put the doll under the jar at least so I could live with it.

I worked and saw people—dinner with Milton, once—and the days went by the way they do, and then one night it occurred to me to look at the doll again.

It was in pretty sorry shape. I'd tried to keep it fairly cool, but it seemed to be melting and running all over. For a moment I worried about what Kelley might say, and then I heartily damned Kelley and put the whole mess down in the cellar.

And I guess it was altogether two months after Hal's death that I wondered why I'd assumed Kelley would have to call for the little horror before he did what he had to do. He said he was going to get what got Hal, and he intimated that the doll was that something. He said he was going to get what got Hal, and he intimated that the doll was that something.

Well, that doll was being got, but good. I brought it up and put it under the light. It was still a figurine, but it was one unholy mess. "Attaboy, Kelley," I gloated. "Go get 'em, kid."

Milton called me up and asked me to meet him at Rudy's. He sounded pretty bad. We had the shortest drink yet.

He was sitting in the back booth chewing on the insides of his cheeks. His lips were gray and he slopped his drink when he lifted it.

"What in time happened to you?" I gasped.

He gave me a ghastly smile. "I'm famous," he said. I heard his glass chatter against his teeth. He said, "I called in so many consultants on Hal Kelley that I'm supposed to be an expert on that—on that . . . condition." He forced his glass back to the table with both hands and held it down. He tried to smile and I wished he wouldn't. He stopped trying and almost whimpered, "I can't nurse one of 'em like that again, I can't."

"You going to tell what happened?" I asked harshly. That works sometimes.

"Oh, oh yes. Well they brought in a . . . another one. At General. They called me in. Just like Hal. I mean *exactly* like Hal. Only I won't have to nurse this one, no I won't, I won't have to. She died six hours after she arrived."

"*She?*"

"You know what you'd have to do to someone to make them look like that?" he said shrilly. "You'd have to tie off parts so they mortified. You'd have to use a wood rasp, maybe; a club; filth to rub into the wounds. You'd have to break bones in a vise."

"All right, all right, but nobody—"

"And you'd have to do that for about two months, every day, every night." He rubbed his eyes. He drove his knuckles in so hard that I caught at his wrists. "I *know* nobody did it; did I say anyone did it?" he barked. "Nobody did anything to Hal, did they?"

"Drink up."

He didn't. He whispered, "She just said the same thing over and over every time anyone talked to her. They'd say, 'What happened?' or 'Who did this to you?' or 'What's your name?' and she'd say. 'He called me Dolly.' That's all she'd say, just 'He called me Dolly'."

I got up. "Bye, Milt."

He looked stricken. "Don't go, will you, you just got—"

"I got to go," I said. I didn't look back. I had to get out and ask myself some questions. Think.

Who's guilty of murder, I asked myself, the one who pulls the trigger, or the gun?

I thought of a poor damn pretty, empty little face with greedy hot brown eyes, and what Kelley said, "I don't care about her one way or the other."

I thought, when she was twisting and breaking and sticking, how did it look to the doll? Bet she never even wondered about that.

I thought, action: A girl throws a fan at a man. Reaction: The man throws the girl at the fan. Action: A wheel sticks on a shaft. Reaction: Knock the shaft out of the wheel. Situation: We can't get inside. Resolution: Take the outside off it.

It's a way of thinking.

How do you kill a person? Use a doll.

How do you kill a doll?

Who's guilty, the one who pulls the trigger, or the gun?

"He called me Dolly."

"He called me Dolly."

"He called me Dolly."

When I got home, the phone was ringing.

"Hi," said Kelley.

I said, "It's all gone. The doll's all gone. Kelley," I said, "stay away from me."

"All right," said Kelley.

The Silken-Swift

THERE'S A VILLAGE BY THE BOGS, and in the village is a Great House. In the Great House lived a squire who had land and treasures and, for a daughter, Rita.

In the village lived Del, whose voice was a thunder in the inn when he drank there; whose corded, cabled body was golden-skinned, and whose hair flung challenges back to the sun.

Deep in the Bogs, which were brackish, there was a pool of purest water, shaded by willows and wide-wondering aspen, cupped by banks of a moss most marvelously blue. Here grew mandrake, and there were strange pipings in midsummer. No one ever heard them but a quiet girl whose beauty was so very contained that none of it showed. Her name was Barbara.

There was a green evening, breathless with growth, when Del took his usual way down the lane beside the manor and saw a white shadow adrift inside the tall iron pickets. He stopped, and the shadow approached, and became Rita. "Slip around to the gate," she said, "and I'll open it for you."

She wore a gown like a cloud and a silver circlet round her head. Night was caught in her hair, moonlight in her face, and in her great eyes, secrets swam.

Del said, "I have no business with the squire."

"He's gone," she said. "I've sent the servants away. Come to the gate."

"I need no gate." He leaped and caught the top bar of the fence, and in a continuous fluid motion went high and across and down beside her. She looked at his arms, one, the other; then up at his hair. She pressed her small hands tight together and made a little laugh, and then she was gone through the tailored trees, lightly, swiftly, not looking back. He followed, one step for three of hers, keeping pace with a new pounding in the sides of his neck. They crossed a flower-bed and a wide marble terrace. There was an open door, and when he passed through it he stopped, for she was nowhere in sight. Then the door clicked shut behind him and he whirled. She was there, her back to the panel, laughing up at him in the dimness. He thought she would come to him then, but instead she twisted by, close, her eyes on his. She smelt of violets and sandalwood. He followed her into a great hall, quite dark but full of the subdued lights of polished wood, cloisonné, tooled leather and gold-threaded tapestry. She flung open another door, and they were in a small room with a carpet made of rosy silences, and a candle-lit table. Two places were set, each with five different crystal glasses and old silver as prodigally used as the iron pickets outside. Six teakwood steps rose to a great oval window. "The moon," she said, "will rise for us there."

She motioned him to a chair and crossed to a sideboard, where there was a rack of decanters—ruby wine and white; one with a strange brown bead; pink, and amber. She took down the first and poured. Then she lifted the silver domes from the salvers on the table, and a magic of fragrance filled the air. There were smoking sweets and savories, rare seafood and slivers of fowl, and morsels of strange meat wrapped in flower petals, spitted with foreign fruits and tiny soft seashells. All about were spices, each like a separate voice in the distant murmur of a crowd: saffron and sesame, cumin and marjoram and mace.

And all the while Del watched her in wonder, seeing how the candles left the moonlight in her face, and how completely she trusted her hands, which did such deftness without supervision—so composed she was, for all the silent secret laughter that tugged at her lips, for all the bright dark mysteries that swirled and swam within her.

They ate, and the oval window yellowed and darkened while the candlelight grew bright. She poured another wine, and another, and with the courses of the meal they were as May to the crocus and as frost to the apple.

Del knew it was alchemy and he yielded to it without question. That which was purposely over-sweet would be piquantly cut; this induced thirst would, with exquisite timing, be quenched. He knew she was watching him; he knew she was aware of the heat in his cheeks and the tingle at his fingertips. His wonder grew, but he was not afraid.

In all this time she spoke hardly a word; but at last the feast was over and they rose. She touched a silken rope on the wall, and paneling slid aside. The table rolled silently into some ingenious recess and the panel returned. She waved him to an L-shaped couch in one corner, and as he sat close to her, she turned and took down the lute which hung on the wall behind her. He had his moment of confusion; his arms were ready for her, but not for the instrument as well. Her eyes sparkled, but her composure was unshaken.

Now she spoke, while her fingers strolled and danced on the lute, and her words marched and wandered in and about the music. She had a thousand voices, so that he wondered which of them was truly hers. Sometimes she sang; sometimes it was a wordless crooning. She seemed at times remote from him, puzzled at the turn the music was taking, and at other times she seemed to hear the pulsing roar in his eardrums, and she played laughing syncopations to it. She sang words which he almost understood:

> *Bee to blossom, honey dew,*
> *Claw to mouse, and rain to tree,*
> *Moon to midnight' I to you;*
> *Sun to starlight, you to me ...*

and she sang something wordless:

> *Ake ya rundefle, rundefle fye,*
> *Ore! ya rundefie kown,*
> *En yea, en yea, ya bunderbee bye*
> *En sor, en see, en sown.*

which he also almost understood.

In still another voice she told him the story of a great hairy spider and a little pink girl who found it between the leaves of a half-open book; and at first he was all fright and pity for the girl, but then she went on to tell of what the spider suffered, with his home disrupted by this yawping giant, and so vividly did she tell of it that at the end he was laughing at himself and all but crying for the poor spider.

So the hours slipped by, and suddenly, between songs, she was in his arms; and in the instant she had twisted up and away from him, leaving him gasping. She said, in still a new voice, sober and low, "No, Del. We must wait for the moon."

His thighs ached and he realized that he had half-risen, arms out, hands clutching and feeling the extraordinary fabric of her gown though it was gone from them; and he sank back to the couch with an odd, faint sound that was wrong for the room. He flexed his fingers and, reluctantly, the sensation of white gossamer left them. At last he looked across at her and she laughed and leapt high lightly, and it was as if she stopped in midair to stretch for a moment before she alighted beside him, bent and kissed his mouth, and leapt away.

The roaring in his ears was greater, and at this it seemed to acquire a tangible weight. His head bowed; he tucked his knuckles into the upper curve of his eye sockets and rested his elbows on his knees. He could hear the sweet sussurrus of Rita's gown as she moved about the room; he could sense the violets and sandalwood. She was dancing, immersed in the joy of movement and of his nearness. She made her own music, humming, sometimes whispering to the melodies in her mind.

And at length he became aware that she had stopped; he could hear nothing, though he knew she was still near. Heavily he raised his head. She was in the center of the room, balanced like a huge white moth, her eyes quite dark now with their secrets quiet. She was staring at the window, poised, waiting.

He followed her gaze. The big oval was black no longer, but dusted over with silver light. Del rose slowly. The dust was a mist, a loom, and then, at one edge, there was a shard of the moon itself creeping and growing.

Because Del stopped breathing, he could hear her breath; it was rapid and so deep it faintly strummed her versatile vocal cords.

"Rita . . ."

Without answering she ran to the sideboard and filled two small glasses. She gave him one, then, "Wait," she breathed, "oh, wait!"

Spellbound, he waited while the white stain crept across the window. He understood suddenly that he must be still until the great oval was completely filled with direct moonlight, and this helped him, because it set a foreseeable limit to his waiting; and it hurt him, because nothing in life, he thought, had ever moved so slowly. He had a moment of rebellion, in which he damned himself for falling in with her complex pacing; but with it he realized that now the darker silver was wasting away, now it was a finger's breadth, and now a thread, and now, and *now*—.

She made a brittle feline cry and sprang up the dark steps to the window. So bright was the light that her body was a jet cameo against it. So delicately wrought was her gown that he could see the epaulettes of silver light the moon gave her. She was so beautiful his eyes stung.

"Drink," she whispered. "Drink with me, darling, darling ..."

For an instant he did not understand her at all, and only gradually did he become aware of the little glass he held. He raised it toward her and drank. And of all the twists and titillations of taste he had had this night, this was the most startling; for it had no taste at all, almost no substance, and a temperature almost exactly that of blood. He looked stupidly down at the glass and back up at the girl. He thought that she had turned about and was watching him, though he could not be sure, since her silhouette was the same.

And then he had his second of unbearable shock, for the light went out.

The moon was gone, the window, the room, Rita was gone.

For a stunned instant he stood tautly, stretching his eyes wide. He made a sound that was not a word. He dropped the glass and pressed his palms to his eyes, feeling them blink, feeling the stiff silk of his lashes against them. Then he snatched the hands away, and it was still dark, and more than dark; this was not a blackness. This was like trying to see with an elbow or with a tongue; it was not black, it was *Nothingness*.

He fell to his knees.

Rita laughed.

An odd, alert part of his mind seized on the laugh and understood it, and horror and fury spread through his whole being; for this was the laugh which had been tugging at her lips all evening, and it was a hard, cruel, self-assured laugh. And at the same time, because of the anger or in spite of it, desire exploded whitely within him. He moved toward the sound, groping, mouthing. There was a quick, faint series of rustling sounds from the steps, and then a light, strong web fell around him. He struck out at it, and recognized it for the unforgettable thing it was—her robe. He caught at it, ripped it, stamped upon it. He heard her bare feet run lightly down and past him, and lunged, and caught nothing. He stood, gasping painfully.

She laughed again.

"I'm blind," he said hoarsely. "Rita, I'm blind!"

"I know," she said coolly, close beside him. And again she laughed.

"What have you done to me?"

"I've watched you be a dirty animal of a man," she said.

He grunted and lunged again. His knees struck something—a chair, a cabinet—and he fell heavily. He thought he touched her foot.

"Here, lover, here!" she taunted.

He fumbled about for the thing which had tripped him, found it, used it to help him upright again. He peered uselessly about.

"Here, lover!"

He leaped, and crashed into the doorjamb: cheekbone, collarbone, hip bone, ankle were one straight blaze of pain. He clung to the polished wood.

After a time he said, in agony, "Why?"

"No man has ever touched me and none ever will," she sang. Her breath was on his cheek. He reached and touched nothing, and then he heard her leap from her perch on a statue's pedestal by the door, where she had stood high and leaned over to speak.

No pain, no blindness, not even the understanding that it was her witch's brew working in him could quell the wild desire he felt at her nearness. Nothing could tame the fury that shook him as she laughed. He staggered after her, bellowing.

She danced around him, laughing. Once she pushed him into a clattering rack of fire irons. Once she caught his elbow from behind and spun him. And once, incredibly, she sprang past him and, in midair, kissed him again on the mouth.

He descended into Hell, surrounded by the small, sure patter of bare feet and sweet cool laughter. He rushed and crashed, he crouched and bled and whimpered like a hound. His roaring and blundering took an echo, and that must have been the great hall. Then there were walls that seemed more than unyielding; they struck back. And there were panels to lean against, gasping, which became opening doors as he leaned. And always the black nothingness, the writhing temptation of the pat-pat of firm flesh on smooth stones, and the ravening fury.

It was cooler, and there was no echo. He became aware of the whisper of the wind through trees. The balcony, he thought; and then, right in his ear, so that he felt her warm breath, "Come, lover . . ." and he sprang. He sprang and missed, and instead of sprawling on the terrace, there was nothing, and nothing, and nothing, and then, when he least expected it, a shower of cruel thumps as he rolled down the marble steps.

He must have had a shred of consciousness left, for he was vaguely aware of the approach of her bare feet, and of the small, cautious hand that touched his shoulder and moved to his mouth, and then his chest. Then it was withdrawn, and either she laughed or the sound was still in his mind.

Deep in the Bogs, which were brackish, there was a pool of purest water, shaded by willows and wide-wondering aspens, cupped by banks of a moss most marvelously blue. Here grew mandrake, and there were strange pipings in mid-summer. No one ever heard them but a quiet girl whose beauty was so very contained that none of it showed. Her name was Barbara.

No one noticed Barbara, no one lived with her, no one cared. And Barbara's life was very full, for she was born to receive. Others are born wishing to receive, so they wear bright masks and make attractive sounds like cicadas and operettas, so others will be forced, one way or another, to give to them. But Barbara's receptors were wide open, and always had been, so that she needed no substitute for sunlight through a tulip petal, or the sound of morning-glories climbing, or the tangy sweet smell of formic acid which is the only death cry possible to an ant, or any other of the thousand things overlooked by folk who can only wish to receive. Barbara had a garden and an orchard, and took things in to market when she cared to, and the rest of the time she spent in taking what was given. Weeds grew in her garden, but since they were welcomed, they grew only where they could keep the watermelons from being sunburned. The rabbits were welcome, so they kept to the two rows of carrots, the one of lettuce, and the one of tomato vines which were planted for them, and they left the rest alone. Goldenrod shot up beside the bean hills to lend a hand upward, and the birds ate only the figs and peaches from the waviest top branches, and in return patrolled the lower ones for caterpillars and egg-laying flies. And if a fruit stayed green for two weeks longer until Barbara had time to go to market, or if a mole could channel moisture to the roots of the corn, why it was the least they could do.

For a brace of years Barbara had wandered more and more, impelled by a thing she could not name—if indeed she was aware of it at all. She knew only that over-the-rise was a strange and friendly place, and that it was a fine thing on arriving there to find another rise to go over. It may very well be that she now needed someone to love, for loving is a most receiving thing, as anyone can attest who has been loved without returning it. It is the one who is loved who must give and give. And she found her love, not in her wandering, but at the market. The shape of her love, his colors and sounds, were so much with her that when she saw him first it was without surprise; and thereafter, for a very long while, it was quite enough that he lived. He gave to her by being alive, by setting the air athrum with his mighty voice, by his stride, which was, for a man afoot, the exact analog of what the horseman calls a "perfect seat."

After seeing him, of course, she received twice and twice again as much as ever before. A tree was straight and tall for the magnificent sake of being straight and tall, but wasn't straightness a part of him, and being tall? The oriole gave more now than song, and the hawk more than walking the wind, for had they not hearts like his, warm blood and his same striving to keep it so for tomorrow?

And more and more, over-the-rise was the place for her, for only there could there be more and still more things like him.

But when she found the pure pool in the brackish Bogs, there was no more over-the-rise for her. It was a place without hardness or hate, where the aspens trembled only for wonder, and where all contentment was rewarded. Every single rabbit there was *the* champion nose-twinkler, and every waterbird could stand on one leg the longest, and proud of it. Shelf-fungi hung to the willow-trunks, making that certain, single purple of which the sunset is incapable, and a tanager and a cardinal gravely granted one another his definition of "red."

Here Barbara brought a heart light with happiness, large with love, and set it down on the blue moss. And since the loving heart can receive more than anything else, so it is most needed, and Barbara took the best bird songs, and the richest colors, and the deepest peace, and all the other things which are most worth giving. The chipmunks brought her nuts when she was hungry and the prettiest stones when she was not. A green snake explained to her, in pantomime, how a river of jewels may flow uphill, and three mad otters described how a bundle of joy may slip and slide down and down and be all the more joyful for it. And there was the magic moment when a midge hovered, and then a honeybee, and then a bumblebee, and at last a hummingbird; and there they hung, playing a chord in A sharp minor.

Then one day the pool fell silent, and Barbara learned why the water was pure.

The aspens stopped trembling.

The rabbits all came out of the thicket and clustered on the blue bank, backs straight, ears up, and all their noses as still as coral.

The waterbirds stepped backwards, like courtiers, and stopped on the brink with their heads turned sidewise, one eye closed, the better to see with the other.

The chipmunks respectfully emptied their cheek pouches, scrubbed their paws together and tucked them out of sight; then stood still as tent pegs.

The pressure of growth around the pool ceased: the very grass waited.

The last sound of all to be heard—and by then it was very quiet—was the soft *whick!* of an owl's eyelids as it awoke to watch.

He came like a cloud, the earth cupping itself to take each of his golden hooves. He stopped on the bank and lowered his head, and for a brief moment his eyes met Barbara's, and she looked into a second universe of wisdom and compassion. Then there was the arch of the magnificent neck, the blinding flash of his golden horn.

And he drank, and he was gone. Everyone knows the water is pure, where the unicorn drinks.

How long had he been there? How long gone? Did time wait too, like the grass?

"And couldn't he stay?" she wept. "Couldn't he stay?"

To have seen the unicorn is a sad thing; one might never see him more. But then—to have seen the unicorn!

She began to make a song

It was late when Barbara came in from the Bogs, so late the moon was bleached with cold and fleeing to the horizon. She struck the high road just below the Great House and turned to pass it and go out to her garden house.

Near the locked main gate an animal was barking. A sick animal, a big animal. . . .

Barbara could see in the dark better than most, and soon saw the creature clinging to the gate, climbing, uttering that coughing moan as it went. At the top it slipped, fell outward, dangled; then there was a ripping sound, and it fell heavily to the ground and lay still and quiet.

She ran to it, and it began to make the sound again. It was a man, and he was weeping.

It was her love, her love who was tall and straight and so very alive—her love, battered and bleeding, puffy, broken, his clothes torn, crying.

Now of all times was the time for a lover to receive, to take from the loved one his pain, his trouble, his fear. "Oh, hush, hush," she whispered, her hands touching his bruised face like swift feathers. "It's all over now. It's all over."

She turned him over on his back and knelt to bring him up sitting. She lifted one of his thick arms around her shoulder. He was very heavy, but she was very strong. When he was upright, gasping weakly, she looked up and down the road in the waning moonlight. Nothing, no one. The Great House was dark. Across the road, though, was a meadow with high hedgerows which might break the wind a little.

"Come, my love, my dear love," she whispered. He trembled violently.

All but carrying him, she got him across the road, over the shallow ditch, and through a gap in the hedge. She almost fell with him there. She gritted her teeth and set him down gently. She let him lean against the hedge, and then ran and swept up great armfuls of sweet broom. She made a tight springy bundle of it and set it on the ground beside him, and put a corner of her cloak over it, and gently lowered his head until it was pillowed. She folded the rest of the cloak about him. He was very cold.

There was no water near, and she dared not leave him. With her kerchief she cleaned some of the blood from his face. He was still very cold. He said, "You devil. You rotten little devil."

"Shh." She crept in beside him and cradled his head. "You'll be warm in a minute."

"Stand still," he growled. "Keep running away."

"I won't run away," she whispered. "Oh, my darling, you've been hurt, so hurt. I won't leave you. I promise I won't leave you."

He lay very still. He made the growling sound again.

"I'll tell you a lovely thing," she said softly. "Listen to me, think about the lovely thing," she crooned.

"There's a place in the bog, a pool of pure water, where the trees live beautifully, willow and aspen and birch, where everything is peaceful, my darling, and the flowers grow without tearing their petals. The moss is blue and the water is like diamonds."

"You tell me stories in a thousand voices," he muttered.

"Shh. Listen, my darling. This isn't a story, it's a real place. Four miles north and a little west, and you can see the trees from the ridge with the two dwarf oaks. And I know why the water is pure!" she cried gladly. "I know why!"

He said nothing. He took a deep breath and it hurt him, for he shuddered painfully.

"The unicorn drinks there," she whispered. "I *saw* him!"

Still he said nothing. She said, "I made a song about it. Listen, this is the song I made:

> *And He — suddenly gleamed! My dazzled eyes*
> *Coming from outer sunshine to this green*
> *And secret gloaming, met without surprise*
> *The vision. Only after, when the sheen*
> *And splendor of his going fled away,*
> *I knew amazement, wonder and despair,*
> *That he should come — and pass — and would not stay,*
> *The Silken-swift — the gloriously Fair!*
> *That he should come — and pass — and would not stay,*
> *So that, forever after, I must go,*
> *Take the long road that mounts against the day,*
> *Travelling in the hope that I shall know*
> *Again that lifted moment, high and sweet,*
> *Somewhere — on purple moor or windy hill —*
> *Remembering still his wild and delicate feet,*
> *The magic and the dream — remembering still!*

His breathing was more regular. She said, "I truly saw him!"

"I'm blind," he said. "Blind, I'm blind."

"Oh, my dear . . ."

He fumbled for her hand, found it. For a long moment he held it. Then, slowly, he brought up his other hand and with them both he felt her hand, turned it about, squeezed it. Suddenly he grunted, half-sitting. "You're here!"

"Of course, darling. Of course I'm here."

"Why?" he shouted. "Why? *Why?* Why all of this? Why blind me?" He sat up, mouthing, and put his great hand on her throat. "Why do all that if . . ." The words ran together into an animal noise. Wine and witchery, anger and agony boiled in his veins.

Once she cried out.

Once she sobbed.

"Now," he said, "you'll catch no unicorns. Get away from me." He cuffed her.

"You're mad. You're sick," she cried.

"Get away," he said ominously.

Terrified, she rose. He took the cloak and hurled it after her. It almost toppled her as she ran away, crying silently.

After a long time, from behind the hedge, the sick, coughing sobs began again.

Three weeks later Rita was in the market when a hard hand took her upper arm and pressed her into the angle of a cottage wall. She did not start. She flashed her eyes upward and recognized him, and then said composedly, "Don't touch me."

"I need you to tell me something," he said. "And tell me you *will!*" His voice was as hard as his hand.

"I'll tell you anything you like," she said. "But don't touch me."

He hesitated, then released her. She turned to him casually. "What is it?" Her gaze darted across his face and its almost healed scars. The small smile tugged at one corner of her mouth.

His eyes were slits. "I have to know this: why did you make up all that ... prettiness, that food, that poison ... just for me? You could have had me for less."

She smiled. "Just for you? It was your turn, that's all."

He was genuinely surprised. "It's happened before?"

She nodded. "Whenever it's the full of the moon—and the squire's away."

"You're lying!"

"You forget yourself!" she said sharply. Then, smiling, "It is the truth, though."

"I'd've heard talk—"

"Would you now? And tell me—how many of your friends know about your humiliating adventure?"

He hung his head.

She nodded. "You see? They go away until they're healed, and they come back and say nothing. And they always will."

"You're a devil ... why do you do it? Why?"

"I told you," she said openly. "I'm a woman and I act like a woman in my own way. No man will ever touch me, though. I am virgin and shall remain so."

"You're *what?*" he roared.

She held up a restraining, ladylike glove. "Please," she said, pained.

"Listen," he said, quietly now, but with such intensity that for once she stepped back a pace. He closed his eyes, thinking hard. "You told me—the pool, the pool of the unicorn, and a song, wait. 'The Silken-swift, the gloriously Fair ...' Remember? And then I— I saw to it that *you'd* never catch a unicorn!"

She shook her head, complete candor in her face. "I like that, 'the Silken-swift.' Pretty. But believe me—no! That isn't mine."

He put his face close to hers, and though it was barely a whisper, it came out like bullets. "Liar! Liar! I couldn't forget. I was sick, I was hurt, I was poisoned, but I know what I did!" He turned on his heel and strode away.

She put the thumb of her glove against her upper teeth for a second, then ran after him. "Del!"

He stopped but, rudely, would not turn. She rounded him, faced him. "I'll not have you believing that of me—it's the one thing I have left," she said tremulously.

He made no attempt to conceal his surprise. She controlled her expression with a visible effort, and said, "Please. Tell me a little more—just about the pool, the song, whatever it was."

"You don't remember?"

"I don't *know!*" she flashed. She was deeply agitated.

He said with mock patience, "You told me of a unicorn pool out on the Bogs. You said you had seen *him* drink there. You made a song about it. And then I—"

"Where? Where was this?"

"You forget so soon?"

"Where? Where did it happen?"

"In the meadow, across the road from your gate, where you followed me," he said. "Where my sight came back to me, when the sun came up."

She looked at him blankly, and slowly her face changed. First the imprisoned smile struggling to be free, and then—she was herself again, and she laughed. She laughed a great ringing peal of the laughter that had plagued him so, and she did not stop until he put one hand behind his back, then the other, and she saw his shoulders swell with the effort to keep from striking her dead.

"You animal!" she said, good-humoredly. "Do you know what you've done? Oh, you . . . you *animal!*" She glanced around to see that there were no ears to hear her. "I left you at the foot of the terrace steps," she told him. Her eyes sparkled: "Inside the gates, you understand? And you . . ."

"Don't laugh," he said quietly.

She did not laugh. "That was someone else out there. Who, I can't imagine. But it wasn't I."

He paled. "You followed me out."

"On my soul I did not," she said soberly. Then she quelled another laugh.

"That can't be," he said. "I couldn't have . . ."

"But you were blind, blind and crazy, Del-my-lover!"

"Squire's daughter, take care," he hissed. Then he pulled his big hand through his hair. "It can't be. It's three weeks; I'd have been accused . . ."

"There are those who wouldn't," she smiled. "Or—perhaps she will, in time."

"There has never been a woman so foul," he said evenly, looking her straight in the eye. "You're lying—you know you're lying."

"What must I do to prove it—aside from that which I'll have no man do?"

His lip curled. "Catch the unicorn," he said.

"If I did, you'd believe I was virgin?"

"I must," he admitted. He turned away, then said, over his shoulder, "But—*you?*"

She watched him thoughtfully until he left the marketplace. Her eyes sparkled; then she walked briskly to the goldsmith's, where she ordered a bridle of woven gold.

If the unicorn pool lay in the Bogs nearby, Rita reasoned, someone who was familiar with that brackish wasteland must know of it. And when she made a list in her mind of those few who travelled the Bogs, she knew whom to ask. With that, the other deduction came readily. Her laughter drew stares as she moved through the marketplace.

By the vegetable stall she stopped. The girl looked up patiently. Rita stood swinging one expensive glove against the other wrist, half-smiling. "So you're the one." She studied the plain, inward-turning, peaceful face until Barbara had to turn her eyes away. Rita said, without further preamble, "I want you to show me the unicorn pool in two weeks."

Barbara looked up again, and now it was Rita who dropped her eyes. Rita said, "I can have someone else find it, of course. If you'd rather not." She spoke very clearly, and people turned to listen. They looked from Barbara to Rita and back again, and they waited.

"I don't mind," said Barbara faintly. As soon as Rita had left, smiling, she packed up her things and went silently back to her house.

The goldsmith, of course, made no secret of such an extraordinary commission; and that, plus the gossips who had overheard Rita talking to Barbara, made the expedition into a cavalcade. The whole village turned out to see; the boys kept firmly in check so that Rita might lead the way; the young bloods ranged behind her (some a little less carefree than they might be) and others snickering behind their hands. Behind them the girls, one or two a little pale, others eager as cats to see the squire's daughter fail, and perhaps even ... but then, only she had the golden bridle.

She carried it casually, but casualness could not hide it, for it was not wrapped, and it swung and blazed in the sun. She wore a flowing white robe, trimmed a little short so that she might negotiate the rough bogland; she had on a golden girdle and little gold sandals, and a gold chain bound her head and hair like a coronet.

Barbara walked quietly a little behind Rita, closed in with her own thoughts. Not once did she look at Del, who strode somberly by himself.

Rita halted a moment and let Barbara catch up, then walked

beside her. "Tell me," she said quietly, "why did you come? It needn't have been you."

"I'm his friend," Barbara said. She quickly touched the bridle with her finger. "The unicorn."

"Oh," said Rita. "The unicorn." She looked archly at the other girl. "You wouldn't betray all your friends, would you?"

Barbara looked at her thoughtfully, without anger. "If—when you catch the unicorn," she said carefully, "what will you do with him?"

"What an amazing question! I shall keep him, of course!"

"I thought I might persuade you to let him go."

Rita smiled, and hung the bridle on her other arm. "You could never do that."

"I know," said Barbara. "But I thought I might, so that's why I came." And before Rita could answer, she dropped behind again.

The last ridge, the one which overlooked the unicorn pool, saw a series of gasps as the ranks of villagers topped it, one after the other, and saw what lay below; and it was indeed beautiful.

Surprisingly, it was Del who took it upon himself to call out, in his great voice, "Everyone wait here!" And everyone did; the top of the ridge filled slowly, from one side to the other, with craning, murmuring people. And then Del bounded after Rita and Barbara.

Barbara said, "I'll stop here."

"Wait," said Rita, imperiously. Of Del she demanded "What are you coming for?"

"To see fair play," he growled. "The little I know of witchcraft makes me like none of it."

"Very well," she said calmly. Then she smiled her very own smile. "Since you insist, I'd rather enjoy Barbara's company too."

Barbara hesitated. "Come, he won't hurt you, girl," said Rita. "He doesn't know you exist."

"Oh," said Barbara, wonderingly.

Del said gruffly, "I do so. She has the vegetable stall."

Rita smiled at Barbara, the secrets bright in her eyes. Barbara said nothing, but came with them.

"You should go back, you know," Rita said silkily to Del, when she could. "Haven't you been humiliated enough yet?"

He did not answer.

She said, "Stubborn animal! Do you think I'd have come this far if I weren't sure?"

"Yes," said Del, "I think perhaps you would."

They reached the blue moss. Rita shuffled it about with her feet and then sank gracefully down to it. Barbara stood alone in the shadows of the willow grove. Del thumped gently at an aspen with his fist. Rita, smiling, arranged the bridle to cast, and laid it across her lap.

The rabbits stayed hid. There was an uneasiness about the grove. Barbara sank to her knees, and put out her hand. A chipmunk ran to nestle in it.

This time there was a difference. This time it was not the slow silencing of living things that warned of his approach, but a sudden babble from the people on the ridge.

Rita gathered her legs under her like a sprinter, and held the bridle poised. Her eyes were round and bright, and the tip of her tongue showed between her white teeth. Barbara was a statue. Del put his back against his tree, and became as still as Barbara.

Then from the ridge came a single, simultaneous intake of breath, and silence. One knew without looking that some stared speechless, that some buried their faces or threw an arm over their eyes.

He came.

He came slowly this time, his golden hooves choosing his paces like so many embroidery needles. He held his splendid head high. He regarded the three on the bank gravely, and then turned to look at the ridge for a moment. At last he turned, and came round the pond by the willow grove. Just on the blue moss, he stopped to look down into the pond. It seemed that he drew one deep clear breath. He bent his head then, and drank, and lifted his head to shake away the shining drops.

He turned toward the three spellbound humans and looked at them each in turn. And it was not Rita he went to, at last, nor Barbara. He came to Del, and he drank of Del's eyes with his own just as he had partaken of the pool deeply and at leisure. The beauty and wisdom were there, and the compassion, and what looked like a bright white point of anger. Del knew that the creature had read everything then, and that he knew all three of them in ways unknown to human beings.

There was a majestic sadness in the way he turned then, and dropped his shining head, and stepped daintily to Rita. She sighed, and rose up a little, lifting the bridle. The unicorn lowered his horn to receive it—

—and tossed his head, tore the bridle out of her grasp, sent the golden thing high in the air. It turned there in the sun, and fell into the pond.

And the instant it touched the water, the pond was a bog and the birds rose mourning from the trees. The unicorn looked up at them, and shook himself. Then he trotted to Barbara and knelt, and put his smooth, stainless head in her lap.

Barbara's hands stayed on the ground by her sides. Her gaze roved over the warm white beauty, up to the tip of the golden horn and back.

The scream was frightening. Rita's hands were up like claws, and she had bitten her tongue; there was blood on her mouth. She screamed again. She threw herself off the now withered moss toward the unicorn and Barbara. "She can't be!" Rita shrieked. She collided with Del's broad right hand. "It's wrong, I tell you, she, you, I. . . ."

"I'm satisfied," said Del, low in his throat. "Keep away, squire's daughter."

She recoiled from him, made as if to try to circle him. He stepped forward. She ground her chin into one shoulder, then the other, in a gesture of sheer frustration, turned suddenly and ran toward the ridge. "It's mine, it's mine," she screamed. "I tell you it can't be hers, don't you understand? I never once, I never did, but she, but she—"

She slowed and stopped, then, and fell silent at the sound that rose from the ridge. It began like the first patter of rain on oak leaves, and it gathered voice until it was a rumble and then a roar. She stood looking up, her face working, the sound washing over her. She shrank from it.

It was laughter.

She turned once, a pleading just beginning to form on her face. Del regarded her stonily. She faced the ridge then, and squared her shoulders, and walked up the hill, to go into the laughter, to go through it, to have it follow her all the way home and all the days of her life.

Del turned to Barbara just as she bent over the beautiful head. She said, "Silken-swift . . . go free."

The unicorn raised its head and looked up at Del. Del's mouth opened. He took a clumsy step forward, stopped again. "*You!*"

Barbara's face was wet. "You weren't to know," she choked. "You weren't ever to know . . . I was so glad you were blind, because I thought you'd never know."

He fell on his knees beside her. And when he did, the unicorn touched her face with his satin nose, and all the girl's pent-up beauty flooded outward. The unicorn rose from his kneeling, and whickered softly. Del looked at her, and only the unicorn was more beautiful. He put out his hand to the shining neck, and for a moment felt the incredible silk of the mane flowing across his fingers. The unicorn reared then, and wheeled, and in a great leap was across the bog, and in two more was on the crest of the farther ridge. He paused there briefly, with the sun on him, and then was gone.

Barbara said, "For us, he lost his pool, his beautiful pool."

And Del said, "He will get another. He must." With difficulty he added, "He couldn't be . . . punished . . . for being so gloriously Fair."

The Clinic

THE POLICEMEN AND THE DOCTORS MEN and most of the people outside, they all helped me, they were very nice but nobody helped me as many-much as Elena. De la Torre liked me very nice I think, but number one because what I am is his work. The Sergeant liked me very nice too but inside I think he say not real, not real. He say in all his years he know two for-real amnesiacs but only in police book. Unless me. Some day, he say, some day he find out I not-real amnesiac trying to fool him. De la Torre say I real. Classic case, he say. He say plenty men forget talk forget name forget way to do life-work but *por Dios* not forget buttons forget eating forget every damn thing like me. The Sergeant say yes Doc you would rather find a medical monstrosity than turn up a faker. De la Torre say yes you would rather find out he is a fugitive than a phenomenon, well this just shows you what expert opinion is worth when you get two experts together. He say, one of us has to be wrong.

Is half right. Is both wrong.

If I am a fugitive I must be very intelligent. If I am an amnesiac I could be even intelligenter as a fugitive. Anyway I be intelligent better than any man in the world, as how could conversation as articulo-fluent like this after only six days five hours fifty-three minutes?

Is both wrong. I be Nemo.

But now comes Elena again, de la Torre is look happy-face, the Sergeant is look watch-face, Elena smile so warm, and we go.

"How are you tonight, Nemo?"

"I am very intelligent."

She laughs. "You can say that again," and then she puts hand on my mouth and more laughs. "No, don't say it again. Another figure

297

of speech. . . . Remember any yet?"

"What state what school what name, all that? No."

"All right." Now de la Torre, he ask me like that and when I no him, he try and try ask some other how. The Sergeant, he ask me like that and when I no him, he try and try ask me the same asking, again again. Elena ask and when I no her, she talk something else. Now she say, "What would you like to do tonight?"

I say, "Go with you whatever."

She say, "Well we'll start with a short beer," so we do.

The short beer is in a room with long twisty blue lights and red lights and a noise-machine looks like two sunsets with bubbles and sounds unhappy out loud. The short beer is wet, high as a hand, color like Elena's eyes, shampoo on top, little bubbles inside. Elena drink then I drink all. Little bubbles make big bubble inside me, big bubble come right back up so roaring that all people look to see, so it is bigger as the noise-machine. I look at people and Elena laugh again. She say, "I guess I shouldn't laugh. Most people don't do that in public, Nemo."

"Was largely recalcitrant bubble and decontrolled," I say. "So what do—keep for intestinals?"

She laugh again and say, "Well, no. Just try to keep it quiet." And now come a man from high long table where so many stand, he has hair on face, low lip flaccid, teeth brown black and gold, he smell as waste-food, first taste of mouth-thermometer, and skin moisture after drying in heavy weavings. He say, "You sound like a pig, Mac, where you think you are, home?"

I look at Elena and I look at he, I say, "Good evening." That what de la Torre say in first speak to peoples after begin night. Elena quick touch arm of mine, say, "Don't pay any attention to him, Nemo." Man bend over, put hand forward and touches it to ear of me with velocity, to make a large percussive effect. Same time bald man run around end of long high table exhibiting wooden device, speaking the prognosis: "Don't start nothing in my place, Purky, or I'll feed you this bung-starter."

I rub at ear and look at man who smells. He say, "Yeah, but you hear this little pig here? Where he think he's at?"

The man with bung-starter device say, "Tell you where you'll be at, you don't behave yourself, you'll be out on the pavement with a knot on your head," and he walk at Purky until Purky move and walk again until Purky is back to old place. I rub on ear and look at Elena and Elena has lip-paint of much bigger red now. No it is not bigger red, it is face skin of more white. Elena say, "Are you all right, Nemo? Did he hurt you?"

I say, "He is destroyed no part. He is create algesia of the middle ear. This is usual?"

"The dirty rat. No, Nemo, it isn't usual. I'm sorry, I'm so sorry. I shouldn't've brought you in here.... Some day someone'll do the world a favor and knock his block off."

"I have behavior?"

She say, "You what? Oh—did you act right." She gives me diagnostic regard from sides of eyes. "I guess so, Nemo. But . . . you can't let people push you around like that. Come on, let's get out of here."

"But then this is no more short beer, yes?"

"You like it? You want another?"

I touch my larynx. "It localizes a euphoria."

"Does it now. Well, whatever that means, I guess you can have another." She high display two fingers and big bald man gives dispensing of short beer more. I take all and large bubble forms and with concentration I exude it through nostrils quietly and gain Elena's approval and laughter. I say my thanks about the kindlies, about de la Torre and the Sergeant but it is Elena who helps with the large manymuchness.

"Forget it," she say.

"Is figure of speech? Is command?"

She say low-intensity to shampoo on short beer, "I don't know, Nemo. No, I guess I wouldn't want you to forget me." She look up at me and I know she will say again, "You'll never forget your promise, Nemo?" and she say it. And I say, "I not go away before I say, Elena, 'I going away.'"

She say, "What's the matter, Nemo? What is it?"

I say, "You think I go away, so I think about I go away too. I like you think about I here. And that not all of it."

"I'm sorry. It's just that I—well, it's important to me, that's all. I couldn't bear it if you just disappeared some day.... What else, Nemo?"

I say, "Two more short beer."

We drink the new short beer with no talk and with thinks. Then she say she go powder she nose. She nose have powder but she also have behavior so I no say why. When she go in door-place at back angle, I stand and walk.

I walk to high long table where stand the smelly man Purky, I push on him, he turn around.

He say, "Well look what crawled up! What you want, piggy?"

I say, "Where you block?"

He say, "Where's *what?*" He speak down to me from very tall, but he speak more noise than optimum.

I say, "You block. Block. You know, knock off block. Where you block? I knock off."

Big man who bring short beer, he roar. Purky, he roar. Mens jump back, looking, looking. Purky lift high big bottle, approach it at me swiftly. I move very close swiftlier, impact the neck of Purky by shoulder, squeeze flesh of Purky in and down behind pelvis, sink right thumb in left abdomen of Purky—one-two-three and go away again. Purky still swing down bottle but I not there for desired encounter now. Bottle go down to floor, Purky go down to floor, I walk back to chair, Purky lie twitching, men look at he, men look at me, Purky say "Uh-uh-uh." I sit down.

Elena come out of door running, say "What happened? Nemo ..." and she look at Purky and all men looking.

I say, "Sorry. Sorry."

"Did you do that, Nemo?"

I make the head-nod, yes.

"Well what are you sorry about?" she say, all pretty with surprise and fierce.

I say, "I think you happy if I knock block off, but not know block. Where is block? I knock off now."

"No you don't!" she say. "You come right along out of here! Nemo, you're dynamite!"

I puzzle. "Is good?"

"Just now, is good."

We go out and big man call, "Hey, how about one on the house, Bomber?"

I puzzle again. EIena say, "He means he wants to give you a drink."

"Short beer?"

Big man put out short beer, I drink all. Purky sit up on floor. I feel big bubble come; I make it roar. I look at Purky. Purky not talk. Elena pull me, we go.

We walk by lakeshore long time. People foot-slide slowly to pulse from mens with air-vibrators, air-column wood, air-column metal, vibrating strings single and sets. "Dancing," Elena say and I say "Nice. Is goodly nice." We have a happy, watching. Pulse fast, pulse slow, mens cry with pulse and vibrations, womens, two at once, cry together. "Singing," Elena say, and the lights move on the dancing, red and yellow-red and big and little blue; clouds shift and change, pulse shift and change, stars come, stars go and the wind, warm. Elena say, "Nemo, honey, do you know what love is?"

I say no.

She look the lake, she look the lights, she wave the arm of her to show all, with the wind and stars; she make her voice like whisper and like singing too and she say, "It's something like this, Nemo. I hope you find out some day."

I say yes, and I have sleepy too. So she take me back to the hospital.

It is the day and de la Torre is tired with me. He fall into chair, wipe the face of he with a small white weaving.

He say, "*Por Dios,* Nemo, I don't figure you at all. Can I be frank with you?"

I say, "Yes," but I know all he be is de la Torre.

He say, "I don't think you're trying. But you must be trying; you couldn't get along so fast without trying. You don't seem to be interested; I have to tell you some things fifty times before you finally get them. Yet you ask questions as if you *were* interested. What are you? What do you want?"

I lift up the shoulders once, quickly, just like de la Torre when he not know.

He say, "You grasp all the complicated things at sight, and ignore the simple ones. You use terms out of *Materia Medica* and use them right, and all the time you refuse to talk anything but a highly individualized pidgin-English. Do you know what I'm talking about?" I say, "Yes."

He say, "*Do* you? Tell me: what is *Materia Medica*? What is 'Individualized'? What is 'Pidgin-English'?"

I do the shoulders thing.

"So don't tell me you know what I'm talking about."

I turn the head little, raise the one finger like he do sometime, I say, "I do. I do."

"Tell me then. Tell it in your own words. Tell me why you won't learn to talk the way I do."

"No use," I say. Then I say, "No use for me." Then I say, "Not interest me." And still he sit and puzzle at me.

So I try. I say, "De la Torre, I see peoples dancing in the night."

"When? With Elena?"

"Elena, yes. And I see mens make pulse and cries for dancing."

"An orchestra?" I puzzle. He say, "Men with instruments, making noises together?" I make a yes. He say, "Music. That's called music."

I say, "What this?" and I move the arms.

He say, "Violin?"

I say, "Yes. Make one noise, a new noise, a new noise—one and one and one. Now," I say, "what this?" and I move again.

"Banjo," he say. "Guitar, maybe."

"Make many noise, in set. Make a new set. And a new set. Yes?"

"Yes," he say. "It's played in chords, mostly. What are you getting at?"

I bump on side of head. "You have think word and word and word and you make set. I have think set and set and set."

"You mean I think like a violin, one note at a time, and you think like a guitar, a lot of related notes at a time?" He quiet, he puzzle. "Why do you want to think like that?"

"Is my thinks."

"You mean, that's the way you think? Well, for Pete's sake, Nemo, you'll make it a lot easier to convey your thinks—uh—thoughts if you'll learn to come out with them like other people."

I make the no with the head. "No use for me."

"Look," he say. He blow hard through he nostrils, bang-bang on table, eyes close. He say, "You've got to understand this. I'll give you an example. You know how an automobile engine works?"

I say no.

He grab white card and mark-stick and start to mark, start to conversation swift, say all fast about they call this a four-cycle engine because it acts in four different phases, the piston goes down, this valve opens, that valve closes, the piston goes up, this makes a fire . . . and a lot, all so swift. "This the intake cycle," and many words. "This is the crankshaft, spark plug, fuel line, compression stroke . . ." Much and much.

And stops, whump. Points mark-stick. "Now, you and your thinking in concepts. That's how it works, basically. Don't tell me you got any of that, with any real understanding."

"Don't tell?"

"No, no," he say. He tired, he smile. He say, "Name the four cycles of this engine."

I say, "Suck. Squeeze. Pop. Phooey."

He drop he mark-stick. A long quiet. He say, "I can't teach you anything."

I say, "I not intelligent?"

He say, "*I* not intelligent."

Is many peoples in eat-place but I by my own with my plate and my thinks, I am alone. Is big roughness impacting on arm, big noise say, "What's your *name?*"

I bend to look up and there is the Sergeant. I say, "Nemo."

He sit down. He look. He make me have think: he like me, he not believe me. He not believe anybody. He say: "Nemo, Nemo. That's not your name."

I do the thing with the shoulders.

He say, "You weren't surprised when I jolted you then. Don't you ever get surprised? Don't you ever get sore?"

I say, "Surprise, no. Sore?"

He say, "Sore, mad, angry."

I have a think. I say, "No."

He say, "Ought to be something that'll shake you up. Hm.... They pamper you too much around here, you walking around like Little Eva or Billy Budd or somebody. Sweetness and light. Dr. de la Torre says you're real bright."

"De la Torre real bright."

"Maybe. Maybe." He eyes have like coldness, like so cold nothing move. He say, "That Elena. How you like Elena, Nemo?"

I say, "I like." And I say, "High music, big color-gentle."

He say, "Thought so." He poke sharp into my chest. "Now I'm gonna tell you the truth about your Elena. She's crazy as a coot. She went bad young. She was a mainliner, understand me? She was an addict. She did a lot of things to get money for the stuff. She had to do more'n most of 'em, with a face like that, and it didn't get any prettier. De la Torre pulled her through a cure. He's a good man. Three different times he cured her.

"So one time she falls off again and what do you know, she picks up with a looney just like you. A guy they called George. I figured from the start he was a faker. Showed up wandering, just like you. And she goes for him. She goes for him bigger'n she ever went for anything else, even hash. And he went over the hill one fine day and was never seen again.

"So she's off the stuff, sure. And you know what? The only thing she has any use for is amnesiacs. Yeah, I mean it. You're the sixth in a row. They come in, she sticks with 'em until they get cured or fade. Between times she just waits for the next one.

"And that's your Elena. De la Torre strings along with her because she does 'em good. So that's your light o' love, Nemo boy. A real twitch. If it isn't dope it's dopes. You get cured up, she'll want no part of you. Wise up, fella."

He look at me. He has a quiet time. He say, "God awmighty, you don't give a damn for her after all . . . or maybe you just don't know

how to get mad . . . or you didn't understand a word of what I said."
I say, "Every people hurt Elena. Some day Elena be happy, always.
Sergeant hurt every people. Sergeant not be happy. Never."
He look at me. Something move in the cold, like lobster on ice;
too cold to move much. I say, "Poor Sergeant."
He jump up, he make a noise, not word, he raise a big hand. I
look up at him, I say, "Poor Sergeant." He go away. He bump de la
Torre who is quiet behind us.
De la Torre say, "I heard that speech of yours, you skunk. I'd
clobber you myself if I didn't think Nemo'd done it better already.
You'd better keep your big flat feet the hell out of this hospital."
Sergeant run away. De la Torre stand a time, go away. I eat.

It is night by the lake, the moon is burst and leaking yellow to me
over the black alive water and Elena by me. I say, "I go soonly."
She breathe, I hear.
I say, "Tree finish, tree die. Sickness finish, sickness gone. House
finish, workmens leave. Is right."
"Don't go. Don't go yet, Nemo."
"Seed sprout, child grow, bird fly. Something finish, something
change. I finish."
She say, "Not so soon."
"Bury plant? Tie boy to cradle? Nail wings to nest?"
She say, "All right." We sit.
I say, "I promised."
She say, "You kept your promise, Nemo. Thank you." She cry. I
watch leaking moon float free, lost light flattening and flattening at
the black lake. Light tried, light tried, water would not mix.
Elena say, "What world do you live in, Nemo?"
I say, "My world."
She say, "Yes . . . yes, that's the right answer. You live in your
world, I live in my world, a hundred people, a hundred worlds.
Nobody lives with me, nobody. Nemo, you can travel from one world
to another."
I do the head, yes.
"But just one at a time. I'm talking crazy, but you don't mind. I

had a world I don't remember, soft and safe, and then a world that
hurt me because I was too stupid to duck when I saw hurt coming.
And a world that was better than real where I couldn't stay, but I
had to go there ... and I couldn't stay ... and I had to go ... and
then I had a world where I thought, just for a little while—*such a
little while*—I thought it was a world for me and ..."

I say, "—and George."

She say, "*You can read my mind!*"

"No!" I say, big; loud. Hurt. I say, "Truly no, not do that, I can't
do that."

She touch on my face, say, "It doesn't matter. But George, then,
about George ... I was going to be lost again, and this time forever,
and I saw George and spoke right up like a—a—" She shake. "You
wouldn't know what I was like. And instead, George was gentle and
sweet and he made me feel as if I was ... well and whole. In all my
life nobody ever treated me gently, Nemo, except Dr. de la Torre,
and he did it because I was sick. George treated me as if I was healthy
and fine, and he ... admired me for it. Me. And he came to love me
like those lights, those lights I showed you, all the colors, slipping
among the dancers under the sky. He came to love me so much he
wanted to stay with me for ever and ever, and then he went away
sometime between a morning and a snowstorm."

The moon is gone up, finished and full, the light, left on the water
frightened and yearning to it, thinning, breaking and fusing, pointing at the moon, the moon not caring, it finished now.

She say, "I was dead for a long time."

She passes through a think and lets her face be dead until she say,
"Dr. de la Torre was so kind, he used to tell me I was a special princess,
and I could go anywhere. I went in all the places in the hospital, and
I found out a thing I had not known; that I had these hands, these
legs, eyes, this body, voice, brains. It isn't much and nobody wants
it ... now ... but I had it all. And some of those people in there,
without all of it, they were happier than I was, brave and good.
There's a place with people who have their voices taken out of their
throats, Nemo, you know that? And they learn to speak there. You
know how they do it? I tell some people this, they laugh, but you

won't laugh. You won't laugh, Nemo?"

I am not laugh.

She say, "You know that noise you made when you drank the beer so fast? That's what they do. On purpose. They do it and they practice and practice and work hard, work together. And bit by bit they make a voice that sounds like a voice. It's rough and it's all on one note, but it's a real voice. They talk together and laugh, and have a debating society . . .

"There's a place in there where a man goes in without legs, and comes out dancing, yes twirling and swirling a girl around, her ballgown a butterfly and he smiling and swift and sure. There's a place for the deaf people, and they must make voices out of nothing too, and ears. They do it, Nemo! And together they understand each other. Outside, people don't understand the deaf. People don't mean to be unkind, but they are. But the deaf understand the deaf, and they understand the hearing as well, better than the hearing understand themselves.

"So one day I met a soldier there, with the deaf. He was very sad at first. Many of the people there are born deaf, but he had a world of hearing behind him. And there was a girl there and they fell in love. Everyone was happy, and one day he went away.

"She cried, she cried so, and when she stopped, it was even worse.

"And Dr. de la Torre went and found the soldier, and very gently and carefully he dug out why he had run away. It was because he was handicapped. It was because he had lost a precious thing. And he wouldn't marry the girl, though he loved her, because she was as she had been born and he felt she was perfect. She was perfect and he was damaged. She was perfect and he was unfit. And that is why he ran away.

"Dr. de la Torre brought him back and they were married right there in the hospital with such fine banquet and dance; and they got jobs there and went to school and now they are helping the others, together . . .

"So then I went into another world, and this is my world; and if I should *know* that it is not a real world I would die.

"My world is here, and somewhere else there are people like us but different. One of the ways they are different is that they need not speak; not words anyway. And something happens to them sometimes, just as it does to us: through sickness, through accident, they lose forever their way of communicating, like our total deaf. But they can learn to speak, just as you and I can learn Braille, or make a voice without a larynx, and then at least they may talk among themselves. And if you are to learn Braille, you should go among the blind. If you are to learn lip-reading you do it best among the deaf. If you have something better than speech and lose it, you must go among a speaking people.

"And that is what I believe, because I must or die. I think George was such a one, who came here to learn to speak so he could rejoin others who also had to learn. And I think that anyone who has no memory of this Earth or anything on it, and who must be taught to speak, might be another. They pretend to be amnesiacs so that they will be taught *all* of a language. I think that when they have learned, they understand themselves and those like them, and also the normal ones of their sort, better than anyone, just as the deaf can understand the hearing ones better.

"I think George was such a one, and that he left me because he thought of himself as crippled and of me as whole. He left me for love. He was humble with it.

"This is what I believe and I can't ..."

She whisper.

" ... I can't believe it ... very much ... longer ..."

She listen to grief altogether until it tired, and when she can listen to me I say, "You want me to be George, and stay."

She sit close, she put she wet face on my face and say, "Nemo, Nemo, I wish you could, I do *so* wish you could. But you can't be my George, because I love him, don't you see? You can be my de la Torre, though, who went out and found a man and explained why and brought him back. All he has to know is that when love is too humble it can kill the lovers. ... Just tell him that, Nemo. When you ... when you go back."

She look past me at the moon, cold now, and down and out to the water and sky, and she here altogether out of memory and hope-thinks. She say with strong daytime voice, "I talk crazy sometimes, thanks, Nemo, you didn't laugh. Let's have a beer some time."

I wish almost the Sergeant knows where I keep anger. It would please him I have so much. Here in the bare rocks, here in the night, I twist on anger, curl and bite me like eel on spear.

It is night and with anger, I alone in cold hills, town and hospital a far fog of light behind. I stand to watch it the ship and around it, those silents who watch me, eight of them, nine, all silent.

This is my anger: that they are silent. They share all thinks in one thinking instant, each with one other, each with all others. All I do now is talk. But the silents, there stand by ship, share and share all thinks, none talks. They wait, I come. They have pity.

They have manymuch pity, so I angry.

Then I see my angry is envy, and envy never teach to dance a one-legged man. Envy never teach the lip-reading.

I see that and laugh at me, laugh but it sting my eyes.

"*Hello!*"

One comes to me, not silent, but have conversation! Surprise. I say, "Good evening."

He shake hand of me, say, "We thought you were not going to come." His speak slow, very strong, steadily.

I say, "I ready. I surprise you have talk."

He say, "Oh, I spent some time here. I studied very carefully. I have come back to live here."

I say, "You conversation goodly. I have learn talk idea, good enough. You have word and word and word, like Earth peoples. Good. Why you come returning?"

He look my face, very near, say, "I did not like it at home. When you go back there, everyone will be kind. But they will have their own lives to live, and there is not much they can share with you any more. You will be blind among the seeing, deaf among those who hear. But they will be kind, oh yes: very kind."

Then he look back at the silents, who stand watching. He say, "But here, I speak among the speaking, and it is a better sharing than even a home planet gone all silent." He point at watchers. He laugh.

He say, "We speak together in a way they have never learned to speak, like two Earth mutes gesticulating together in a crowd. It is as if we were the telepaths and not they—see them stare and wonder!"

I laugh too. "Not need to telepath here!"

He say, "Yes, on Earth we can be blind with the blind, and we will never miss our vision. While I was here I was happy to share myself by speaking. When I went home I could share only with other . . . damaged . . . people. I had to go home to find out that I did not feel damaged when I was here, so I came back."

I look to ship, to wondering silents. I say, "What name you have here?"

He say, "They called me George."

I think, I have message for you: Elena dying for you. I say, "Elena waiting for you."

He make large shout and hug on me and run. I cry, "Wait! Wait!" He wait, but not wanting. I say, "I learn talk like you, word and word, and one day find Elena for me too."

He hit on me gladly, say, "All right. I'll help you."

We go down hill togetherly, most muchly homelike. Behind, ship wait, ship wait, silents watch and wonder. Then ship load up with all pity I need no more, scream away up to stars.

I have a happy now that I get sick lose telepathy come here learn talk find home, *por Dios.*

Mr. Costello, Hero

"COME IN, PURSER. AND SHUT THE DOOR."

"I beg your pardon, sir?" The Skipper never invited anyone in—
not to his quarters. His office, yes, but not here.

He made an abrupt gesture, and I came in and closed the door.
It was about as luxurious as a compartment on a spaceship can get.
I tried not to goggle at it as if it was the first time I had ever seen it,
just because it was the first time I had ever seen it.

I sat down.

He opened his mouth, closed it, forced the tip of his tongue through
his thin lips. He licked them and glared at me. I'd never seen the Iron
Man like this. I decided that the best thing to say would be nothing,
which is what I said.

He pulled a deck of cards out of the top-middle drawer and slid
them across the desk. "Deal."

I said, "I b—"

"And don't say you beg my pardon!" he exploded.

Well, all right. If the skipper wanted a cozy game of gin rummy
to while away the parsecs, far be it from me to ... I shuffled. Six
years under this cold-blooded, fish-eyed automatic computer with
eyebrows, and this was the first time that he—

"Deal," he said. I looked up at him. "Draw, five-card draw. You
do play draw poker, don't you, Purser?"

"Yes, sir." I dealt and put down the pack. I had three threes and
a couple of court cards. The skipper scowled at his hand and threw
down two. He glared at me again.

I said, "I got three of a kind, sir."

He let his cards go as if they no longer existed, slammed out of
his chair and turned his back to me. He tilted his head back and
stared up at the see-it-all, with its complex of speed, time, position

and distance-run coordinates. Borinquen, our destination planet, was at spitting distance—only a day or so off—and Earth was a long, long way behind. I heard a sound and dropped my eyes. The Skipper's hands were locked behind him, squeezed together so hard that they crackled.

"Why didn't you draw?" he grated.

"I beg your—"

"When I played poker—and I used to play a hell of a lot of poker—as I recall it, the dealer would find out how many cards each player wanted after the deal and give him as many as he discarded. Did you ever hear of that, Purser?"

"Yes, sir, I did."

"You *did*." He turned around. I imagine he had been scowling this same way at the see-it-all, and I wondered why it was he hadn't shattered the cover glass.

"Why, then, Purser," he demanded, "did you show your three of a kind without discarding, without drawing—without, mister, asking me how many cards I might want?"

I thought about it. "I—we—I mean, sir, we haven't been playing poker that way lately."

"You've been playing draw poker without drawing!" He sat down again and beamed that glare at me again. "And who changed the rules?"

"I don't know, sir. We just—that's the way we've been playing."

He nodded thoughtfully. "Now tell me something, Purser. How much time did you spend in the galley during the last watch?"

"About an hour, sir."

"About an hour."

"Well, sir," I explained hurriedly, "it was my turn."

He said nothing, and it suddenly occurred to me that these galley-watches weren't in the ship's orders.

I said quickly, "It isn't *against* your orders to stand such a watch, is it, sir?"

"No," he said, "it isn't." His voice was so gentle, it was ugly. "Tell me, Purser, doesn't Cooky mind these galley-watches?"

"Oh, no, sir! He's real pleased about it." I knew he was thinking about the size of the galley. It was true that two men made quite a crowd in a place like that. I said, "That way, he knows everybody can trust him."

"You mean that way you know he won't poison you."

"Well—yes, sir."

"And tell me," he said, his voice even gentler, "who suggested he might poison you?"

"I really couldn't say, Captain. It's just sort of something that came up. Cooky doesn't mind," I added. "If he's watched all the time, he knows nobody's going to suspect him. It's all right."

Again he repeated my words.

"It's all right." I wished he wouldn't. I wished he'd stop looking at me like that. "How long," he asked, "has it been customary for the deck officer to bring a witness with him when he takes over the watch?"

"I really couldn't say, sir. That's out of my department."

"You couldn't say. Now think hard, Purser. Did you ever stand galley-watches, or see deck-officers bring witnesses with them when they relieve the bridge, or see draw poker played without drawing— before this trip?"

"Well, no, sir. I don't think I have. I suppose we just never thought of it before."

"We never had Mr. Costello as a passenger before, did we?"

"No, sir."

I thought for a moment he was going to say something else, but he didn't, just: "Very well, Purser. That will be all."

I went out and started back aft, feeling puzzled and sort of upset. The Skipper didn't have to hint things like that about Mr. Costello. Mr. Costello was a very nice man. Once, the Skipper had picked a fight with Mr. Costello. They'd shouted at each other in the day-room. That is, the Skipper had shouted—Mr. Costello never did. Mr. Costello was as good-natured as they come. A good-natured soft-spoken man, with the kind of face they call open. Open and honest. He'd once been a Triumver back on Earth—the youngest ever appointed, they said.

You wouldn't think such an easygoing man was as smart as that.

313

Triumvers are usually life-time appointees, but Mr. Costello wasn't satisfied. Had to keep moving, you know. Learning all the time, shaking hands all around, staying close to the people. He loved people.

I don't know why the Skipper couldn't get along with him. Everybody else did. And besides—Mr. Costello didn't play poker; why should he care one way or the other how we played it? He didn't eat the galley food—he had his own stock in his cabin—so what difference would it make to him if the cook poisoned anyone? Except, of course, that he cared about *us*. People—he *liked* people.

Anyway, it's better to play poker without the draw. Poker's a good game with a bad reputation. And where do you suppose it gets the bad reputation? From cheaters. And how do people cheat at poker? Almost never when they deal. It's when they pass out cards after the discard. That's when a shady dealer knows what he holds, and he knows what to give the others so he can win. All right, remove the discard and you remove nine-tenths of the cheaters. Remove the cheaters and the honest men can trust each other.

That's what Mr. Costello used to say, anyhow. Not that he cared one way or the other for himself. He wasn't a gambling man.

I went into the dayroom and there was Mr. Costello with the Third Officer. He gave me a big smile and a wave, so I went over.

"Come on, sit down, Purser," he said. "I'm landing tomorrow. Won't have much more chance to talk to you."

I sat down. The Third snapped shut a book he'd been holding open on the table and sort of got it out of sight.

Mr. Costello laughed at him. "Go ahead, Third, show the Purser. You can trust him—he's a good man. I'd be proud to be shipmates with the Purser."

The Third hesitated and then raised the book from his lap. It was the *Space Code* and expanded *Rules of the Road*. Every licensed officer has to bone up on it a lot, to get his license. But it's not the kind of book you ordinarily kill time with.

"The Third here was showing me all about what a captain can and can't do," said Mr. Costello.

"Well, you asked me to," the Third said.

"Now just a minute," said Mr. Costello rapidly, "now just a minute." He had a way of doing that sometimes. It was part of him, like the thinning hair on top of his head and the big smile and the way he had of cocking his head to one side and asking you what it was you just said, as if he didn't hear so well. "Now just a minute, you *wanted* to show me this material, didn't you?"

"Well, yes, Mr. Costello," the Third said.

"You're going over the limitations of a spacemaster's power of your own free will, aren't you?"

"Well," said the Third, "I guess so. Sure."

"Sure," Mr. Costello repeated happily. "Tell the Purser the part you just read to me."

"The one you found in the book?"

"You know the one. You read it out your own self, didn't you?"

"Oh," said the Third. He looked at me—sort of uneasily, I thought—and reached for the book.

Mr. Costello put his hand on it. "Oh, don't bother looking it up," he said. "You can remember it."

"Yeah, I guess I do," the Third admitted. "It's a sort of safeguard against letting a skipper's power go to his head, in case it ever does. Suppose a time comes when a captain begins to act up, and the crew gets the idea that a lunatic has taken over the bridge. Well, something has to be done about it. The crew has the power to appoint one officer and send him up to the Captain for an accounting. If the Skipper refuses, or if the crew doesn't like his accounting, then they have the right to confine him to his quarters and take over the ship."

"I think I heard about that," I said. "But the Skipper has rights, too. I mean the crew has to report everything by space-radio the second it happens, and then the Captain has a full hearing along with the crew at the next port."

Mr. Costello looked at us and shook his big head, full of admiration. When Mr. Costello thought you were good, it made you feel good all over.

The Third looked at his watch and got up. "I got to relieve the bridge. Want to come along, Purser?"

"I'd like to talk to him for a while," Mr. Costello said. "Do you suppose you could get somebody else for a witness?"

"Oh, sure, if you say so," said the Third.

"But you're going to get someone."

"Absolutely," said the Third.

"Safest ship I was ever on," said Mr. Costello. "Gives a fellow a nice feeling to know that the watch is never going to get the orders wrong."

I thought so myself and wondered why we never used to do it before. I watched the Third leave and stayed where I was, feeling good, feeling safe, feeling glad that Mr. Costello wanted to talk to me. And me just a Purser, him an ex-Triumver.

Mr. Costello gave me the big smile. He nodded toward the door. "That young fellow's going far. A good man. You're all good men here." He stuck a sucker-cup in the heater and passed it over to me with his own hands. "Coffee," he said. "My own brand. All I ever use."

I tasted it and it was fine. He was a very generous man. He sat back and beamed at me while I drank it.

"What do you know about Borinquen?" he wanted to know.

I told him all I could. Borinquen's a pretty nice place, what they call "four-nines Earth Normal"—which means that the climate, gravity, atmosphere and ecology come within .9999 of being the same as Earth's. There are only about six known planets like that. I told him about the one city it had and the trapping that used to be the main industry. Coats made out of *glunker* fur last forever. They shine green in white light and a real warm ember-red in blue light, and you can take a full-sized coat and scrunch it up and hide it in your two hands, it's that light and fine. Being so light, the fur made ideal space cargo.

Of course, there was a lot more on Borinquen now—rare isotope ingots and foodstuffs and seeds for the drug business and all, and I suppose the *glunker* trade could dry right up and Borinquen could still carry its weight. But furs settled the planet, furs supported the city in the early days, and half the population still lived out in the bush and trapped.

Mr. Costello listened to everything I said in a way I can only call respectful.

I remember I finished up by saying, "I'm sorry you have to get off there, Mr. Costello. I'd like to see you some more. I'd like to come see you at Borinquen, whenever we put in, though I don't suppose a man like you would have much spare time."

He put his big hand on my arm. "Purser, if I don't have time when you're in port, I'll make time. Hear?" Oh, he had a wonderful way of making a fellow feel good.

Next thing you know, he invited me right into his cabin. He sat me down and handed me a sucker full of a mild red wine with a late flavor of cinnamon, which was a new one on me, and he showed me some of his things.

He was a great collector. He had one or two little bits of colored paper that he said were stamps they used before the Space Age, to prepay carrying charges on paper letters. He said no matter where he was, just one of those things could get him a fortune. Then he had some jewels, not rings or anything, just stones, and a fine story for every single one of them.

"What you're holding in your hand," he said, "cost the life of a king and the loss of an empire half again as big as United Earth." And: "This one was once so well guarded that most people didn't know whether it existed or not. There was a whole religion based on it—and now it's gone, and so is the religion."

It gave you a queer feeling, being next to this man who had so much, and him just as warm and friendly as your favorite uncle.

"If you can assure me these bulkheads are soundproof, I'll show you something else I collect," he said.

I assured him they were, and they were, too. "If ship's architects ever learned anything," I told him, "they learned that a man has just got to be by himself once in a while."

He cocked his head to one side in that way he had. "How's that again?"

"A man's just got to be by himself once in a while," I said. "So, mass or no, cost or no, a ship's bulkheads are built to give a man his privacy."

"Good," he said. "Now let me show you." He unlocked a hand-case and opened it, and from a little compartment inside he took out a thing about the size of the box a watch comes in. He handled it very gently as he put it down on his desk. It was square, and it had a fine grille on the top and two little silver studs on the side. He pressed one of them and turned to me, smiling. And let me tell you, I almost fell right off the bunk where I was sitting, because here was the Captain's voice as loud and as clear and natural as if he was right there in the room with us. And do you know what he said?

He said, "My crew questions my sanity—yet you can be sure that if a single man aboard questions my authority, he will learn that I am master here, even if he must learn it at the point of a gun."

What surprised me so much wasn't only the voice but the words—and what surprised me especially about the words was that I had heard the Skipper say them myself. It was the time he had had the argument with Mr. Costello. I remembered it well because I had walked into the dayroom just as the Captain started to yell.

"Mr. Costello," he said in that big heavy voice of his, "in spite of your conviction that my crew questions my sanity ..." and all the rest of it, just like on this recording Mr. Costello had. And I remember he said, too, "even if he must learn it at the point of a gun. *That, sir, applies to passengers—the crew has legal means of their own.*"

I was going to mention this to Mr. Costello, but before I could open my mouth, he asked me, "Now tell me, Purser, is that the voice of the Captain of your ship?"

And I said, "Well, if it isn't, I'm not the Purser here. Why, I heard him speak those words my very own self."

Mr. Costello swatted me on the shoulder. "You have a good ear, Purser. And how do you like my little toy?"

Then he showed it to me, a little mechanism on the jeweled pin he wore on his tunic, a fine thread of wire to a pushbutton in his side pocket.

"One of my favorite collections," he told me. "Voices. Anybody, anytime, anywhere." He took off the pin and slipped a tiny bead out of the setting. He slipped this into a groove in the box and pressed the stud.

And I heard my own voice say, "I'm sorry you have to get off there, Mr. Costello. I'd like to see you some more." I laughed and laughed. That was one of the cleverest things I ever saw. And just think of my voice in his collection, along with the Captain and space only knows how many great and famous people!

He even had the voice of the Third Officer, from just a few minutes before, saying, "A lunatic has taken over the bridge. Well, something has to be done about it."

All in all, I had a wonderful visit with him, and then he asked me to do whatever I had to do about his clearance papers. So I went back to my office and got them out. They are kept in the Purser's safe during a voyage. And I went through them with the okays. There were a lot of them—he had more than most people.

I found one from Earth Central that sort of made me mad. I guess it was a mistake. It was a *Know All Ye* that warned consular officials to report every six months, Earth time, on the activities of Mr. Costello.

I took it to him, and it was a mistake, all right—he said so himself. I tore it out of his passport book and adhesed an official note, reporting the accidental destruction of a used page of fully stamped visas. He gave me a beautiful blue gemstone for doing it.

When I said, "I better not; I don't want you thinking I take bribes from passengers," he laughed and put one of those beads in his recorder, and it came out, in my voice, "I take bribes from passengers." He was a great joker.

We lay at Borinquen for four days. Nothing much happened except I was busy. That's what's tough about pursering. You got nothing to do for weeks in space, and then, when you're in spaceport, you have too much work to do even to go ashore much, unless it's a long layover.

I never really minded much. I'm one of those mathematical geniuses, you know, even if I don't have too much sense otherwise, and I take pride in my work. Everybody has something he's good at, I guess. I couldn't tell you how the gimmick works that makes the ship travel faster than light, but I'd hate to trust the Chief Engineer with one of my interplanetary cargo manifests, or a rate-of-exchange table, *glunker* pelts to U.E. dollars.

Some hard-jawed character with Space Navy Investigator credentials came inboard with a portable voice recorder and made me and the Third Officer recite a lot of nonsense for some sort of test, I don't know what. The SNI is always doing a lot of useless and mysterious things. I had an argument with the Port Agent, and l went ashore with Cooky for a fast drink. The usual thing. Then I had to work overtime signing on a new Third—they transferred the old one to a corvette that was due in, they told me.

Oh, yes, that was the trip the Skipper resigned. I guess it was high time. He'd been acting very nervous. He gave me the damnedest look when he went ashore that last time, like he didn't know whether to kill me or burst into tears. There was a rumor around that he'd gone beserk and threatened the crew with a gun, but I don't listen to rumors. And anyway, the Port Captain signs on new skippers. It didn't mean any extra work for me, so it didn't matter much.

We up-shipped again and made the rounds. Boötes Sigma and Nightingale and Caranho and Earth—chemical glassware, black prints, *sho* seed and glitter crystals; perfume, music tape, *glizzard* skins and Aldebar—all the usual junk for all the usual months. And round we came again to Borinquen.

Well, you wouldn't believe a place could change so much in so short a time. Borinquen used to be a pretty free-and-easy planet. There was just the one good-sized city, see, and then trapper camps all through the unsettled area. If you liked people, you settled in the city, and you could go to work in the processing plants or maintenance or some such. If you didn't, you could trap *glunker*s. There was always something for everybody on Borinquen.

But things were way different this trip. First of all, a man with Planetary Government badge came aboard, by God, to censor the music tapes consigned for the city, and he had the credentials for it, too. Next thing I find out, the municipal authorities have confiscated the warehouses—*my* warehouses—and they were being converted into barracks.

And where were the goods—the pelts and ingots for export?

Where was the space for our cargo? Why, in houses—in hundreds of houses, all spread around every which way, all indexed up with a whole big new office full of conscripts and volunteers to mix up and keep mixed up! For the first time since I went to space, I had to request layover so I could get things unwound.

Anyway it gave me a chance to wander around the town, which I don't often get.

You should have seen the place! Everybody seemed to be moving out of the houses. All the big buildings were being made over into hollow shells, filled with rows and rows of mattresses. There were banners strung across the streets: ARE YOU A MAN OR ARE YOU ALONE? A SINGLE SHINGLE IS A SORRY SHELTER! THE DEVIL HATES A CROWD!

All of which meant nothing to me. But it wasn't until I noticed a sign painted in whitewash on the glass front of a barroom, saying—TRAPPERS STAY OUT!—that I was aware of one of the biggest changes of all.

There were no trappers on the streets—none at all. They used to be one of the tourist attractions of Borinquen, dressed in *glunker* fur, with the long tail-wings afloat in the wind of their walking, and a kind of distance in their eyes that not even spacemen had. As soon as I missed them, I began to see the TRAPPERS STAY OUT! signs just about everywhere—on the stores, the restaurants, the hotels and theaters.

I stood on a street corner, looking around me and wondering what in hell was going on here, when a Borinquen cop yelled something at me from a monowheel prowl car. I didn't understand him, so I just shrugged. He made a U-turn and coasted up to me.

"What's the matter, country boy? Lose your traps?"

I said, "What?"

He said, "If you want to go it alone, *glunker*, we got solitary cells over at the Hall that'll suit you fine."

I just gawked at him. And, to my surprise, another cop poked his head up out of the prowler. A one-man prowler, mind. They were really jammed in there.

This second one said, "Where's your trapline, jerker?"

I said, "I don't have a trapline." I pointed to the mighty tower of my ship, looming over the spaceport. "I'm the Purser off that ship."

"Oh, for God's sakes!" said the first cop. "I might have known. Look, Spacer, you'd better double up or you're liable to get yourself mobbed. This is no spot for a soloist."

"I don't get you, Officer. I was just—"

"I'll take him," said someone. I looked around and saw a tall Borinqueña standing just inside the open doorway of one of the hundreds of empty houses. She said, "I came back here to pick up some of my things. When I got done in here, there was nobody on the sidewalks. I've been here an hour, waiting for somebody to go with." She sounded a little hysterical.

"You know better than to go in there by yourself," said one of the cops.

"I know—I know. It was just to get my things. I wasn't going to stay." She hauled up a duffel bag and dangled it in front of her. "Just to get my things," she said again, frightened.

The cops looked at each other. "Well, all right. But watch yourself. You go along with the Purser here. Better straighten him out— he don't seem to know what's right."

"I will," she said thankfully.

But by then the prowler had moaned off, weaving a little under its double load!

I looked at her. She wasn't pretty. She was sort of heavy and stupid.

She said, "You'll be all right now. Let's go."

"Where?"

"Well, Central Barracks, I guess. That's where most everybody is."

"I have to get back to the ship."

"Oh, dear," she said, all distressed again. "Right away?"

"No, not right away. I'll go in town with you, if you want." She picked up her duffel bag, but I took it from her and heaved it up on my shoulder. "Is everybody here crazy?" I asked her, scowling.

"Crazy?" She began walking, and I went along. "I don't *think* so."

"All this," I persisted. I pointed to a banner that said, NO LAD-
DER HAS A SINGLE RUNG. "What's that mean?"

"Just what it says."

"You have to put up a big thing like that just to tell me . . ."

"Oh," she said. "You mean what does it *mean!*" She looked at
me strangely. "We've found out a new truth about humanity. Look,
I'll try to tell it to you the way the Lucilles said it last night."

"Who's Lucille?"

"*The* Lucilles," she said, in a mildly shocked tone. "Actually, I
suppose there's really only one—though, of course, there'll be someone else in the studio at the time," she added quickly. "But on trideo
it looks like four Lucilles, all speaking at once, sort of in chorus."

"You just go on talking," I said when she paused. "I catch on
slowly."

"Well, here's what they say. They say no one human being ever
did *anything*. They say it takes a hundred pairs of hands to build a
house, ten thousand pairs to build a ship. They say a single pair is
not only useless—it's *evil*. All humanity is a thing made up of many
parts. No part is good by itself. Any part that wants to go off by
itself hurts the whole main thing—the thing that has become so
great. So we're seeing to it that no part ever gets separated. What
good would your hand be if a finger suddenly decided to go off by
itself?"

I said, "And you believe this—what's your name?"

"Nola. *Believe* it? Well, it's true, isn't it? Can't you see it's true?
Everybody *knows* it's true."

"Well, *it could* be true," I said reluctantly. "What do you do with
people who want to be by themselves?"

"We help them."

"Suppose they don't want help?"

"Then they're trappers," she said immediately. "We push them
back into the bush, where the evil soloists come from."

"Well, what about the fur?"

"*No*body uses furs any more!"

So that's what happened to our fur consignments! And I was
thinking those amateur red-tapers had just lost 'em somewhere.

She said, as if to herself, "All sin starts in the lonesome dark," and when I looked up, I saw she'd read it approvingly off another banner.

We rounded a corner and I blinked at a blaze of light. It was one of the warehouses.

"There's the Central," she said. "Would you like to see it?"

"I guess so."

I followed her down the street to the entrance. There was a man sitting at a table in the doorway. Nola gave him a card. He checked it against a list and handed it back.

"A visitor," she said. "From the ship."

I showed him my Purser's card and he said, "Okay. But if you want to stay, you'll have to register."

"I won't want to stay," I told him. "I have to get back."

I followed Nola inside.

The place had been scraped out to the absolute maximum. Take away one splinter of vertical structure more and it wouldn't have held a roof. There wasn't a concealed comer, a shelf, a drape, an overhang. There must have been two thousand beds, cots and mattresses spread out, cheek by jowl, over the entire floor, in blocks of four, with only a hand's-breadth between them.

The light was blinding—huge floods and spots bathed every square inch in yellow-white fire.

Nola said, "You'll get used to the light. After a few nights, you don't even notice it."

"The lights never get turned off?"

"Oh, dear, no!"

Then I saw the plumbing—showers, tubs, sinks and everything else. It was all lined up against one wall.

Nola followed my eyes. "You get used to that, too. Better to have everything out in the open than to let the devil in for one secret second. That's what the Lucilles say."

I dropped her duffel bag and sat down on it. The only thing I could think of was, "Whose idea was all this? Where did it start?"

"The Lucilles," she said vaguely. Then, "Before them, I don't know. People just started to realize. Somebody bought a warehouse—

no, it was a hangar—I don't know," she said again, apparently trying hard to remember. She sat down next to me and said in a subdued voice, "Actually, some people didn't take to it so well at first." She looked around. "*I* didn't. I mean it, I really didn't. But you believed, or you had to act as if you believed, and one way or another everybody just came to this." She waved a hand.

"What happened to the ones who wouldn't come to Centrals?"

"People made fun of them. They lost their jobs, the schools wouldn't take their children, the stores wouldn't honor their ration cards. Then the police started to pick up soloists—like they did you." She looked around again, a sort of contented familiarity in her gaze. "It didn't take long."

I turned away from her, but found myself staring at all that plumbing again. I jumped up. "I have to go, Nola. Thanks for your help. Hey—how do I get back to the ship, if the cops are out to pick up any soloist they see?"

"Oh, just tell the man at the gate. There'll be people waiting to go your way. There's always somebody waiting to go everywhere."

She came along with me. I spoke to the man at the gate, and she shook hands with me. I stood by the little table and watched her hesitate, then step up to a woman who was entering. They went in together. The doorman nudged me over toward a group of what appeared to be loungers.

"*North!*" he bawled.

I drew a pudgy little man with bad teeth, who said not one single word. We escorted each other two-thirds of the way to the spaceport, and he disappeared into a factory. I scuttled the rest of the way alone, feeling like a criminal, which I suppose I was. I swore I would never go into that crazy city again.

And the next morning, who should come out for me in an armored car with six two-man prowlers as escort, but Mr. Costello himself!

It was pretty grand seeing him again. He was just like always, big and handsome and good-natured. He was not alone. All spread out in the back corner of the car was the most beautiful blonde woman that ever struck me speechless. She didn't say very much. She would just look at me every once in a while and sort of smile, and then she would look out of the car window and bite on her lower lip a little, and then look at Mr. Costello and not smile at all.

Mr. Costello hadn't forgotten me. He had a bottle of that same red cinnamon wine, and he talked over old times the same as ever, like he was a special uncle. We got a sort of guided tour. I told him about last night, about the visit to the Central, and he was pleased as could be. He said he knew I'd like it. I didn't stop to think whether I liked it or not.

"Think of it!" he said. "All humankind, a single unit. You know the principle of cooperation, Purser?"

When I took too long to think it out, he said, "You know. Two men working together can produce more than two men working separately. Well, what happens when a thousand—a million—work, sleep, eat, think, breathe together?" The way he said it, it sounded fine.

He looked out past my shoulder and his eyes widened just a little. He pressed a button and the chauffeur brought us to a sliding stop.

"Get that one," Mr. Costello said into a microphone beside him.

Two of the prowlers hurtled down the street and flanked a man.

He dodged right, dodged left, and then a prowler hit him and knocked him down.

"Poor chap," said Mr. Costello, pushing the Go button. "Some of 'em just won't learn."

I think he regretted it very much. I don't know if the blonde woman did. She didn't even look.

"Are you the mayor?" I asked him.

"Oh, no," he said. "I'm a sort of broker. A little of this, a little of that. I'm able to help out a bit."

"Help out?"

"Purser," he said confidentially, "I'm a citizen of Borinquen now. This is my adopted land and I love it. I mean to do everything in my power to help it. I don't care about the cost. This is a people that has found the *truth*, Purser. It awes me. It makes me humble."

"I . . ."

"Speak up, man. I'm your *friend*."

"I appreciate that, Mr. Costello. Well, what I was going to say, I saw that Central and all. I just haven't made up my mind. I mean whether it's good or not."

"Take your time, take your time," he said in the big soft voice. "Nobody has to *make* a man see a truth, am I right? A real truth? A man just sees it all by himself."

"Yeah," I agreed. "Yeah, I guess so." Sometimes it was hard to find an answer to give Mr. Costello.

The car pulled up beside a building. The blonde woman pulled herself together. Mr. Costello opened the door for her with his own hands. She got out. Mr. Costello rapped the trideo screen in front of him.

He said, "Make it a real good one, Lucille, real good. I'll be watching."

She looked at him. She gave me a small smile. A man came down the steps and she went with him up into the building.

We moved off.

I said, "She's the prettiest woman I ever saw."

He said, "She likes you fine, Purser."

I thought about that. It was too much.

He asked, "How would you like to have her for your very own?"

"Oh," I said, "she wouldn't."

"Purser, I owe you a big favor. I'd like to pay it back."

"You don't owe me a thing, Mr. Costello!"

We drank some of the wine. The big car slid silently along. It went slowly now, headed back out to the spaceport.

"I need some help," he said after a time. "I know you, Purser. You're just the kind of man I can use. They say you're a mathematical genius."

"Not mathematics exactly, Mr. Costello. Just numbers—statistics—conversion tables and like that. I couldn't do astrogation or theoretical physics and such. I got the best job I could have right now.

"No, you haven't. I'll be frank with you. I don't want any more responsibility on Borinquen than I've got, you understand, but the people are forcing it on me. They want order, peace and order—tidiness. They want to be as nice and tidy as one of your multiple manifests. Now I could organize them, all right, but I need a tidy brain like yours to keep them organized. I want full birth-and death-rate statistics, and then I want them projected so we can get policy. I want calorie-counts and rationing, so we can use the food supply the best way. I want, well, you see what I mean. Once the devil is routed—"

"What devil?"

"The trappers," he said grayly.

"Are the trappers really harming the city people?"

He looked at me, shocked. "They go out and spend weeks alone by themselves, with their own evil thoughts. They are wandering cells, wild cells in the body of humanity. They must be destroyed."

I couldn't help but think of my consignments. "What about the fur trade, though?"

He looked at me as if I had made a pretty grubby little mistake. "My dear Purser," he said patiently, "would you set the price of a few pelts above the immortal soul of a race?"

I hadn't thought of it that way.

He said urgently, "This is just the beginning, Purser. Borinquen is only a start. The unity of that great being, Humanity, will become known throughout the Universe." He closed his eyes. When he opened them, the organ tone was gone. He said in his old, friendly voice, "And you and I, we'll show 'em how to do it, hey, boy?"

I leaned forward to look up to the top of the shining spire of the spaceship. "I sort of like the job I've got. But—my contract's up four months from now . . ."

The car turned into the spaceport and hummed across the slag area.

"I think I can count on you," he said vibrantly. He laughed. "Remember this little joke, Purser?"

He clicked a switch, and suddenly my own voice filled the tonneau. "*I take bribes from passengers.*"

"Oh, that," I said, and let loose one *ha* of a *ha-ha* before I understood what he was driving at. "Mr. Costello, you wouldn't use that against me."

"What do you take me for?" he demanded, in wonderment.

Then we were at the ramp. He got out with me. He gave me his hand. It was warm and hearty.

"If you change your mind about the Purser's job when your contract's up, son, just buzz me through the field phone. They'll connect me. Think it over until you get back here. Take your time." His hand clamped down on my biceps so hard I winced. "But you're not going to take any longer than that, are you, my boy?"

"I guess not," I said.

He got into the front, by the chauffeur, and zoomed away.

I stood looking after him and, when the car was just a dark spot on the slag area, I sort of came to myself. I was standing alone on the foot of the ramp. I felt very exposed.

I turned and ran up to the airlock, hurrying, hurrying to get near people.

That was the trip we shipped the crazy man. His name was Hynes. He was United Earth Consul at Borinquen and he was going back to report. He was no trouble at first, because diplomatic passports are easy to process. He knocked on my door the fifth watch out from Borinquen. I was glad to see him. My room was making me uneasy and I appreciated his company.

Not that he was really company. He was crazy. That first time, he came busting in and said, "I hope you don't mind, Purser, but if I don't talk to somebody about this, I'll go out of my mind." Then he sat down on the end of my bunk and put his head in his hands and rocked back and forth for a long time, without saying anything. Next thing he said was, "Sorry," and out he went. Crazy, I tell you.

But he was back in again before long. And then you never heard such ravings.

"Do you know what's happened to Borinquen?" he'd demand. But he didn't want any answers. He had the answers. "I'll tell you what's wrong with Borinquen—Borinquen's gone mad!" he'd say.

I went on with my work, though there wasn't much of it in space, but that Hynes just couldn't get Borinquen out of his mind.

He said, "You wouldn't believe it if you hadn't seen it done. First the little wedge, driven in the one place it might exist—between the urbans and the trappers. There was never any conflict between them—never! All of a sudden, the trapper was a menace. How it happened, why, God only knows. First, these laughable attempts to show that they were an unhealthy influence. Yes, laughable—how could you take it seriously?

"And then the changes. You didn't have to prove that a trapper had done anything. You only had to prove he was a trapper. That was enough. And the next thing—how could you *anticipate* anything as mad as this?"—he almost screamed—"the next thing was to take anyone who wanted to be alone and lump him with the trappers. It all happened so fast—it happened in our sleep. And all of a sudden you were afraid to be alone in a room for a *second*. They left their homes. They built barracks. Everyone afraid of everyone else, afraid, afraid . . .

"Do you know what they *did?*" he roared. "They burned the paintings, every painting on Borinquen they could find that had been done by one artist. And the few artists who survived as artists—I've seen them. By twos and threes, they work together on the one canvas."

He cried. He actually sat there and cried.

He said, "There's food in the stores. The crops come in. Trucks run, planes fly, the schools are in session. Bellies get full, cars get washed, people get rich. I know a man called Costello, just in from Earth a few months, maybe a year or so, and already owns half the city."

"Oh, I know Mr. Costello," I said.

"Do you now! How's that?"

I told him about the trip out with Mr. Costello. He sort of backed off from me. "*You're* the one!"

"The one what?" I asked in puzzlement.

"*You're* the man who testified against your Captain, broke him, made him resign."

"I did no such a thing."

"I'm the Consul. It was my hearing, man! I was *there!* A recording of the Captain's voice, admitting to insanity, declaring he'd take

330

a gun to his crew if they overrode him. Then your recorded testimony that it was his voice, that you were present when he made the statement. And the Third Officer's recorded statement that all was not well on the bridge. The man denied it, but it was his voice."

"Wait, wait," I said. "I don't believe it. That would need a trial. There was no trial. I wasn't called to any trial."

"There would have been a trial, you idiot! But the Captain started raving about draw poker without a draw, about the crew fearing poisoning from the cook, about the men wanting witnesses even to change the bridge-watch. Maddest thing I ever heard. He realized it suddenly, the Captain did. He was old, sick, tired, beaten. He blamed the whole thing on Costello, and Costello said he got the recordings from you."

"Mr. Costello wouldn't do such a thing!" I guess I got mad at Mr. Hynes then. I told him a whole lot about Mr. Costello, what a big man he was. He started to tell me how Mr. Costello was forced off the Triumverate for making trouble in the high court, but they were lies and I wouldn't listen. I told him about the poker, how Mr. Costello saved us from the cheaters, how he saved us from poisoning, how he made the ship safe for us all.

I remember how he looked at me then. He sort of whispered, "What has happened to human beings? What have we done to ourselves with these centuries of peace, with confidence and cooperation and no conflict? Here's distrust by man for man, waiting under a thin skin to be punctured by just the right vampire, waiting to hate itself and kill itself all over again . . .

"My *God!*" he suddenly screamed at me. "Do you know what I've been hanging onto? The idea that, for all its error, for all its stupidity, this One Humanity idea on Borinquen was a *principle?* I hated it, but because it was a principle, I could respect it. It's Costello—Costello, who doesn't gamble, but who uses fear to change the poker rules—Costello, who doesn't eat your food, but makes you fear poison—Costello, who can see three hundred years of safe interstellar flight, but who through fear makes the watch officers doubt themselves without a witness—Costello, who runs things without being seen!

"My God, Costello doesn't *care!* It isn't a principle at all. It's just Costello spreading fear anywhere, everywhere, to make himself strong!"

He rushed out, crying with rage and hate. I have to admit I was sort of jolted. I guess I might even have thought about the things he said, only he killed himself before we reached Earth. He was crazy.

We made the rounds, same as ever, scheduled like an interurban line: Load, discharge, blastoff, fly and planetfall. Refuel, clearance, manifest. Eat, sleep, work. There was a hearing about Hynes. Mr. Costello sent a spacegram with his regrets when he heard the news. I didn't say anything at the hearing, just that Mr. Hynes was upset, that's all, and it was about as true as anything could be. We shipped a second engineer who played real good accordion. One of the inboard men got left on Carànho. All the usual things, except I wrote up my termination with no options, ready to file.

So in its turn we made Borinquen again, and what do you know, there was the space fleet of United Earth. I never guessed they had that many ships. They sheered us off, real Navy: all orders and no information. Borinquen was buttoned up tight; there was some kind of fighting going on down there. We couldn't get or give a word of news through the quarantine. It made the skipper mad and he had to use part of the cargo for fuel, which messed up my records six ways from the middle. I stashed my termination papers away for the time being.

And in its turn, Sigma, where we lay over a couple of days to get back in the rut, and, same as always, Nightingale, right on schedule again.

And who should be waiting for me at Nightingale but Barney Roteel, who was medic on my first ship, years back when I was fresh from the Academy. He had a potbelly now and looked real successful. We got the jollity out of the way and he settled down and looked me over, real sober. I said it's a small Universe—I'd known he had a big job on Nightingale, but imagine him showing up at the spaceport just when I blew in!

"I showed up *because* you blew in, Purser," he answered.

Then before I could take that apart, he started asking me questions. Like how was I doing, what did I plan to do.

I said, "I've been a purser for years and years. What makes you think I want to do anything different?"

"Just wondered."

I wondered, too. "Well," I said, "I haven't exactly made up my mind, you might say—and a couple of things have got in the way—but I did have a kind of offer." I told him just in a general way about how big a man Mr. Costello was on Borinquen now, and how he wanted me to come in with him. "It'll have to wait, though. The whole damn Space Navy has a cordon around Borinquen. They wouldn't say why. But whatever it is, Mr. Costello'll come out on top. You'll see."

Barney gave me a sort of puckered-up look. I never saw a man look so weird. Yes, I did, too. It was the old Iron Man, the day he got off the ship and resigned.

"Barney, what's the matter?" I asked.

He got up and pointed through the glass door-lights to a white monowheel that stood poised in front of the receiving station. "Come on," he said.

"Aw, I can't. I got to—"

"Come *on!*"

I shrugged. Job or no, this was Barney's bailiwick, not mine. He'd cover me.

He held the door open and said, like a mind reader, "I'll cover you."

We went down the ramp and climbed in and skimmed off.

"Where are we going?"

But he wouldn't say. He just drove.

Nightingale's a beautiful place. The most beautiful of them all, I think, even Sigma. It's run by the UE, one hundred per cent; this is one planet with no local options, but *none*. It's a regular garden of a world and they keep it that way.

We topped a rise and went down a curving road lined with honest-to-God Lombardy poplars from Earth. There was a little lake down there and a sandy beach. No people.

The road curved and there was a yellow line across it and then a red one, and after it a shimmering curtain, almost transparent. It extended from side to side as far as I could see.

"Force-fence," Barney said and pressed a button on the dash.

The shimmer disappeared from the road ahead, though it stayed where it was at each side. We drove through and it formed behind us, and we went down the hill to the lake.

Just this side of the beach was the coziest little Sigma cabana I've seen yet, built to hug the slope and open its arms to the sky. Maybe when I get old they'll turn me out to pasture in one half as good.

While I was goggling at it, Barney said, "Go on."

I looked at him and he was pointing. There was a man down near the water, big, very tanned, built like a space-tug. Barney waved me on and I walked down there.

The man got up and turned to me. He had the same wide-spaced, warm deep eyes, the same full, gentle voice. "Why, it's the Purser! Hi, old friend. So you came, after all!"

It was sort of rough for a moment. Then I got it out. "Hi, Mr. Costello."

He banged me on the shoulder. Then he wrapped one big hand around my left biceps and pulled me a little closer. He looked uphill to where Barney leaned against the monowheel, minding his own business. Then he looked across the lake, and up in the sky.

He dropped his voice. "Purser, you're just the man I need. But I told you that before, didn't I?" He looked around again. "We'll do it yet, Purser. You and me, we'll hit the top. Come with me. I want to show you something."

He walked ahead of me toward the beach margin. He was wearing only a breech-ribbon, but he moved and spoke as if he still had the armored car and the six prowlers. I stumbled after him.

He put a hand behind him and checked me, and then knelt. He said, "To look at them, you'd think they were all the same, wouldn't you? Well, son, you just let me show you something."

I looked down. He had an anthill. They weren't like Earth ants. These were bigger, slower, blue, and they had eight legs. They built nests of sand tied together with mucus, and tunneled under them so that the nests stood up an inch or two like on little pillars.

"They look the same, they act the same, but you'll see," said Mr. Costello.

He opened a synthine pouch that lay in the sand. He took out a dead bird and the thorax of what looked like a Caranho roach, the one that grows as long as your forearm. He put the bird down here and the roach down yonder.

"Now," he said, "watch."

The ants swarmed to the bird, pulling and crawling. Busy. But one or two went to the roach and tumbled it and burrowed around. Mr. Costello picked an ant off the roach and dropped it on the bird. It weaved around and shouldered through the others and scrabbled across the sand and went back to the roach.

"You see, you *see?*" he said, enthusiastic. "Look."

He picked an ant off the dead bird and dropped it by the roach. The ant wasted no time or even curiosity on the piece of roach. It turned around once to get its bearings, and then went straight back to the dead bird.

I looked at the bird with its clothing of crawling blue, and I looked at the roach with its two or three voracious scavengers. I looked at Mr. Costello.

He said raptly, "See what I mean? About one in thirty eats something different. And that's all we need. I tell you, Purser, wherever you look, if you look long enough, you can find a way to make most of a group turn on the rest."

I watched the ants. "They're not fighting."

"Now wait a minute," he said swiftly. "Wait a minute. All we have to do is let these bird-eaters know that the roach-eaters are dangerous."

"They're not dangerous," I said. "They're just different."

"What's the difference, when you come right down to it? So we'll get the bird-eaters scared and they'll kill all the roach-eaters."

"Yes, but why, Mr. Costello?"

He laughed. "I like you, boy. I do the thinking, you do the work. I'll explain it to you. They all look alike. So once we've made 'em

drive out these—" he pointed to the minority around the roach—
"they'll never know which among 'em might be a roach-eater. They'll
get so worried, they'll do anything to keep from being suspected of
roach-eating. When they get scared enough, we can make 'em do
anything we want."

He hunkered down to watch the ants. He picked up a roach-eater
and put it on the bird. I got up.

"Well, I only just dropped in, Mr. Costello," I said.

"I'm not an ant," said Mr. Costello. "As long as it makes no difference to me what they eat, I can make 'em do anything in the world
I want."

"I'll see you around," I said.

He kept on talking quietly to himself as I walked away. He was
watching the ants, figuring, and paid no attention to me.

I went back to Barney. I asked, sort of choked, "What is he doing,
Barney?"

"He's doing what he has to do," Barney said.

We went back to the monowheel and up the hill and through the
force-gate. After a while, I asked, "How long will he be here?"

"As long as he wants to be." Barney was kind of short about it.

"Nobody wants to be locked up."

He had that odd look on his face again. "Nightingale's not a jail."

"He can't get out."

"Look, chum, we could start him over. We could even make a
purser out of him. But we stopped doing that kind of thing a long
time ago. We let a man do what he wants to do."

"He never wanted to be boss over an anthill."

"He didn't?"

I guess I looked as if I didn't understand that, so he said, "All his
life he's pretended he's a man and the rest of us are ants. Now it's
come true for him. He won't run human anthills any more because
he will never again get near one."

I looked through the windshield at the shining finger that was
my distant ship. "What happened on Borinquen, Barney?"

"Some of his converts got loose around the System. That Humanity One idea had to be stopped." He drove a while, seeing badly out

of a thinking face. "You won't take this hard, Purser, but you're a thick-witted ape. I can say that if no one else can."

"All right," I said. "Why?"

"We had to *smash* into Borinquen, which used to be so free and easy. We got into Costello's place. It was a regular fort. We got him and his files. We didn't get his girl. He killed her, but the files were enough."

After a time I said, "He was always a good friend to me."

"Was he?"

I didn't say anything. He wheeled up to the receiving station and stopped the machine.

He said, "He was all ready for you if you came to work for him. He had a voice recording of you large as life, saying 'Sometimes a man's just *got* to be by himself.' Once you went to work for him, all he needed to do to keep you in line was to threaten to put that on the air."

I opened the door. "What did you have to show him to me for?"

"Because we believe in letting a man do what he wants to do, as long as he doesn't hurt the rest of us. If you want to go back to the lake and work for Costello, for instance, I'll take you there."

I closed the door carefully and went up the ramp to the ship.

I did my work and when the time came, we blasted off. I was mad. I don't think it was about anything Barney told me. I wasn't especially mad about Mr. Costello or what happened to him, because Barney's the best Navy psych doc there is and Nightingale's the most beautiful hospital planet in the Universe.

What made me mad was the thought that never again would a man as big as Mr. Costello give that big, warm, soft, strong friendship to a lunkhead like me.

The Education of Drusilla Strange

THE PRISON SHIP, UNDER FULL SHIELDS, slipped down toward the cove, and made no shadow on the moonlit water, and no splash as it slid beneath the surface. They put her out and she swam clear, and the ship nosed up and silently fled. Two wavelets clapped hands softly, once, and that was the total mark the ship made on the prison wall.

For killing the Preceptor, she had been sentenced to life imprisonment.

With torture.

She swam toward the beach until smooth fluid sand touched her knee. She stood up, flung her long hair back with a single swift motion, and waded up the steep shingle, one hand lightly touching the bulging shoulder of the rocks which held the cove in their arms.

Ahead she heard the slightest indrawn breath, then a cough. She stopped, tall in the moonlight. The man took a half-step forward, then turned his head sidewise and a little upward away from her, into the moon.

"I'm—I beg your—sorry," he floundered.

She sensed his turmoil, extracted its source, delved for alternative acts, and chose the one about which he showed the most curious conflict. She crouched back into the shadows by the rock.

I didn't see you there.

"I didn't see you until you ... I'm sorry. Why am I standing here like this when you ... I'll move on down the ... I'm sorry."

She took and fanned out his impressions, sorted them, chose one. *My clothes—*

He started away from the rocks, looking about him, as if he might have been leaning against something hot, or something holy. "Where are they? Am I in the way? Shall I put them near the ... I'll just move on down."

No ... no clothes. Directly from him she took *Where are they?*

"I don't see any. Somebody must've—are you sure you put them—where did you put them?" He was floundering again.

She caught and used the phrase *Why, who would ... what low-down trick!*

"Is your—do you have a car up there?" he asked, peering up at the grassy rim of the beach. He added immediately, "But even if you got to the car ..."

I have no car.

"My God!" he said indignantly. "Anybody that would ... here, what am I standing here yapping for? You must be chilled to the bone."

He was wearing a battered trench coat. He whipped it off and approached her, three-quarters backward, the coat dangling from his blindly extended arm like a torn jib on a bowsprit. She took it, shook it out, turned it over curiously, then slipped into it so that it fell around her the way it had covered him.

Thank you.

She stepped out of the shadows, and the huge relief he felt, and the admixture of guilty regret that went with it made her smile.

"Well!" he said, rubbing his hands briskly. "That's better, now, isn't it?" He looked up the lonely beach, and down. "Live around here somewhere?"

No.

"Oh." He said it again, then, "Friends bring you down?" he asked diffidently.

She hesitated. *Yes.*

"Then they'll be back for you!"

She shook her head. He scratched his. Suddenly he stepped away from her and demanded, "Look, you don't think I had anything to do with stealing your clothes, do you?"

Oh, no!

"Well, all right, because I didn't, I mean I couldn't do a thing like that, even in fun. What I was going to say, I mean, now I don't want you to think anyth . . ." He ground to a stop, took a breath and tried again. "What I mean is, I have a little shack over the rise there. You'd be perfectly safe. I have no phone, but there's one a mile down the beach. I could go and call your friends. I mean I'm not one of those . . . well, look, you do just what you think is best."

She searched. She felt it emerged correctly: *I really mustn't put you to that trouble. But you're very kind.*

"I'm not kind. You'd do exactly the same thing for me, now wouldn't . . ."

He stopped because she was laughing silently, her eyes turned deep into the corners to look at him. She laughed because she had sensed his startled laughter at what he was saying even before it had uncurled.

"I—can't say you would at that," he faltered, and then his laughter surfaced. By the time it had run its course, she was striding lithely beside him.

They walked for a while in silence, until he said, "I do the same thing myself, go swimming in the—I mean without . . . at night. But generally not this late in the year."

She found this unremarkable and made no reply.

"Uh," he began, and then faltered and fell silent again.

She wondered why he felt it so necessary to talk. She probed, and discovered that it was because he was excited and frightened and guilty and happy all at once, full of little half-finished plans concerning cold odds and ends of food and the contents of a clothes closet, the breathless flash of a mental picture of her emerging from the water with certain details oddly highlighted, the quick blanking of the picture and the stern frown that did it, the timid hope that she did not suspect feelings that he could not control . . . Oh, yes, he must talk.

"You have a—do you mind if I say something personal?"

She looked up attentively.

"You have a funny sort of way of talking. I mean—" he leaned close—"you hardly move your lips when you talk."

She turned her head slightly and flexed her lips. She made the effort and said aloud, "Oh?"

"Maybe it's the moonlight," he informed himself. Inwardly he pictured her still face and said *Strange, strange, strange.* "What's your name?"

"Dru. Drusilla," she said carefully. It was not her name, but she had probed and discovered that he liked it. "Drusilla Strange."

"Beautiful," he breathed. "Say, that's a beautiful name, did you know that? Drusilla Strange. That's just . . . just exactly *right*." He looked about at the cool white blaze of the beach, at the black grass under the moon. "Oh!" he said abruptly, "I'm Chan. Chandler Behringer. It's a clumsy sort of name, hard to say, not like—"

"Chandler Behringer," she said. "It sounds like a little wind catching its tail around a—" she dipped into him swiftly—"palm frond."

"Huh!" he shouted. It was one syllable of a laugh, and it was sheer delight. Then he found the rest of the laugh.

He put his hand on her arm just above the elbow and steered her off the beach. The feel of her flesh under the flat close fabric caused a shock that ran up his arm and straight through his defenses.

"Here's my place," he said, with all the wind and none of the cordal vibration necessary to make a voice. He moved away from her and marched up the slope, frowning, leading the way. He ducked into a lean-to porch and fumbled too busily with a latch. "You'd better wait for a moment while I light the lamp. It's sort of cluttered."

She waited. The doorway swallowed him, and there was a fumbling, and a scratching, and suddenly the cabin had an interior. She moved inside.

"You needn't be afraid to look around," he said presently, watching her.

She did, immediately. She had been looking straight at him, following his critical inventory of the entire place, and she now knew it every bit as well as he. But, "Oh," she said, "this is—" she hesitated—"cozy."

"A small place," he said, "but it's dismal." He laughed, and explained apologetically, "I got that line from a movie."

She sorted out the remark, wondered detachedly why he had

made it, half-heartedly probed for the reason, then dropped it as unessential effort.

"A nice soft blanket," he said, lifting it. Her hands went reflexively to the top button of the trench coat and fell away at his next words. "When I go out, you just wrap yourself up nice and snug. I won't be long. Now give me the number."

His mental code for "number" was so brief and so puzzling—a disk with holes in it superimposed on ruled paper—that she was quite at a loss. "Number?"

"Your friends. I'll phone them. They can bring you some clothes, take you home." He laughed self-consciously. "I'll try to say it so that ... I mean, make it sound ... Do you know, I haven't the first idea of just what I'll tell them?"

"Oh," she said. "My friends ... have no phone."

"No—oh. What, no phone?" He looked at her, around at the walls, and inevitably at the bed. It was a very small bed. He gestured weakly at the door. "A ... telegram, maybe, but that would take a long time, and ... Oh, I know. I have clothes, dungarees and things. A lumberjack shirt. Why didn't I think of it? Girls wear all that kind of—but shoes, I don't know ... And then I'll get you a taxi!" he finished triumphantly, and the chaos within him was, to misuse the term, deafening.

She considered very, very carefully and then said, "No taxi could take me back. It's much too far for a taxi to travel."

"Isn't there anyone that—"

"There isn't anyone," she said firmly.

After a long, complicated pause, he asked gently, "What happened?"

She averted her face.

"It was something sad," he half-whispered, and although he was quite still, she could feel the tendrils of his sympathy reaching out toward her. "That's all right, don't worry. Don't," he said loudly, as if it were the first word of a very important pronouncement; but it would not form. He said at last, inanely, "I'll make coffee."

He crossed the room, raising his hand to pat her shoulder as he passed, checking it, not touching her at all, while the echo of that first shock bounded and rebounded within him. He bent over the stove, and in a moment the evil smell of the lamp, which had been pressing closer and closer upon her consciousness, was eclipsed completely by what was to her a completely overpowering, classic, catastrophic and symphonic stench. Her eyelids flickered and closed as she made a tremendous nervous effort and at last succeeded in the necessary realignment of her carbon-oxygen dynamic. And in a moment she could ignore the fumes and open her eyes again.

Chan was looking at her.

"You'll have to stay."

"Yes," she said. She looked at his eyes. "You don't want me to."

"I want you to," he said hurriedly, "I want..." He thought *She's in trouble and she's afraid I'm going to take advantage of it.*

"I'm in trouble," she said, "but I'm not afraid you'll take advantage of it."

He flashed a startling white grin. *She trusts me.* Then the grin faded and the internal frown clamped down. But it could not hide the thought: *She's ... she expects ... she's maybe the kind who ...*

"I'm not the kind," she said levelly, "who—"

"Oh, I know I know I know!" he interrupted rapidly, and with it he thought *Why is she so damned sure of herself?*

"I just don't know *what* to do!" she said.

He smiled again. "You just leave everything to me. We'll make out fine, I mean you're quite safe, you know. And in the morning everything will look a lot brighter. Oh, that coat, that wet old coat. Here," he bustled, "here—here."

From curtained clothes-pole and paper-lined orange crate came blue denims, a spectral holocaust in woolen plaid, a pair of socks of a red that did not belong within four miles of any color in the shirt. She looked at the clothes and at him. He turned his back.

"I'll go on with the ... cook-cook-coffee and you know," he said nervously.

She took off the trench coat and while her fingers solved the logical problem called buttons and the topological one whereby a foot enters a sock, she pondered Chandler Behringer's extraordinary sen-

344

sitivities. Either this species must overpopulate its planet in nine generations, she thought whimsically, or it must die from nervous exhaustion in four. The dungarees gouged and rasped her skin until she damped its sensitivity, but the feel of the heavy, washed wool of the shirt was delightful.

He set out plates and in a moment slid a handsome orange-and-white edible onto them. She looked at it with interest, and then her eyes traveled to the small table by the stove, and she saw the shells. *By the Fountain Itself,* she said silently, *eggs! They eat EGGS!*

She forced her feelings into a desensitized compartment of her mind and corked it. Then she sat opposite Chandler and ate heartily. The coffee was bitter and, to her palate, gritty, but she drank her second cup with composure. *He's so very pleased that I eat with him,* she thought. *They probably do everything gregariously, even where cooperation is not involved.* She was conscious of no disgust, for that, too, was insulated—and so it must stay for the rest of her imprisonment, which is to say the rest of her life.

The food seemed to have relaxed him; a sphygmomanetic allocation, she deduced. And involuntary. How very confining. His chatter had eased and he was taking a silent pleasure in watching her. When she met his eyes finally, he leaped up nervously and scraped and washed the plates energetically. He thought, *I wonder if she liked it.* And: *She knows how to be a guest, and how to keep herself from plunging into the dish-washing, putting them back in the wrong place and all.* And: *I like doing things for her. I wish I could do everything for . . .* And then the frown.

Suddenly in a rush of embarrassment and self-accusation, he spun around and said, "I haven't even asked you, I mean told you, if you, I mean, well, this is just a shack and we haven't all the fixtures."

She looked at him blankly, then probed.

Oh. This is loaded, too. But not eating. Amazing.

She made it as easy for him as she could. She rose and gave him the quick nervous smile that was correct.

"It's outside," he said. "To your left. That little path."

She slipped outside, stalked directly down to the water's edge and with as little effort and even less distress than a polite cough might have cost her, she vomited up the eggs and the coffee. She had eaten, after all, only two days ago.

He had the bed made up when she came in, the pillow smooth, crisp sheets flat and diagonally folded at the head end. "I bet you're as tired as I am," he said. "And that's a whole lot." "Oh," she said, looking at the bed. For sleeping! What would she want sleep for? Because of a phylic habit unbroken in these savages since they were forced to spend the dark hours immobile in a rocky hole to save themselves from nocturnal carnivores? But she said, "Oh, how neat. But I can't take your bed. I'll sit up."

"You'll do no such thing," he said severely, and her eyes widened. He busied himself with a blanket roll and sleeping bag, which he put on the floor just as far—four feet or so—as it could possibly go from the bed. "I love this old bag. Look, nylon and down—the only expensive thing I own. Except my guitar."

She visualized "guitar" and immediately put it down as something to investigate. The flash she got in his coding was brief, but sufficient for her to recognize its size, shape and purpose, and to conclude that although its resonant volumes were gross and its vents inaccurately placed, it was closer to the engineering she knew and understood than most things she had glimpsed here so far.

"You didn't tell me you played the guitar," she said politely.

"I get paid for it," he said, yawning, and she knew that this yawn belonged to this remark and not to the circumstance of somnolence. "Ready for bed?"

Patiently she bowed to his formalities. "You're very kind."

He went to the lamp and turned it out. The low moon streamed in.

He hesitated, slid into his sleeping bag after removing only his shoes. There ensued a considerable amount of floundering, ducking, and thumping on the floor, and at last he brought his trousers out, folded as small as possible. He wadded them between the corner of the sleeping bag and the wall as if they were a secret. Then he sat up and took off his shirt. He hung it on the corner of the window sill, lay down, zipped the bag up to his neck, and ostentatiously turned on his side with his face to the wall. "Good night."

"Good night," she said. Resignedly she got between the sheets, as indicated by the folded-down corner, pulled up the blanket, porpoised out of her trousers, folded them, brought them out and hid them; removed her shirt, reached out a long arm and hung it on the other corner of the window sill. Did he still have his socks on? He did. She wriggled her toes and slightly desensitized her ankles where the weave pressed them.

"You're perfectly safe. Don't worry about a thing."

"Thank you, Chan. I feel safe. I'm not worried. Good night."

"Good night. *Dru,*" he said suddenly, lifting himself on one elbow.

"What is it?"

He lay down again. "Good night."

She watched with deep interest the downward spiralings of his thoughts into the uprising tides of sleep. It happened to him suddenly, and the "noise" factor of his conscious presence slumped away out of the room.

And the torture began.

She had known it was there, but Chandler Behringer was a fine foil for it. He alleviated nothing, but he set up a constant distraction purely by the bumbling, burrowing busyness of his mind. Now it had faded to a whisper, to an effective nothing, and her torture poured down on her. From the warp-shielded, indetectible satellites which guarded the prison planet and administered the punishment, agony poured down to her.

Thus it will be tonight, and the next and next nights, and every night for all of my own forever. Hushed in the day and hungry and sweet at night, it will rain down on me. And I can lie and relax, and I can harbor my anger and anchor my anguish, but the tide will rise, the currents will tug until they break me; if it takes two hundred years. And when I'm broken by it, the torture will go on and on— and on.

Most of the torture was music.

Some of the torture was singing.

And a little of the torture was a thing hardly describable in Earthly terms, which made pictures—not on a screen, not on the mind like memories, however poignant—but pictures so clear and true that the sudden whip of a pennant brought, a second later, spent wind to buffet the eyelids, pictures wherein one walked barefoot on turf and knew a mottling of heat and coolth in the arches, with the moisture of the grass its broken green bleeding. These were pictures where to loose a sling was to know the draw of the pectorals and the particled bite of soil under the downdriven toenails, and to picture a leap was to kick away a very planet, to have that priceless quarter-second of absolute float, and to come back to a cushioning of one's own litheness.

This was music of an ancient planet peopled by a race far older. This was music with the softness and substance of weathered granite, and the unwinding intricacies of a fern. It was ferocious music with a thick-wristed control of its furies so sure that it could be used for laughter. And altogether it was music that rose and cycled and bubbled and built like the Fountain Itself.

This was the high singing of birds beauty-lost in altitude, and the heavier, upward voices expressed by the reaching of trees. It was the voice of the tendon burst for being less strong than the will, and the heart of the sea, and its base was the bass of pulsations of growth (for even a shouldering tree trunk has a note, if listened to for years enough) and altogether these were the voices that made and were made by the Fountain Itself.

And these were the pictures of the Fountain Itself . . .

And such were the tortures of those who were exiled, imprisoned and damned.

She lay there and hated the moonlight; the moon she regarded as ugly and vulgar and new. It seemed to her an added lash, as were all things similar and all things contrasting to the world she had lost. She turned eyes grown cold on the sleeping man, and curled her lip; the creature was a clever counterpart, a subtle caricature, of the worst of the men of her race, in no way perfect, in no way magnificent, but in no way so crude an artifact as to permit her to forget what was surely its original.

By comparison and by contrast, Earth, this muddy, uncouth ball of offal, pinioned her soul to her home. Earth had everything that could be found on her world—after a fashion—racecourses comparatively an armspan wide, racing dun rats ridden by newts in sleazy silks ... men whose eyes sparkled in the sun not quite as much as her racial brother's might when he, with only his shaded hand to help him, sought and found a ghostly nebula.

Cell by interlocking cell, ion by osmotic particle, she belonged elsewhere. And Earth, which was her world falsified; and the endless music, which was her world in truth—these would never let her forget it.

So she cursed the moonbeams and the music sliding down them, and swore that she would not be broken. She could soak herself in this petty planet, zip it up to her neck to conceal anything of her real self in her pettiest acts; she could don the bearing and the thoughts themselves of Earth's too-fine, too-empty puppets and still inwardly she would be herself, a citizen of her world, part of the Fountain Itself. As long as she was that, in any fiber, she could not be completely an exile. Excommunicated she might be; bodily removed, wingless and crawling, trembling under the dear constant breath of her home; but until she broke, her jailers had failed for all their might and righteousness.

The sun rose and turned her away from her bitterness, a little.

Chan's sleeping consciousness came close and roared around her, fell back into blacknesses. She rose and went to the door. The sea was rose-gold and breathing and the sun was aloft, a shade too near, too yellow, and too small. She damned it heartily with a swift thought that spouted and spread and hung in the air like the mist from a fountain, and went and dressed.

She glanced at the percolator, understood it, and deftly made coffee. At its first whisper in the tube, Chan sighed and his consciousness came upward with a rush. Drusilla slipped outside. Patience she had in full measure, but she felt it unworthy to tap it for such unwieldy formalities as she knew she must witness if she stayed in the room during the cracking of his nylon chrysalis.

There was a hoarse shout from inside, a violent floundering, and then Chandler Behringer appeared. He was tousled and frightened. His panic, she noted, had been sufficient to drive him outdoors without his shirt, but not without his trousers. He squeezed his eyelids so tight shut that his cheekbones seemed to rise; then opened them and saw her standing by the beach margin. The radiance that came from his face competed for a moment with the early tilting sunlight.

"I thought you'd gone."

She smiled. "No."

She came to him. His eyes devoured her. He raised both hands together and placed them, one on the other, on his left collarbone. She understood that he was concealing the vestigial nipples (which were absent in males of her race) with his wrists. She examined this reflex with some curiosity, and filed away for future puzzlement the fact that he did this because he wore trousers; had they been bathing trunks, the reflex would not have appeared. He took a breath so deep that she empathized his pain.

"You are the most beautiful woman I have ever seen," he said. She did not doubt it, and had no comment.

"The most beautiful woman who ever lived," he murmured.

Abruptly she turned her back, and now it was her eyes which squeezed shut. "I am *not!*" she said in a tone so saturated with hatred and violence that he stepped back almost into the doorway.

Without another word she strode off, down the beach, her direction chosen solely by the way she happened to be facing at the time. In a moment she was conscious of his feet padding after her.

"Dru, Dru, don't go!" he panted. "I'm sorry, I didn't mean, *hah!* to do anything that *hah!* oh, I was only "

She stopped and turned so abruptly that had he taken two more steps they would have collided. Far from taking steps, however, he had all he could do to stay upright.

She stood looking at him, unmoving. On her face was no particular expression; but there was that in the high-held head, the slightly distended nostrils, the splendid balance of her stance, and her gracefully held, powerful hands that made approach impossible. His eyes were quite round and his lips slightly parted. He extended one hand and moved his mouth silently, then let the hand fall. His knees began to tremble visibly.

She turned again and walked away. He stood there for a long time watching her go. When she was simply a brilliant fleck on the brightening dunes, the purposeless hand came forward again.

"Dru?" he said, in a voice softened to soprano inaudibility by all the cautions of awe. And she was gone, and he turned slowly, as if he had a tall and heavy weight on his rounded shoulders, and plodded back to the cabin.

She found a road which paralleled the beach and climbed to it. Fools cluster about the Universe, she thought, like bubbles about the fountain pool, shifting and pulsing at random, without design, purpose or function. She had left such a fool and she was such a fool. There was far more culpability in her folly than in that of the man. He had little control over what he might say, and less understanding, because of his nature and his limitations. Neither his faculties nor his conditioning could enable him to understand why she felt such fury.

She stabbed her heels into the sandy roadbed as she walked. She ground her teeth. *The most beautiful woman who ever lived . . .*

Her beauty!

Where, exile—where, criminal, has your beauty brought you?

She strode on, her mood so black it all but eclipsed the torture music.

Perhaps fifteen minutes later, she became conscious of a shrill ultrasonic, a rapidly pulsing, urgent, growing thing that would be a silence to all but her. She slowed, stopped finally. The sound came from behind her, but she would not confuse her analysis by looking back. She listened as an intervening wind carried the vibrations away and then let them come back again, nearer, stronger. She sensitized her bare feet; she raised an arm and took the vibrations on the back of her hand. She became conscious of synchronous sounds.

Something rotated at approximately thirty-eight hundred and forty rpm. Something was chain-driven and the chain was not a metal. Something pounded . . . no, paced—something rolled endless soft cleats on the earth. She heard the straining of coil springs, the labored slide of heavy transverse leaf-springs, the make-and-break in the meniscus of the oil guarding busy pistons.

The utter stupidity of so complex a thing as an automobile was, to her, more wondrous than a rainbow.

At last she turned to look, and in a moment she saw it climb a rise some two miles away. The piercing ultrasonic was beyond bearing, and she adjusted her hearing to eliminate everything between eighty-six and eighty-eight thousand cycles.

More comfortable now, she waited patiently. The car slid down a straight and gentle grade toward her, spitting sunlight through its chromium teeth, palming aside the morning air and pressing it back and down its sleek flanks, while underneath, where there was no hint of fairing, air shocked and roiled and shuddered and troubled what dust it could find in the sandy road. It was a very large and very new car. Drusilla watched it, wide-eyed. She came to wonder what conclusions one would have regarding these—these savages, if one knew nothing of them but such a vehicle. What manner of man streamlines only where he can see?

The lovely thought, then: *It's a world of clowns.*

She smiled; the driver saw it and his foot came down on the brake pedal. The car threw down its glittering baroque nose, slid a hand's breadth, and lowered itself sitzwise into its warm bath of springs.

The driver's eyes were long and flat and his nose and chin were sharp. Drusilla watched what he was doing, which was watching himself watch her.

Suddenly he said, "How far is it to—" and before the first word was spoken, she knew he was completely familiar with these roads.

She said, "Your—" and raised her hand to point accurately at the hood, while she searched him for the term. "Your rocker-arm's not getting oil. The third one from the front." Even while the motor idled, the soundless shriek of that dry friction would have been unbearable had she let it.

"Sounds all right to me," he shrugged. He looked—he journeyed, rather—down from her eyes, down until he saw that her feet were bare. He left his gaze where it was and said, "Let me give you a lift." He half turned then, reached one thin spidery arm back and across without looking, and the rear door swung open.

Drusilla took one step forward and only then saw that the man was not alone in the car. She stopped, amazed—not at the woman who sat there, but at the fact that perceptions such as hers had missed so much. She glanced at the man, and realized that it was his feeling, or lack of it, that had numbed and blinded her to everything about the woman who sat beside him. She was companion reduced to presence, minified to fixture, reduced to a very limbo of familiarity. Drusilla stared at her, and the woman stared back.

She was a small woman, compact, so coiffed and clad that she was only a blandness. What kept her from being featureless as an egg was a pair of achingly blue eyes large enough for a being half again her size, and a perfect mouth painted such a transcendental, pupil-shrinking red that surely it would melt fuse-wire. Her wide eyes were blank.

To Drusilla's horror, a growth like an iridescent liver sprang into being between the flaming lips, grew to the size of a fist and collapsed limply. The lips parted a pink tongue deftly caught, cleared, and drew the limp matter back between an even flicker of paper-white teeth. And again the face was molded and smooth and motionless.

"My wife," said the man, "so you're chaperoned. My God, Lu, you got bubble gum again." The woman took her gaze away from Drusilla and placed it on the driver, but there was otherwise no change. "Get in."

Drusilla's mind played back a fleeting inner sensation she had taken from him when he had said "My wife." It was ... pride? No. Admiration? Hardly! *Compliment*; that was it. This woman was a compliment he paid himself. He had no tiny fleck of doubt that he was admired for her careful finish.

The big blue eyes swung to her again and she probed.

For a ghastly micro-second, she had all the sensations of walking into a snakepit with chloroform on her scarf. She recoiled violently, moved far back to the low bank; and she shuddered.

"Come on, uh, hey, what's the matter?" the driver called.

Drusilla shook her head twice, not so much in refusal as in an attempt to escape from something that was laying clammy strands of silk on her face and hair. Without another word, she turned and walked away down the road, behind the car.

"Hey!"

Drusilla did not look back.

He started the car and drove off slowly. In a moment, the woman leaned forward and tugged hard on the wheel. The car heeled back on the road, and at last he took his eyes from the rear view mirror. "Now what's with her?" he demanded of the windshield wiper.

Lu blew another bubble.

When the car was gone, Drusilla went slowly back and past the place she had met it, and on toward the town. From her marrow she swore a mighty oath that never again would she be trapped into sending her probes into such a revolting mess. The driver hadn't been like that; Chan Behringer hadn't. Yet she knew with a terrible certainty that there must be thousands like that creature here on the prison planet.

So as she walked she devised something, a hair-triggered synaptic structure, a reaction pattern that could, even without her conscious knowledge, detect the faintest beginnings of a presence such as this; and it would snap down her shields, isolate her, protect her, keep her clean.

She was badly shaken. The presence of that woman had shaken her, but the most devastating thing of all was the knowledge that she could be shaken. It was a realization most difficult for her to absorb; it had little precedent in her cosmos.

Walking, she shuddered again.

Drusilla came to the town and wandered until she found a restaurant which needed a waitress. She borrowed the price of a pair of beach sandals from the weary cashier and went to work. She found a little room and at the end of the second day she had the price of a cotton dress.

In the second week she was a stenographer and, in the second month secretary to the head of a firm which made boat-sails and awnings. She invested quietly, sold some poems, a song, two articles and a short story. In terms of her environment, she did very well indeed, very fast. In her own estimate, she did nothing but force her attention randomly away from her torture.

For the torture, of course, continued. She bore it with outward composure, shucked it off as casually as, from time to time, she changed her name, her job, her hair-styling and her accent. But like the lessons she learned, like the knowledge of the people she met and worked with, the torture accumulated. She could estimate her capacity for it. It was large, but not infinite. She could get rid of none of it, any more than she could get rid of knowledge. It could be compacted and stored. As long as she could do this with the torture, she was undefeated. But she was quite capable of calculating intake against capacity and she had not much time. A year and a half, two ...

She would stand at the window, absorbing her punishment, staring up into the night sky with her bright wise eyes. She could not see the guardian ships, of course, but she knew they were there. She knew of their killer-boats which could, if necessary, slip down in moments and blast a potential escapee, or one about to violate the few simple rules of a prisoner's conduct.

Sometimes, objectively, she marveled at the cruel skill of the torture. Music alone, with its ineffable spectrum of sadness and longing and wild nostalgic joy, could have been enough and more than enough for a prisoner to bear; but the sensory pictures, the stimulative and restimulative flow and change of taste and motion and all the subtleties of the kinetic senses—these, mixed and mingled with music, charging in where music lulled, marching in the footprints of the music's rhythmic stride—these were the things which laughed at her barriers, sparred with her, giggling; met her fists with a breeze, her rapier with a gas, her advances with a disappearance.

There was no fighting attacks like these. Ignorance would have been a defense, but was of no use to her who was so nerve-alive to all the torture's sense and symbolism. All she could do was to absorb, compact, and hope that she could find a defense before she broke.

So she lived and outwardly prospered. She met some humans who amused her briefly, and others she avoided after one or two meetings because they reminded her so painfully of her own people—a smile, a stride, a matching of colors. If she met any others with the terrifying quality of the woman in the car, she was not aware of it; that part of her defense, at least, was secure.

But the torture still poured down upon her, and after half a year she knew she must take some steps to counteract it. At base, the solution was simple. If she did nothing, the torture would crush her, and there was no surcease in that, for having broken, she would go on suffering it. She could kill herself, but that in itself would fulfill the terms of her sentence—"life imprisonment—with torture." There was only one way—to be killed, and to be killed by the guardians. She was not under a death sentence. If she forced one, they would have; to violate their own penalty, and she would be able to die unbroken, as befits a Citizen of the Fountain Itself.

More and more she studied the sky, knowing of the undetectible presence of the guardians and their killer-boats, knowing that if she could think of it, there must be a way to bring one of them careening silently down on her to snuff her out. She made sendings of many kinds—even of the kind she had used to extinguish the life-force of the Preceptor—without altering the quality or degree of torture in the slightest.

Perhaps the guardians sent, but did not receive; perhaps nothing could touch them. Geared to the pattern of a Citizen's mind and conditioning, they patiently produced that which must, in time, destroy it. The destruction would be because of the weakness of the attacked. Drusilla wanted to be destroyed through the strength of the attacker. The distinction was, to her, clear and vital.

There had to be a way, if only she could think of it.

There was, and she did.

He came onstage grinning like a boy, swinging his guitar carelessly.

The set was a living room. He plumped down on a one-armed easy-chair and hooked a brown-and-white hassock toward him with his heel. There was applause.

"Thank you, Mother," said Chan Behringer. He slipped the plectrum from under the first and second strings. Dru thought *Your low D is one one-hundred-twenty-eighth tone sharp.*

Deftly, out of sight of the audience, he plugged in the pickup cable. Dru watched attentively. She had never seen a twelve-string guitar before.

He began to play. He played competently, with neither mistakes nor imagination. There was a five-stage amplifier built into his chair and a foot-pedal tone control and electronic vibrato in the hassock. A rough cutoff at twenty-seven thousand cycles, she realized, and then remembered that, to most humans, response flat to eight thousand is high fidelity.

She was immensely pleased with the electrical pickups; she had not noticed them at first, which was a compliment to him. One was magnetic, sunk into the fingerboard at the fourteenth fret. The other was a contact microphone, obviously inside the box, directly under the bridge. The either-or-both switch was audible when he moved it, which she thought disgraceful.

He finished his number, drawled a few lines of patter, asked for and played a couple of requests and an encore, by which time Drusilla had left the theater and was talking to the stage doorman. He took the paper parcel she handed him and sent it to the dressing rooms via the callboy.

In a matter of seconds, there was a wild whoop from backstage and Chan Behringer came bounding down the iron steps, clutching a wild flannel shirt, a pair of blue dungarees, and some tatters of paper and string.

"Dru! Dru!" he gasped. He ran to her, his arms out. Then he stopped, faltered, put his head very slightly to one side. "Dru," he said again, softly.

"Hello, Chan."

"I never thought I'd see you again."

"I had to return your things."

"Too good to be true," he murmured. "I—we—" Suddenly he turned to the goggling doorman and tossed clothes to him. "Hang on to these for me, will you, George?" To Drusilla he said, "I should take 'em backstage, but I'm afraid to let you out of my sight."

"I won't run away again."

"Let's get out of here," he said. He took her arm, and again there was the old echo of a shock he had once felt at the touch of her flesh through fabric.

They went to a place, all soft lights and leather, and they talked about the beach and the city and show business and guitar music, but not about her strange fury with him the morning she had stalked out of his life.

"You've changed," he said at length.

"Have I?"

"You were like—like a queen before. Now you're like a princess."

"That's sweet."

"More . . . human."

She laughed. "I wasn't exactly human when you first met me. I'd had a bad time. I'm all right now, Chan. I—didn't want to see you until I was all right."

They talked until it was time for his next act, and after that they had dinner.

She saw him the next day, and the next.

The chubby man with a face like a cobbler and hands like a surgeon made the most beautiful guitars in the world. He sprang to his feet when the tall girl came in. It was the first time he had paid such a courtesy in fourteen years.

"Can you cut an F-slot that looks like this?" she demanded.

He looked at the drawing she laid on the counter, grunted, then said, "Sure, lady. But why?"

She launched into a discussion which, at first, he did not hear, for it was in his field and in his language and he was too astonished to think. But once into it, he very rapidly learned things about resonance, harmonic reinforcement, woods, varnishes and reverse-cantilever designs that were in no book he had ever heard about.

When she left a few minutes later, he hung gasping to the counter. In front of him was a check for work ordered. In his hand was a twenty-dollar bill for silence. In his mind was a flame and a great wonderment.

She spilled a bottle of nail polish remover on Chan's guitar. He was kind and she was pathetically contrite. It was all right, he said; he knew a place that could retouch it before evening. They went there together. The little man with the cobbler's face handed over the new instrument, a guitar with startling slots, an ultra-precision bridge, a fingerboard that crept into his hand as if it were alive and loved him. He chorded it once, and at the tone he put it reverently down and stared. His eyes were wet.

"It's yours," Drusilla twinkled. "Look—your name inlaid on the neck-back."

"I know your guitars," said Chan to the chubby man, "but I never heard of anything like this."

"Tricks to every trade," said the man, and winked.

Drusilla slipped him another twenty as they left.

The electronics engineer stared at the schematic diagram. "It won't work."

"Yes, it will," said Drusilla. "Can you build it?"

"Well, gosh, yes, but who ever heard of voltage control like this? Where's the juice supposed to go from . . ." He leaned closer. "Well, I'll be damned. Who designed this?"

"Build it," she said.

He did. It worked. Drusilla wired it into the prop armchair and Chan never knew anything had been changed. He attributed everything to the new instrument as he became more familiar with it and began to exploit its possibilities. Suddenly there were no more layoffs. No more road trips, either. The clubs began to take important notice of the shy young man with the tear-your-heart-out guitar.

She stole his vitamin pills and replaced them with something else. She invited him to dinner at her apartment and he fainted in the middle of the fish course.

He came to seven hours later on the couch, long after the strange induction baker and the rack of impulse hypodermics had been hidden away. He remembered absolutely nothing. He was lying on his left arm and it ached.

Dru told him he had fallen asleep and she had just let him sleep it out.

"Poor dear, you've been working too hard."

He told her somewhat harshly that she must *never* let him sleep like that, cutting off the circulation in his fingering arm. The next day, the arm was worse and he had to cancel a date. On the third day, it was back to normal, one hundred per cent, and on the fourth, fifth, and sixth days it continued to improve. And what it could do on the fingerboard was past description. Which was hardly surprising: there was not another arm on Earth like it, with its heavier nerve-fibers, the quadrupling of the relay-nodes on the medullary sheaths, the low-resistance, super-reactive axones, and the isotopic potassium and sodium which drenched them.

"I don't play this damn thing any more," he said. "I just think the stuff and that left hand reads my mind."

He made three records in three months, and the income from them increased cubically each time. Then the record company decided to save money and put him under a long-term contract at a higher rate than anyone had ever been paid before.

Chan, without consulting Drusilla, bought one of a cluster of very exclusive houses just over the city line. The neighbors on the left were the Kerslers, whose grandfather had made their money in off-the-floor sanitary fixtures. The neighbors on the right were the Mullings you know, Osprey Mullings, the writer, two books a year, year in and year out, three out of four of them making Hollywood.

Chan invited the Kerslers and the Mullings to his housewarming, and took Drusilla out there to surprise her.

She was surprised, all right. Kersler had a huge model railroad in his cellar and his mind likewise contained a great many precise minutiae, only one of which was permitted to operate at a time. Grace Kersler's mind was like an empty barn solidly lined with pink frosting. Osprey Mullings' head contained a set of baby's blocks of limited number, with which he constructed his novels by a ritualistic process of rearrangement. But Luellen Mullings was the bland-faced confection who secretly chewed bubble gum and who had so jolted Drusilla that day on the beach road.

It was a chatty and charming party, and it was the very first time that humans had been capable of irritating Drusilla so much that she had to absorb the annoyance rather than ignore it. She bore this attack on her waning capacities with extreme graciousness, and at parting, the Kerslers and the Mullings pressed Chan's hand and wished him luck with that *beautiful* Drusilla Strange, you lucky fellow you.

And late at night, full to bursting with success and security and a fine salting of ambition, Chan drove her back to town and at her apartment, he proposed to her.

She held both his hands and cried a little, and promised to work with him and to help him even more in the future—but, "Please, please, Chan, never ask me that again."

He was hurt and baffled, but he kept his promise.

Chan studied music seriously now—he never had before. He had to. He was giving concerts rather than performances, and he played every showcase piece ever composed by one virtuoso to madden and frustrate the others. He played all of the famous violin cadenzi on his guitar as well. He made arrangements of the arrangements. He did all this with the light contempt of a Rubinstein examining a two-dollar lesson in chord-vamping. So at length he had no recourse but to compose. Some of his stuff was pretty advanced. All of it took you by the throat and held you.

One Sunday afternoon, "Try this," said Drusilla. She hummed a tone or two, then burst into a cascade of notes that brought Chan up standing.

"*God*, Dru!"

"Try it," she said.

He got his guitar. His left hand ran over the fingerboard like a perplexed little animal, and he struck a note or two.

"No," she said, "this." She sang.

"Oh," he whispered. Watching her, he played. When she seemed not pleased, he stopped.

"No," she said. "Chan, I can only sing one note at a time. You have twelve strings." She paused, thoughtfully, *listening.* "Chan, if I asked you to play that theme, and then to—to paint pictures on it with your guitar, would that make sense?"

"You usually make sense."

She smiled at him. "All right. Play that theme, and with it, play the way a tree grows. Play the way the bud leads the twig and the twig cuts up into space to make a hole for the branch. No," she said quickly, as his eyes brightened and his right thumb and forefinger tightened on the plectrum, "not yet. There's more."

He waited.

She closed her eyes. Almost inaudibly, she hummed something. Then she said, "At the same time, put in all the detail of a tree that has already grown." She opened her eyes and looked straight at him. "That will consolidate," she said factually, "because a tree is only the graphic trajectory of its buds."

He looked at her strangely. "You're quite a girl."

"Never mind that," she said quickly. "Now put those three things together with a fountain. And that's all."

"What kind of a fountain?"

She paled, but her voice was easy. "Silly. The only kind of fountain that could *be* with that theme, the tree growing, and the tree grown."

He struck a chord. "I'll try."

She hummed for him, then brought one long forefinger down. He picked up the theme from her voice. He closed his eyes. The guitar, of all instruments the most intimately expressive, given a magic sostenuto by its electronic graft, began to speak.

The theme, the tree growing, the tree grown.

Suddenly, the fountain, too.

What happened then left them both breathless. Music of this nature should never be heard in a cubic volume smaller than its subject.

When the pressured stridency of the music was quite gone, Chan looked at a cracked window pane and then turned to watch a talc-fine trickle of plaster dust stream down from the lintel of the french window.

"Where," he said, shaken, "did you get *that* little jangle?"

"Thin air, darling," said Drusilla blithely. "All the time, everywhere, whenever you like. Listen."

He cocked his head. There was an intense silence. His left hand crept up to the frets and spattered over them. In spite of the fact that he had not touched the strings with his right hand, a structure of sound hung in the room, reinforcing itself, holding, holding ... finally dying.

"That it?" he asked, awed.

She held up a thumb and forefinger very close together. "About so much of it."

"How come I never heard it before?"

"You weren't ready."

His eyes suddenly filled with tears. "Damn it, Drusilla ... you're—you've done ... Oh, hell, I don't know, I love you so much."

She touched his face. "Shh. Play for me, Chan."

He breathed hard, thickly. "Not in here."

He put down his guitar and went to get the portable amplifier. They set it upon the rolling lawn and plugged in the guitar. Chan held the instrument for a silent moment, sliding his hand over its polished flank. He looked up suddenly and met Drusilla's eyes. Chan's face twisted, for her ecstasy and gaiety and triumph added up to something very like despair, and he did not understand.

He would have thrown down the guitar then, for his heart was full of her, but she backed away, shaking her head lightly, and bent to the amplifier to switch it on. Her fingers pulled at the rotary switch as she turned it, and only she knew the nature of the mighty little transmitter that began to warm up along with the audio. She moved back still further; she did not want to be close to him when it—happened.

He watched her for a moment, then looked down at the guitar. He watched his four enchanted left fingers hook and hover over the fingerboard; he looked at them with a vast puzzlement that slowly turned to raptness. He began to sway gently.

Drusilla stood tall and taut, looking past him to the trees, to the scudding clouds and beyond. She dropped her shields and let the music pour in. And from the guitar came a note, another, two together, a strange chord. *For this I shall be killed,* she thought. To bring to the mighty scorn her people had of Earth and all things Earthly, this molded savage who could commune like a Citizen ... this was the greatest affront.

A foam of music fell and feathered and rushed inward to the Fountainhead Itself, and every voice of it smashed and hurtled upward. The paired sixth strings of the guitar flung up with them in a bullroar *glissando* that broke and spread glistening all over the keyboard, falling and falling away from a brittle high spatter of doubled first strings struck just barely below the bridge, metallic and needly; and if those taut strings were tied to a listener's teeth, they could not be more intimate and shocking.

The unique sound box found itself in sudden shrill resonance, and it woke the dark strings, the deep and mighty ones. They thrummed and sang without being touched; and Chan's inhuman fingers found a figure in the middle register, folded it in on itself, broke it in two, and the broken pieces danced ... and still the untouched strings hummed and droned, first one loud and then another as the resonances altered and responded.

And all at once the air was filled with the sharp and dusty smell of ozone.

With it all, the music, hers and Chan's, settled itself down and down like some dark giant, pressing and sweeping and gathering in its drapes and folds as it descended to rest, to collect its roaring and crooning and tittering belongings all together that they may be pieced and piled and understood; until at last the monster was settled and neat, leaving a looming bulk of silence and an undertone of pumping life and multi-level quiet stripes of contemplation. The whole structure breathed, slowly and more slowly, held its breath, let a tension develop, rising, painful, agonizing, intolerable ...

"Play Red River Valley, hey, Chan?"

Drusilla gasped, and the ozone rasped her throat. Chan's fingers faltered, stopped. He half-turned, with a small, interrogative whimper.

Standing on the other side of the far hedge, near her house, was

Luellen Mullings, her doll-figure foiled like a glass diamond in a negligible playsuit, her golden hair free, her perfect jaw busy on her sticky cud.

There was born in Drusilla a fury more feral, more concentrated, than any power of muscle or mind she had ever conceived of. Luellen Mullings, essence of all the degradation Earth was known for, all the cheapness, shallowness, ignorance and stupidity. She was the belch in the cathedral; she would befoul the Fountain Itself.

"Hi, Dru, honey. Didn't see you. Hey, I saw a feller at the Palace could play guitar holding it behind his back." She sniffed. "What's that funny smell? Like lightning or something."

"Get back in your house, you cheap little slut," Drusilla hissed.

"Hey, who you calling—" Luellen dipped down and picked up a smooth white stone twice the size of her fist. She raised it. Even Drusilla's advanced reflexes were not fast enough to anticipate what she did. The stone left her hand like a bullet. Drusilla braced herself—but the stone did not come to her. It struck Chan just behind the ear. He pivoted on his heel three-quarters of a revolution, and quietly collapsed on the grass, the guitar nestling down against him like a loving cat.

"Now look at what you made me do!" Luellen cried shrilly.

Drusilla uttered a harpy's scream and bounded across the lawn, her long hands spread out like talons. Luellen watched her come, round-eyed.

There is a force in steady eyes by which a tiger may be made to turn away. It can make a strong man turn and run. There is a way to gather this force into a deadly nubbin and hurl it like a grenade. Drusilla knew how to do this, for she had done it before; she had killed with it. But the force she hurled at Luellen Mullings now was ten times what she had dealt the Preceptor.

For a moment, the Universe went black, and then Drusilla became aware of a pressure on her face. There was another sensation, systemic, pervasive. Her legs, her arms, were weighted and tingly, and she seemed to have no torso at all.

She gradually understood the sensation on her face. Moist earth and grass. She was lying on her stomach on the lawn. She absorbed this knowledge as if it were a complicated matrix of ideas which, if comprehended, might lead to hitherto unheard-of information. At last she realized what was wrong with her body. Oxygen starvation. She began to breathe again, hard, painful gasps, inflations that threatened to burst the pulmonary capillaries, exhalations that brought her diaphragm upward until it crushed in panic against the pounding cardium.

She moved feebly, pulled a limp hand toward her, rested a moment with it flat on the grass near her shoulder. She began to press herself upward weakly, failed, rested a moment, and tried again. At last she raised herself to a sitting position.

Chan lay where he had fallen, still as death, guitar nearby.

Pop!

Drusilla looked up. Over the hedge, like an artificial flower, nodded Luellen's bright head. The quick deft tongue was retrieving the detritus of a broken bubble.

Drusilla snarled and formed another bolt, and as it left her something like a huge soft mallet seemed to descend on her shoulder blades. Seated as she was, it folded her down until her chest struck the ground. Her hip joints crackled noisily. She writhed, straightened out, lay on her side gasping.

Pop!

Drusilla did not look up.

Presently she heard Luellen's light footsteps retreating down the gravel path. She gave herself over to a wave of weakness, and relaxed completely to let the strength flow back.

Shh ... shh ... approaching footsteps.

Drusilla rolled over and sat up again. Her head felt simultaneously pressured and fragile, as if any sudden move would make it burst like a faulty boiler. She turned pain-blinded eyes to the footsteps. When the jagged ache receded, she saw Luellen sauntering toward her on this side of the hedge, swinging her hips, humming tunelessly.

"Feeling better, honey?"

Drusilla glared at her. The killer-bolt began to form again. Luellen sank gracefully to the grass, near but not too near, and chose a grass-stem to pull up.

"I wouldn't if I were you, hon," she said pleasantly. "I can keep this up all day. You're just knocking yourself out."

She regarded the grass stem thoughtfully from her wide vacant eyes, poked out a membrane of gum, hesitated a moment, and drew it back in without blowing a bubble. The gum clicked wetly twice as she worked it.

"*Damn* you," said Drusilla devoutly.

Luellen giggled. Drusilla struggled upward, leaned heavily on one arm, and glared. Luellen said, without looking at her, "That's far enough, sweetie."

"Who are you?" Drusilla whispered.

"Home makuh," said Luellen, with a trace of Bronx accent. "Leisure class type home makuh."

"You know what I mean," Drusilla growled.

"Whyn't you look and see?"

Drusilla curled her lip.

"Don't want to get your pretty probes dirty, huh? Know what you are? You're a snob."

"A—a what?"

"Snob," said Luellen. She stretched prettily. "Just too good for *anybody*. Too good for him."

She pointed to Chan with a gesture of her head. "Or me." She shrugged. "*Anybody*."

Drusilla glanced at Chan and probed anxiously.

"He's all right," said Luellen. "Just unplugged."

Drusilla swung her attention back to the other girl. Reluctantly she dropped her automatic shield and reached out with her mind. *What are you?*

Luellen put her hands out, palms forward. "Not that way. I don't do that any more. Look if you want to, but if you want to talk to me, talk out loud."

Drusilla probed. "A criminal!" she said finally, in profound disgust.

"Sisters under the skin," said Luellen. She popped her gum. Drusilla shuddered. Luellen said, "Tell you what I did."

"I'm not interested."

"Tell you, anyway. Listen," Luellen said suddenly, "you know if you try to do anything to me, you'll go flat on your bustle. Well, the same thing applies if you don't listen to me. Hear?"

Drusilla dropped her eyes and was furiously silent. Reluctantly she realized that this creature could do exactly as she said.

"I'm not asking you to like it," Luellen said more gently. "Just listen, that's all."

She waited a moment, and when Drusilla offered nothing, she said, "What I did, I climbed over the wall at school."

Drusilla gasped. "You went outside?"

Luellen rolled over onto her stomach and propped herself on her elbows. She pulled another blade of grass and broke it. "Something funny happened to me. You know the feeling-picture about jumping?"

Drusilla recognized it instantly, the sweet, strong, breathless sensation of being strong and leaping from soft grass, floating? landing lithely.

"You do," said Luellen, glancing at Drusilla's face. "Well, I was having that picture one fine morning when it—*stuck*. I mean like one of the phonograph records here when it gets stuck. There I was feeling a jump. Just off the ground, and it all froze."

She laughed a little. "I was real scared. After a while, it started again. I went and asked my tutor about it. She got all upset and went to the Preceptor. He called me in and there was no end of hassle about it." Again she laughed. "I'd have forgotten the whole thing if he hadn't made such a fuss. He wanted me to forget it in the *worst* way. Tried to make me think it happened because there was something wrong with me.

"So I got to thinking about it. When you do that, you start looking pretty carefully at *all* the pictures. And you know, they're full of scratches and flaws, if you look.

"But all time they were teaching us that this was the world

over the Wall—perfect green grass, beautiful men, the fountain and the falls and all the rest of it, that we were supposed to graduate to when the time came. I wondered so much that I wouldn't wait any more. So I went over the wall. They caught me and sent me here."

"I don't wonder," said Drusilla primly.

Luellen put pink fingers to her lips, hauled the gum out almost to arm's length, and chewed it back in as she talked. "And all you did was knock off the Preceptor!"

Drusilla winced and said nothing.

Luellen said, "You been here about two years, right? How many of us prisoners have you run into?"

"None!" said Drusilla, with something like indignation. "I wouldn't have anything to do with—" She clamped her lips tight and snorted through her nostrils. "Will you *stop* that giggling?"

"I can't help it," said Luellen. "It's part of the pattern for home makuhs. All home makuhs giggle."

" . . . And that voice!"

"That's part of the pattern too, hon," said Luellen. "How do you think I'd go over at the canasta table if I weren't a-flutter and a-twitter, all coos and sighs and gentle breathings? My God, the girls'd be scared right out of their home permanents!" She tittered violently.

"Again!" Drusilla winced.

"You might as well get used to it, hon. I had to. You'll be doing something equally atrocious yourself, pretty soon. It goes under the head of camouflage . . . Look, I'll stop fooling around. There's a couple of hard truths you have to get next to. I know what you did. You set up a reflex to blank out any ex-Citizen you might meet. Right?"

"One must keep oneself decent," insisted Drusilla.

Luellen shook her head wonderingly. "You're just dumb, girl. I don't like you, but I have to be sorry for you."

"I don't need your pity!"

"Yes, you do. You've been asleep for a whole lot of years and you just have to snap out of it." Luellen knelt and sat back on her heels. "Tell me—up to the time they shipped you here, where did you go?"

"You know perfectly well. The Great Hall. My garden. My dormitory. That's all."

"Um-hmm. That's all. And every minute since you were born, you've been conditioned: a Citizen is the finest flower of creation. Be a good obedient girl and you'll gambol on the green for the rest of your life. Meanwhile there are criminals who get sent to prison, and the prison is the lowest cesspool in the Universe where you live out your life being reminded of the glory of the world you lost."

"Of course, but you make it sound—"

"Did you ever see any of those big muscular beautiful men the pictures told you about? Did you ever see that old-granite and new-grass landscape, or get warm under that nice big sun?"

"No, I was sent here before I had—"

Luellen demonstrated her ties to Earth by uttering a syllable which was, above all else, Earthy. "You're the dumbest blind kitten I ever saw. And tell me, when they took you to the ship, did you get a chance to look around?"

"I wasn't . . . worthy," said Drusilla miserably. "If a—a criminal was privileged to see outside the Wall—"

"They blindfolded you. Yes, and you never got a chance to look out of the ship when it left, either. Look, Citizen," she said scornfully, "if you hadn't had the good sense to get yourself sent here, you never would have gotten over the Wall!"

"I had only six more years before I—"

"Before you'd be quietly moved to another Walled Place with your age group. And maybe you'd have been bred, and maybe not, and by the time you realized there was no release for you, you'd be so old you wouldn't care any more. And they call that a world and this a prison!"

Drusilla suddenly put her hands over her ears. "I won't listen to this! I won't!"

Luellen grasped her wrist in a remarkably powerful little hand. "Yes, by God, you will," she said between her perfect teeth. "Our race is old and dying, rotten to the core. Know why you never saw any men? Because there are only a few hundred of them left. They lie in their cubicles and get fat and breed. And most of their children are girls, because that's the way it was arranged so long ago that we've forgotten how it was done or how to change it. You know what's over the Wall? Nothing! It's an ice world, with a dying sun and thinning air, and a little cluster of Walled Places to breed women for the men to breed with, and a few old, old, worn transmitters for music and pictures to condition the blindworms who live and die there!"

Drusilla began to cry. Luellen sat back and watched her, a great softness coming into her eyes.

"Cry, that's good, sweetie," she said huskily. "Ah, you poor brat. You could've gotten straightened out the day you arrived. But no. Criminals were the lowest of the low, and you wouldn't associate with them. Earth and humans were insects and savages, because that's what you were taught. To be a Citizen was to be a god among gods, and to hear the music was your torture, for what you'd lost."

"What about the torture?"

"Transmitters in the guardian ships. You know about that."

"But the Citizens on board them—"

"What? Oh, for Pete's sake, hon! They're machines, that's all."

"They're not! The killer-boats are—"

"The killer-boats home on any human mind that begins to operate near the music bands. You had a close call, kitten."

"I wish one had come," Drusilla said miserably. "That's what I wanted."

"One did come, silly. But I don't get you. What did you want?"

"I wanted it to kill me. That's why I taught Chan to—"

Luellen clapped her hands to her face. "I thought that, but I couldn't really believe it! Sweetie, I got news for you. That boat wouldn't have killed you. It was after your boy-friend there."

Drusilla's face went almost as white as her teeth. She put her fist to her mouth and bit it, her eyes round, full of horror.

"It's all right," Luellen murmured. "It's gone. It was homing on him, and when he stopped radiating, it stopped coming. It's just a machine."

"You stopped it," Drusilla breathed. Slowly she sat up straight, staring at the little blonde as if she had never seen her before.

"Pity if one of us couldn't out-think a machine," said Luellen deprecatingly. Then, "What is it, Dru? What's the matter?"

"He might have been ... killed."

"You only just thought of that. Really thought of it."

Drusilla nodded.

"I'll bet this is the first time you ever thought of someone else. See what snobbery can do?"

"I feel awful."

Luellen laughed at her. "You feel fine. Or you will. What you've got is an attack of something called humility. It rushes in to fill the hole when the snobbery is snatched out. You'll be all right now."

"Will I?" She licked her lips. She tried to speak and could not. She pointed a wavering finger at the unconscious man.

"Him?" Luellen answered the unspoken question. "Just you keep him asleep for a while. Give him more music, but keep him away from that." She pointed to the sky. "He won't know the difference."

"Humility," said Drusilla, thoughtfully. "That's when you feel ... not good enough. Is that it?"

"Something like that."

"Then I don't ... I don't think I understand. Lu, do you know why I killed the Preceptor?"

Luellen shook her head. "It was a good idea, whatever."

Drusilla said with difficulty, "My group went to be chosen for breeding. There's a—custom that the ... ugliest girl must be sent back to her garden. He pointed me out. I was the ugliest one there. He said I was the ugliest woman in the world. I went ... kind of ... crazy, I guess. I killed him."

Suddenly she was in Luellen's strong small arms. "Oh, for God's sake," said Luellen with a roughness that made Drusilla cry again. "You're the sorriest most mixed-up little chicken ever. Don't you know that a perfect necklace has to have an ugliest diamond in it somewhere?" She thumped Drusilla's heaving shoulder. "We've been bred for beauty for more generations than this Earth has years, Dru. On Earth you're one of the most beautiful women alive."

"He told me that once, and I could have . . . killed him," Drusilla squeaked. She swallowed hard, moved back to peer piteously into Luellen's face. "Is that humility? To feel you're not good enough?"

"That's humiliation," said Luellen. She paused thoughtfully. "And here's the difference: Humility is knowing something is finer and better than you can ever be, so it's worth putting everything you have behind that something. Everything! Like . . ."

She laughed. "Like me and that ham novelist of mine. Bit by bit, year by year, he gets better. I give him exactly what he needs, in his own time. Right now what he wants is an irresponsible little piece of candy he can pick up or put down, and meantime get envied all over the neighborhood for. He's got it in him to do some really important work some day, and when he does he'll need something else from me, and I'll be here to give it to him. If, fifty years from now, he comes doddering up to me and tells me I've grown with him through the years, I'll know I did the thing right."

Drusilla worried at the statement, turning it over, shaking it. She parted her lips, closed them again.

Luellen said, "Go ahead. Ask me."

Drusilla looked to her timidly, dropped her eyes. "Is he really finer and better?"

"Snob!" said Luellen, and this time it was all kindliness. "Of course! He's an Earthman, Dru. Earth is young and crude and raw, but it's strong and it's good. Do you call an infant stupid because it can't talk, or is a child bad because it hasn't learned reason? We have nothing but decadence to bring to Earth. So instead we help Earth with the best it has. You keep your eyes open from now on, Dru. Nine women out of ten who truly help their men to realize themselves are what you've been calling criminals.

"You'll find them all over, up and down the social scale, through and through the history of this culture. Put up your shields again—for fun—and watch the women you meet. See how some seem to understand one another on sight—how they pass a glance that seems to be full of secrets. They're the hope of the world, Dru darling, and this world is the hope of the Galaxy." She followed Drusilla's gaze and smiled. "Now that you come to think of it, you love him, don't you?"

"Now that I come to think of it ..."

She raised her head and looked at the sky. Gradually a smile was born on her trembling lips. She shook herself and took a deep breath of the warm evening air.

"Listen," she said. She laughed unevenly. "It *is* sort of scratchy, isn't it?"

Story Notes

by Paul Williams

"A Saucer of Loneliness": first published in *Galaxy Science Fiction*, February 1953. Probably written early autumn 1952.

"A Saucer of Loneliness" was adapted as a radio drama for the "X Minus One" program (aired Sept. 1, 1957). It was adapted as a television drama in France in 1982, under the title "La Soucoupe de Solitude." An American TV adaptation (starring Shelley Duvall, Richard Libertini and Nan Martin) was aired Sept. 27, 1986 in the (revived) Twilight Zone series. In 1975, Sturgeon wrote to the French production company that had purchased "Saucer": *I would be most pleased if the film carried the following dedication, to precede my own credits: THIS FILM IS DEDICATED TO THE MEMORY OF "MAMA" CASS ELLIOTT, WHO LOVED THE STORY, AND WHO WAS VERY MUCH LOVED BY ALL THE WORLD. It happens that I received the first word of your interest in this story on the very day of Cass's tragic death* [July 29, 1974]. *Had I not heard the sad news, I would have called her immediately and asked her to get in touch with you. Indeed she loved SAUCER; it had special meanings for her. As an actress of increasing accomplishment, she had desired for years to play the heroine of SAUCER, and for years I have been trying to make it possible. She was a warm and lovely person and a dear friend, and much beloved around the world as she was by all who knew her, and it would please me beyond measure to have this dedication made in this way.*

A note from TS to *Galaxy* editor H. L. Gold after this story was accepted indicates that Gold wanted to delete the "A" in the title and requested a new closing paragraph. Sturgeon replied: *Title: I still like A Saucer of Loneliness, because of its connotation of quantity, which is lost by dropping the article. What it means to me is "measure" or "portion." Closing: This is squeezed out of me like toothpaste out of a tube with the cap on tight: because of too much pressure, emerging unexpectedly from the wrong place, and rather damaging to the source; but for all that, containing precisely the right material:* [This is followed by

375

the story's present closing paragraph. The original manuscript ended, "You're beautiful."]

In one of Sturgeon's 1955 or '56 "maunderings" (in which he talked to himself on paper in an effort to come up with story ideas or further develop an idea that hasn't jelled), he speaks longingly of the ease (and speed) with which certain powerful stories flowed out of him: *BIANCA'S HANDS and SAUCER OF LONELINESS were so easy . . . and IT, though I recall a certain amount of trouble doing the most inferior part of it, the crap about the will . . . WORLD WELL LOST was good but really took forever to set itself up . . . it's all very well to say all right, just write, but dammit you need just something to go on, a setting, something . . .* On another "maundering" page from the same era, TS reinforces this by saying: *I'm still haunted by SAUCER OF LONELINESS, and somehow am sure I'm right in sticking to this chore until I can bust loose with such a thing.*

On July 13, 1953, Sturgeon wrote a letter to J. Donald Adams at *The New York Times Book Review* in response to a column Adams had written the day before about "science fiction and its implications for our time." Sturgeon approved of Adams's comments and added, in his letter:

Probably the most widespread idea about the nature of science fiction is that it is cold-blooded, mechanistic, gadget-happy . . . Evolved and refined, science fiction is today even more preoccupied with human beings than with machines and technologies. After some fifteen years of arduous filtering, one of S-F's more widely-read practitioners has come up with a definition of science fiction designed to include all that is worthy in the field, and exclude the cowboy story which occurs on Mars instead of in Arizona. "A good story is good science fiction," he says, "when it deals with human beings with a human problem which is resolved in terms of their humanity, cast in a narrative which could not occur without the science element."

(To show you that this definition is not merely wishful, I'm committing the enormity of sending you two examples of S-F which follow it. They are both very short. One is Judith Merril's ". . . That Only a Mother . . ." and the other is my "A Saucer of Loneliness."

Editor's blurb from the first page of the original magazine appearance [where the story was titled "Saucer of Loneliness"; Sturgeon restored his preferrred title "A Saucer of Loneliness" in his collection *E Pluribus Unicorn*, published in November 1953]: THERE ARE SECRETS THAT CAN

BE REPEATED ENDLESSLY AND REMAIN WHOLLY AND AB-
SOLUTELY SECRET!

"His story 'A Saucer of Loneliness' kept me from suiciding when I
was 16."—science fiction writer Spider Robinson, in *Locus* magazine after
Sturgeon's death. In the same tribute issue, A.C. Crispin told of meeting
Sturgeon at a convention: "'Hello,' he said. 'Why haven't you come over
to talk to me?' I managed to mumble that it was because I was shy. 'No,'
he said. 'That won't do. Shy is noplace, you know. You have things inside
you must communicate, and you'll never manage it if you're shy. I wrote
a story once called "A Saucer of Loneliness," and that's what it was all
about: communication. There must be communication, or there can never
be love.'"

"The Touch of Your Hand": first published in *Galaxy Science Fiction*,
September 1953. Written in October 1952. A handwritten note on the
author's carbon copy of the manuscript indicates that he finished writing
it, or submitted it to an editor, on November 3, 1952.

In a biographical profile of Theodore Sturgeon I wrote for *Rolling
Stone* magazine in 1976 (they never published it; it appeared in a 1981
paperback called *The Berkeley Showcase, Vol. 3*, Schochet and Silber-
sack, editors) I said, "Sturgeon's vision in "The Touch of Your Hand" of
a limited telepathic linkage that allows each person's skills to become
everyman's is at least as important an idea as the notion of going to the
moon, which originated in science fiction (thousands of years ago) and
has been repeated over the years until somebody finally went ahead and
acted it out. It is *the idea*, not the technology, that is the force behind
human progress."

TS built another story around this same idea: "The Skills of Xanadu"
(1956). In a 1957 letter to a book editor describing stories available for a
new collection, Sturgeon wrote: THE TOUCH OF YOUR HAND *and*
THE SKILLS OF XANADU *will be seen by the discerning eye to be the
same story. A third, now in preparation for* Astounding [and apparently
never completed], *says the same thing again. This results from a deep conviction that the basic statement of these stories needs to be made.*

Sturgeon's introduction to "The Touch of Your Hand" in his 1984 collection *Alien Cargo*: *This is from the fertile postwar period, when I was
writing the likes of* More than Human. *It's about love and authoritari-
anism, as is so much of my work since.*

Editor's blurb from the first page of the original magazine appearance: OSSER KNEW EXACTLY WHAT HE WANTED, WHY HE WANTED IT, AND HOW TO GET IT—EXCEPT THAT EACH ONE OF HIS REASONS WAS TOTALLY WRONG!

"The World Well Lost": first published in *Universe Science Fiction*, June 1953. Written late 1952 or early 1953.

In an unpublished note in 1980 TS pointed out the similarity between Grunty in "The World Well Lost" and characters in his 1949 story "Minority Report" and his 1960 story "Need" (*This guy is very real to me— more so than many I have met in the flesh*). The full quote can be found on p. 381 of Volume V. of *The Complete Stories of Theodore Sturgeon.*

"The World Well Lost" is included in an anthology of "Gay Stories from Alice Munro to Yukio Mishima," *Meanwhile, in Another Part of the Forest*, edited by Alberto Manguel and Craig Stephenson. In the editors' introduction to Sturgeon's story, they write: "Theodore Sturgeon was a science fiction writer who revolutionized the genre.... One subject that Sturgeon legitimized for science fiction was sex, in all its astounding diversity. 'The World Well Lost' was ground-breaking when it was published in 1953—the first science fiction story to sympathetically portray homosexuality. According to the 'Prime Directive' which Sturgeon later created for the Star Trek television series, the overriding law of the United Federation of Planets 'prohibits Federation interference with the normal development of alien life and societies.' In his fiction, Sturgeon gleefully challenges our reading of this directive again and again by asking: in any society, what does the notion of 'normal development' signify? And under whose social code—in 'The World Well Lost' there is more than one—is any of us allowed the fulfilment of personal freedom?"

James Gunn in *Alternate Worlds, The Illustrated History of Science Fiction* says, in regard to "Sturgeon's explorations in personal statement, such as those that turn upon physical abnormality or human taboos": "Because of Sturgeon other writers have been freer to write what they wished to write and able to find a market for it."

In his 1953 essay "Why So Much Syzygy?" Sturgeon said, *"Bianca's Hands" and "The World Well Lost" cause the violently extreme reactions they do because of the simple fact that the protagonist was happy with the situation.*

In a "Postscript" included in his 1960 novel *Venus Plus X*, Sturgeon says:

Story Notes

I once wrote a fairly vivid story about a man being unfaithful to his wife and no one made any scandalous remarks about me. I then wrote a *specific kind of narrative about a woman being unfaithful to her husband and nobody had anything scandalous to say about my wife.* But I wrote *an empathetic sort of tale about some homosexuals and my mailbox filled up with cards drenched with scent and letters written in purple ink with green capitals. As good Philos says herein:* you cannot be objective about *sex, especially when it's outside certain parameters. Hence this disclaimer, friend: keep your troubles to yourself. I wear no silken sporran* (The latter is the clothing of the bisexual beings in *Venus Plus X*; the "empathetic sort of tale" referred to is "The World Well Lost."

"**. . . And My Fear Is Great . . .**": first published in *Beyond Fantasy Fiction*, July 1953 (first issue of a short-lived fantasy magazine edited by H. L. Gold). A handwritten notation on the carbon copy of the manuscript of this story indicates that it was sent to *Galaxy* (i.e., to Gold, possibly because he'd requested a fantasy for his new magazine) on Jan. 17, 1953. Given Sturgeon's writing-and-marketing habits, we can be fairly sure it was written in the first two weeks of January, 1953.

Introducing this story in his 1979 collection *The Golden Helix*, Sturgeon wrote:

This is one of my favorite stories. It appeared a long time ago in a hardcover collection, which (like most such) disappeared fairly soon, and when the collection went into paperback, this story was dropped. It was a convention at the time to fill up tables of contents with as many titles as possible, and the longer stories filled up the book with fewer titles. A great many went to limbo because of that, and it is gratifying to have this one back in the light.

I've been a "wordaholic" all my life, reveling in the texture and feel and shape and music of words; and outside of Whitman's "I Sing the Body Electric," I know of no more exquisite and moving passage than "The Irish Girl's Lament," included in this story, and also the title-giver. I found it in an essay by W. B. Yeats called "What Modern Poetry?" in which he decried artifice and artificiality in poetry, and said that the best poetry, the real poetry, came from the lips and hearts of the people, speaking in their own idiom. He quoted this lament as an example, affirming that he did not write it; it is not his. Therefore I cannot acknowledge it as his, but can only express my gratitude to him for leading me to such a treasure.

As Sturgeon notes above, the prose poem Joyce recites to the tattered man, the source for this story's title, can be found in a 1901 essay by William Butler Yeats (titled "What Is 'Popular Poetry'?" in his volume *Essays and Introductions*). Yeats does not indicate that he heard this lament and wrote it down. He introduces it (without clarifying the source) into his argument by saying, "If men did not remember nor half remember impossible things, and, it may be, if the worship of sun and moon had not left a faint reverence behind it, what Aran fisher-girl would sing:—'It is late last night the dog was speaking of you . . .'" The entire lament quoted by Sturgeon's heroine follows. As the Aran Islands are off the west coast of Ireland and Yeats in 1901 was already spending much time with one Lady Gregory, a collector of the lore of the west of Ireland, perhaps Lady Gregory acquainted Yeats with this extraordinary fisher-girl's lament.

Among Sturgeon's papers is a letter from Richard Lovelace at Yale University, dated May 2, 1953, which begins: "Thank you for writing the novella in the first issue of *Beyond*. It is the finest work of literature that I've seen in any popular magazine. I don't just say that because I like Yeats and have come very recently to accept the beliefs behind the story, either, although of course that's a large part of it. I think it is better writing than Bradbury's ever done, in both expression and construction. You have the power to do a great service by writing fiction like this."

The source for the all-night cafe Don went to night after night, where he first saw Joyce, is Sturgeon's life as an impecunious young writer in New York City in 1940. In a 1972 interview, TS told David Hartwell:

I used to hang out in a place called Martin's 57th Street Cafeteria. It was an all-night cafeteria, where all kinds of bums and weirdos used to hang out and talk all night, and they'd drink the ketchup and eat the sugar, nobody had any money whatsoever. You could nurse one cup of coffee all night long and pay a nickel and go out, y'know. And there were all kinds of very interesting conversations that developed in Martin's.

It seems likely that some aspects of this story, for example Don's rat story and his revelation about the wasps, are partly a reflection of TS's experiences as a Dianetics suditor and auditee.

On the first page of this story's appearance in *Beyond Fantasy Fiction*, the title is followed by an editor's blurb which reads: AS WHOSE WOULDN'T BE, WHEN THE DEMON WITHIN MEETS AN EVEN MORE FRIGHTFUL MONSTER WITHOUT!

There are some slight textual differences between this story as it appears here and previously published versions, because we have made use of Sturgeon's original ms. instead of the published text, which had been edited, sometime clumsily, by Gold. The differences are minor except for the restoration of six important sentences in the paragraph near the end of the story that begins: *Right. We're goin' to make mistakes.* With this restoration, one can see here the seeds of the final page of the last section of *More than Human*, which was written soon after this story and which shares some other thematic links with "... And My Fear Is Great ..."

"The Wages of Synergy": first published in *Startling Stories*, August 1953. Probably written early in 1953 and submitted to Gold and rejected, before it was ultimately purchased by Samuel Mines, editor of *Startling Stories*.

"The Dark Room": first published in *Fantastic*, July-August 1953. Written in late winter or early spring 1953.

Sturgeon's 1979 introduction to this story:

I would like to state here and now that the above was not my title; there is a room in the story but at no time is it dark, nor is darkness of any particular significance to the story. I called it "Alien Bee," which is probably not the best possible title for it either, but a better one, I think, than the one the editor chose. Anyway, I am keeping his title for bibliographical purposes.

Written in 1953, this story is one of my first efforts to develop different styles. Anyone with any verbal facility can develop a style, polish and perfect it until it becomes that writer's special trademark, and you can come a long way in the writing business by doing that. However, like any specialization, it can inhibit and even imprison you, so that all the characters speak like each other and like the author. The writers I admire most—Samuel R. Delany, to name a single one—are masters of many styles, not just one, and no one will ever write one-paragraph pastiches or lampoons of his work.

So here is a hard-heeling, fast-paced, brawling, macho Sturgeon story. And if it turns out that you don't like this kind of person—well, neither do I.

When the parasite entity in this story tells Tom, "we are free to pass and repass in front of their silly eyes," Sturgeon may be consciously alluding to a similar phrase in the poem "Brahma" by his distant relative Ralph Waldo Emerson.

"**Talent**": first published in *Beyond Fantasy Fiction*, September 1953 Written in spring 1953.

Magazine blurb: EXTERMINATING PESTS WAS JOKEY'S SPECIALTY—AND HE WAS 100% EFFICIENT AT IT!

"**A Way of Thinking**": first published in *Amazing Stories*, October-November 1953. Written in spring 1953.

In 1981 Sturgeon wrote the following introduction to "A Way of Thinking" when it was reprinted by *Amazing Stories* as part of a "Hall of Fame" series:

Before I was a writer I was a sailor in the U.S. Merchant Marine. I went to some strange places and met some strange people. One of the most memorable of all was the man you're about to meet (if you haven't met him before). My description of him, and the episodes of the deck winch, the tarpaper cat-house, and the flying fan, are not fiction, but reportage. Tall, feline, soft-voiced, always laid-back and relaxed, with those long green eyes, Kelley is unforgettable, even though I've not see him for many years. I'm quite sure I have more to say about him; one of these days he will slide gently into my typewriter and amaze me.

It says in this story that "he's in Atlanta now." That's Atlanta Penitentiary, I'm sorry to say. I quite forget who told me that, and I never did learn why that was so, and I've always wondered. I am sure, however, that what got him there was the result of his unique way of thinking. I am also sure that his stay could not have been long; as he once took the outside off a building to get in, he was quite capable of taking the inside out of a jail to get out. Don't ask me how. Ask Kelley.

The line "he's in Atlanta now" is not actually in this story; TS may have been thinking of other times he'd written about Kelley: for example in the 1950 essay "Author, Author," included as an appendix in Volume VI of *The Complete Stories of Theodore Sturgeon*.

In an interview on Dec. 6, 1975 Sturgeon told me: *my father died of Parkinson's Disease, which is a horrible thing. Every day you know you're going to be worse than the day before. And he finally turned into just a mush. His brother took care of him. He had to be fed, and he had to be taken to the bathroom. It was sad.*

"**The Silken-Swift**": first published simultaneously in *The Magazine of Fantasy and Science Fiction*, November 1953 and in *E Pluribus Unicorn* by Theodore Sturgeon, a collection of stories published by Abelard Press in November 1953. Written in spring 1953. The song Barbara shares with Del is credited on the copyright page of *E Pluribus Unicorn*, where TS writes: *I should like to express my profound gratitude to Christine Hamilton, who, as a poet, authored the poem "Unicorn" and permitted its use here, and, as a mother, authored the undersigned.* Christine Hamilton Sturgeon was an ambitious (but mostly unpublished) novelist and short story writer as well as a poet.

On the Science Fiction Radio Show in 1983, Sturgeon was asked, "What works of your own do you think are particularly good? Which ones are you proudest of?" He replied: *"The Silken-Swift," the unicorn story, for example, I'm very proud of. I love that story.* He then mentions a story he's just written, "Seasoning," and then goes on: *Let's see, looking for others of what I would call my favorite stories ... I do like that unicorn story. I like the way it's written; it's a very passionate story and it has something I consider very important to say. There again I was combating the assumption that a woman who is not a virgin is not as good a woman as she might be. That was the basic statement of the story. It's a wonder that it came out intact that way.*

On one of his sheets of "maundering" notes from the mid-1950s, TS wrote: *BIANCA'S HANDS and THE SILKEN-SWIFT were, in my own personal category, fables for grown-up people. They had this in common: a legendary, but not fabulous scene: some time in the past, somewhere (probably England, but not for sure). I almost found the same "country"* *in that* Weird Tales *thing about the skull and the hoof—one foot in the grave, or some such title.*

Lucy Menger in her 1981 book *Theodore Sturgeon* says, "In 'The Silken-Swift,' as in few of his prose works, the poet in Sturgeon dominates the prosaist. This story is a mosaic of poetic devices and sensory appeals riding atop a fluctuating tide of subtle rhythms."

"The Clinic": first published in a book (an anthology of "original"—previously unpublished, written especially for the anthology—stories) entitled *Star Science Fiction Stories No. 2*, edited by Frederik Pohl. Written in spring or summer 1953.

Sturgeon's 1979 introduction to this story:
Standing on a street corner waiting for the light to change, I noticed the man next to me gesticulating rapidly and with swift precision while

he stared intently across the street. Following his gaze, I saw a woman watching him with great attention. When he stopped his gestures, her hands flickered swiftly in response, and they both laughed. They were deaf-mutes, and it came to me then that in this situation they were not handicapped. I was, and so were the dozens of hearing people around us, who could not possibly accomplish such a feat.

So I turned the coin over—as you will see.

In his August 13, 1957 letter to Walter Bradbury at Doubleday describing stories available for a new Sturgeon collection, TS said "The Clinic" *is one of the few really successful efforts to tell a tale from the point of view of an extra-terrestrial.*

"**Mr. Costello, Hero**": first published in *Galaxy Science Fiction*, December 1953. Written in summer 1953. Adapted as a radio drama for the "X Minus One" program (aired March 7, 1956).

The story behind the writing of "Mr. Costello, Hero," was told by its author in a 1977 interview with Darrell Schweitzer:

I had a deadline for a novelette of twenty thousand words or so, and Horace Gold called me up and said, "Hey, where's the novelette?" And I began to cry a lot over the telephone. This was the time of the McCarthy hearings. The whole country was in a grip of terror that, not having been through it you just would never understand how awful that was. It was a frightening thing. It crept into all the corners of the houses and everybody's speech and language. Everybody started to get super-careful about what they said, what they wrote and what they broadcast. The whole country was in a strange type of fear, some great intangible something that nobody could get hold of. A very frightening thing.

I became aware by that time that I had a fairly high-caliber typewriter and I became alarmed by the fact that I wasn't using it for anything but what I call "literature of entertainment." I don't want to knock entertainment at all, but I felt I had the tool to do something but I didn't know what to do with it.

Horace listened to me with great care, and he said, "I'll tell you what you do, Sturgeon. You write me a story about a guy whose wife has gone away for the weekend, and he goes down to the bus station to meet her and the bus arrives and the whole place is full of people. He looks across the crowd and he sees his wife emerge from the exit talking to a young man who is talking earnestly back to her. And he is carrying her suitcase

She looks across the crowd, sees her husband, speaks a word to the young man and the young man hands her her suitcase, tips his hat, and disappears into the crowd, and she comes across to him and kisses him. Now then, Sturgeon, write me that story, and by the time you're finished the whole world will know how you feel about Joseph McCarthy."

For the moment I didn't know what the hell he was talking about, and it comes right back to what I said earlier. If a writer really and truly believes in something, if he is totally convinced, if he has a conviction, it really doesn't matter what he writes about. That conviction is going to come through. At that point I sat down and wrote a story called "Mr. Costello, Hero" which was as specific and as sharply-edged a portrait of Joe McCarthy as anyone has ever written. Not only the man himself and his voice and his actions and his speech, but his motivations, where he was coming from, what made him do what he did, which I had never analyzed before.

In my book The 20th Century's Greatest Hits (by Paul Williams, Tor Books, 2000) *I quote Sturgeon as above, and go on to say: "Actually the story does more than that. It is one of the most valuable (*and* entertaining) pieces of political fiction ever written, because it gives us a diagram, it demonstrates in much detail precisely how an Adolf Hitler or Joe McCarthy or Jim Jones or Charles Manson or Slobodan Milosevic can charm and seduce a handful of people who become his lieutenants so that they and soon whole nations start jumping to his tune and even believe they wrote it themselves. The more insight we gain into how this is done, the more opportunity we have to protect ourselves and others from this human peril. 'Mr. Costello, Hero' is a great story as a story, as a narrative and a work of language, but more than that it offers direct insight into the methodology by which psychopathic and power-hungry personalities manipulate other persons by engaging their fears and hatreds, even of people or things they never thought of fearing or hating until the manipulator caught them in his web."*

On August 13, 1953, Sturgeon wrote to Horace Gold: *Here's the rewrite of the ending of the work-in-progress tentatively titled "Never Alone."*

Now let me get something off my chest. Everything that follows necessarily bears the prefix "in my opinion," so don't take any of it too much to heart. It's only me, and who the hell am I?

First, the title. THE EVIL SOLOIST *or* THE EVIL SOLOISTS *are okay as far as they might look on a table of contents. But in terms of the* story they won't do. In the first place the title implies that the soloists (i.e. "trappers" or people who were so accused) _were_ evil, or that I the author so imply. One of the two important (to me) purposes of this story is to show that they were not evil; or, to put it more generally, that to be accused and to be guilty are two very different things. Though the title might conceivably state only Costello's warped teaching, this aspect is not treated strongly enough to make a switch out of it (i.e., the reader is not likely to review the story in his mind and recognize such a title as Costello's view rather than as the story's basic theme.)

Besides, the story is _not_ about the evils of being alone, in anyone's view. That "never alone" thesis on Borinquen was simply a tactic, as the suspicion of poison and of cheating were on the ship. I think it is quite clear that the elimination of privacy is no principle of Costello's; it's simply a means he uses to his megalomaniacal end.

NEVER ALONE [Sturgeon's original title] is therefore wrong as a title, and I freely kick it out. My two suggestions are based on the fact that this story, more than anything I ever wrote, requires the participation of its readers. Therefore, the less the title says, the better. My first choice: MR. COSTELLO. My second: HERO. Don't forget that after reading a story, the story makes the title, not the other way around. THE OLD MAN AND THE SEA is clumsy and arhythmic, AS YOU LIKE IT is meaningless in terms of plot, FROM HERE TO ETERNITY has nothing to say at the outset and in retrospect seems inept. Yet each of these is now touched with magic. So: leave me be tacit. MR COSTELLO or HERO.

Now, as to the ending—specifically, Costello's treatment on Nightingale. You have absolutely no right to assume a different conclusion from my extrapolations. Pleading logic is beside the point. Human progress, mike-or-macrocosmically, frequently departs from a logical chain; if it didn't, we word-merchants would be hard put to it to create characters. The isolation treatment Costello got is consistent in terms of the story. Inventing a machine to make him like ants instead violates the story's main message. He has _got_ to be seen, in essence, "doing what he has to do." The fact that he will do it with ants if he can't do it with men is the strongest single statement about his character.

Your editor wishes to point out that much of the power of this story results from Sturgeon's decision to tell the story from the viewpoint of a good-natured fool, the sucker/victim who is still under the influence of the psychopath's charm in the brilliantly insightful and chilling last sentence of the story (which could almost be the epitaph for our era).

"The Education of Drusilla Strange": first published in *Galaxy Science Fiction*, March 1954. Written in autumn 1953.

Sturgeon's 1979 introduction to this story:

This is one of my very favorite stories, for a number of reasons.

Novelettes were for a long time "lost"; once they had appeared in a magazine, book publishers were chary of using them because of a conviction that the moron reader couldn't sustain his attention span for more than five thousand words, and that he would feel cheated if he didn't get a dozen or fourteen items in the Table of Contents. This is the chief reason that Drusilla has gotten so little exposure.

My dream for Drusilla is to see her education as a major motion picture, and then to spin off as a television series dealing with the educated *Drusilla Strange. It isn't the glory (of which my readers have given me fulsomely) or the money (because I have found out that the line between owning money and being honestly broke is the line between owning money and being owned by it) but because it's a prime opportunity for a strong dramatic role to be given to a woman. I discount imitation bionic men and imitation male police officers, and of course sitcom pie-in-the-face, perennial teases, and Daddy-is-an-oaf so-called comedies. Drusilla is a super-woman, with super-empathy, super-compassion, super-libido (if you like), but also super-responsibility, so that, because she knows she will live for a thousand years, she knows that with ethical responsibility, she must always move on. The* educated *Drusilla Strange has a prime drive: her deeply convinced and passionate love for humanity, and her desire, with all her powers, to solve human problems.*

Oh, well ... when Hollywood is through with 1927 to 1935 science fiction, and is ready to look at inner space instead of outer space, perhaps it will do right by our Drusilla.

The biographical note included in the back of some of Sturgeon's books starting in 1956 says, "He lives with his wife, son and daughter, twelve-string guitar and hot-rod panel truck in Rockland County ... " His 1950 autobiographical essay "Author, Author" mentions that *I played guitar with a square-dance orchestra once, in the Poconos.*

Original magazine blurb: THE GRASS INVARIABLY IS GREENER ON YOUR OWN PLANET—EVEN IF THERE IS NO GRASS THERE

AND IT WOULD NOT BE THAT COLOR IF THERE WERE ANY!

In a 1972 interview published in the French language edition of *Galaxy*, Sturgeon told Patrice Duvic about a letter he once received from an architecture student who said that one line in one of Sturgeon's stories had totally changed the course of his life and of his studies, and his whole attitude towards his work. The line was Drusilla Strange's thought upon first seeing an automobile: *What manner of man* [or race] *streamlines only where he can see?*